Abraham James Fretz

A Brief History of John Valentine Kratz

And a Complete Genealogical Family Register

Abraham James Fretz

A Brief History of John Valentine Kratz
And a Complete Genealogical Family Register

ISBN/EAN: 9783337098209

Printed in Europe, USA, Canada, Australia, Japan

Cover: Foto ©Raphael Reischuk / pixelio.de

More available books at **www.hansebooks.com**

A BRIEF HISTORY

OF

JOHN VALENTINE KRATZ,

AND A COMPLETE

GENEALOGICAL FAMILY REGISTER

WITH

BIOGRAPHIES OF HIS DESCENDANTS FROM THE
EARLIEST AVAILABLE RECORDS TO THE
PRESENT TIME.

WITH PORTRAITS AND OTHER ILLUSTRATIONS.

BY

REV. A. J. FRETZ,

OF MILTON, N. J.

With an Introduction by R. W. KRATZ, of Pomona, Kan.

We dedicate this book to the memory of our worthy ancestor JOHN VALENTINE KRATZ and his descendants.

PREFACE.

Genealogies are profitable, inasmuch as they are of great interest to all descendants, and become more and more so to future generations in tracing back their lineage.

There is a growing feeling in many families in this respect, and family pride is increasing with a desire to know more of one's ancestors.

In this our second attempt to prepare a family genealogy, it has been our aim and purpose to make it as correct, accurate, and complete as possible.

However, in some respects the work is incomplete owing to the failure of a very few of the connections to respond to inquiries for information and data.

The design of this genealogy is to perpetuate the memory of our worthy ancestor, John Valentine Kratz, and to gather in one volume the names of his many descendants.

We acknowledge ourselves indebted to many of the friends for their kindness in furnishing information for this genealogy. Prominent among those who have shown great interest in the work, and furnished us much information are the following: Abraham F. Kratz, Harleysville, Pa., E. A. Kratz, M. D., Champaign, Ill., Reuben W. Kratz, Pomona, Kansas, H.W. Kratz, Norristown, Pa., H. M. Kratz, Dublin, Pa., Prof. A. B. Fretz, Singac, N. J., Rev. H. A. Hunsicker, Mount Bethel, Pa., J. B. Honsberger, Fenwick, Ont., D. K. Cassel, Philadelphia, Pa., Mrs. Catharine Martin, Jordan Station, Ont., and others.

Milton, N. J., 1892.　　　　　THE AUTHOR.

INTRODUCTION.

Religious principles have been important factors in American civilization.

Indeed it may be questioned if any other source could have supplied the strength necessary to endure the hardships and dangers braved by the first settlers on our Atlantic seaboard. They have also performed an equally important work in the upbuilding of every section of our great country, in all that glorifies it and makes it the home of a free, intelligent, and virtuous people.

It was said of the Christ, "Herod will seek the young child to destroy him," which illustrates the animus of the world toward principles claiming regnant authority by virtue of inherent right, as it sometimes seems the only way to debase a hated principle is to persecute its living enbodiment. Such persons are subjected to all the indignities that malicious cunning may regard necessary to accomplish its purpose.

Persecution makes conspicuous the principles, surrounds with a halo the brow of its martyrs, who, as the world progresses, are lifted to their niche in the temple of fame.

We make then, but a modest affirmation when we declare the name of our first ancestor on American soil. John Valentine Kratz, worthy of Honorable mention. He was a native of Germany* as shown by an old family Bible, handed down direct from him, and held as an heirloom by his family.

His religious principles were those of the Mennonites, for which he was driven by persecution from his native land to find a home in America, where he arrived Oct. 16, 1727, as shown by a book *entitled* "Rupp's Thirty Thousand Emigrants into Pennsylvania from 1727 to 1776."

As advocates of peace principles, the Mennonites are far in advance of the prevailing sentiment in this last decade of the Nineteenth Century, and our ancestors were fully a century and a half in advance of the times. But, although, so far in advance their ideas must not be regarded chimerical, for inspiration has declared, "They shall beat their swords into plowshares, and their spears into pruning-hooks, nation shall not lift up sword against nation, neither shall they learn war any more."

When this prediction has received its fulfillment, the man who centuries before believed its underlying principles, advocated it, and suffered for it, will be honored more than a Cæsar, or a Napoleon. "He shall be called a son of God."

The influence of such a man on his posterity, can hardly be overestimated, and justifies the expectation of an honest, courageous, and intelligent people, which has been fully realized in a family that has spread over nearly every portion of the United States.

---

* See foot note page 11.

and Canada, and is represented in every profession
and walk in life, from the farm, the workshop, up
to the higher schools, Colleges and Universities.

The family is fortunate in having a Historian in
the person of Rev. A. J. Fretz, who is connected
with it through both of his parents, and has proven
himself competent for the work. May his work prove
such an incentive to the further representatives of
the family that all may lead such noble lives as shall
prove them worthy descendants of a noble sire.

REUBEN W. KRATZ.

Pomona, Kansas, April 1891.

LIST OF EXPLANATIONS AND ABBREVIATIONS.

In the preparation of this work it will be observed that all descendants are recorded in the regular order of birth, from the oldest to the youngest, each generation being marked consecutively from first to last. The Roman numerals placed before each name indicates the generation to which they belong, as

    I.   John Philip Kratz, (First generation).
    II.   John Valentine Kratz, (Second generation).
    III.   John Kratz, (Third generation).
    IV.   Valentine Kratz, (Fourth generation), etc.

Beginning with the first (I.) ancestor John Philip Kratz, all his children are named in the order of their birth. Then follows his youngest son John Valentine Kratz, (the ancestor in America), (II. Generation) and his children (III. Generation) next. John being the oldest, is followed down to the last of his descendants. Then the other children of John Valentine Kratz having issue, are taken in the order of birth and carried down to the last of their descendants in like manner.

Where marriages occur between members of the connection the husband carries the record. In all such cases a numbered reference is placed after the name and marriage of the wife, as for example (See Index of References No. 1). In the Index of References will be found No. 1, Martha Cline, Page —. On the page given, in the body of the book, the family records will be found. In the general Index will be found the names of all the males of eighteen years and over, and the maiden names of all the females of eighteen years and over; also the pages on which their family records are given in the body of the book.

To find family records See *Index* of *Branches*, where names of all that had issue of the second, third and fourth generations are given.

Abbreviations: Mrd. signifies married; Dec'. deceased; Ch. church; Twp. township; Montg. Co., Montgomery Co.; S. single; Ev. Assoc. Evangelical Association.

THE KRATZ FAMILY HISTORY.

I. John Philip Kratz, father of the ancestor of the Kratz family in America, was born in Germany, Oct. 8th, 1665, and died there in 1746, aged 80 years. His wife, died in 1710. Their children were (II.) Anna Eliza. born in 1695. (II.) John, born 1697. died 1704. (II.) John Philip, born 1699. (II.) Anna Maria. born 1703. (II.) Anna. born 1705. (II.) John Valentine. born 1707. (II.) Anna Elizabeth. born 1709.

II. John Valentine Kratz, youngest son of John Philip Kratz, was born in 1707. in the Palatinate, a province of Germany. bordering on the east side of the Rhine.* He died in 1780, aged about 73 years. He emigrated to Pennsylvania in 1727. when he was 20 years old. and arrived in the ship "Friendship". on the 16th of October of said year.

The vessel set sail on the 20th of June. making the voyage in nearly four months. It is said that one of his sisters came with him to this country. Of her we have been unable to learn anything further.

Like many others. persecuted in the land of his nativity. on account of his religious faith. he turned his face toward the new world. the land of religious freedom. leaving the parental roof, the scenes of his youth. and all the kindred associations of the old home, to make his abode among strangers in a strange land.

---

* By some of the connection, it is thought that John Valentine Kratz was a native of Switzerland, but of this we have no positive proof. According to Rupp's 30.000 names, he was one of 46 emigrants, who emigrated with their families, in all about 200 persons, from the Palatinate to Pennsylvania in 1727. However, during the persecution of the Mennonites in Switzerland by the Calvinists, many of them found refuge for a time in the Palatinate, and afterwards emigrated to other countries.

Here he braved the trials and hardships incident to a new and sparsely settled country, in which wild beasts and savage red men abounded. Here, he with others who like himself had been driven from their homes across the sea by the cruel hand of persecution, aided in erecting shrines and altars around which they worshiped the God of their fathers. Here he prospered and enjoyed the fruit of his labors. Here he lived the quiet unassuming life of an American citizen, and during the period that tried men's souls, he remained true, and loyal to the American cause. He yet lived when the colonies began the arduous struggle for freedom from crowned tyranny, and died amid the thunders of the battles of the Revolution which brought the freedom his children after him enjoyed.

John Valentine Kratz settled in what was then Salford Township, Philadelphia County, now Montgomery County, Pa., where he purchased two tracts of land, one from Gerhart Clemens, and one from the commissioners of property. By warrant granted under the lesser seal bearing date Aug. 3, 1734, there was surveyed to John Valentine Kratz on the 12th day of March following a tract of land in Salford Township, containing 163 acres and 71 perches, with allowance of six percent. for roads and highways, and for which he paid £25, 6s., 8d., and received a patent therefor on Feb. 14, 1736, and is located in Upper Salford. It extended on both sides of the Skippack road to the crossroad below Salfordsville. The other tract which he purchased from Gerhard Clemens and wife, Jan. 30, 1736, contained 53 acres, and for which he paid £53. This tract is located in Lower Salford, and was adjoining his first purchase. Here he built the first house where Milton H. Alderfer now lives.

He also purchased another tract of land containing 68 acres.

In the tax list of 1776 John Valentine Kratz was assessed for 150 acres in Upper Salford,* and 150 acres in Lower Salford. After the death of John Valentine Kratz, the Old Homestead and 150 acres of land were held by his youngset son, Isaac, who was born in 1749. On the other farm of 150 acres in Upper Salford, John Valentine Kratz built the residence where Henry Weber now lives, for his son Valentine.

By his descendants it is said that John Valentine Kratz married Ann Clemens, presumably the daughter of Gerhart Clemens†. She died in 1793.

They were among the original members of the Mennonite church of Salford.

The first meeting house in Salford, in which they worshiped was probably built in 1738. This becoming too small was taken down and built larger about 1770.

The present meeting house was built in 1850. In the adjoining grave-yard to this church were laid to rest all that was mortal of our worthy ancestor, John Valentine Kratz. one hundred and eleven years ago, and his wife Ann ninety-eight years ago. There undisturbed may their ashes rest until the final gathering of the faithful to come forth to inherit the kingdom prepared for them. Their children. in the order of their birth. were as follows: John, Michael, Gerhart, Philip, Abraham. Isaac. Anna, *a daughter*, Valentine and Isaac.

---

* Salford Township was divided into Upper and Lower Salford in 1741.

† Gerhart Clemens, born in 1680; died about 1745. Emigrated from Europe to Pennsylvania in 1709. Settled in Montgomery Co., where he made various purchases of lands until he owned in all about 1000 acres.

DESCENDANTS OF JOHN KRATZ SON OF JOHN VALENTINE KRATZ.

III. John Kratz, born in Montgomery Co., in 1732; died in 1812, aged 80 years. He was married to **Anna Moyer**, daughter of Samuel Moyer. He was a farmer, and lived in Hilltown Twp., Bucks Co., opposite the Creamery, on the farm occupied by the late Isaac Moyer, and adjoining lands of Rev. Abraham F. Moyer. He and wife were members of the Mennonite church at Blooming Glen, and are buried there. Children: Christian, Anna, Valentine, Jacob, Barbara, Magdalena.

IV. Christian Kratz, born—; died—. Mrd. Catharine Geil—. No issue.

IV. Anna Kratz, born—; died—. Mrd. John High—. No issue.

IV. Valentine Kratz, born—; died—. Mrd.—. Lederach-. Farmer. They emigrated to Canada in 1799; settled in Lincoln Co., Ont. In 1801 the first Mennonite church was established in Canada known as Moyer's church. Of this church he was ordained minister the same year, 1801, and consequently was the first mennonite minister in Canada. Children: Anna, Mary, Barbara, John, Susanna, Magdalena, Catharine, Elizabeth, Abraham, Margaret.

V. Anna Kratz, born Apr. 14, 1787; died Nov. 20, 1848, aged 61 yrs., 6 mos. and 6 days. Mrd. Samuel Honsberger. Farmer. Mennonites. Children: Susanna, Margaret, Samuel.

VI. Susanna Honsberger, born in Lincoln Co., Ont., Oct. 9, 1815; died Feb. 20, 1880. Mrd. Moses R. Overholt, Oct. 27, 1836; died Feb. 20, 1880. Farmer. Mennonites. Children: Samuel, Mary, Gabriel, Nancy, Moses, Freeman, Daniel.

VII. Samuel Overholt, born Jan. 28, 1837; died July 7, 1842.

VII. Mary Overholt, born Dec. 26, 1840; died Aug. 25, 1855.

VII. Gabriel Overholt, born Aug. 2, 1842. Mrd. Anna Margaret Spears, Feb. 2, 1869. P. O., Jordan, Ont. Farmer, and lives on the old homestead in Lincoln Co., Ont. Children: (**VIII.**) Courtland Overholt, born Mar. 18, 1870. (**VIII.**) Lucetta Overholt, born Jan. 19, 1874. (**VIII.**) Samantha Overholt, born Feb. 18, 1881.

VII. Nancy Overholt, born Feb. 1, 1845; died May 2, 1888. Mrd. Jonas Albright, Feb. 22, 1871. P. O., Campden, Ont. Farmer. Mem. Ev. Assoc. Children: Susan, Moses, Mary.

VIII. Susan Albright, born Sept. 3, 1871. Mrd. Alfred Tallboys, Dec. 17, 1890. P. O., International Bridge, Ont. Mem. Ev. Assoc.

VIII. Moses Albright, born Sept. 27, 1874.

VIII. Mary Margaret Albright, born Jan 24, 1881.

VII. Moses H. Overholt, born Oct. 27, 1847. Mrd. Barbara Moyer, Oct. 28, 1873. She died May 24, 1874. Mrd. second, Eva Valeria (Wills) Wismer (widow), Jan. 11, 1881. P. O., Jordan, Ont. Farmer. One child: (**VIII.**) Galen Stanley Overholt, born July 9, 1891.

VII. Freeman H. Overholt, born Sept. 15, 1849. Mrd. Mary Honsberger, Nov. 2, 1875. P. O., Jordan, Ont. Farmer. One child: (**VIII.**) Edith Eloria Overholt, born Dec. 20, 1880.

VII. Daniel Overholt, born Oct. 2, 1855; died Apr. 23, 1885. S.

VI. Margaret Honsberger, born in 1820; died in 1851. Mrd. Jacob H. High. Children: (**VII.**) Solomon High. S. (**VII.**) Anna High. S.

VI. Samuel Honsberger, born about 1830; died 1888. Mrd. Margaret Honsberger. Children: (**VII.**) Melvina Honsberger. S. (**VII.**) Susanna Honsberger. S. (**VII.**) George Hunsberger. S.

V. Mary Kratz, born Jan. 19, 1788; died June 8, 1862, aged 74 yrs., 4 mos. 22 days. Mrd. Isaac Honsberger, about 1815 or 1816. He died Mar. 19, 1844, aged 57 yrs., 5 mos. 1 day. Miller and farmer.

Mennonites. Children: Anna, Magdalena, Henry, Valentine, Susan, Catharine.

VI. Anna Honsberger, born in 1818; died in 1888. Mrd. Rev. Abraham High. No issue.

VI. Magdalena Honsberger, born Aug. 17, 1820; died in 1873. Mrd. Christian High—. He died June 18, 1844. Farmer. Mennonites, one child: Isaac. Magdalena mrd. for her second husband John Fry, Nov. 28, 1852. One child: Mary.

VII. Isaac High, born Jan. 11, 1844. Mrd. Caroline Fender, Jan. 7, 1891. P. O. South Cayuga, Ont. Farmer. Wife Lutheran.

VII. Mary Fry, born Aug. 1855; died Dec. 1882. Mrd. Emerson High, Feb. 1882. Farmer. Mennonites, one child: (VIII.) Orpha Jane High, born Dec. 1882.

VI. Henry Honsberger, born Oct. 21, 1822. Mrd. Mary Fry, Oct. 29, 1851. P. O. Jordan, Ont. Farmer. Ev. Assoc. Children: Mary, Jacob, Saloma, William.

VII. Mary Honsberger, born Sept. 6, 1852. Mrd. Freeman M. Moyer, Dec. 4, 1875. He died Nov. 22, 1887. Children: (VIII.) Milton Leslie Moyer, born June 29, 1879. (VIII.) William Arden Moyer, born Sept. 4, 1887.

VII. Jacob Honsberger, born July 25, 1855; died Aug. 28, 1884. Mrd. Saphronia C. Culp, Feb. 18, 1880. One child: (VIII.) Eva Dell Honsberger, born Dec. 9, 1882.

VII. Saloma Honsberger, born Apr. 14, 1859; died June 28, 1890. Mrd. William H. Crowe, Dec. 21, 1887. P. O. Jordan, Ont. Children: (VIII.) Ellie Crowe, born Dec. 16, 1888. (VIII.) Ethel Crowe, born Dec. 24, 1889.

VII. William Honsberger, born Jan. 30, 1862. Mrd. Minnie A. Haist, Jan. 25, 1888. P. O. Jordan, Ont. Farmer. Ev. Assoc. No children (1891).

VI. Valentine Honsberger, born in 1824. Mrd. Catharine Fry, Nov. 26, 1851. P. O. South Cayuga, Ont. Farmer. Ev. Assoc. Children: Solomon, Annie, Henry, Jerome, Isaac, Samuel, Oscar, Edward, Martha, George, Elsie.

VII. Solomon Honsberger born in 1853; died in 1853.

VII. Annie Honsberger, born in 1854. Mrd. Freeman H. Moyer, Dec. 25, 1879. He was born in 1848. Methodists. Children: (**VIII.**) Mary Elsie Moyer, born Feb. 12, 1881. (**VIII.**) Hugh Ellis Moyer, born Feb. 5, 1883. (**VIII.**) Fred Clare Moyer, born Nov. 6, 1887. (**VIII.**) John Wray Moyer, born Nov. 4, 1889.

VII. Henry F. Honsberger, born in 1857.

VII. Jerome F. Honsberger, M. D., born in Haldimand Co., Ont. Oct. 6, 1859. Mrd. Alberta C. Stoddard, of Delhi, Ont., Oct. 14, 1890. P. O., Delhi, Ont. Methodists. Dr. Honsberger received his early education in the district schools, going to school during the winter months, and during the summer assisted on his father's farm. But his ambitious young mind soon made him dissatisfied with his limited education, and the small opportunities which a farm life afford for advancement; accordingly at the age of 17, he, with his brother, began to prepare himself for the 3d class teachers' examination, and with the help of the lady teacher who boarded in their home, by improving every spare moment, often studying till midnight after a hard day's work on the farm, they passed the examination successfully. In the fall succeeding the examination he attended the Model school in Caledonia, obtained his certificate, and at the beginning of the New Year, began teaching. After teaching for three years, he spent a term at the Collegiate Institute, Brantford, and in July 1880 passed the 2d class teachers' examination there, carrying off a scholarship given by that Institution for proficiency. He next attended the Normal School in Toronto, obtained his Professional 2d class certificate, and taught for two years more. But as is often the case he was only using the profession of teaching as a stepping-stone to something higher. Ever since his boyhood he had made up his mind to be a doctor, and now he was about to enter upon the fulfillment of that dream. In the fall of 1882 he began his medical course at Trinity Medical College, Toronto, passed his examinations successfully at the end of each year, and graduated in March, 1886, both from Trinity Medical

College and Trinity University, standing at the head of his class at the University. A few weeks later he sailed for England, where he spent six months continuing his studies in the largest hospital, and under the most distinguished physicians of London. Here he passed another examination, taking the degree of Licentiate of the Royal College of Physicians, England. He returned in November, and in the following spring located in Delhi, a thriving little town in Norfolk Co., Ont., where he has worked a large and lucrative practice. Though he has been less than four years in actual practice, Dr. Honsberger is already widely known throughout that district as a clever young physician, whose ability is sure to gain for him a leading place in his profession.

VII. Isaac Honsberger, born and died in 1861.

VII. Samuel Honsberger, born and died in 1863.

VII. J. Oscar Honsberger, born in 1864.

VII. Edward Honsberger, born in 1866; died in 1871.

VII. Martha Honsberger, born in 1869; died in 1869.

VII. George H. Honsberger, born in 1871.

VII. Elsie Honsberger, born and died in 1873.

VI. Susan Honsberger, born in 1826; died about 1830.

VI. Catharine Honsberger, born March 16, 1831. Mrd. Michael Schisler, Nov. 30, 1852. P. O., South Cayuga, Ont. Farmer. Ev. Assoc. Children: Mary, Solomon, Salome, George, Annie, William, Emily.

VII. Mary Frances Schisler, born March 31, 1855.

VII. Solomon Schisler, born Apr. 29, 1859; died Sept. 23, 1859.

VII. George Isaac Schisler, born Apr. 8, 1861; died June 3, 1864.

VII. Salome Catharine Schisler, born Nov. 16, 1862. Mrd. William Mitchell, March 15, 1888. P. O., South Cayuga, Ont. Carriage builder. Ev. Assoc. One child: (**VIII.**) Tennison Mitchell, born Jan. 9, 1889.

VII. Annie Dalena Schisler, born Nov. 10, 1865.

VII. William Franklin Schisler, born May 26, 1868.

VII. Emily Jane Schisler, born July 30, 1870.

V. Barbara Kratz, born Nov. 15, 1789; died Nov. 14, 1878. Mrd. Abraham Honsberger, in 1812. He was born Apr. 5, 1788; died Oct. 11, 1866. Farmer. Mennonites. Children: Isaac, Valentine, Abraham, John, Susanna, Michael, Jacob, Magdalena, William.

VI. Isaac Honsberger, born Jan 30, 1814; died Oct. 9, 1881. Mrd. Lutia Ann Fessenden, May 20, 1841. Tailor and Merchant, was Post Master, and had also served as Clerk of the Court. Baptists. Children: Ellen, Barbara, Arthur, Olive, Paul.

VII. Ellen A. Honsberger, born Sept. 20, 1842. Mrd. Christopher Sevenpiper. Shoemaker. Disciples. Nine children.

VII. Barbara C. Honsberger, born March 27, 1844. Mrd. Timothy Wardell, Dec. 22, 1868. Farmer. Disciples. Children: .

VII. Arthur E. Honsberger, born May 11, 1846. Mrd. Susan Zimmerman, Jan. 20, 1868. Shoemaker. Methodists. Seven Children.

VII. Olive L. Honsberger, born March 10, 1848. Mrd. John Walker, Sept. 22, 1885. Harness maker, and Post Master at Rainham, Ont. Methodists. No children.

VII. Paul J. Honsberger, born Aug. 18, 1850. Mrd. Lucy Kindee, May 14, 1879. Wagon maker. Methodists. Children: .

VI. Valentine Honsberger, born in Lincoln Co., Ont., June 13, 1816. Mrd. Julia Vannatta, Dec. 12, 1837. She was born July 20, 1820; died Aug. 1, 1869. Blacksmith. Methodists. Children: Isaac, Alfred, Richard, Sarah, Barbara, Sarah, Phebe, Abraham, John, Emma, Carrie, Nelson.

VII. Isaac J. Honsberger, born Oct. 8, 1838.

VII. Alfred Honsberger, born in 1841; died 1853.

VII. Richard Honsberger, born May 5, 1843. Mrd. Caroline Esther Bird, May 28, 1863. She died May 26, 1881. Farmer. Presbyterians. Children: Reuben, Dora, Ida, Bertha, Ada, Edna, Calvin, William. Richard mrd. his second wife, Isabella McCormack (widow), July 4, 1884. One child: James.

VIII. Reuben Adelbert Honsberger, born in Welland Co., Ont., March 27, 1865. Mrd. Louisa B. Furman, May 16, 1888. P. O., Gaines, Pa. Manufacturer and dealer in Hard wood. Attends Methodist ch. One child: (IX.) Esther Gertrude Honsberger, died aged 34 years.

VIII. Dora Louretta Honsberger, born July 16, 1867; died Aug. 2, 1889. Mrd. William Eberhart, of Collinswood, Ont., June 13, 1888. One child, still born.

VIII. Ida Honsberger, born May 1, 1870.

VIII. Bertha Frances Honsberger, born Sept. 9, 1872.

VIII. Ada Alice Honsberger, born Feb. 13, 1875.

VIII. Edna A. Honsberger, born Feb. 9, 1877.

VIII. Calvin Bruce Honsberger, born May 5, 1879.

VIII. William Verness Honsberger, born March 13, 1881.

VIII. James Richard Beattie Honsberger, born Oct. 30, 1887.

VII. Sarah Honsberger, born 1845; died 1848.

VII. Barbara Honsberger, born 1847; died 1862.

VII. Sarah Ann Honsberger, born — 1849. Mrd. William Marshall.

VII. Phebe Jane Honsberger, born — 1851. Mrd. George Deamude.--.

VII. Abraham Honsberger, born Aug. 5, 1853. Mrd. Mary A. Hitz, Dec. 22, 1875. P. O., Banda, Ont. Farmer. Children: (VIII.) Charlotta Jane Honsberger, born July 10, 1877; died July 12, 1877. (VIII.) Selena May Honsberger, born Nov. 10, 1878. (VIII.) Marshall Honsberger, born June 24, 1881; died Dec. 18, 1881. (VIII.) Daniel Bertram Honsberger, born Nov. 9, 1883. (VIII.) Lewis Erwin Honsberger, born July 16, 1891.

VII. John Honsberger, born in 1855,--.

VII. Emma Honsberger, born in 1857. Mrd. Thomas Deamude,—.

VII. Carrie Honsberger, born in 1859. Mrd. James Ryckman.

VII. Nelson Elliott Honsberger, born — 1861.

VI. Abraham Honsberger, born in Lincoln Co., Ont., May 1, 1818; died May 7, 1887. Mrd. Elizabeth Brower, Mar. 17, 1844. She was born Apr. 23, 1821.— Children: Mary, Barbara, Susan, William, John, Sarah, Rebecca.

VII. Mary Catharine Honsberger, born Aug. 30, 1845. Mrd. Andrew Couthers, Apr. 7, 1882. P. O., Mansfield, Ont.

VII. Barbara Ellen Honsberger, born Aug. 30, 1845. Twin with Mary.

VII. Susan Ann Honsberger, born Feb. 24, 1848; died Mar. 1, 1889. Mrd. Vernon V. Bishop, Jan. 1865. P. O., Baldwin, Kan. Turner and wheelwright. Christian Ch. Children: (**VIII.**) Ettie May Bishop, born May 9, 1866. (**VIII.**) Verdman Houghton Bishop, born Feb. 9, 1870. (**VIII.**) George Ethelbert Bishop, born May 23, 1872. (**VIII.**) Edwey Bishop, born Dec. 1, 1873; died Dec. 28, 1873. (**VIII.**) Elmer Bishop, born Dec. 3, 1874; died Dec. 26, 1874. (**VIII.**) Linda Elizabeth Bishop, born Dec. 4, 1875. (**VIII.**) Abraham Franklin Bishop, born July 5, 1878. (**VIII.**) Florence Emeline Bishop, born Dec. 2, 1880. (**VIII.**) James Bidwell Bishop, born Apr. 12, 1883. (**VIII.**) Susan Elsie Bishop, born Mar. 4, 1885. (**VIII.**) Wilbur Ross Bishop, born July 29, 1887.

VII. William Nelson Honsberger, born Aug. 3, 1850.

VII. John Henry Honsberger, born Nov. 19, 1853.

VII. Sarah Elizabeth Honsberger, born May 15, 1857. Mrd. Oliver Perry Clabaugh, Dec. 6, 1883. P. O., Republic, Kan. Carpenter. United Brethren. Children: (**VIII.**) Benjamin Ray Clabaugh, born Dec. 17, 1884, and (**VIII.**) Belva Fay Clabaugh, born Dec. 17, 1884, Twins. (**VIII.**) Fleetah May Clabaugh, born Nov. 25, 1886. (**VIII.**) Harriet Argina Clabaugh, born June 14, 1890.

VII. Rebecca Jane Honsberger, born Nov. 10, 1860. Mrd. James H. Stinson, Mar. 24, 1880. P. O. Strathaven, Ont.

VI. John Honsberger, born July 13, 1820. Retired. Mem. Methodist Ch. Unmarried.

VI. Susanna Honsberger, born Jan. 10, 1822; died June 2, 1883. Mrd. Martin Orth, Nov. 30, 1838. He was born Jan. 15, 1815. Children: Mary, William, John, Abraham, Barbara, Alfred, Rhoda, Keturah, Ada, Frank.

VII. Mary Catharine Orth, born Feb 9, 1839. Mrd. Edwin Zimmerman, Jan. 5, 1859. P. O., Alto, Mich. Farmer. Baptists. Children: James M., M. E., W.T.

VIII. James M. Zimmerman, born Aug. 20, 1860. Mrd. . P. O., Bridgeport, Ala. Supt. and partner in Handle Factory. Children:—.

VIII. M. E. Zimmerman, born Nov. 3, 1862. Mrd.—. P. O., Tecumseh, Mich. Proprietor of Handle Factory. Children:—.

VIII. W. T. Zimmerman, born Jan. 10, 1866. Prof. of Music at Pueblo, Colo., and lay preacher in the Episcopal church.

VII. William W. Orth, born in Lincoln Co., Ont., Sept. 26, 1841. Mrd. Mary F. Knox, Dec. 2, 1879. Res., Detroit, Mich.; Railway Passenger Conductor for 27 years with Grand Haven & Milwaukee Railway. Baptists. Children: (**VIII.**) Sophia Compton Orth, born Nov. 3, 1870. (**VIII.**) Ada Belle Orth, born Jan. 14, 1880; died June 27, 1880.

VII. John H. Orth, born June 4, 1843. Mrd. Hila Brown, of Mich., June 18, 1873. Steam Laundry in Portland, Ore. Church of Christ. Chidren: (**VIII.**) Ruby Melwayn Orth, born Apr. 29, 1885; died Mar. 31, 1886. (**VIII.**) Harold William Orth, born Nov. 1, 1887. (**VIII.** Iva Orth and (**VIII.**) Ila Orth, twins, born Oct. 28, 1891.

VII. Abraham H. Orth, born Dec. 30, 1845. Mrd. Samantha McIntyre, Oct. 25, 1870. She was born Mar. 22, 1846. P. O., Campden, Ont. Engineer. Children: (**VIII.**) Naomi Orth, born Feb. 25, 1871. (**VIII.**) Clara Orth, born May 14, 1872. (**VIII.**) Ida Orth, born Apr. 16, 1876. (**VIII.**) Edna Orth, born July 24, 1878.

VII. Barbara A. Orth, born in Lincoln Co., Ont., Feb. 13, 1847. Mrd. Robert Tubbs in 1874. P. O., East Saginaw, Mich. Farmer. Baptists. No issue.

VII. Alfred Orth, born Oct. 4, 1849. P. O., Campden, Ont.

VII. Rhoda Ann Orth, born Oct. 1, 1852. Mrd. William G. McIntyre, Jan. 19, 1871. P. O., Campden, Ont. Farmer. Disciples. No issue.

VII. Keturah Margaret Orth, born at Campden, Ont., Oct. 18, 1854. Mrd. John William Boulton, Dec. 24, 1878. He was born Dec. 10, 1851. P. O., Campden, Ont. Painter. Children: (**VIII.**) Ada Boulton, born Oct. 10, 1879. (**VIII.**) Sophia Myrtle Boulton, born Sept. 9, 1886.

VII. Ada L. Orth, born Dec. 7, 1858. P. O. Campden, Ont.

VII. Frank Orth, born Feb. 20, 1864; died Sept. 15, 1864.

VI. Michael Honsberger, born in Lincoln Co., Ont., Aug. 8, 1825. Mrd. Elizabeth Ann Orth, Oct. 6, 1857. She was born June 16, 1837. P. O., Campden, Ont. Baptists. Children: Orpha, Frank, Margaret, John, Andrew, Allen, Henry, Alpheus.

VII. Orpha I. Honsberger, born July 13, 1858. Mrd. Albert Singer, May 7, 1888—.

VII. Frank Honsberger, born Jan. 15, 1860.

VII. Margaret Honsberger, born May 31, 1862.

VII. John A. Honsberger, born June 27, 1864. Mrd. Nelly Fry in 1885—. Baptists.

VII. Andrew Dean Honsberger, born in 1866.

VII. Allen Mack Honsberger, born July 20, 1868.

VII. Henry James Honsberger, born Nov., 1873.

VII. Alpheus Honsberger, born Dec. 29, 1875.

VI. Magdalena Honsberger, born Apr. 18, 1827. Mrd. Abraham Swartz, Nov. 20, 1847. He died Mar. 14, 1882. Tailor. Disciples. No issue.

VI. Jacob B. Honsberger, born Apr. 18, 1827. Mrd. Barbara Culp, July 17, 1849. P. O., Fenwick, Ont. Sawyer. Methodists. Children: Anna, Mary, Menno, Augusta, Joshua, Jacob, Jonathan, Barbara, Almer.

VII. Anna Margaret Honsberger, born Apr. 13, 1850. Mrd. Charles Fester, Dec. 25, 1870. P. O., Fenwick, Ont. Children: (**VIII.**) John Ezra Fester, born Dec. 8, 1872. (**VIII.**) Jacob Wesley Fester, born June 25, 1875. (**VIII.**) Mary Ann Fester, born Mar. 15, 1880.

VII. Mary Magdalena Honsberger, born Sept. 12, 1853. Mrd. Henry Hamson in 1878. Employed in Coal Yard at Lockport, N. Y. Children: (**VIII.**) Allas,

(**VIII.**) William.   (**VIII.**) George.   (**VIII.**) Archibald. (**VIII.**) Grace.

VII. Menno Simon Honsberger, born Dec. 22, 1855.

VII. Augusta Honsberger, born Jan. 3, 1858.

VII. Joshua C. Honsberger, born Aug. 17, 1860.

VII. Jacob Remandas Honsberger, born June 16, 1863; died June 4, 1873.

VII. Jonathan M. Honsberger, born Dec. 21, 1866.

VII. Barbara Clarenda Honsberger, born Oct. 21, 1868.

VII. Almer Honsberger, born Apr. 26, 1871.

VI. William Honsberger, born in Lincoln Co., Ont., July 1, 1830. Mrd. Barbara Kinsey in 1856. She died . P. O., Campden, Ont. Farmer. Methodist. Children: Mary, Sarah, James, Lydia. William married for his second wife Mary High, May 3, 1864. Children: Samantha, Emma, Ezra, William.

VII. Mary Catharine Honsberger, born Feb. 3, 1857. Mrd. Joseph Kreish, June, 1884. P. O., Preston, Ont. One child. (**VIII.**) Wilford Kreish, born July, 1889.

VII. Sarah Ann Honsberger, born Sept. 23, 1858. Mrd. Simeon Kratz. (See Index of Refer nces No. 1.)

VII. James Honsberger, born Nov. 15, 1860. Mrd. Fannie Fretz, Mar. 3, 1886. P. O., Campden, Ont. Farmer. Children: (**VIII.**) Ernest Honsberger, born Feb. 3, 1887. (**VIII.**) Bertha Honsberger, born July 25, 1888.

VII. Lydia Margaret Honsberger, born Oct. 6, 1862. Mrd. Jacob H. Schweitzer, Dec. 21, 1889. P. O., Niagara Falls Centre, Ont. One child. (**VIII.**) Charles E. Schweitzer, born May 5, 1890.

VII. Samantha Honsberger, born Mar. 28, 1865; died Mar. 19, 1883. Methodist.

VII. Emma Honsberger, born Sept. 9, 1867. Mrd. Wilford Moyer, Dec. 21, 1887. P. O., Brantford, Ont. Painter. One child: (**VIII.**) Alleta May Moyer born Mar. 17, 1891.

VII. Ezra Honsberger, born May 16, 1871.

VII. William Honsberger, born Aug. 21, 1877.

V. John Kratz, born in Bucks Co., Pa., Aug. 29, 1791; died Mar. 26, 1850. Mrd. Magdalena Honsberger about 1813. Farmer in Lincoln Co., Ont. Mennonite. Children: Valentine, Magdalena, John, Anna, Catharine, Susanna, Agnes, Elizabeth, Abraham, Christian, Margaret.

VI. Valentine Kratz, born Nov. 16, 1814; died Oct. 3, 1890. Mrd. Susanna Fretz, daughter of Samuel and Catharine (Honsberger) Fretz, Mar. 14, 1840. Children: Henry, Anna, William.

VII. Henry Kratz, born June 4, 1842.

VII. Anna Kratz, born June 7, 1849. Mrd. Atter.

VII. William Kratz, born Sept. 13, 1857.

VI. Magdalena Kratz, born Mar. 16, 1817. Mrd. Henry Price,—. Farmer. Children: Margaret, Eliza, Catharine, Solomon.

VII. Margaret Price, born May 19, 1838. Mrd. John W. Tufford, Sept. 26, 1855. He was born Sept. 26, 1827. Mennonites. Children: Mary, Jerome, Sarah Philip.

VIII. Mary Elizabeth Tufford, born Feb. 28, 1856. Mrd.—.

VIII. Jerome Tufford, born Feb. 8, 1861. Mrd. .

VIII. Sarah Caroline Tufford, born Oct. 21, 1863. Mrd. Alonzo L. Benson, May 10, 1884 Farmer in Monroe Co., N. Y. Attend Methodist church. One child: (**IX.**) Harvey L. Benson, born May 28, 1888.

VIII. Philip Tufford, born June 18, 1867.

VII. Eliza Ann Price, born Feb. 1, 1841. Mrd. Peter H. Cline, Feb. 24, 1857. P. O., Jordan, Ont. Horticulturist. Disciples. Children: Martha, Henry, Mary, John, Charles, Maggie, Olive, Ella, Eliza, Gertrude, James.

VIII. Martha Cline, born Oct. 22, 1858. Mrd. James Honsberger. (See Index of References No. 2.)

VIII. Henry F. Cline, born Sept. 19, 1860.

VIII. Mary C. Cline, born Dec. 19, 1862.

VIII. John W. Cline, born Mar. 3, 1865.

VIII. Charles W. Cline, born Dec. 4, 1867. Mrd. Ellen Morrison, May 24, 1889. Blacksmith. Children: (**IX.**) Harold Cline, (**IX.**) Gertrude Cline.

VIII. Maggie E. Cline, born Apr. 23, 1870.

VIII. Olive S. E. Cline, born Feb. 20, 1873; died Nov. 16, 1875.

VIII. Ella M. Cline, born Apr. 22, 1876.

VIII. Eliza A. Cline, born Apr. 21, 1878; died Oct. 23, 1879.

VIII. Gertrude M. Cline, born Mar. 8, 1881.

VIII. James J. Cline, born Sept. 30, 1883.

VII. Catharine Price, born June 25, 1842. Mrd. Levi Myers, Dec. 24, 1867. He died April 24, 1875. Children: (VIII.) William A. Myers, born Feb. 5, 1869. (VIII.) Birdie M. Myers, born Dec. 28, 1874.

VII. Solomon Price, born Sept. 24, 1851. Mrd. Flora Walrath, June 15, 1872. She died July 13, 1889. Farmer. One child: (VIII.) Mary E. Price, born Dec. 5, 1878.

VI. John Kratz, born Oct. 22, 1819; died May 31, 1866. Mrd. Saloma Moyer, —. Farmer. Mennonites. Children: Alma, Mary, Maggie, Jacob, Susan, Barbara, Sarah.

VII. Alma Kratz, born —. Mrd. Solomon Overholt. —, P. O., Jordan, Ont. Fruit Grower. Children: (VIII.) Anna Maud Overholt. (VIII.) Cora Mabel Overholt.

VII. Mary Kratz, born —. Mrd. Thomas Easterbrook, —.

VII. Maggie Kratz, born . Mrd. Alfred Warder, .

VII. Jacob M. Kratz, born June 1, 1859. P. O. Freeman, Ont. Farmer. Ev. Assoc. Single.

VII. Susan Kratz, born Sept. 10, 1866. Mrd. Franklin H. Eckhardt, Dec. 16, 1885. P. O., Campden, Ont. Painter. Ev. Assoc. Children: (VIII.) Lena Eckhardt, born Apr. 23, 1887. (VIII.) Salome Eckhardt, born Apr. 8, 1890; died Sept. 11, 1891.

VII. Barbara Kratz, born Aug. 16, 1861; died May 3, 1863.

VII. Sarah Kratz, born Jan. 22, 1864; died Sept. 8, 1865.

VI. Anna Kratz, born June 25, 1821. Mrd. Henry Wismer, in 1845. He was born June 29, 1821; died May 14, 1884. Farmer. In 1861 he was elected a member of the Township Council by a majority of one vote, and was a member of the Township Council for eight successive years, having been elected by acclamation. In 1870 he was elected Reeve of Louth Twp., which office he held for seven years, and in

1875 he was elected Warden of Lincoln County. He served as a member of the Louth Township Council for 16 years. He lived on the shore of Lake Ontario, where he owned a farm of 80 acres. No issue.

VI. Catharine Kratz, born Jan. 19, 1823. Mrd. Abraham Martin, Mar. 15, 1846. P. O., Jordan, Ont. Farmer. Baptists. Children: Barbara, Mary, John, Abraham.

VII. Barbara Ellen Martin, born June 29, 1848. Mrd. Courtland High, May 18, 1870. P. O., Beamsville, Ont. Farmer. Baptists. One child: (**VIII.**) Archie Martin High, born Feb. 15, 1875.

VII. Mary Margaret Martin, born May 21, 1852. Mrd. Aaron Wismer, Jan. 19, 1876. P. O., Jordan, Ont. Farmer. Baptists. No issue.

VII. John Franklin Martin, born Sept. 23, 1854. Mrd. Samantha E. Price, Dec. 10, 1879. P. O., Jordan, Ont. Farmer. Baptists. One child: (**VIII.**) Nellie May Martin, born May 19, 1885.

VII. Abraham Judson Martin, born Mar. 28, 1863; died Mar. 27, 1882.

VI. Susanna Kratz, born July 27, 1826. Mrd. Jacob H. Moyer, May 12, 1850. P. O., Jordan, Ont. Farmer. Children: Solomon, Magdalena, Barbara, Mahlon, Anna, Agnes, Catharine, Norman.

VII. Solomon K. Moyer, born Jan. 27, 1851. Fruit Merchant. Single.

VII. Magdalena Moyer, born Oct. 24, 1853. Mrd. Ephraim Wismer, Aug. 1, 1872. P. O., St. Catharines, Ont. Book-keeper. Baptists. Children: (**VIII.**) Clara Euretta Wismer, born Oct. 9, 1873. (**VIII.**) Norman Howard Wismer, born Dec. 8, 1875. (**VIII.**) Cora Mabel Wismer, born Oct. 6, 1876. (**VIII.**) Effie Gertrude Wismer, born Feb. 7, 1880. (**VIII.**) Hilliard Grove Wismer, born July 1, 1886; died Aug. 21, 1887. (**VIII.**) Walter Stanley Wismer, born July 21, 1887.

VII. Barbara Moyer, born Aug. 19, 1855. Mrd. Alfred Wismer, Jan. 8, 1874. P. O., Portdalhousie, Ont. Farmer. Baptists. Children: (**VIII.**) Elsie Maud Wismer, born June 3, 1877. (**VIII.**) Herbert Stanley

Wismer, born Mar. 27, 1882. (**VIII.**) Eva Florence Wismer, born Feb. 20, 1886.

VII. Mahlon K. Moyer, born Oct. 16, 1856. Mrd.—.

VII. Anna K. Moyer, born Nov. 28, 1858. Mrd. Jesse Pawling,—.

VII. Catharine Moyer, born Aug. 3, 1862. Mrd. William Fegan.

VII. Agnes Moyer, born July 17, 1865. Mrd. John Fegan.

VII. Norman K. Moyer, born 1867. Single.

VI. Agnes Kratz, born Mar. 16, 1828. Mrd. Michael Hunsberry, —. He died—. Farmer. Mrs. Hunsberry, Disciple. Children: William, John.

VII. William Albert Hunsberry, born Aug. 6, 1849. Mrd. Margaret Martin, Mar. 19, 1873. Horticultur ist. Disciple. One child: (**VIII.**) Wellington Henry Hunsberry, born Apr. 22, 1876.

VII. John Oscar Hunsberry, born Dec. 25, 1851. Mrd. Celia Ann Fegan, Feb. 21, 1876. She was born Nov. 7, 1857. Laborer. Methodists. Children: (**VIII.**) William Curtis Hunsberry, born Apr. 12, 1878. (**VIII.**) Aggie Minerva Hunsberry, born Mar. 29, 1880. (**VIII.**) Herbert Hunsberry, born Aug. 14, 1882; died Nov. 20, 1882. (**VIII.**) Henry Earl Hunsberry, born Oct. 7, 1883. (**VIII.**) Claire Hunsberry, born Oct. 1, 1890.

VI. Elizabeth Kratz, born in Lincoln Co., Ont., Apr. 9, 1830. Mrd. Samuel W. Moyer, Dec. 15, 1850. He was born Feb. 19, 1830. P. O., Welland, Ont. Children: Reuben, Daniel, Lavina, Magdalena, Anna, Mary.

VII. Reuben K. Moyer, born Sept. 11, 1851. Mrd. Matilda Grant, Dec. 21, 1875. She was born Nov. 18, 1853. P. O., Fonthill, Ont. Children: (**VIII.**) Alberta Moyer, born July 24, 1877. (**VIII.**) James Franklin Moyer, born Sept 3, 1879. (**VIII.**) Lillie May Moyer, born Apr. 25, 1884.

VII. Daniel Moyer, born May 30, 1853.

VII. Lavina Moyer, born Nov. 17, 1855; died Apr. 11, 1868.

VII. Magdalena Moyer, born Apr. 30, 1857. Mrd. Mangus Haist, Jan. 11, 1876. He was born in Baden, Germany, Sept. 3, 1852. P. O., Fonthill, Ont. Children: (**VIII.**) Samuel Arthur Haist, born Nov. 21, 1876. (**VIII.**) Curtis Haist, and (**VIII.**) Courtland Haist (twins), born June 21, 1879.

VII. Anna Catharine Moyer, born Sept. 21, 1866.

VII. Mary Agnes Moyer, born Sept. 20, 1871.

VI. Abraham Kratz, born July 16, 1832; died Jan. 10, 1890. S.

VI. Christian Kratz, born Feb. 7, 1835. P. O., Jordan, Ont. S.

VI. Margaret Kratz, born June 21, 1837; died in her fifth year.

V. Magdalena Kratz, born in Bucks Co., Pa., Apr. 2, 1795; died in Canada, Dec. 28, 1873. Mrd. Rev. Jacob Culp, May 18, 1819. He was born in Bucks Co., Pa.; died in Canada. Farmer, and for many years a minister in the Mennonite church. Children: Elizabeth, Isaac, Valentine, Anna, Barbara, Susanna, Jacob.

VI. Elizabeth Culp, born Apr. 21, 1820. Mrd. John Fretz, son of Samuel and Catharine (Honsberger) Fretz, Nov. 23, 1841. He was born Feb. 6, 1820; died Aug. 15, 1847. Farmer. Mennonites. Children: Matilda, Moses, John. For second husband Elizabeth mrd. Jacob H. High,—.

VII. Matilda Fretz, born in Lincoln Co., Ont., Sept. 17, 1843. Mrd. Henry H. Honsberger, Feb. 5, 1867. P. O., Jordan, Ont. Farmer. Mennonites. Children: (**VIII.**) Franklin Honsberger, born Dec. 10, 1867. (**VIII.**) Sylvina Honsberger, born Aug. 31, 1869. (**VIII.**) Elizabeth Honsberger, born March 7, 1871. (**VIII.**) Jacob Honsberger, born July 19, 1872. (**VIII.**) Sarah Honsberger, born Feb. 15, 1876. (**VIII.**) Wesley Honsberger, born Aug. 28, 1877; died Sept. 25, 1877. (**VIII.**) James E. Honsberger, born Feb. 27, 1880. (**VIII.**) Anna S. Honsberger, born May 12, 1883; died June 22, 1884. (**VIII.**) Effie Honsberger, born June 4, 1885.

VII. Moses Fretz, born Oct. 16, 1845; died Aug. 6, 1847.

VII. John Fretz, born in Lincoln Co., Ont., Jan. 29, 1848. P. O., Jordan, Ont. Farmer. S.

VI. Isaac Culp, born Jan. 1, 1822; died Nov. 5, 1840.

VI. Valentine Culp, born Nov. 10. 1823. P. O., Jordan, Ont. S.

VI. Anna Culp, born Oct. 13, 1825. Mrd. Isaac M. Culp. Mar. 8, 1846. P. O., Jordan, Ont. Farmer. Mennonites. Children: Tillman, Saphronia.

VII. Tillman Culp, born Mar. 23, 1847; died Sept. 8, 1847.

VII. Saphronia Culp, born Mar. 8, 1859. Mrd. Jacob Honsberger. (See Index of References No. 3.)

VI. Barbara Culp, born Feb. 4, 1827: died Jan. 21. 1882. Mrd. Jacob B. Honsberger. (See Index of References No. 4.)

VI. Susanna Culp, born July 14, 1829: died--. Mrd. James Hodgkin— P. O., Cottam, Ont. Children: Malinda. Alfred. Lenorah. Magdalena. Jacob, Anna, Mary.

VII. Malinda Hodgkin, born June 11, 1851. Mrd. William Logan, Apr. 22. 1877 .P. O., Kingsville, Ont. Children: (VIII.) Errie Logan. (VIII.) James Logan. (VIII.) Beatrice Logan. (VIII.) Gracie Logan. (VIII.) Electa Logan.

VII. Alfred J. Hodgkin. born Apr. 4, 1854. Mrd. Emma Gertrode. Sept. 16. 1890. P. O., Cottam. Ont.

VII. Lenorah Hodgkin, born Aug. 16, 1856. Mrd. Albert Colthorp.— .P. O., St. Louis. Mich. Children: (VIII.) Mabel Irene. (VIII.) Pathena Pearl. (VIII.) Homer Roy. (VIII.) Albert Ray. (VIII.) Orvilla Grant.

VII. Magdalena Hodgkin, born Apr. 2. 1859. Mrd. Leamington Burns Stewart, M. D., Sept. 24, 1883. P. O., Sparta, Mich. Physician. Attend Congregational Ch. Children: (VIII.) Augusta Burns Stewart, born Apr. 28, 1886. (VIII.) Lyman Bruce Stewart, born Mar. 5, 1889.

VII. Jacob Hodgkin, born Jan. 29, 1862. Mrd. Jennie Broner.--. P. O., Vancouver. B C. Children: (VIII.) Nina Hodgkin. (VIII.) Sybilla Hodgkin.

VII. Anna Margaret Hodgkin. born July 29, 1864. Mrd. Wesley Langheed.—. P. O., Ridgeway, Mich.

VII. Mary Jane Hodgkin, born June 5, 1867. P. O., Sparta. Mich. Teacher. Single.

VI. Jacob W. Culp, born Jan. 25, 1838. Mrd. Barbara Beck, May 27, 1862. P. O., South Cayuga, Ont. Farmer. Children: John, Martha, Frederick.

VII. John Ezra Culp, born June 5, 1863. P. O., Brantford, Ont. S.

VII. Martha Jane Culp, born Feb. 11, 1865. Mrd. John Easton, Feb. 22, 1888. P. O., Appleby, Ont. Farmer. Wesleyan Methodists. One child: (**VIII.**) Eva Edna Luella Easton, born Feb. 2, 1889.

VII. Frederick Tennyson Culp, born Dec. 13, 1882.

V. Susanna Kratz, born : died —. Mrd. Abraham H. High,—. No issue.

V. Catharine Kratz, born Aug. 25, 1800; died Mar. 25, 1880, aged 79 y. 7 mo., never married.

V. Elizabeth Kratz, born —: died—. Mrd. John Honsberger. . Children: Jacob, John, Valentine, Abraham, Daniel, Samuel, Enos, Joseph.

VI. Jacob K. Honsberger, born Oct. 24, 1820. Mrd. Anna Culp, in 1846. P. O., Tilsonburg, Ont. Farmer. Methodists. Children: Elizabeth, Matilda, Anna, John, Sarah, Mary, Isaac, Alfred, Jacob, Frank.

VII. Elizabeth Honsberger, born Feb. 10, 1847. Mrd. Jacob Fry, May 19, 1866. P. O., Dunville, Ont. Veterinary Surgeon. Mrs. Fry, Baptist. Children: Harry, William, Myrtle.

VIII. Harry W. Fry, born Jan. 5, 1869. Mrd. Frances Michener, May 23, 1889. P. O., Dunville, Ont. Veterinary Surgeon. Methodists

VIII. William A. Fry, born Sept. 7, 1872. Printer.

VIII. Myrtle E. Fry, born May 30, 1879.

VII. Matilda Honsberger, born in 1848. Mrd. David Moyer, in 1865. P. O., Maybee, Ont. Farmer. Children: Ella, Levi, Mary, Michael, Jane.

VIII. Ellen Moyer, born 1865. Mrd. William Hays in 1885. P. O., Dorchester, Ont. Children: (**IX.**) Elgin Hays, (**IX.**) Albert Hays, (**IX.**) Clarence Hays.

VIII. Levi Moyer, born in 1867. Farmer. S.

VIII. Mary Moyer, born in 1872.

VIII. Michael Moyer, born in 1875.

VIII. Jane Moyer, born in 1877.

VII. Anna Honsberger, born in 1849. Mrd. Martin Raible. . P. O., Eden, Ont. No issue.

VII. John Honsberger, born in 1851. Methodist. S.

VII. Sarah Honsberger, born in 1854. Mrd. Samuel Culp. Farmer. Methodist. Children: Anna, Frederick.

VIII. Anna Culp, born —. Mrd. Almer Ostrander—. 1890. P. O., Guysboro, Ont. Farmer. Methodist.

VIII. Frederick Culp, born—.

VII. Mary Honsberger, born in 1856. Mrd. Daniel Steward in 1883. Farmer. Methodist. One child: (**VIII.**) Alla Steward.

VII. Isaac Honsberger, born in 1858. Mrd. Adaline Steward—. P. O., Brownsville, Ont. Children: (**VIII.**) Virgil Honsberger. (**VIII.**) Mabel Honsberger. (**VIII**) Frank Honsberger.

VII. Alfred Honsberger, born in 1864. Mrd. Phœbe Townsend,—. P. O., Maybee, Ont. Children: (**VIII.**) Ivan Honsberger. (**VIII.**) Alva Honsberger. (**VIII.**) Charles Honsberger. (**VIII.**) Clarence Honsberger. (**VIII.**) John Honsberger.

VII. Jacob Honsberger, born in 1866. S.

VII. Frank Honsberger, born in 1868. S.

VI. John Honsberger, born in 1822; died —. Farmer. Methodist. S.

VI. Valentine Honsberger, born—. Mrd. Magdalena Swartz. P. O., Rainham, Ont. Farmer. Members Disciple Ch. Children: Simeon, Abram, Alice, Ralph, William, Mary.

VII. Simeon Honsberger, born—. S.

VII. Abram Honsberger, born—. Mrd.—. One child.

VII. Alice Honsberger, born—. Mrd.—. One child.

VII. Ralph Honsberger, born—. S.

VII. William Honsberger, born—. S.

VII. Mary Matilda Honsberger, born—; died—.

VI. Rev. Abraham Honsberger, born in 1826; died Mar. 30, 1889. Mrd. Mary Albright, in 1852. Farmer and minister. He was ordained minister of the Old Mennonite church in 1857, and served as pastor of the church in Clinton Twp., Ont. Children: James, Jonas, Martha, John.

VII. James H. Honsberger, born in 1853. Mrd. Martha Cline, daughter of Peter Cline. . P. O., —, Ont. Farmer. Disciples. No children.

VII. Jonas A. Honsberger, born Mar. 14, 1858. Engaged in the mercantile business in Buffalo, N. Y.

VII. Martha Honsberger, born in Lincoln Co., Ont., in 1861. Mrd. William A. Caskey, in 1887 P. O., Jordan, Ont. Farmer. Mrs. Caskey, Methodist. One child: **(VIII.)** Mary Catharine Caskey, born and died same day in 1889.

VII. John Honsberger, M. D., born in Lincoln Co., Ont., June 5, 1867. Attends Protestant Episcopal Ch. At the age of five he began to attend the district schools. He soon became passionately fond of studying and always stood well. In 1880 or 1881 he went up for the high school entrance examination at Beamsville, Ont., which he passed. From that time public school was neglected, and in a short time he ceased attendance, preferring to study at home on the farm. In the fall of 1883 he started to high school at Beamsville, and the following year took out a teacher's certificate. In the fall of 1884 he attended Normal school and received his Professional teacher's certificate. He then attended Canada Business College at Hamilton, until the following April, when he returned to high school. In the summer of 1886 he matriculated in medicine at Toronto University, and in October of the same year he entered Trinity Medical College. After a four year's course he was graduated at Trinity University with honors and received the degree of M. D.eey. In the spring of 1889 his father died, before witnessing what had been his life long ambition, viz: to see him made a physician. His vacations during his course were spent in the office of his highly esteemed preceptor, Dr. Jessup of St. Catharines, to whom he is deeply indebted for much most valuable assistance. On May 24, 1890, he removed to Buffalo, N. Y., where he has since been engaged in the practice of his profession, and where he is receiving his share of fame and shekels. S.

VI. Daniel Honsberger, born—. Mrd. Sarah Honsberger—. She died.—. P. O., Dunnville, Ont. Farmer. United Brethren. Children: William, Julia, Harriet. Mary. John. Susan. Adda, Joseph.

VII. William Honsberger. born--. S.

VII. Julia Honsberger. born--. Mrd.--.

VII. Harriet Honsberger. born--. Mrd.--.

VII. Mary Jane Honsberger. born--. S.

VII. John Henry Honsberger. born--. Mrd.--.

VII. Susan Honsberger. born--: died--.

VII. Adda Honsberger. born--. S.

VII. Joseph Honsberger, born--. S.

VI. Samuel Honsberger. born--. P. O.. Rainham, Ont. Carpenter. Disciple. S.

VI. Enos Honsberger, born--. Mrd.--. P. O. Langton, Ont. Farmer. Methodist. Children: (**VII.**) Mary Honsberger. (**VII.**) Emma Honsberger. (**VII.**) Rosa Honsberger. (**VII.**) Minnie Honsberger. (**VII.**) Austin Honsberger. (**VII.**) Sylvester Honsberger. (**VII.**) Alberta Honsberger. dec'd. (**VII.**) Sanford Honsberger. All single.

VI. Joseph Honsberger. born--. P. O.. Dunnville, Ont. Printer and operator.

V. Abraham Kratz. born Oct. 3, 1805; died Sept. 30, 1885. Mrd. Mary Swartz. Dec. 17. 1826. She was born Jan. 22, 1809; died Oct. 25. 1872. Farmer. Mennonites. Mr. Kratz was ordained deacon of the Mennonite church in 1835 and served the church in that capacity for many years. Children: Andrew. Christian. Anna. Isaac. Jacob. Barbara. Mary. Abraham. Elizabeth. Margaret. Joseph. Catharine, Ephraim.

VI. Andrew Kratz, born Mar. 22, 1828. Mrd. Margaret High, Jan. 23, 1855. She was born Mar. 5. 1833; died Oct. 1. 1878. P. O.. Jordan. Ont. Farmer. Mennonites. Children: Simeon. Rachel. Augusta, John, Austin. Emerson. Jane. Minnie. Margaret, Abraham. For his second wife Andrew mrd. Barbara Fretz. Feb. 14. 1884.

VII. Simeon Kratz, born July 12. 1857. Mrd. Sarah Ann Honsberger, Dec. 21, 1887. One child: (**VIII.**) Meta Kratz. born July 21. 1890.

VII. Rachel Kratz. born Jan. 25. 1859.

VII. Augusta Kratz. born Dec. 4. 1860. Mrd. Robert Carl. Sept.. 1883. P. O., Jordan. Ont. Farmer.

VII. John Kratz, born Aug. 12. 1862. Farmer.

VII. Austin Kratz. born June 19. 1864. Farmer.

VII. Emerson Kratz. born June 15. 1866: died Mar. 7. 1891. Book-keeper and Shorthand writer.

VII. Jane Kratz. born Aug. 12. 1868.

VII. Minnie Kratz. born Apr. 27. 1872.

VII. Margaret Kratz. born June 15. 1874.

VII. Abraham Kratz. born Apr. 20. 1877.

VI. Christian Kratz. born May 4. 1830. Mrd. Barbara Moyer. Mar. 19. 1871. She was born Sept. 27. 1838. P. O.. Jordan. Ont. Farmer. He became blind in 1851 from a cataract. No issue.

VI. Anna Kratz. born Nov. 27. 1831. Mrd. Henry Fretz. Nov. 2. 1852. He was born Mar. 19. 1830. P. O.. Campden. Ont. Farmer. Mennonites. Children: Sarah. Mary. Levi. Annie. Maggie. Fannie. Emma. Martha.

VII. Sarah Fretz. born Jan. 3. 1854: died Sept. 9. 1856.

VII. Mary Fretz. born Nov. 28. 1855. Mrd. Mahlon H. Myers. June 30. 1873 (his second wife). Farmer in Bucks Co.. Pa. Mennonites. Children:

VIII. Anna F. Myers. born Feb. 25. 1875.

VIII. Beulah Eldora Myers. born July 25. 1876.

VIII. Maggie F. Myers. born Sept. 30. 1878: died Mar. 8. 1886.

VIII. Hannah F. Myers. born July 24. 1880.

VIII. William H. Myers. born July 1. 1882: died Mar. 8. 1886.

VIII. Henry F. Myers. born Oct. 29. 1884: died Mar. 11. 1886.

VIII. Mary Emma Myers. born Mar. 4. 1887: died June 6. 1890.

VIII. Ezra F. Myers. born Apr. 1. 1889: died May 19. 1890.

VIII. Elmer Clayton Myers. born Apr. 29. 1891.

VII. Levi Fretz, born Sept. 1. 1857. Mrd. Madilla Moyer, Oct. 11. 1880. P. O.. Campden. Ont. Fruit Grower. Methodists. Children: (VIII.) Beatrice Fretz, born Jan. 7, 1884. (**VIII.**) Cora Fretz, born Aug. 21, 1888.

VII. Annie Fretz, born Jan. 26, 1859. Single.

VII. Maggie Fretz, born July 3, 1861. Mrd. Francis M. Fretz (see Index of References No. 5).

VII. Fannie Fretz, born Nov. 15, 1864. Mrd. James H. Honsberger (see Index of References No. 6).

VII. Emma Fretz, born Sept. 15, 1868.

VII. Martha Fretz, born May 3, 1874.

VI. Isaac Kratz, born Aug. 18, 1834. Mrd. Anna Moyer, Mar. 27, 1866. She was born June 15, 1844. Farmer. One child: (**VII.**) Sylvester Kratz, born Sept. 2, 1870.

VI. Jacob S. Kratz, born Aug. 4, 1836. Mrd. Tryphena Beam, Aug. 25, 1883. She was born Sept. 19, 1848. He has always been partially blind. Fruit grower and farmer. One child: (**VII.**) Levi Kratz, born June 7, 1888.

VI. Barbara Kratz, born Aug. 4, 1838. Mrd. Jacob F. Rittenhouse, Nov. 30, 1865 (his second wife). P. O., Campden, Ont. Farmer. Mennonites. Children:

VII. Franklin K. Rittenhouse, born Sept. 24; 1866. Engineer in Chicago, Ill.

VII. Moses K. Rittenhouse, born July 8, 1869.

VII. Mary K. Rittenhouse, born June 2, 1872.

VI. Mary Kratz, born in Lincoln Co., Ont., Jan. 23, 1841. Mrd. Freeman Wismer, Jan. 8, 1866. P. O., St. Catharines, Ont. Farmer. Mrs. Wismer member Mennonite Brethren in Christ. Children: (**VII.**) Salina Wismer, born Dec. 9, 1866. (**VII.**) Morgan Wismer, born July 10, 1869. (**VII.**) Albert Wismer, born May 11, 1872. (**VII.**) Archibald Wismer, born Oct. 14, 1875. (**VII.**) Hattie Wismer, born Feb. 11, 1879. (**VII.**) Mary Wismer, born Nov. 8, 1881.

VI. Abraham Kratz (twin to Mary), born Jan. 23, 1841; died Feb. 13, 1841.

VI. Elizabeth Kratz, born Jan. 29, 1843; died Aug. 29, 1846.

VI. Margaret Kratz, born July 23, 1845. Mrd. Jacob Sievenpiper, Jan. 9, 1866. He was born May 2, 1844; died Jan. 27, 1885. Farmer. Children: (**VII.**) Joel Sievenpiper, born Dec. 1, 1866. (**VII.**) Ephraim

Sievenpiper, born Jan. 29, 1870. (**VII.**) Sophronia Sievenpiper, born Oct. 22, 1874. (**VII.**) Abraham Sievenpiper, born Feb. 26, 1876. (**VII.**) Salina Sievenpiper, born Apr. 21, 1877. (**VII.**) Minnie Sievenpiper, born June 29, 1879. (**VII.**) Melvin Sievenpiper, born Aug. 12, 1881. (**VII.**) Franklin Sievenpiper, born July 24, 1884.

VI. Joseph Kratz, born Sept. 7, 1847; died Feb. 11, 1889. Mrd. Agnes Cordelia Hill, Apr. 20, 1869. Children: (**VII.**) Charles S. Kratz, born July 12, 1871. Clerk. S. (**VII.**) Alexander A. Kratz, born July 3, 1873.

VI. Catharine Kratz, born Oct. 1, 1849. Mrd. John W. Nunn, Dec. 3, 1872. He was born Apr. 1, 1851. P. O., Jordan, Ont. Fisherman. Children: (**VII.**) Emily Nunn, born Feb. 20, 1874. (**VII.**) Ervin Nunn, born Sept. 21, 1875. (**VII.**) Louisa Nunn, born June 8, 1877. (**VII.**) Mary Nunn, born Dec. 24, 1879.

VI. Ephraim Kratz, born Jan. 29, 1852. Mrd. Hannah Vaughn, Apr. 25, 1882. She was born May 23, 1849. Fruit grower. Children: (**VII.**) James Clayton Kratz, born Apr. 27, 1883. (**VII.**) Lidie Kratz, born Feb. 17, 1885. (**VII.**) Mabel Kratz, born May 17, 1887.

V. Margaret Kratz, born in Lincoln Co., Ont., Feb. 23, 1808; died Apr. 15, 1875. Mrd. Rev. Daniel High, Dec. 20, 1826. Farmer and minister. He was ordained a minister of the Mennonite church in 1831. He was born about 1805; died—. Children: Anna, Catharine, Daniel, Maria, Valentine, Jacob, John, Samuel, Catharine, Benjamin, Margaret, Jessa, William.

VI. Anna High, born May 15, 1828. Mrd. Jacob L. Kinsey, Oct. 17, 1854. P. O., Doon, Ont. Farmer. Mennonites. Chidren: Maria, Jacob, Daniel.

VII. Maria Kinsey, born Apr. 7, 1859; died Oct. 22, 1859.

VII. Jacob H. Kinsey, born Mar. 26, 1863. Mrd. Louisa Smith, May 14, 1889. P. O., Doon, Ont. Farmer. Attends Mennonite Ch. No children.

VII. Daniel Kinsey, born Apr. 17, 1866. P. O., Doon, Ont. Farmer. Attends Mennonite Ch. S.

VI. Catharine High, born Dec. 20, 1829; died May 4, 1839.

VI. Daniel K. High, born in Lincoln Co., Ont., Sept. 4, 1831. Mrd. Nancy Moyer, May 9, 1854. She died Mar. 22, 1891. P. O., Jordan, Ont. Farmer. Members of E. M. Ch. Children: Infant, Mary, Wendell, Emma, Clara.

VII. Infant son, born and died Dec. 2, 1855.

VII. Mary Ann High, born May 26, 1857; died Oct. 7, 1862.

VII. Wendell High, born Dec. 13, 1860. Mrd. Augusta Moore, Dec. 23, 1884. P. O., Jordan, Ont. Farmer. Mrs. High, Ev. Assoc. No. issue.

VII. Emma High, born Jan. 5, 1868.

VII. Clara High, born May 22, 1874.

VI. Maria High, born in Lincoln Co., Ont., Feb. 7, 1834. Mrd. Christian Moyer, Esq., Oct. 9, 1859. P. O., Campden, Ont. Farmer. Mennonites. Children: Ezra, Alfred, Matilda, Loetta, Rowland.

VII. Ezra Moyer, born Nov. 26, 1860. Mrd. Martha Robins,—. P. O., Campden, Ont.

VII. Alfred H. Moyer, born July 11, 1862. Bookkeeper and stenographer in Chicago, Ill. Methodist Episcopal.

VII. Matilda Moyer, born Aug. 1, 1868.

VII. Loetta Moyer, born Aug. 1, 1872; died Apr. 2, 1880.

VII. Rowland J. Moyer, born Dec. 13, 1878.

VI. Valentine High, born May 3, 1835. Mrd. Della Pope, May, 1862. She was born in 1845; died May, 1873. Res. Chicago, Ill. Traveling Ag't. Baptists. Children: Emma, William.

VII. Emma High, born June 9, 1863. Mrd. Christian G. Moyer,—. P. O., Campden, Ont. Farmer. Ev. Assoc. Children: (**VIII.**) Enoch Moyer, born Nov. 2, 1886. (**VIII.**) Elmer Moyer, born June 9, 1889.

VII. William High, born Dec. 1867. S.

VI. Jacob K. High, born in Lincoln Co., Ont., Feb. 20, 1839. Mrd. Matilda Moyer, Mar. 12, 1867. P. O., Jordan, Ont. Farmer. Children: (**VII.**) Lodema High, born Jan. 28, 1869. S. (**VII.**) Lucetta High, born Oct. 21, 1870. S. (**VII.**) Cora Belle High, born July

11, 1880. **(VII.)** Norman High, born July 15, 1883; died July 18, 1883.

VI. John K. High, M. D., born Sept. 25, 1840. Practicing Physician at Bridgeport, Mich. S.

VI. Samuel K. High, born July 6, 1842. Mrd. Mary Ann Detwiler, Jan. 3, 1871. P. O., Blair, Ont. Farmer. New Mennonite. Children: **(VII.)** Ezra High, still born Jan 7, 1872. **(VII.)** Ephraim D. High, born Jan. 15, 1873. **(VII.)** Maggie Abigail High, born Apr. 29, 1875. **(VII.)** Maria High, born Dec. 13, 1877. **(VII.)** Almeda High, born Apr. 22, 1880; died June 10, 1880. **(VII.)** Eliza Ann High, born Jan. 20, 1882. **(VII.)** Daniel D. High, born Nov. 14, 1887.

VI. Catharine High, born Aug. 2, 1843. Mrd. Franklin Albright, Mar. 3, 1863. P. O., Berlin, Ont. Sawyer. Children: Susan, Jasbina, Mary, Daniel.

VII. Susan Amanda Albright, born May 20, 1864. Mrd. D. B. Detweiler, June 1886. P. O., Berlin, Ont. Commercial traveler. Children: **(VIII.)** Bertha Detweiler, born Feb. 1887. **(VIII.)** Irene Detweiler, born Apr. 1888; died July 1888.

VII. Jasbina Albright, born June 23, 1866. Mrd. George House, Jan. 1891. P. O., Woodstock, Ont. Shirt manufacturer.

VII. Mary Margaret Albright, born Aug. 16, 1871. S.

VII. Daniel Webster Albright, born Sept. 30, 1873. Grocery clerk. S.

VI. Benjamin K. High, born Oct. 6, 1844. Mrd. Sarah Catharine Hoffman, Oct. 31, 1876. P. O., Smithville, Ont. Farmer. Ev. Assoc. Children: **(VII.)** Alfred Leslie H. High, born Sept. 16, 1877. **(VII.)** Philip H. High, born Aug. 18, 1881. **(VII.)** Margaret Ellen High, born Jan. 30, 1884; died Feb. 10, 1885. **(VII.)** Daniel H. High, born Apr. 5, 1886.

VI. Margaret K. High, born July 3, 1846; died May 19, 1876.

VI. Jessa K. High, born Sept. 30, 1847; died May 25, 1856.

VI. William K. High, born July 20, 1850; died Jan. 27, 1861.

IV. Jacob Kratz, born Feb. 5, 1771; died about 1823. Mrd. —— Latchaw.—. Farmer, and lived on the old

homestead near Blooming Glen. Children: Abraham.
Catharine. Jacob. John. Barbara. Elizabeth. Maria.

V. Abraham Kratz. born —; died —. Mrd. Catharine.
daughter of Martin Fretz. of Hilltown Twp. Farmer.
Mennonites. No issue.

V. Catharine Kratz. born May 30. 1809; died May
8. 1891. Mrd. *Jacob S. Yeakel. in 1829. He was
born Mar. 17. 1803; died May 5. 1864. Weaver and
farmer. Children: Samuel. Mary. John. Catharine.

VI. Samuel K. Yeakel. born Mar. 25. 1832. Mrd.
Sophia Reitz. Oct. 4. 1858. P. O.. 950. 5th St. Beloit.
Wis. Carpenter. Children: Mary. Anna. John, Sam-
uel. Harvey. infant.

VII. Mary Ella Yeakel. born June 25. 1860. Mrd.
John F. Warehime. Nov. 24. 1881. P. O.. Lake City.
Iowa. Farmer. Mrs. Warehime. Methodist. One
child: (**VIII.**) George O. Warehime. born Jan. 16. 1882.

VII. Anna Martha Yeakel. born Oct. 18. 1861; died
Apr. 3. 1864.

VII. John H. Yeakel, born Mar. 12. 1866.

VII. Samuel G. Yeakel, born Dec. 11. 1868.

VII. Harvey R. Yeakel, born Oct. 22. 1871.

VII. Infant. still born.

VI. Mary A. Yeakel. born Sept. 18. 1839. Mrd.
Henry S. Moyer. Jan. 28. 1866. He was born Aug.
15. 1840; died May 27. 1882. Farmer. Mennonites.
Children: (**VII.**) Ella Moyer. born Jan. 17. 1867.
(**VII.**) Hannah Moyer. born Mar. 5. 1870. (**VII.**) Harvey Moyer. born Aug. 15. 1872. (**VII.**) Erwin Moyer.
born Mar. 30. 1875.

VI. John K. Yeakel. born Mar. 28. 1843. Mrd. Minnie VanGilder. in 1875. Tinsmith. No issue.

VI. Catharine Yeakel. born May 27. 1847. Mrd.
Quincey A. Fretz. Oct. 10. 1873. He was born July
18, 1847. P. O.. Bedminster. Pa. Farmer. New
Mennonites. One child: (**VII.**) Alice Y. Fretz. born
—; died in infancy.

V. Jacob Kratz. born in Bucks Co.. Pa.. Aug. 13.
1811; died Feb. 1. 1872. Mrd. Catharine Wismer.
She was born in Bucks Co.. Pa., Sept. 20. 1813. In

---

* A descendant of the Schwenkfelders.

May 1839 they moved to Wayne Co., Ohio, and purchased a farm on which they lived until his death. Mennonites. Children: Samuel, Maria, Reuben, Henry, Jacob, Lee.

VI. Samuel W. Kratz, born in Bucks Co., Pa., in 1836. P. O., Acme, Ohio. Retired teacher, and farmer. Mennonite. S.

VI. Maria Kratz, born in Wayne Co., Ohio, Sept. 17, 1840. Mrd. John C. Steiner, Apr. 20, 1863. P. O., Sterling, Ohio. Farmer. Mennonites. Children: Reuben, Edwin, Kate, Harvey, Alice, Franklin, Lizzie.

VII. Reuben K. Steiner, born Dec. 6, 1863.

VII. Edwin L. Steiner, born Aug. 3, 1866.

VII. Kate A Steiner, born June 20, 1869. Mrd. Andrew D. Blough, in 1888. He was born Oct. 17, 1863. P. O., Fredericksburg, Ohio. Druggist. Disciple. One child: (**VIII.**) Walter H. Blough.

VII. Harvey J. Steiner, born July 8, 1872.

VII. Alice C. Steiner, born Feb. 11, 1876.

VII. Franklin K. Steiner, born Apr. 11, 1879; died July 6, 1879.

VII. Lizzie May Steiner, born Nov. 10, 1882.

VI. Reuben N. Kratz, born in Wayne Co., Ohio, July 2, 1845. In early life he taught in the public schools, and also conducted singing schools in the vicinity of his former home in Wayne Co., Ohio. He was mrd. to Amanda M. Miller, of Akron, Ohio, Sept. 11, 1873. In 1882 they moved to Mitchell, South Dakota. He has been variously occupied as Lumber Merchant, Land Office Clerk, Land Attorney, and at present occupies the position of Register of U. S. Office at Mitchell. He was also one of the founders of the University of Dakota, and is a member of its managing board. Methodists. Children: (**VII.**) Frank E. Kratz, born Oct. 11, 1874; died July 6, 1878. (**VII.**) Fred. M. Kratz, born Feb. 21, 1879. (**VII.**) Carl Samuel Kratz, born Feb. 13, 1888.

VI. Henry Elton Kratz, M. A. Ph. D., born in Medina Co., Ohio, Oct. 14, 1849. He prepared himself for college in the common and high schools of his native State, and supported himself by teaching. He first entered Denison University, Granville, Ohio, where he remained two years, and then completed his college course at Wooster University, Wooster, Ohio, graduating with the degree of B. S., in 1874. Later the degree of M. A. was granted him by his Alma Mater, for subsequent work performed. He at once entered upon the work of teaching and has been superintendent and principal of schools in several important cities, principally those of Bucyrus, Ohio, and Dexter, Michigan. In both of these States he was frequently engaged in the institute work by the side of their best educators. In 1881 he went abroad, taking his family with him, and during two years resided in London. While in Europe he made a special study of systems of education, and methods of instruction. He met many of the leading educators of the old world and became familiar with their theories. Opportunities were offered him to observe school work there which he readily and profitably availed himself of and returned to this country much broadened in his views of education. The year 1885 found him installed in the schools of Mitchell, Dakota, as superintendent, a position he held for four years. He organized and graded these schools, and put them in a condition second to none in the country. His pupils have found easy admission to the schools of our leading cities. He promptly identified himself with the educators of the state, and has been present at every important educational meeting in Dakota since 1886. When the Educational Association organized the reading circle department he was made the chief officer, and in turn made the reading circle one of the vital educational forces of the State. He was three times unanimously chosen president of the State Educational Association, an honor not before conferred on any member. He was also prominently mentioned for the position of Territorial Superintendent of Public Instruction. At the first election for State officers, the leading educators and teachers all over the State made urgent appeal to him to consent to become a candidate for the office of State Superintendent of Public Instruction. Against his better judgment he was finally induced to make an effort to secure the Republican nomination. Unfortunately preceding nominations on the ticket, bunched the nominees in his part of the State, and he was defeated, although even then he received a large number of votes in the convention.

In the spring of 1889, he was called to the chair of Pedagogy and Principalship of the Normal Department of the University of South Dakota, which position he still occupies. Recently he completed a post graduate course in Philosophy and Pedagogy in Wooster University and received the degree of Doctor of Philosophy. "In November 1891, he was unanimously chosen Superintende t of the city schools, to succeed Prof. Charles W. Deane, resigned." at an increase of salary, which was fixed at $2,100 a year. In addition to his other duties he has the chief management of the S. Dakota State Teacher's Circle, conducts Teachers' Institutes, lectures from time to time, and occasionally contributes on educational topics to the press. At the first South Dakota Chautauqua held in the summer of 1891 at Lake Madison, he was director of the summer school, and was unanimously re-elected as director for 1892. Taken altogether it may be seen that Dr. Kratz is an exceedingly busy man.

He was married to Lizzie M. Deal, of Bucyrus, Ohio, July 19, 1876. They are members of the Methodist Episcopal church. Children: (VII.) Horace Elton Kratz, born Nov. 12, 1877. (VII.) Bessie May Kratz, born Jan. 2, 1879. (VII.) Arthur Murray Kratz, born Nov. 5, 1880.

VI. Jacob Kratz, born Feb. 7, 1855. Mrd. Acelia Kindig, Mar. 1, 1876. P. O., Shepherd, Mich. Farmer. Methodists. Children: (VII.) Anna M. Kratz, born Jan 1, 1878. (VII.) Harvey D. Kratz, born Sept. 27, 1879. (VII.) Infant born July 9; died Sept. 19, 1881.

VI. Lee G. Kratz, born July 27, 1858. Mrd. Frankie Curtiss, Nov. 30, 1887. Res. Omaha, Neb. Musician, and Director of the "T. K." Quartette, of Omaha, Neb. Methodists. No children.

V. John Kratz, born— : died –. Mrd.––. Children: Mary, Hannah, Amanda, John.

VI. Mary Ann S. Kratz, born Jan. 8, 1846; died in 1870. Mrd. John L. Fretz, Dec. 16, 1863. (See Index of References No. 7.)

VI. Hannah Kratz, born—. Mrd. Tobias O. Landis, —. They have issue.

VI. Amanda Kratz, born—; died young.

VI. John Kratz, born—; died young.

V. Barbara Kratz, born—; died—, advanced in years. Unmrd.

V. Elizabeth Kratz, born—; died—.

V. Maria Kratz, born—; died—. Mrd. Henry S. Moyer. Two children, son and daughter.

VI. The son enlisted in the army, and died from wounds received in battle. S.

VI. Barbara Moyer, born—; died–. Mrd. John M. Hunsberger, . (See Index of References No. 8.)

IV. Barbara Kratz, born—; died–. Mrd. David High. No children.

IV. Magdalena Kratz, born Aug. 30, 1776; died Jan. 9, 1840, aged 63 yrs., 4 mos., 10 ds. Mrd. Abraham Fretz, son of Christian and Barbara (Oberholtzer) Fretz, Apr. 30, 1793. He was born Mar. 30, 1769; died Mar. 7, 1844, aged 74 yrs., 11 mos., 7 ds. They lived and died on the old "Weaver" John Fretz homestead in Bedminster Twp., Bucks Co., Pa. The farm consisting of about 255 acres was inherited from his father. They were honest, upright people, conscientious Christians, and held in high esteem by the community in which they lived. It is related that while Mr. Fretz was working in the field one day, a man rode up, and seeing his fine cows, wanted to buy one, but he did not want to sell. The man, however, insisted, and asked him to set a price. He then thought that if he should ask double what the cow was worth, the man would leave without buying. But, contrary to his expectations, the man laid down the money and drove the cow off. After the man was gone, he talked the mater over with his wife and they decided it was "Usury," so he mounted a horse, rode after the man, and gave him back half of the money, say-

ing. "I don't want to be damned for a cow." They
were members of the Mennonite church at Deep Run,
of which he was for many years a Deacon. Children:
Anna, Rebecca, Jacob, Christian, John, Isaac, Martin,
Elizabeth, Barbara, Abraham.

V. Anna Fretz, born Jan. 22, 1795; died Mar. 18,
1873. Mrd. Henry Meyers, Dec. 23, 1830. He was
born Sept. 7, 1795; died Mar. 25, 1870. Farmer.
Mennonites. Children: Abraham, John, Christian.

VI. Abraham F. Meyers, born Oct. 14, 1831; died
Oct. 21, 1877. Mrd. Susanna Smith, Nov. 10, 1855.
She died Feb. 9, 1877. Farmer. Mennonite. Children:
(VII.) Anna Catharine Myers, born Nov. 12, 1856;
died May 21, 1882. **(VII.)** Joseph S. Meyers, born
Oct. 25, 1858; died Nov. 15, 1877. **(VII.)** Andrew L.
Meyers, born Oct 3, 1863; died May 24, 1881.

VI. John F. Meyers, born Nov. 1, 1833; died Sept.
11, 1855.

VI. Christian F. Meyers, born Jan. 4, 1841. Mrd.
Sarah Baum, Jan 18, 1883. P. O., Dublin, Pa. Mennonites at Deep Run. No issue.

V. Rebecca Fretz, born Sept. 29, 1796; died Feb. 2,
1798.

V. Jacob Fretz, born Aug. 9, 1799; died Mar. 11,
1800.

V. Christian Fretz, born Jan. 13, 1801; died Sept. 5,
1875. Mrd. Mary Leatherman, Oct. 24, 1824. She
died Apr. 24, 1864. Children: Ely, Abraham, Eliza,
Mary. Christian mrd. for his second wife Elizabeth
Nash, Oct. 6, 1867. She died— . He was a farmer of
large means, a man of thriving energy, a director of
the Doylestown Bank, and an honored member of the
Old Mennonite church at Deep Run.

VI. Ely Fretz, born Sept. 9, 1825. Mrd. Mary Meyers, daughter of William Meyers, in 1850. He is a
prosperous farmer of Bedminster Twp., and a director
of the Sellersville Bank. He and his wife are influen-
tial members of the Second Mennonite church, Deep
Run. Children: Allen, Lucinda, Emeline, Mahlon,
Francis, Barbara, Susan Mary.

VII. Rev. Allen M. Fretz, born Dec. 12, 1853, in
Tinicum Twp., Bucks Co. When 16 years old he was

sent by his parents to the Mennonite Seminary at Wadsworth, Ohio. He subsequently attended one term at the Excelsior Normal Institute at Carversville, Pa., after which he taught school eleven terms, working on his father's farm during the summer months. On Sept. 18, 1880, he was mrd. to Sarah, daughter of Abraham L. Leatherman. She died Mar. 21, 1882. An infant son died soon after birth without name. In the fall of 1882 he accepted the nomination of the Republican party as a candidate for the State Legislature, which was tendered him; but his party being in the minority in that year's campaign, he was, with the rest of the ticket defeated. In 1883, the Second Mennonite church at Deep Run called him to be their minister, and he was accordingly ordained by Bishop Moses Gottschall on Oct. 13, 1883, and installed pastor of same. Feeling the pressing need of an English paper in the interest of his branch of the Mennonite church, he with the aid of N. B. Grubb, pastor of the church in Philadelphia, succeeded in October, 1885 in getting out the prospectus of "*The Mennonite*," which was laid before the conference and accepted as one of the periodicals of the church. He is still one of the editors of the paper, which has steadily increased in popularity and circulation since it was started.

On Mar. 5, 1884, he was mrd. to Anna, daughter of Jacob F. Rittenhouse, of Campden, Ont. Children: (VIII.) Jacob Rittenhouse Fretz, born July 22, 1886. (VIII.) Ely R. Fretz, born Nov. 27, 1888. (VIII.) Viola Fretz, born Mar. 22, 1891.

VII. Lucinda Fretz, born Aug. 5, 1855. Mrd. Edward L. Yost, May 16, 1874. Harness-maker and farmer. Lutherans. Children: (VIII.) William F. Yost, born Nov. 15, 1874. (VIII.) Stella May Yost, born Apr. 28, 1884.

VII. Emeline Fretz, born Dec. 14, 1857. Member second Mennonite Ch., Deep Run. Resides with her parents. S.

VII. Mahlon M. Fretz, born Aug. 21, 1859. Mrd. Amanda, daughter of Joseph M. Fretz of Trumbauersville, Pa., Dec. 22, 1883. Farmer. Lives on the old

"Weaver" John Fretz homestead in Bedminster Twp. New Mennonites. No issue.

VII. Francis M. Fretz, born May 25, 1863. Mrd. Maggie, daughter of Henry Fretz, of Campden, Ont., Mar. 3, 1886. Farmer in Bucks Co. Mennonites. One Child: **(VIII.)** Martha Fretz, born Aug. 30, 1887.

VII. Barbara Fretz, born May 20, 1866. Mrd. Irwin Wasser, Apr. 21, 1888. Farm laborer. Mennonites. Children: **(VIII.)** Mary Wasser, born Jan. 26, 1889. **(VIII.)** Clarence Wasser, born .

VII. Susan Fretz, born Dec. 1, 1869. S.

VII. Mary Etta Fretz, born Dec. 1, 1869 (twin). Mrd. Jacob M. Landis, Feb. 21, 1891.

VI. Abraham Fretz, born Dec. 16, 1829; died Dec. 13, 1876. S.

VI. Eliza Ann Fretz, born Apr. 1, 1835. Mrd. Reuben Stover, Oct. 15, 1854. He died Mar. 25, 1871. Farmer. He was Ger. Reformed. She is New Mennonite. One child:

VII. Louisa Stover, born in 1855. Mrd. John S. Bissey, Aug. 26, 1873. Farmer. Lutherans. Children: **(VIII.)** Clara S. Bissey, born Feb. 22, 1877. **(VIII.)** Alvin S. Bissey, born Dec. 22, 1879. **(VIII.)** Sadie S. Bissey, born Oct. 30, 1882; died Feb. 12, 1886. **(VIII.)** Alma Bertha Bissey, born Oct. 23, 1888.

VI. Mary Fretz, born Oct. 18, 1842. Mrd. John M. Fretz. (See Index of references No. 9.)

V. John Fretz, born in Bucks Co., Pa., Apr. 21, 1803; died Nov. 17, 1866. Mrd. Ann Fretz (daughter of Abraham and Rachel Fretz), May 4, 1830. She died—. Farmer in Bedminster Twp. New Mennonites. One child:

VI. Susan Fretz, born May 4, 1831; died Feb. 25, 1873. Mrd. Lafayette Yost, Dec. 8, 1855. He died Jan. 21, 1880. Children: Annetta, Rachel, John, Linford, Ulysses, Lizzie.

VII. Annetta Yost, born Aug. 27, 1857. Mrd. Samuel High, Dec. 3, 1881. Farmer in Bedminster Twp. Mennonites. Children: **(VIII.)** Gertrude High, born July 5, 1883. **(VIII.)** Jacob Freeman High, born Nov. 13, 1884. **(VIII.)** Chester Arthur High, born Oct. 16, 1886.

VII. Rachel Yost, born Oct. 8, 1860. Mrd. Leidy Harpel, in 1883. Merchant. Lutherans. One child: **(VIII.)** Maggie Harpel, born Sept. 28, 1883.

VII. John Fretz Yost, born Mar. 28, 1863. Mrd. Jennie Fulmer, Oct. 6, 1883. Farmer. Children: **(VIII.)** Fretz Yost, born Feb. 15, 1884; died Sept. 4, 1884. **(VIII.)** Edgar Yost, born Feb. 15, 1885. **(VIII.)** Harry Yost, born Sept. 2, 1886. **(VIII.)** Raymond Yost, born Jan. 17, 1888; died Sept. 13, 1888.

VII. Linford Yost, born Mar. 12, 1866. S.

VII. Ulysses Grant Yost, born Nov. 4, 1868; died Mar. 24, 1869.

VII. Lizzie Fretz Yost, born Nov. 13, 1870.

V. Isaac K. Fretz, born in Bedminster, Bucks Co., Dec. 16, 1805; died July 7, 1882. Mrd. Annie Leatherman (daughter of Christian and Annie Leatherman), Oct. 1, 1833. She was born Apr. 15, 1809; died Oct. 14, 1883. Farmer. New Mennonites at Deep Run, where he led the singing for upwards of twenty years. Children: Abraham, William, Magdalena, Sarah, John, Maria, Annie, Isaac.

VI. Abraham L. Fretz, born Sept. 6, 1834. Mrd. Leanna Orr (daughter of Samuel and Elizabeth Orr, of Rockhill, Pa.,) Jan. 2, 1856. She was born Feb. 12, 1840. Farmer. New Mennonites at Deep Run. Children: Adina, Samuel.

VII. Adina Fretz, born Feb. 11, 1861; died Feb. 20, 1867.

VII. Samuel O. Fretz, born Dec. 7, 1862. Mrd. Minerva, daughter of John H., and Emeline Stout, of Rockhill, Pa., Feb. 13, 1886. She was born Jan. 31, 1865. Farmer, resides with his father in Bedminster Twp. New Mennonites at Deep Run. One child: **(VIII.)** Nero Stout Fretz, born May 27, 1888.

VI. William L. Fretz, born May 13, 1837; died Aug. 25, 1840.

VI. Magdalena Fretz, born July 19, 1839; died Aug. 19, 1840.

VI. John L. Fretz, born Jan. 13, 1841. Mrd. Mary Ann S. Kratz, Dec. 16, 1863. She was born Jan. 18, 1846; died in 1870. Farmer. Children: **(VII.)** Isaiah K. Fretz, born Dec. 26, 1864; died Sept. 11, 1865. **(VII.)**

CHRISTIAN MEYER, SR., HOMESTEAD, IN MONTGOMERY COUNTY, PA.

Emma Jane. K. Fretz. born Jan. 27. 1866; died Mar. 27, 1868. (**VII.**) Isaac K. Fretz. born Dec. 14, 1867; died in 1869. By a second wife he had one child: (**VII.**) John Fretz. born—; died, aged about 6 months. He married for his third wife, Sarah Ann Leicy. June 12. 1875. They have one child: (**VII.**) Horace L. Fretz, born, Nov. 27. 1879.

VI. Sarah Fretz. born July 9. 1843; died Jan. 25. 1847.

VI. Maria Fretz. born Mar. 19. 1846. Mrd. Henry K. Hockman,—. He was born Aug. 15. 1840. Carpenter. Children: (**VII.**) Lillie Hockman, born Mar. 1. 1867; died Jan. 7. 1872. (**VII.**) William Henry Hockman, born Dec. 17. 1869. (**VII.**) Ella Hockman. born in 1874. (**VII.**) Clinton Hockman, born May 25. 1885.

VI. Annie L. Fretz, born Oct. 19. 1848. Mrd. John B. Kratz, Sept. 7. 1876. Saddler and farmer. New Mennonites. Children: (**VII.**) Isaac F. Kratz. born Jan. 31. 1881. (**VII.**) Irene F. Kratz. born Sept. 6. 1884.

VI. Isaac L. Fretz, born Jan. 30. 1851. Mrd. Minerva, daughter of John K., and Maria Meyers. May 1. 1875. Farmer. Ger. Ref. Children: (**VII.**) Mary Lizzie Fretz. (**VII.**) Grace Alice Fretz.

V. Martin Fretz, born on the old Fretz homestead in Bedminster. Pa., Sept. 12. 1808. Mrd. Elizabeth Kratz (daughter of John Kratz. of Skippack. Pa.). Oct. 6. 1831. She was born Aug. 31, 1813; died Mar. 21. 1855. He was variously occupied. as farmer, weaver, miller. and merchant. He at first lived on a farm in Montgomery Co.. and afterwards purchased sixty acres of the old Fretz homestead, and some adjoining lands in Bedminster, Bucks Co., where in 1838, he built a dwelling-house, and subsequently a barn, tenant house and other buildings. The farm is now owned and occupied by Reuben Miller. In early life he and wife were members of the Old Mennonite church at Deep Run. About 1847 a division took place in that congregation, and a new meeting-house was built a few hundred yards from the old one. At the time of the division he was a trustee of the old church. but cast his lot with the new church, and was subsequently chosen one of its first ministers. In 1853 he purchased a mill property in Sussex Co., New Jersey, and moved thereon with his family in the spring of 1854. He married for his second wife, widow Margaret E. Hill (maiden name Wintamute), Feb. 14, 1857. She was born Apr. 30, 1817. Soon after marriage, in the spring of 1857, having rented their mill property, he moved to his wife's farm in Warren Co., N. J., where he engaged in farming until the spring of 1862, having disposed of his mill property, he removed to Newton, Sussex Co., where he had built a house and engaged in the commission business. About 1866 he removed to Stillwater, Sussex Co., where he had purchased a home and engaged in merchandise. In the spring of 1882, he again removed to the farm in Warren Co., where he died July 13, 1882. Some years prior to his death he was ordained a Ruling Elder in the Presbyterian church of Stillwater. Amid all the trials and turmoils of his long and eventful life he maintained a strict integrity and died highly respected by the community in which he lived, and honored in the church. The children by the first wife are: Mary, Magdalena, Catharine, Leah, Elizabeth. John, Anna, Theodore, Abraham, Martha, Edwin, Albert. The children by the second wife are: Alva, Lucilla, David.

VI. Mary Ann Fretz, born Nov. 4, 1832; died Mar. 8, 1842.

VI. Magdalena Fretz, born in Montgomery Co., Pa., Aug. 16, 1834; died May 18, 1876. Mrd. Frank Strohme, about 1853. Ger. Ref. Children: Lydia, Mary, Hannah, Elias, Henry, Sallie, John. Magdalena mrd. second husband, Samuel Lear, of Tinicum Twp., in 1865. Carpenter and Farmer. Children: Martha, Abraham, and infant died unnamed.

VII. Lydia Strohme, born in 1853; died in 1854.

VII. Mary Fretz Strohme, born in Stillwater Twp., Sussex Co., N. J., Oct. 4, 1854. Mrd. Alfred D. Wilt, May 7, 1873. Mrs. Wilt, Lutheran. Children: **(VIII.)** Anna Mabel Wilt, born in 1873. S. **(VIII.)** James Henry Wilt, born Oct. 26, 1875.

VII. Hannah Strohme, born in Sussex Co., N. J., May 2, 1856. Mrd. William Hillpot, Jan. 8, 1879. Mrs. Hillpot Ger. Ref. Children: (VIII.) Mary Belle Hillpot, born —; died —. (VIII.) Annie Hillpot. (VIII.) William Dayton Hillpot. (VIII.) Frank Hillpot. (VIII.) Hannah Hillpot.

VII. Elias Strohme, born in Bucks Co., Feb. 19, 1858. Mrd. P. O., Erwinna, Pa. One child. (VIII.) —, born —; died —.

VII. Henry F. Strohme, born Aug. 18, 1859. Mrd. Amanda Shelly, of Lawndale, Pa., Oct. 8, 1887. P. O., Souderton, Pa. Mennonites. Children: (VIII.) Harvey Strohme. (VIII.) Mary Strohme.

VII. Sallie F. Strohme, born in Bucks Co., Feb. 3, 1861. Mrd. John D. Miller, Jan. 13, 1883. P. O., Dyerstown, Pa. Farmer. Children: (VIII.) Mary Strohme, born Jan. 7, 1885. (VIII.) Barty Strohme, born Feb. —, 1889.

VII. John Strohme, born Apr. 29, 1862. Mrd.—. One child: (VIII.) Henry Strohme.

VII. Martha Fretz Lear, born Aug. 5, 1866. S.

VII. Abraham F. Lear, born Nov. 24, 1868. S.

VI. Catharine Fretz, born in Montgomery Co., Pa., Apr. 20, 1836, died Oct. 20, 1853. One child: (VII.) Lavina Fretz, born in Bucks Co., July 12, 1853. P. O., Creamery, Pa. Tailoress. New Mennonite. S.

VI. Leah Fretz, born June 20, 1838; died Aug. 1, 1840.

VI. Elizabeth Fretz, born in Bedminster, Bucks Co., Apr. 18, 1840. Mrd. Levi C. Hefler, in 1857. He died Mar. 13, 1870. Miller and merchant. Children: Irwin, Ellsworth, Elmer.

VII. Irwin F. Hefler, born in Bucks Co., Mar. 23, 1857. Mrd. Mary Borger, Sept. 30, 1886. Clerk in Phila. One child: (VIII.) Emma Hefler, born Mar. 23, 1887.

VII. Ellsworth Hefler, born—; died in infancy.

VII. Elmer Hefler, born Mar. 6, 1869; died Oct. 5, 1876.

VI. John Kratz Fretz, born in Bucks Co., Apr. 19, 1843. At the age of fourteen years he left home and served as farm laborer. In 1862 he enlisted in the

15th Regiment N. J. Vol. for three years. In 1863 he was appointed Corporal. He was engaged in some of the severest battles of the war,—the two battles at Fredricksburg. Chancellorsville, and others. In the great battle of Spottsylvania C. H., in which his regiment was nearly annihilated. he fell a martyr to his country's cause on May 12, 1864, from a bayonet wound in the mouth and a rifle ball which entered his right eye. "A brave and gallant soldier, and a true patriot."

VI. Anna Fretz, born May 17, 1845; died Mar. 7, 1846.

VI. Theodore E. Fretz, born in Bucks Co., Pa., Dec. 1. 1846. After leaving home he served as a farm la borer for a time. then engaged for several years as clerk, until about 1869, when he was tendered a position with the Newark and Orange Railway Co., which position he accepted and very satisfactorily filled until his death. which occurred in the City of Orange, N. J., Dec. 14, 1872. He was a member of Lafayette Lodge No. —, I. O. O. F. of Orange.

VI. Abraham James Fretz, born in Bedminster Twp., Bucks Co., Pa., Feb. 7, 1849. At the age of thirteen years he left home and worked as farm laborer, attending school in winter. He was converted in 1865, during the great revival at Newton, N. J. He united with the Presbyterian church and soon after felt called to preach the Gospel. He accordingly entered the Newton Collegiate Institute Jan. 3, 1867, with the ministry of the Presbyterian church in view. In the winter of 1868 he taught school at Mount Benevolence, Sussex Co., N. J. Disagreeing with the doctrines of the Presbyterian church, he subsequently united with the Methodist Episcopal church. July 4, 1868. He was licensed an exhorter Oct. 18, 1869, and a local preacher Mar. 7, 1870. In Sept. 1870 he went to Ohio and attended the Mennonite Seminary at Wadsworth for a year. After visiting friends in Canada, he returned east in the fall of 1872. In the spring of this year (1872) he was appointed pastor of Middle Smithville charge, in Monroe and Pike Co's., Pa., by Rev. N. Vansant. P. E. His labors as pastor

MARY H. FRETZ.

See Page 53.

- 53 -

of this charge were attended with great spiritual success. He conducted several revival meetings and received into the churches under his care 121 souls. Since then he has served as pastor of the following charges: Stockholm. N. J.. 1873; Libertyville and Coleville. 1874; Unionville and Westtown, N. Y.. 1875. In the fall of 1876 he attended Wyoming Seminary at Kingston. Pa. Appointed to Hamburgh and Ogdensburg. 1877; Hurdtown and Hopatcong. 1878 1879. In 1880 he built a house and went to farming. which he has since followed in connection with the ministry. He is at present pastor at Longwood and Dodge Mine. N. J. He was ordained Deacon by Bishop John F. Hurst. Apr. 2. 1882. and Elder by Bishop Charles H. Fowler. Apr. 1. 1888. He was married to Elizabeth C. Headley* (daughter of Joseph and Almeda Headley. of Milton, N. J.). Nov. 14. 1877. In August. 1890. he was appointed Township Clerk. and later Assessor to fill vacancies. In the spring of 1891 he received the Republican nomination for Township Clerk. and was elected. receiving every Republican vote except one. and several Democratic votes. and was re-elected Township Clerk by the unanimous vote of his party. Mar. 8. 1892. Children: **(VII.)** Mary Headley Fretz. born Dec. 13. 1878. **(VII.)** Joseph Martin Fretz. born Sept. 27. 1881: died May 10. 1883. **(VII.)** Ervin Kratz Fretz. born Dec. 19. 1883: died June 7. 1884.

VI. Martha Fretz. born in Bedminster. Pa.. July 25 1850. Mrd. Andrew E. Newbaker. of Hardwick Twp.. N. J.. Dec. 25. 1869. Carpenter in Philadelphia. Pa. Methodists. Children: **(VII.)** Mary Belle Newbaker. born in Bucks Co.. Pa.. Apr. 20. 1871. Methodist. **(VII.)** Florence Ellen Newbaker. born in Bucks Co.. Nov. 26. 1876. Methodist.

---

* She is a descendant of Robert Headley, who settled at Milton during the Revolution. He was a native of England and emigrated to this country, settled in the Wyoming Valley, Pa. Prior to the Wyoming Massacre he received timely warning of the impending danger from a friendly squaw and made his escape.

VI. Edwin Fretz, born in Pa., Sept. 15, 1853; died in N. J., Apr. 28, 1855.

VI. Albert Fretz, born in N. J., Mar. 15, 1855; died Apr. 3, 1855.

VI. Alva Bennett Fretz, born in Hardwick Twp., Warren Co., N. J., July 23, 1858. His early school days were spent in the Academy and Collegiate Institute, both of Newton, N. J. He next attended the Select school of Rev. T. B. Condit, at Stillwater, until the doors of that institution were closed forever. He then attended the Academy in that village until the age of sixteen, when he left school and for a year worked as day laborer, after which he continued his studies under his Preceptress, Miss Anna M. Condit. During this his last year at home he decided to make teaching his profession, which he has since followed with but few periods of relaxation, up to the present. He began his career as a teacher in 1876, has been very successful as such, and is at present Principal of a Graded school in Essex Co., N. J. He has always been a profound reader and an indefatigable student. He has held positions of trust and honor in various social, Dramatic, Musical and Literary Societies to which he belongs, and received many encomiums of merit, ability and talent from his patrons and superiors. He is a member of Arcana Lodge No. 60, F. and A. M. at Boonton, N. J. He was married to Lillian Isabel Williams, daughter of Matthew Williams of Hampton, Sussex Co., N. J., in 1881. She was born Jan. 15, 1862. Mrs. Fretz is a member of the Christian Ch., towards which the husband is also strongly inclined. Children: (**VII.**) Harold Norman Fretz, born Jan. 30, 1882. (**VII.**) Arthur Raymond Fretz, born Apr. 25, 1885; died May 16, 1885. (**VII.**) Ethel May Fretz, born Aug. 2, 1888; died Feb. 9, 1890. (**VII.**) Leo Fretz, born June 11, 1891.

VI. Lucilla Fretz, born June 9, 1860; died Mar. 12, 1861.

VI. David Elmer Fretz, born in Newton, Sussex Co., N. J., Dec. 7, 1862. Mrd. Harriet C. Swisher, July 26, 1890. Farmer. Presbyterians.

V. Elizabeth Fretz, born in Bedminster Twp., Bucks Co., Pa., Jan. 12, 1812; died Apr. 30, 1877. Mrd. Benjamin D. Hendricks, Mar. 16, 1839. Farmer. Mennonites. Children: Mary, Abraham, Aaron, John, William, Sarah, Jacob.

VI. Mary Ann Hendricks, born Feb. 22, 1840; died Sept. 30, 1887. Mrd. Jacob L. Dimmig, Sept. 13, 1862. Carpenter. Lutherans. Children: Lydia, Emma, Mahlon, Isaac, Maria, Lavina, Benjamin, Lavina, Morrison, Mabel.

VII. Lydia Ann Dimmig, born Nov. 28, 1863; died Apr. 5, 1888. Mrd. Darius Sine—. One child: (**VIII.**) Harry Sine, born Mar. 1, 1887.

VII. Emma Elizabeth Dimmig, born Feb. 28, 1865. Mrd. Thos. King (dec'd). One child: (**VIII.**) Mamie Susan King, born Apr. 12, 1885.

VII. Mahlon Dimmig, born May 13, 1866.

VII. Isaac Dimmig, born July 13, 1867.

VII. Maria Dimmig, born May 13, 1870.

VII. Lavina Dimmig, born July 20, 1873.

VII. Benjamin Dimmig, born Nov. 11, 1874.

VII. Laura Cora Dimmig, born Aug. 27, 1878.

VII. Morrison Dimmig, born Mar. 7, 1881; died Nov. 27, 1881.

VII. Mabel Albuirtus Dimmig, born May 11, 1883.

VI. Abraham Hendricks, born Jan. 12, 1842; died Apr. 19, 1842.

VI. Aaron Hendricks, born July 29, 1844; died Oct. 17, 1862.

VI. John Hendricks, born June 29, 1846; died Nov. 20, 1862.

VI. William Hendricks, born Dec 26, 1848; died Mar. 6, 1859.

VI. Sarah Hendricks, born Sept. 1, 1851; died Oct. 20, 1862.

VI. Jacob Freeman Hendricks, A. M., born in Bedminster, May 15, 1854. He was the youngest, and is now the only surviving child of Benjamin D. and Elizabeth (Fretz) Hendricks. When he became of school age he was sent to the district school. In 1862, through the visitation of death of seven children, but two—the oldest and the youngest—remained. The oldest was led forth from beneath the parental roof the same year. leaving the subject of our sketch the only child at the family fireside.

In '65 his father sold the farm on which he had lived for many years and bought a property near the village of Line Lexington in the Township of Hilltown. and moved thereon. Here the boy resumed his attendance at district school. assisting his father when school was not in session in the work on the farm and in the chores about the place. Between the years of '65 and '70 he induced his father to send him for several short terms to Line Lexington Seminary. then a select school for boys and girls. In the spring of '70. thirsting for still wider educational advantages he induced his father to send him for a twelve weeks' term to the Excelsior Normal Institute at Carversville. then under the principalship of Rev. F. R. S. Hunsicker, D. D. In the fall he entered the profession of teaching. taking charge of a school in Hilltown Township. In the spring of '71 he entered Millersville State Normal school and remained there twelve weeks. In the fall he again took charge of a school in Hilltown Township. and continued teaching in that Township for three successive terms. In the spring of '74 he returned to Millersville and remained one term. In the fall he was examined by County Superintendent Knauss of Lehigh county and granted a provisional certificate with No. 1 in every branch. He was thereupon elected Principal of the schools of Rittersville in that county. After teaching there several months he was granted a professional certificate. In the spring of '75 he once more returned to Millersville and remained to finish his course. graduating in the classs of '76. He graduated with the degree of Bachelor of the Elements. and had conferred upon him one of the honors of his class. In the fall he took charge of a school at Breinigsville. Lehigh Co. During this term he gained prominence among the teachers of the county. At Teachers' Institute of that year he was made Secretary of the Institute. appointed to open the discussion on one of the topics.

chosen delegate to the State Teachers' Association, and selected as one of the evening lecturers.

In the fall of '77 he took charge of a school in East Donegal Township, Lancaster Co. During this time he gave some attention to public lecturing, appearing among other audiences before the Page Literary Society of Millersville. At the commencement of '78 he received from his *Alma Mater* the degree of Master of the Elements. In the fall of this year he was elected teacher of the Intermediate Department of the Doylestown Borough Public Schools and before the close of the term was made Principal and Borough Superintendent. In the summer of '79, after winning golden testimonials as a teacher, he left the school-room and turned his face in the direction of the legal profession. He entered the office of Alfred Fackenthall, Esq., Doylestown, and was duly registered as a student at law. In '81 he was admitted to the Bucks County Bar and he at once entered upon the practice of the law at the County Capital. In the spring of '83 Doylestown Borough elected him Justice of the Peace by an overwhelming majority when his party was hopelessly in the minority. The same year he was admitted to the Bryant Literary Union of New York, and again he entered the lecture field. For several years he appeared before County Teachers' Institutes and other distinguished audiences and won the strongest testimonials. At the commencement of '86, Ursinus College conferred upon him the degree of Master of Arts. From the time he turned to the law, he has been closely identified with politics and has been on the stump for his party in every campaign. He has been an ardent believer and zealous worker in the Republican League and has been signally honored by that organization. He has been President of the Doylestown League for two years, delegate from his league to all four of the State conventions, delegate from the State League to the last two National conventions, and for two years the Pennsylvania member of the National League Executive Committee. He is now Notary Public, Clerk of the Town Council, and Chairman of the Republican County Committee. He is Presbyterian in religion, a warm friend of the Sunday-school cause, and an ardent believer in the Society of Christian Endeavor. He has figured prominently as a speaker at public gatherings. In '90 he delivered the annual address before the Literary Societies at the Millersville State Normal School and Ursinus College. He still resides at Doylestown pursuing his several lines of work with courage and vigor, and looking into the future with hope and faith.

V. Barbara Fretz, born in Bedminster, Pa., Mar. 24, 1813; died—. Mrd. Joseph F. Myers, Mar. 22, 1838. He was born Mar. 17, 1811; died May 12, 1882. Mason and farmer. New Mennonites. Children: Henry, Abraham, Enos, Aaron, Mary, Mahlon, Infant, Susanna.

VI. Henry F. Myers, born Feb. 24, 1839. Mrd. Emma S. Harpel, Oct. 3, 1863. She was born Sept. 23, 1837; died Apr. 4, 1886. Farmer. Lutherans. Children: (**VII.**) Livera Myers, born Dec. 9, 1864. Lutheran. (**VII.**) Erwin H. Myers, born Oct. 17, 1866; died in 1889. (**VII.**) Anna Barbara Myers, born Nov. 16, 1868; died Feb. 1890. Lutheran. (**VII.**) Edgar H. Myers, born Mar. 3, 1872. (**VII.**) Nora Myers, born July 5, 1877.

VI. Abraham F. Myers, born Oct. 12, 1842. Mrd. Susanna High, Nov. 18, 1872. She was born Sept. 7, 1849; died Oct. 13, 1883. P. O., Hagersville, Pa. Farmer. New Mennonite. Children: (**VII.**) Anna Belle Myers, born June 24, 1875; died Aug. 28, 1875. (**VII.**) Clara V. B. Myers, born Aug. 6, 1877. (**VII.**) Josephine Myers, born Sept. 15, 1880. Abraham mrd. for his second wife, Caroline Miener, widow of Aaron K. Sine, Feb. 8, 1890.

VI. Enos F. Myers, born Sept. 19, 1844; died June 22, 1857.

VI. Aaron F. Myers, born July 10, 1846. Mrd. Lydia M. Moyer, May 1, 1869. P. O., Bedminster, Pa. Farmer. New Mennonites. Children: (**VII.**) Oscar M. Myers, born Dec. 12, 1869. New Mennonite (**VII.**) Joseph M. Myers, born Mar. 17, 1871. New Mennonite. (**VII.**) Titus M. Myers, born July 5, 1873. (**VII.**)

Christian Meyer (Jr.) Homestead, in Montgomery County, Pa.

Barbara A. Myers, born Aug. 14, 1875; died Aug. 21, 1876. (VII.) Susan M. Myers, born May 25, 1877; died June 4, 1877. (VII.) Pierson M. Myers, born Jan. 11, 1879. (VII.) Isaiah M. Myers, born Oct. 13, 1881. (VII.) Henry M. Myers, born July 12, 1884; died Sept. 28, 1884. (VII.) Sevinus M. Myers, born Jan. 9, 1886. (VII.) Abraham M. Myers, born Feb. 22, 1888.

VI. Mary Ann Myers, born Feb. 27, 1848; died Mar. 29, 1848.

VI. Mahlon F. Myers, born May 31, 1849; died June 21, 1849.

VI. Infant, born Jan. 25, 1851; died unnamed.

VI. Susanna Myers, born Mar. 12, 1853; died Feb. 26, 1863.

V. Abraham Fretz, son of Deacon Abraham and Magdalena (a born Kratz), was born on the Fretz Homestead in Bedminster Twp., Oct. 9, 1815. Mrd. Sarah Detweiler in 1840. She was born Jan. 5, 1818; died July 18, 1850. Children: Oliver, Titus, Lavina, Clayton, Clementine, Sarah. He mrd. for his second wife, Catharine Fry, in Mar. 1859. She was born Jan. 12, 1827; died July 5, 1886. Children: Lewis, Sybilla, Laura, Alice, Abraham, Katie. He is one of a few surviving members of the fourth generation from his ancestor John Fretz. Being the youngest of the children, he remained at home with his parents to be their comfort and stay in their declining years. He remained on the old homestead for the first seventy-one years of his life, carrying on the business of farming, and during the summer months that of droving. In his business transactions he is noted for his honesty and integrity. He is a member of the New Mennonite church at Deep Run.

VI. Oliver D. Fretz, born in Bedminster, Nov. 13, 1840. Mrd. Susanna Meyers, Dec. 3, 1870. Shoemaker at Bedminsterville, Pa. New Mennonites. Children: (VII.) Abbie Fretz, born July 27, 1875. (VII.) William James Fretz, born Aug. 6, 1877.

VI. Titus Fretz, born Apr. 9, 1842; died Oct. 7, 1842.

VI. Lavina D. Fretz, born in Bedminster Twp., May 2, 1843. Mrd. Jonas S. Myers, Jan. 19, 1864. P. O.,

Dublin, Pa. Farmer. New Mennonites. Children: Rosella, Annie, Clayton, Lamech, Sallie, Abraham, Henry, William, Lavina.

VII. Rosella Myers, born June 29, 1864. Mrd. Henry S. Shelly, Nov. 22, 1884. Farmer. Mennonites. Children: (**VIII.**) Ervin F. Shelly, born May 7, 1886. (**VIII.**) Charles Shelly, born Nov. 29, 1889.

VII. Annie F. Myers, born Nov. 21, 1865; died Dec. 7, 1868.

VII. Clayton F. Myers, born Oct. 26, 1867.

VII. Lamech F. Myers, born May 7, 1869.

VII. Sallie F. Myers, born Dec. 16, 1871.

VII. Abraham Myers, born July 7, 1874; died Aug. 19, 1875.

VII. Henry Myers, born June 8, 1877.

VII. William Myers, born Mar. 6, 1879.

VII. Lavina Myers, born Oct. 20, 1881.

VI. Clayton D. Fretz, M. D., son of Abraham and Sarah (Detweiler) Fretz, was born on the old John Fretz homestead in Bedminster, Nov. 16, 1844. At the age of six years his mother died of a lingering illness. He remained at home with his father until the spring of 1855, when he was hired out on the farm of the late Jonas Myers, of Bedminster, where he remained nearly two years. The following year he was with the late Reuben Stover, and the succeeding year with Aaron Tyson, working on the farm in the summer months, and attending school at Bedminster, during the winter terms. His father having resumed farming he returned home in the spring of 1859, and assisted on the farm, attending school during the winter months at Fretz Valley. In the spring of 1862 he attended a term at "The North Wales Institute," under the principalship of A. S. Overholt. He also attended the spring term of 1863, at the same institution. In the summer of 1864 he took a course at Eastman Business College at Poughkepsie, N. Y., graduating July 12. In the autumn of 1862 he sesured a sertificate of County Superintendent S. S. Overholt, and taught his first term of school in the "Old Octagon" school-house, near Fountainville. He continued teaching for the next three years—teaching at the Monroe School, Durham, and the Fretz Valley school, Bedminster, closing his career as teacher at Crout's school, Rockhill. During this last term he commenced reading medicine under his preceptor, Dr. I. S. Moyer, then at Plumsteadville, Bucks Co. After the close of the school term he devoted all his time to medicine, entered the office of his preceptor as a regular student, and in the autumn of 1866 he matriculated at the Medical Department of the University of Pennsylvania, Philadelphia. During the succeeding two years he applied himself closely to study, attended the lectures and graduated March 13, 1868. Ten days thereafter, on the 23d of March, he located at Sellersville, Pa., and entered into partnership with Dr. Nelson Applebach, for the practice of his profession. He met with success, and in a few years succeeded in acquiring a lucrative practice, establishing himself in the confidence and esteem of the community. In the autumn of 1871, he dissolved the business partnership with Dr. Applebach to enter into a life partnership with Miss Kate B. Everhart, daughter of the late Dr. Charles W. Everhart, of Sellersville.

The study of Botany and the collection of specimens of plants and flowers has been one of his favorite pursuits. He has added many new and rare plants to the known flora of Bucks county, besides having discovered one new to the State flora and also a variety not before known to science. His herbarium not only contains a complete set of all the plants in Bucks county, but a very large majority of the plants growing east of the Mississippi, including not less than ten thousand specimens and about four thousand different species and varieties.

Dr. Fretz is a member of the Bucks county Medical Society, the Lehigh Valley Medical Association, the Bucks county Historical Society, and the Bucks county branch of the Pennsylvania Forestry Association. He was married to Kate B. Everhart, Nov. 16, 1871. She was born in Sellersville, May 2, 1846. Ger. Ref. Ch. Children: (VII.) Charles Raymond Fretz, born July 19, 1873; died June 19, 1877, aged

3 yrs. 11 mos. (**VII.**) Alfred Everhart Fretz, born Aug. 30, 1874. Teacher in public schools. (**VII.**) Samuel Edward Fretz, born Aug. 30, 1878. (**VII.**) Eva Catharine Fretz, born Feb. 17, 1885; died Nov. 25, 1885, aged 9 m. 8 d.

VI. Clementine Fretz, born June 14, 1846. Mrd. William J. Meyers. He was born Sept. 1, 1846; died Mar. 22, 1867. One child: (**VII.**) Susan Meyers: died aged 9 days. Clementine Mrd. second husband, William. K. Hockman. (See Index of References No. 10.)

VI. Sarah Ellen Fretz, born Oct. 24, 1848; died Jan. 3, 1871. Mrd. Amos Myers. (See Index of References No. 11.)

VI. Lewis F. Fretz, born in Bedminster, Jan. 13, 1860. Mrd. Sallie Stahr, Nov. 29, 1884. She died Dec. 3, 1885. One child: (**VII.**) Nellie Victoria Fretz, born June 30, 1885. Lewis Mrd. second wife, Jeannette Stokes Buchanan, June 6, 1888. She was born Mar. 16, 1868. Painter in Philadelphia, Pa. One child: (**VII.**) Lewis Buchanan Fretz, born Apr. 26, 1889.

VI. Sybilla F. Fretz, born Nov. 18, 1861. Mrd. William L. Fenton, of Chaltenham, Pa., Oct. 20, 1880. R. R. Engineer. Children: (**VII.**) Marion Alice Fenton, born Jan. 31, 1882; died Jan. 6, 1886. (**VII.**) Clarence L. Fenton, born Nov. 30, 1883; died Jan. 21, 1886. (**VII.**) Clarion Myrtle Fenton, born Dec. 15, 1886.

VI. Laura Fretz, born Feb. 22, 1863; died Jan. 9, 1886.

VI. Alice Fretz, born in Bedminster Twp., Sept. 26, 1865. Mrd. Harvey B. Lewis, Nov 6, 1886. He was born July 5, 1864. Tailor. Lutheran. Children: (**VII.**) Genella Lewis, born Dec. 6, 1887. (**VII.**) Laura Lugertia Lewis, born Nov. 23, 1889; died Apr. 1, 1890.

VI. Abraham Fretz, born Oct. 29, 1867; died Dec. 19, 1869.

VI. Katie Fretz, born in Bedminster Twp., Mar. 18, 1870. Mrd. Richard R. Hudson, June 26, 1889. Fireman on Railroad. Ger. Ref. One child: (**VII.**) Miriam F. Hudson, born July 3, 1890.

III. Michael Kratz, born in 1834. Probably left no issue.

III. Gerhart Kratz, born in 1736. It is thought that he also died without issue.

III. Philip Kratz, born in Montgomery Co., in 1739; died in 1818, aged 79 years. Mrd. Susanna Krout, of Bedminster, Pa., about 1760. She was born in 1739, died Oct. 1831, aged 92 years. They settled in Bucks Co., near Plumsteadville, where he purchased the farm known as the "Jessup farm" consisting of 200 or more acres. It is still in the family name, and is known as the "Valley Park farm," and occupied by his great-grandson, Reuben Kratz.

He always spelled his name "Fillip Crots." In his old days he became very childish. It is related that as his daughter-in-law was busy at work one day, she thought it would be company for both of them to have him near her. He sat and looked at her very sharply for some time, and then said to his son Philip who had just come in, "Philip, I think you are old enough to get married," to which he replied, "Yes, father, I think I am." Then he said, "here is a nice young woman who seems right industrious, and I think she would make you a very good wife. They then had been married ten years.

During the Revolutionary war, a company or detatchment of the Federal army was stationed at Danborough, Pa., and owing to their foraging raids, were known as the "Press Gang." While the ancestors were loyal to the American cause, they did not relish losing their property, and acted accordingly. Upon one occasion a young calf was gobbled up and taken away by the "Press Gang," whereupon Anna, the oldest daughter, saddled her pony and rode over to Danboro, three miles distant, to claim it as her individual property, but before she could make her errand known to the justice, she saw it "knocked in the head," and she sorrowfully returned. During her absence from home word came that the "Press Gang" were returning for horses. Her father and the boys accordingly hid them in the dense thicket close by. Her mother, Susanna, invited the foragers in, and while she was entertaining them at lunch, Anna arrived and took in the situation. All she could do to prevent discovery was to take the pony in the cellar from the outside, which was done, and she kept the horse company, fearful all the time that he might whinny, during her mother's frequent visits to the cellar for refreshments. They finally left empty handed.

Philip, and his wife Susanna, were members of the Mennonite church at Deep Run, and are buried there. Children: Anna, John, Elizabeth, Mary, Henry, Rachel, Susanna, Philip.

IV. Anna Kratz, born in Bucks Co., Nov. 4, 1764; died Aug. 4, 1813, aged 48 y. 9 m. Mrd. John Fretz, son of Christian and Barbara Fretz, of Bedminster, Pa. He was born May 24, 1758; died Dec. 20, 1804, aged 46 y., 6 m. 26 d. They at first lived in Bedminster, Twp., and later in Warwick Twp., where in 1792 he purchased 299½ acres of land, for which he paid 1200 pounds, "in good gold and silver money." On this farm he built a barn in 1794, and a house in 1795. The house is still standing and occupied as a dwelling. To this he added by various purchases, so at his death he owned 800 acres. The old homestead in Warwick is now owned in part by his granddaughter Mrs. Elizabeth F. Farren. Mennonites, and buried at Doylestown. Children: Christian, Susan, Rachel, Barbara, Eliza, Mary, John, Anna, Philip.

V. Christian Fretz, born in Bedminster, Nov. 17, 1782; died in Warwick, Jan. 28, 1840. Mrd. Mary, daughter of Ralph Stover, of Bedminster, Apr. 14, 1808. She was born Dec. 15, 1787; died in New York, Nov. 27, 1855. Farmer and Hotel-keeper, and resided in Warwick on the old homestead, now owned and occupied by his daughter, Mrs. Elizabeth F. Farren, and where he died Jan. 28, 1840. Children: Ralph, John, Philip, Elizabeth, Christian, Mary.

VI. Ralph Stover Fretz, born on the homestead in Warwick, Nov. 13, 1809. He sailed from the Isthmus of Panama in 1849, and landed at San Francisco, Cali-

Franconia Mennonite Meetinghouse.

fornia, where he established a bank, and amassed a fortune of about a half million dollars, which he bequeathed to relatives, except $20,000 which he willed to the United States to liquidate the National debt caused by the late war. He was never married, and died in California, June 6, 1867, aged 58 years.

VI. John Fretz, born Oct. 2, 1811, also went to California where he died unmrd., June 26, 1863, at the White Sulphur Springs. He owned and operated a gold quartz mill in Calaveras Co., California.

VI. Philip K. Fretz, born Sept. 14, 1813. Mrd. Annie Stover, Feb. 18, 1841. He lived on a part of the old homestead in Warwick. Farmer. Was also extensively engaged in contract work, and was one of the contractors to build the Horse Shoe curve over the Allegheny Mountains, on the Pa. R. R. He was one of the prominent men of the company, and a member of the Doylestown, Presbyterian church. He died on Steamship "Henry Chauney" on voyage to California, Mar. 13, 1867. Buried in the Atlantic, off the coast of North Carolina. Had four children: Charles, Mary, Philip, John.

VII. Charles Augustus Fretz, born May 31, 1843. Mrd. Susie Derby. He owns and occupies a part of the old homestead that belonged to his father, and is engaged in farming. No issue.

VII. Mary Catharine Fretz, born Jan. 9, 1845. Mrd. Theodore P. Austin, Sept. 8, 1868. Mr. Austin employs his time in looking after his woodlands, and mining property in Maine. Residence 95, Fifth Avenue, New York city. Mrs. Austin is a member of the Presbyterian church; Mr. Austin and one daughter are members of the Protestant Episcopal church, of which the family are regular attendants. Children: (**VIII.**) Altia Rheua Austin, born Sept. 15, 1869, at 95, Fifth Avenue, N. Y. City. (**VIII.**) Neva Ethel Aus'in, born Oct. 18, 1876, at their country residence, Portland, Conn.

VII. Philip Henry Fretz, born Nov. 22, 1846. Mrd. Margaret Nilla Johnston, daughter of Robert and Nilla (McHenry) Johnston, Sept. 19, 1871. She was born June 1, 1848. They reside on a farm near

Doylestown, known as the Hough Property, where they have built and occupy a handsome residence. Presbyterians. Children: (VIII.) John Edgar Fretz, born Nov. 29, 1872. (VIII.) Anna Leola Fretz, born Nov. 1, 1875. (VIII.) Ralph Johnston Fretz, born Feb. 25, 1878.

VII. John S. Fretz born Sept. 22, 1850. Mrd. Mary W. Long, of Doylestown. Resides on a portion of the old John Fretz homestead in Warwick. Occupation, farming and running sawmill. One child: (VIII.) Harry Fretz.

VI. Elizabeth Fretz, daughter of Christian Fretz of Warwick, born Feb. 23, 1818. Mrd. John Farren, of Elizabethtown, Lancaster Co., Pa., Jan. 1, 1844. He was born Mar. 1, 1809. He was a contractor, being one of the contractors in constructing the Penn. R. R., on the Allegheny Mountains. The last years of his life were spent at Warwick homestead, where he died Dec. 16, 1878. Mrs. Farren owns, and still resides on a portion of the old homestead. Roman Catholics. Children: Mary, Frances, John, Mary.

VII. Mary Janetta Farren, born May 7, 1851; died infant.

VII. Frances Annetta Farren, born Apr. 1, 1853; died infant.

VII. John Augustus Farren, born Apr. 21, 1855; died Dec. 12, 1884, aged 29 yrs. Roman Catholic. He mrd. Alletta Bleiler, of Doylestown, Bucks Co., Pa., Jan. 25, 1882. She attends Prot. Ep. Ch. No issue.

VII. Mary Celicia Farren, born Feb. 21, 1858. Mrd. Samuel J. Penrose, of Horsham, Pa., June 16, 1881. Farmer. Member of the Society of "Friends." Mrs. Penrose and son Roman Catholics. One Child: (VIII.) Cyril Farran Penrose, born May 5, 1882.

VI. Christian Augustus Fretz, born Nov. 25, 1824; died in Bucks Co., Pa., Dec. 1, 1859. Provision merchant on Isthmus of Panama for seven years previous to his death.

VI. Mary Catharine Fretz, born Jan. 13, 1827; died Mar. 4, 1842.

V. Susan Fretz, born Sept. 1, 1784; died Sept. 9,

1829. Mrd. William Garges, July 30, 1805. Merchant at Bridge Point, Pa. Moved to Fairfax Co., Va., where he bought a farm on which he remained until his death. Mrs. Garges, Mennonite. Children: Anna, Sarah, Margaret, John, William, Susan, Abraham, Mary.

VI. Anna Fretz Garges, born in Bucks Co., Pa., Nov. 23, 1806. Spent the early part of her life at the old home; later in life moved to Zanesville, Ohio, where she died in 1869. Methodist. Unmrd.

VI. Sarah Garges, born in Bucks Co., Pa., July 29, 1808. Lived for many years with her sister, Mrs. Ball, in Muskingum Co., Ohio; died in Washington, D. C., July 15, 1883. Methodist. Unmrd.

VI. Margaret Garges, born in Bucks Co., Pa., Aug. 22, 1810. Mrd. Edward Ball, of Fairfax Co., Va., Jan. 8, 1840. They moved to Zanesville, Ohio, where he was for a time sheriff, afterwards farmer. Later practiced law, finally went into politics, and was elected to Congress two terms. Methodists. Children: Virginia, Sarah, Margaret, William, Thomas, Susan, John.

VII. Virginia Fairfax Ball, born Nov. 7, 1840. Employed as clerk in Patent Office at Washington, D. C.

VII. Sarah A. Ball, born Apr. 16, 1843. Mrd. Charles A. Stevenson, of Versailles, Ky., June 15, 1875. Farmer. Mrs. Stevenson, Presbyterian. Resides in Washington, D. C. Children: (VIII.) Fred Ball Stevenson, born Sept. 13, 1877. (VIII.) Pauline Stevenson, born Nov. 12, 1881. (VIII.) Vincent Moore Stevenson, born Mar. 1, 1883.

VII. William E. Ball, born Sept. 6, 1844; died June 19, 1850.

VII. Susan Ball, born Dec. 17, 1846; died next day.

VII. Thomas Smith Ball, born Apr. 1, 1849; died June 1, 1850.

VII. John Alfred Ball, born Sept. 15, 1851. Mrd. Georgie C. Bradshaw, of Somerton, Ohio, June 20, 1876. Book-keeper. Attend M. E. Ch. Children: (VIII.) Cornelia Virginia Ball, born Sept. 27, 1878. (VIII.) Edward Ball, born Aug. 9, 1880; died Feb. 13, 1884.

VII. Margaret Anna Ball, born at Zanesville, Ohio, Jan. 3, 1854. Mrd. in Washington, D. C., Oct. 24, 1876, to Philip T. Dodge, Patent Attorney in Washington, D. C. Mrs. Dodge Ref. Lutheran. Children: (VIII.) Norman Dodge, born Sept. 27, 1877. (VIII.) Olive Van Patten Dodge, born July 17, 1882.

VI. John Henry Garges, born in Bucks Co., Pa., Feb. 14, 1813. Mrd. Martha Ann Scott, of Fairfax Co., Va., Dec. 16, 1842. She died Apr. 9, 1886. His occupation formerly, wheelright and engineer. He bought the old homestead farm at Anandale, Va. It grew to be a village on his hands, and became a place of note in the history of the late war. Mr. Garges being a Union man had to seek protection in Washington, D. C., where he still resides. His property was destroyed, being held first by the Confederates then by the Union forces. Finally the whole village was burned by the Union troops as they fell back, not willing that the Confederates should protect themselves, and hold the place. Mrs. Garges, Methodist. Children: Eugene, Robert, William, Thomas, John, Otto, Edwin, Martha, Abraham.

VII. Eugene Boyle Garges, born Oct. 18, 1843. Mrd. Josephine M. Langley, Jan. 17, 1870. Children: (VIII.) John Henry Garges, born Oct. 17, 1870. (VIII.) William Warren Garges, born Jan. 27, 1872. (VIII.) Geo. Washington Garges, born Dec. 3, 1873. (VIII.) Margaret H. Garges, born Nov. 20, 1876. (VIII.) Thomas Smith Garges, born Aug. 13, 1879. (VIII.) Virginia Fairfax Garges, born Feb. 12, 1882. (VIII.) Chandler Garges, born Feb. 1, 1885. (VIII.) Ellen Garges, born May 15, 1887. All Roman Catholics.

VII. Robert Emmet Garges, born Nov. 30, 1844; died Mar. 21, 1886. During the late war he was captured by the Confederates and imprisoned at Richmond, Va., for many months, where he lay ill for a long time with pneumonia. When permitted to leave the prison, he went almost in a state of nudity to his uncle Thomas Smith, of Va.

VII. William H. Garges, born in Fairfax Co., Va., Feb. 23, 1846. When a youth of about 15 during the late war he was captured by the Confederates and confined in Libby Prison for nine months, during which time he endured many hardships. He mrd. Mary A. Mullen, Oct. 24, 1871. Coach-maker. Mrs. Garges and children Roman Catholics. Children: (**VIII.**) Martha Magdalena Garges, born Aug. 21, 1872. (**VIII.**) Daniel Edward Garges, born Mar. 6, 1874. (**VIII.**) Mary Adelia Garges, born Oct. 2, 1876. (**VIII.**) Willliam Henry Garges, born Aug. 26, 1878. (**VIII.**) Samuel Miller Garges, born Oct. 25, 1880. (**VIII.**) Francis Garges, born June 8, 1882. (**VIII.**) Eugene Boid Garges, born Nov. 1, 1883. (**VIII.**) Sarah Jane Garges, born Feb. 9, 1887.

VII. Thomas Smith Garges, born Jan. 6, 1848. Mrd. Rebecca Carvithen, May 8, 1874. He is supervisor of Metropolitan R. R. No issue.

VII. John Henry Garges, born Jan. 19, 1850; died in Washington, D. C. 1862.

VII. Otto Goldsmith Garges, born in Fairfax Co., Va., Apr. 22, 1852. Mrd. Annie B. Faley, of Irish descent. Mr. Garges is in the livery business in Washington, D. C. Methodists. Children: (**VIII.**) John Henry Garges born Jan. 22, 1872. (**VIII.**) Abraham A. Garges, born Jan. 24, 1874. (**VIII.**) Ellen Catharine Garges, born Mar. 2, 1876. (**VIII.**) Edwin Brooke Garges, born Jan. 29, 1877; died Mar. 30, 1879. (**VIII.**) James Foley Garges, born Jan. 2, 1880.

VII. Edwin Brooke Garges, born Apr. 22, 1852. Mrd. Margaret E. Herrity, June 12, 1877. Proprietor of a hotel at Richmond, Va. Children: (**VIII.**) Ida Theressa Garges, born Oct. 17, 1878. (**VIII.**) William Henry Garges, born Oct. 12, 1880; died Oct. 18, 1880.

VII. Martha W. Garges, born Nov. 19, 1859. She graduated from the Washington Normal School, June 8, 1877, and is now a teacher in the 6th Grade public school of Washington, D. C. She has taught boys ever since her graduation, from the lowest grade up. Member of Prot. Ep. Ch., and resides with her father in Washington.

VII. Abraham Lincoln Garges, born Apr. 22, 1861. Mrd. Leone Walde, Nov. 5, 1881. Coach-painter. Children: (**VIII.**) Charles Otto Garges, born Apr. 10,

1883. **(VIII.)** Martha Leone Garges, born Aug. 16, 1884.

VI. William Garges, Jr., born in Bucks Co., Pa., Mar. 19, 1816. Mrd. Elizabeth Laughlin, of Lexington, Va., in 1835. She died—. Children: A son and daughter, Mary. Mr. Garges mrd. for his second wife, Isabella Bryan, of Fincastle, Va., May 21, 1846. Children: Sarah, William, Susan, Charles, John, Rose, Harry, Annie, Milton, Alfred. Mr. Garges has been variously occupied as stage driver in Rockbridge Co., Va., and for several years in the livery business and farming. At the beginning of the Rebellion he enlisted as a three years' Volunteer in the 78th Ohio Regiment. At the expiration of this enlistmen the re-enlisted in the same Regt. and remained with it, until the close of the war, when he was mustered out at Washington, D. C. United Presbyterians. Reside at Zanesville, Ohio. Children: A son, Mary E.

VII. A son; died in infancy.

VII. Mary E. Garges, born Jan. 1, 1842. Mrd. W. H. Hardy, of Winchester, Va., Oct. 10, 1866, Merchandise,—dealer in Harness, saddles and leather. Mrs. Hardy, Methodist. Children: **(VIII.)** Harry Hardy, born Oct. 18, 1867. **(VIII.)** Rose Lee Hardy, born Nov. 23, 1869. **(VIII.)** Mary N. Hardy, born Mar. 19, 1871 (dec'd). **(VIII.)** Bessie Hardy, born Mar. 26, 1873. **(VIII.)** William G. Hardy, born Oct. 26, 1876. **(VIII.)** Maggie B. Hardy, born Sept. 9, 1880. **(VIII.)** Lucy L. Hardy, born April 11, 1883 (dec'd). **(VIII.** Francis L. Hardy, born Nov. 20, 1884.

VII. Sarah Bertha Garges, born Aug. 16, 1847. Mrd. L. P. Minier, May 15, 1873. Superintendent of Telegraphy in Cincinnati, Ohio. Swedenborgians. Children: **(VIII.)** Estella Minier, born Mar. 8, 1874. **(VIII.)** Chester Minier, born Mar. 2, 1877. **(VIII.)** Edith Minier, born April 12, 1880; died Jan. 20, 1885. **(VIII.)** Waite Minier, born Feb., 8, 1882. **(VIII.)** Bessie Minier, born Oct. 19, 1885.

VII. Rev. William Louis Garges born Apr. 10, 1849, at Fincastle, Va. At the age of fourteen he was apprenticed to John L. Shryock, with whom he learned

the printer's trade, at which he worked one year after
serving apprenticeship. He then went to the country
and worked as a farm hand for three years. In the
winter of 1870 he entered the preparatory department of Muskingum College, of New Concord, Ohio,
from which college he graduated, June 24, 1876, paying his own way through college by teaching, having
received no financial aid from any one. In the summer of 1869, he joined the U. Presbyterian Church at
Rix's Mills, Ohio. In the winter of 1876 and 1877, he
entered the Theological Seminary of the U Presbyterian Ch., at Xenia, Ohio, from which he graduated
in Mar. 1880. He was licensed by the Presbytery of
Muskingum June 17, 1879 and ordained to the ministry of the U. Presbyterian Ch., by the southern Ill.
Presbytery, Sept. 6, 1880. He has served as pastor
at Hopewell, Parry Co., Ill., from ordination to Dec.
6, 1881. At Beulah, Crawford Co., Kan., from Oct.
18, 1882 to Apr. 8, 1885, and Nortonville, since June
16, 1885. Now financial ag't. When he entered
college it was his intention to fit himself for teaching.
In order to do this he determined to take the full
classical course. But during his college career his
mind was turned toward the ministry, and when he
entered the junior year it was with the desire, if the
way opened to enter upon this work. This desire
grew until, like Paul, he could exclaim, "Woe is me
if I preach not the Gospel," and therefore he decided,
before the junior year had closed that if the Lord was
willing, he would give himself to this work. He was
married to Miss Alice E. Kelley, of Muskingum Co.,
Ohio, June 29, 1875. Children:
(VIII.) Eva Belle Garges, born Oct. 8, 1876. (VIII.)
Hettie Myrtle Garges, born August. 22, 1878.
(VIII.) Martha Lorene Garges, born May 4, 1881.
(VIII.) Homer Bruce Garges, born June 7, 1883. (VIII.)
Mary Gertrude Garges, born Jan. 4, 1886. (VIII.)
Herbert Kelley Garges, born July 24, 1888.

VII. Susan Louisa Garges, born May 7, 1851. Unmarried. She resides in Cincinnati, Ohio. Dressmaker. Methodist.

VII. Charles M. Garges, born Feb. 21, 1853. Mrd. —. Children: (VIII.) Walter Garges, aged 7 yrs. (VIII.) Fannie Garges, aged 9 yrs.

VII. John Andrew Garges, born Dec. 27, 1854. Mrd. Ella Karr, of Knobnoster, Mo. Watchmaker. Mrs. Garges, Baptist. Children: (VIII.) Freddie Garges, aged 7 yrs. (VIII.) Margaret Garges, aged 2 mos.

VII. Rose Gertrude Garges, born Feb. 2, 1857. Mrd. Roscoe E. Thomas— . Farmer in Ohio. Mrs. Thomas is a member of the Baptist Ch. Children: (VIII.) Mabel Thomas. (VIII.) Ralph Thomas.

VII. Harry Letcher Garges, born May 7, 1859. Mrd. Anna Magrie, Aug. 25, 1885. She was born of English parents, Dec. 7, 1864. Salesman in St. Paul, Minn. Mr. Garges, Methodist, and Mrs. Garges, Episcopalian. One child: (VIII.) Matilda Ann Garges, born Mar. 22, 1886.

VII. Anna Margaret Garges, born June 3, 1861. Resides in Zanesville, O. Unmrd.

VII. Milton Garges, born at Norwich, Ohio, Sept. 5, 1867. Mrd. Kate Fitzgerald, of Zanesville, O., Oct. 10, 1888. He is employed as day Telegraph Operator by the Associated Press, the largest concern of the kind in the world, for furnishing press dispatches to newspapers, at their office in St. Paul, Minn. He is a believer in the Christian religion.

VII. Alfred Ball Garges, born Dec. 25, 1869. Single (1888).

VI. Susan Garges, born in Bucks Co., Pa., July 24, 1818. She came with her parents to Fairfax Co., Va., in 1819, and lived at Annandale until after her father's death, which occurred two or three years before the war, when they left the old home and went to Ohio, where she remained until 1882. She then came to Washington, D. C., where she has her residence at the present time. Methodist. Unmrd.

VI. Abraham Garges, born in Fairfax Co., Va., Jan. 6, 1821. He spent the early part of his life with his brother John, working the homestead farm, at Annandale, Va. He afterwards moved to Ohio, where he took charge of quite a large business, owned and carried on by the "Coal Dale Mining Company."

See Page 4

THE NEW YORK
PUBLIC LIBRARY

ASTOR, LENOX AND
TILDEN FOUNDATIONS.

He afterwards mrd Mary Stark, of Muskingum Co., Ohio. He has retired from business and has a very pleasant home near Zanesville, Ohio. No issue.

VI. Mary Elizabeth Garges, born in Fairfax Co., Va., Oct. 14, 1825; died Jan. 11, 1827.

V. Rachel Fretz, born in Bucks Co., Pa., Mar. 30, 1787. Mrd. Abraham F. Stover, in 1808 or 9. He was born Mar. 10, 1786. Rachel died in 1870, aged 83 years less 13 days. Children: John, Ralph, Infant, Charles, Albert.

VI. John Stover, died in childhood.

VI. Ralph Stover, born Sept. 28, 1811. Mrd. Oct. 4, 1838, Eliza (born Aug. 31, 1815), daughter of Henry S. Stover, of Erwinna, and Barbara, daughter of Isaac Stout, of Williams, Northampton Co., Pa. Occupation, farming, milling and lumber business. Baptists. Residence, Point Pleasant, Pa. Children: Robert, Mary, John, Rachel, Emaline, Horace, Eliza, Ellie, Adelaide, R. Chester, Annie, Albert.

VII. Robert C. Stover, born in Faquier Co., Va., Oct. 28, 1839. Mrd. Ellie Carrington of Va., Jan. 8, 1873. In mill business. Attends Baptist church. Children: (**VIII.**) Lydia Antrim Stover, born Jan. 25, 1874. (**VIII.**) Charles Stover, born Feb. 19, 1876; died Sept. 25, 1877. (**VIII.**) Maggie Chen Stover, born Aug. 4, 1878; died June 8, 1884. (**VIII.**) Linwood Carrington Stover, born Sept. 6, 1880. (**VIII.**) Maud Alma Stover, born Mar. 6, 1882. (**VIII.**) Claribel Stover, born Feb. 2, 1884. (**VIII.**) May Pearl Stover, born Nov. 2, 1885; died Aug. 24, 1887. (**VIII.**) Robert Stover and (**VIII.**) Ralph Stover, twins, born Apr. 3, 1888.

VII. Mary Gill Stover, born Feb. 21, 1842. Mrd. Eugene Keyser. (See Index of References No. 12.)

VII. John Henry Stover, born May 13, 1843. Teacher in public schools. Enlisted in the 3d Pennsylvania Artillery. Was wounded at the battle of Cold Harbor, Va., June 2, 1864. Died at Campbell Hospital, Washington, D. C., June 30, 1864.

VII. Rachel Virginia Stover, born Sept. 2, 1844; died Sept. 11, 1848.

VII. Emaline Stover, born Dec. 19, 1845; died Sept. 9, 1856.

VII. Horace Stover, born June 2, 1847; died July 30, 1847.

VII. Eliza Barbara Stover, born Nov. 30, 1848. Mrd. Frederick W. Troemner, Dec. 21, 1870. Manufacturer of scales and weights. They reside in Philadelphia, Pa. Baptists. Children: **(VIII.)** Florence M. Troemner, born Nov. 14, 1871. **(VIII.)** Clara L. Troemner, born Nov. 11, 1873. **(VIII.)** Henry Troemner, born Feb. 14, 1880; died Feb. 10, 1885.

VII. Ella Stover, born Oct. 9, 1850. Mrd. John B. Lequear, of Hunterdon Co., N. J., Sept. 14, 1876. Merchant. Reside in Philadelphia, Pa. Baptists. No issue.

VII. Adelaide Stover, born Feb. 1, 1852. Mrd. Adelbert Thomson, of East Avon, Livingston Co., N. Y. Farmer. Presbyterians at East Avon, N. Y. Children: **(VIII.)** Mary Eliza Thomson, born Feb. 28, 1881. **(VIII.)** Ella May Thomson, born May 2, 1882. **(VIII.)** Leland Stover Thomson, born Oct. 12, 1884. **(VIII.)** Adelbert L. Thompson, Jr., born May 18, 1888.

VII. R. Chester Stover, born Feb. 19, 1853. Mrd. Mary E., daughter of Findley and Anna M. Bush, of Shawnee, Monroe Co., Pa., June 14, 1881. Occupation, Miller. Children: **(VIII.)** John Henry Stover, born Apr. 14, 1883. **(VIII.)** Ralph Chester Stover, born Nov. 12, 1885.

VII. Annie Stover, born Sept. 8, 1854. Mrd. Albert Stover, of Kintnersville, Bucks Co., Pa., Sept. 30, 1885. Lumber merchant. No issue.

VII. Albert F. Stover, born Aug. 20, 1860. Mrd. Lucy W. Rugler, of Hunterdon, N. J., Dec. 31, 1881. Farmer. Baptists. Children: **(VIII.)** Leland Stover, born 1882. **(VIII.)** Clarence A. Stover, born 1884; died Jan. 14, 1886.

VI. Died unnamed.

VI. Charles Stover, born Sept. 13, 1816; died Mar. 30, 1872. Unmrd. Occupation, miller and farmer in Va. After his brother Albert's death he ran his store for a time. Successful in business he enjoyed the unlimited confidence and respect of the community in which he lived, so much so that at . . close of the war, which left the rebel states without the protection of law and order of any kind, the whole community insisted on his acting as County Magistrate, which office he filled until reconstruction of the state government was effected under authority of Congress of U. S. It was well understood all through the war that he was a Union man, but he did not make himself obnoxious by ill-judged intrusion of his sentiments upon others in that section, where it could do no good. Thus he was left alone during the war except that the armies of both sides encamped on his place at Thoroughfare Gap, repeatedly, and left neither fence nor living thing of stock on the place. His losses in property and money caused by the war was about $40,000.

VI. Albert F. Stover, born Aug. 12, 1829; died Dec. 17, 1854. Merchant. Unmrd.

V. Barbara Fretz, born in Bucks Co., Pa.,   ; died in 1862. Mrd. John Smith.   . He died in 1844. Farmer. Children: Richard, Elizabeth, Rachel, John.

VI. Richard Smith, born about 1817. Mrd. Resides near Portland, Mo. Children: **(VII.)** J. R. Smith. **(VII.)** C. H. Smith (deceased). **(VII.)** Sallie Smith (deceased).

VI. Elizabeth Smith born —; died 1887. Mrd. Col. Darnes, —. He died in 1847. One child: **(VII.)** Ella Darnes, born about 1844. Mrd.—.

VI. Rachel Smith, born . Mrd.— Buehler, of Harrisburgh, Pa.—. Children: Eliza, and child. Barbara married for her second husband Daniel Grisson,—. editor of the *St. Louis Republican*, a Democratic paper.

VII. Eliza Buehler, born —; died—. Mrd.— . No issue.

VII. (Child) Buehler, died quite young.

VI. John Andrew Smith, born—; died in California about 1855 or 6.

V. Elizabeth Fretz, born Feb. 25, 1795; died—. Mrd. Thomas Z. Smith, of Buckingham, Bucks Co., Pa., Nov. 18, 1817. Children: Mary, John.

VI. Mary F.—— Smith, born Sept. 9, 1818, in Alexandria, District of Columbia; died Aug. 16, 1824, in

Fairfax Co., Va. Father and daughter lie buried in Friend's yard, Alexandria, D. C.

VI. John Fretz Smith, born Jan. 14, 1825, in Bedminster Twp., Bucks Co., Pa.; died while on a visit at his Uncle John Fretz's house at Warwick, Oct. 9, 1838. Mother and son lie buried in the Mennonite yard, near Doylestown, Pa. No living issue of above family.

V. Mary Kratz Fretz, born in 1798; died—. Mrd. Henry Gill, of Northampton Twp., Bucks Co., Pa., May 24, 1821. Farmer. Attended Dutch Ref. Ch. Children: Abraham Stover, Mary Ann, Elizabeth Smith, Henry Z., Susan, Samuel.

VI. Abraham Stover Gill, born June 22, 1824. Mrd. Mary H. Praul, Oct. 29, 1846, both of Northampton Township, Bucks Co., Pa. Farmer. Presbyterian. Moved to Illinois in 1853, where he died Apr. 30, 1857. Children: John Fretz, Thomas Smith.

VII. John Fretz Gill, born Oct. 10, 1847; died Sept. 19, 1859.

VII. Thomas Smith Gill, born Aug. 26, 1850. Mrd. Annie Sudbrack, Jan. 6, 1878. Wagon-maker. Attends Presbyterian Ch. Children: (**VIII.**) Nora Rosanna Gill, born May 7, 1879. (**VIII.**) Nellie B. Gill, born Dec. 4, 1881. (**VIII.**) Arthur Gill, born Dec. 14, 1883. (**VIII.**) Lettie Gill, born Mar. 29, 1886. (**VIII.**) Frederick W. Gill, born Nov. 7, 1888.

VI. Mary Ann Gill, born June 23, 1827; died May 31, 1871. Mrd. John Addis, Jan. 1, 1851. He died Sept. 3, 1887. Farmer. Member Dutch Ref. Ch. Children: Mary E., Miles, Susie G.

VII. Mary E. Addis, born Aug. 8, 1852. Mrd. Will A. Yerkes, of Richboro, Pa., Feb. 3, 1874. Farmer. Dutch Ref. No issue.

VII. Miles Addis, born July 30, 1854; died Apr. 26, 1855.

VII. Susie G. Addis, born Jan. 2, 1860; died Feb. 5, 1883. Unmrd.

VI. Elizabeth S. Gill, born July 19, 1829. Mrd. Isaac Carrell, Nov. 21, 1855. She died in Trenton, N. J., Aug. 15, 1882, without issue. Buried at Richboro, Pa., cemetery.

VI. Henry Z. Gill, M. D., born in Northampton
Township, Bucks Co., Pa., Oct. 6, 1831. Mrd. Miss
Mattie W. Carpenter, of Columbus, Ohio, April 21,
1869; she being the only daughter of Timothy R. Carpenter. After completing his 21st year at home (at
the place of birth), he went to a select school kept by
John Clark, A. M., about two miles north of New
Britain church, remaining several months. He then
returned home, taught school for ten months in
Plymouth Twp., Montg'y Co., Pa. Some time in
1854 he taught a term of school near Columbus, Ohio.
Having injured his eyes by too close application to
study, he consulted a physician connected with a College Eye Infirmary, commenced treatment, and after
his school term was completed, by the physician's
suggestion and recommendation he commenced the
study of medicine; his original purpose having been
to study civil engineering. After attending a course
and a half of lectures, and close reading till the fall of
1856, he went to Jefferson Medical College at Philadelphia, Pa., from which he graduated in March 1857.
During his time of study in Columbus, Ohio, he had
charge of the dissecting room, and aided in the Eye
Infirmary. These two circumstances gave him a taste
for surgery and diseases of the eye, which were not
neglected, and were of much advantage to him in the
general practice of his profession. After graduating
he returned to Columbus, Ohio, and commenced to
practice, giving especial attention to the eye and ear,
though not abandoning the general practice.

The war breaking out in 1861, a call was made
for medical men, a law being passed requiring all to
pass examination; five years of practice being required, or its equivalent in Hospital for assistants,
and ten years for surgeons. Although in the examinations he and another stood equal (third) in the list
of over fifty admitted to examination, yet he could be
appointed assistant only. In the summer campaign
in West Virginia he had the entire work of the regiment until winter, when he had the first severe sickness of his life, and from which he probably never
fully recovered. The next summer (1862), foreseeing

the probable same experience of all the work with
part of the pay of surgeon, he resigned, and was in a
few days appointed surgeon of another Regiment, the
95th Ohio, the former being the 11th Ohio Infantry.
They were immediately sent to the field in Kentucky,
and on Aug. 30, 1862, engaged in the battles (three
engagements in one day) of Richmond, Ky., where a
large part of the regiment were captured, and many
killed and wounded. Remaining six weeks in the en-
emy's hands with the wounded, they returned paroled
to Columbus, Ohio, in October and prepared for the
work of 1863 down the Mississippi River, and the
siege of Vicksburgh, in all of which he (Dr. Gill) participated. After that campaign and the second attack
on Jackson, Miss., they spent the fall and winter in
scouting and doing guard duty. He had applied for
permission to appear before the United States Medical Board for examination for Surgeon of Volunteers,
a higher position than Surgeon of a Regiment, though
of the same rank (Major of Cavalry). The number of
such was limited by law of Congress. A ten days' examination satisfied the authorities and he received his
commission from Abraham L'ncoln. (It is believed
the first vacancy.) He was at once sent to the Atlanta Campaign, and very early assigned as Surgeon
in Chief of the First Division, 20th Army Corps,
Gen. Joe Hooker's fighting corps. This position he
held to the close of the war, finishing the Atlanta
Campaign, the famous march to the sea, the Carolina
Campaign, and so on to the great review at Washington in 1865. He went with the Western troop, west
to Louisville, Ky., and was honorably mustered out
in August, 1865. Spent the fall in traveling, the
winter at the Jefferson Medical College.

In May, 1866, he sailed for Europe, where he
spent two years of hard study in hospitals; 16 months
in Germany, the remainder of the time in Paris, Geneva and London, and returned to New York in May,
1868. Re-commenced the practice of his profession in
St. Louis, in Oct. 1868. There he practiced and was
Associate Editor of the St. Louis Medical and Sur-
gical Journal until 1873, when at the solicitation of

friends he removed to Jerseyville, Ill. About 1875 or 6 the degree of A. M. was conferred on Dr. Gill by McKendree College, Lebanon, Ill., and the degree of L.L. D. by the University of Wooster, Ohio, in 1883, the Medical Department of which was located at Cleveland, Ohio, where he was living and lecturing in the Medical College, occupying the chair of Clinical Surgery. In 1881 he was appointed Physician to Southern Illinois Penitentiary, where he did some of his best work. In March 1865 he received the first Brevet (Lt. Colonel) of any medical officer from the state of Ohio. From Chester, Ill. (Southern Ill. Penitentiary), he was urged to take the chair Surgery in the Medical Department of the University of Wooster, at Cleveland, Ohio, which position he filled for over two years; then resigned on account of over-work and severity of climate. In Oct. 1886 he removed to El Dorado, Butler Co., Kansas, having at that time just completed his work on "Diphtheria, Croup and Tracheotomy," a work which cost him much labor. In the spring of 1855, Dr. Gill joined the M. E. church, of which he has been a member ever since, and has held every official position up to President of the "Lay Electoral Conference" of Southern Ill. Conference in 1883. Their children are: (VII.) Amos Carpenter Gill, born May 6, 1871; died Feb. 22, 1872. (VII.) Elizabeth Carrell Gill, born Sept. 21, 1873. (VII.) Randolph Foster Gill, born Aug. 6, 1880.

VI. Susan Fretz Gill, born in Bucks Co., Pa., April 3, 1835. Mrd. James Gill, Oct. 1, 1855. For some years they lived in California. In 1860 they returned to Bucks Co., Pa., having purchased the old Gill homestead. He was in the lumber business until 1865, when he retired. Mrs. Gill, Dutch Reformed. Children: Harry, Joseph, Charles, James, Mary.

VII. Harry Clay Gill, born Aug. 3, 1857. Mrd. Kate C. Coffman, Dec. 28, 1887, daughter of William and Mary J. Coffman, of Philadelphia. Book-keeper and accountant in Law Department of the City of Philadelphia, Pa. They attend the Baptist church. No children.

VII. Joseph Swift Gill, born Nov. 17, 1859. Mrd. Florence Elizabeth Cooper (daughter of Wm. S. and Mary H.), Oct. 20, 1886. In lumber business. Children: (**VIII.**) Joseph Raymond Gill, born June 2, 1887. (**VIII.**) William Cooper Gill, born Dec. 15, 1888.

VII. Charles Stover Gill, born Sept. 4, 1861; died, aged 2 years and 8 months.

VII. James William Gill, born Feb. 5, 1864. Machinist. Resides in St. Louis, Mo. Unmrd.

VII. Mary Lillian Gill, born July 27, 1866. Mrd. John Marsden, Mar. 9, 1887. Dry goods business. Attends Ref. church. One child: (**VIII.**) Ethel Gill Marsden, born Feb. 15, 1888.

VI. Samuel Gill, born Sept. 2, 1837; died Sept. 15, 1838.

V. John Fretz, born Aug. 10, 1802; died Dec. 4, 1872. He married Martha Carver, of Buckingham, Pa., in 1825. He owned and lived on a part of the old homestead in Warwick, Bucks Co., Pa, where he engaged in farming, until within a few years of his death, when he sold his farm to Samuel Larzelere, and bought a house in Doylestown, where he lived retired until his death. He died without issue.

V. Anna Fretz, born — , 1805; died Sept. 10, 1875. Mrd. Samuel Dungan, of Southampton, Pa. Baptists. Children: Charles S., Emeline F.

VI. Charles S. Dungan, born May 18, 1826. Mrd. Mary Jane Fau, Oct. 2, 1850. Mrs. Dungan died July 16, 1873. Mr. Dungan's occupation is Paymaster. Baptist. Residence, Philadelphia, Pa. Children: William, Charles, John, Thomas, Ida, William, Robert, Mary, Charles, Louisa, Samuel.

VII. William Weightman Dungan, born Sept. 25, 1851; died Aug. 22, 1856.

VII. Charles Henry Dungan, born Sept. 12, 1853; died July 13, 1859.

VII. John Fau Dungan, born May 27, 1855. Mrd. —, May 19, 1884. Occupation, Florist. Residence, Maryland. No issue.

VII. Thomas Fau Dungan, born May 27, 1855. Mrd. . Clerk. Residence, San Francisco, Cal.

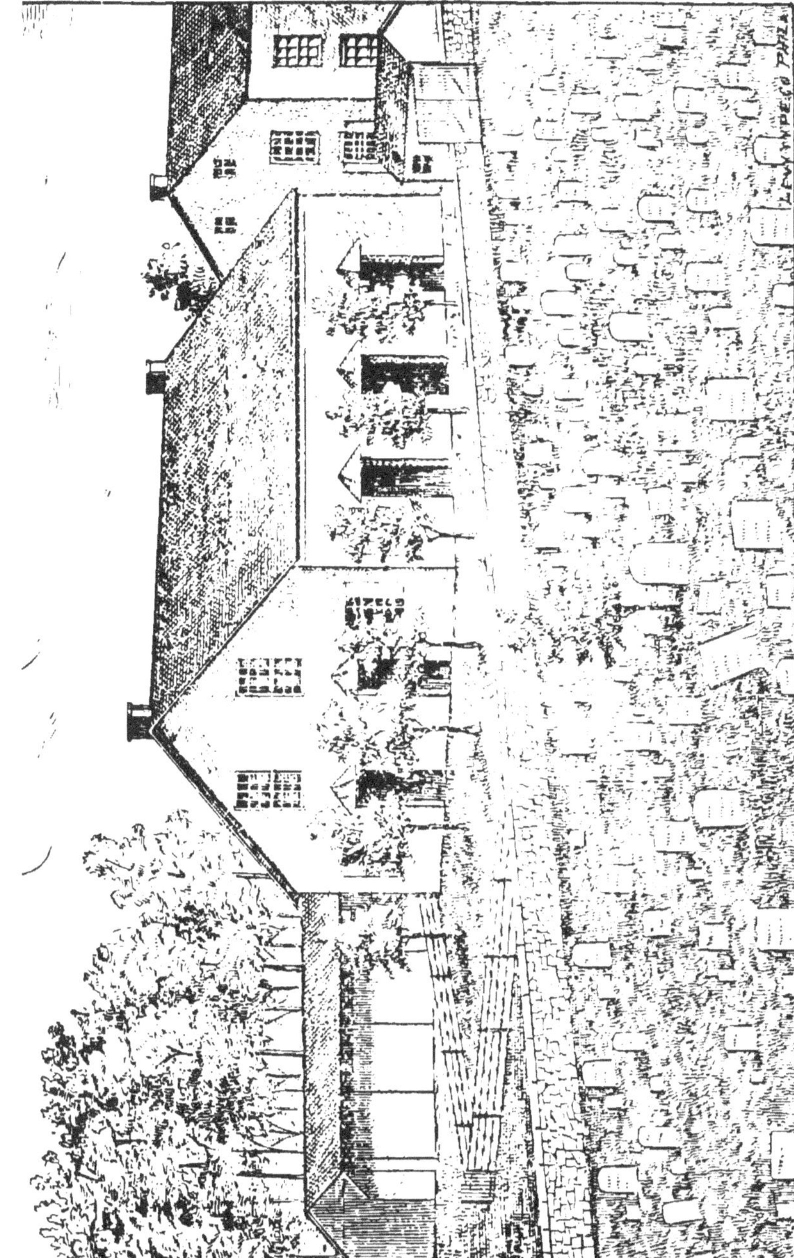

VII. Ida Virginia Dungan, born Nov. 10, 1857. Mrd. John H. H. Poole, Aug. 10, 1882. Occupation, manufacturer. Res., Haddenfield, N. J. Children: **(VIII.)** Irene May Poole, born May 5, 1883. **(VIII.)** Horatio Nelson Poole, born Jan. 16, 1885. **(VIII.)** John Chapin Poole, born April 9, 1887.

VII. William Weightman Dungan, born Dec. 22, 1859. Mrd. —, June 11, 1885. Painter. Res. San Francisco, Cal. No issue.

VII. Robert Q. Dungan, born Nov. 5, 1861; died Nov. 6, 1861.

VII. Mary Emma Dungan, born Dec. 19, 1862. Mrd. W. R. Perry, Apr. 10, 1882. Occupation, gentleman. Res., Maryland. Children: **(VIII.)** Mary Agnes Perry, born May 26, 1883. **(VIII.)** Geneva Ethelberta Perry, born April 24, 1884. **(VIII.)** Helen Perry, born June 15, 1887.

VII. Charles Samuel Dungan, born July 18, 1864; died Oct. 27, 1867.

VII. Louisa Trottee Dungan, born Aug. 2, 1866. Mrd. Charles F. Esher, June 16, 1886. Merchant. Res., Girard Ave., Philadelphia, Pa. One child: **(VIII.)** Ida Louisa Esher, born June 12, 1887.

VII. Samuel Grant Dungan, born July 27, 1869.

Charles S. Dungan **(VI.)** mrd. for his second wife Amanda Heinig, Jan. 1, 1876.

VI. Emeline F. Dungan, born—; died July 20, 1830.

V. Philip Fretz, born—; died young.

IV. John Kratz, born in Bucks Co., Pa., Nov. 22, 1765; died Jan. 27, 1844, aged 78 yrs., 2 mos. 5 d. Mrd. Anna Freed—. She died Feb. 11, 1799. Farmer. Mennonite. Children: Abraham, Saloma, Deborah, Susanna, Magdalena. John mrd. for his second wife Magdalena Swartzlander (a half sister to his first wife). She died Mar. 9, 1814. Children: David, Philip, Joseph, Anna, Isaac, Catharine, Rachel, John, Jr.

V. Abraham Kratz, born Mar. 7, 1791.

V. Saloma Kratz, born May 8, 1792.

V. Deborah Kratz, born Nov. 6, 1793.

V. Susanna Kratz, born Feb. 18, 1796; died— . Mrd. John Riale, of New Britain, Pa., in 1828. He died—.

Moved West. Children: Joshua, Clayton. Susanna mrd. second husband, — McDonnell—. One son: (VI.) Alexander.

VI. Joshua Riale, born— . Mrd.—. Lives somewhere in Nebraska. Children: (VII.) Frank N. Riale, born about 1859. (VII.) Mittie Riale, born about 1862. (VII.) Mary Ella Riale, born about 1869.

VI. Clayton K. Riale, born—.

VI. Alexander McDonnell, born—. Mrd.—. Lives somewhere in Missouri. Farmer. Children: (VII.) Clayton McDonnell. (VII.) Annie McDonnell. (VII.) Welford McDonnell. (VII.) Frances McDonnell.

V. Magdalena Kratz, born Mar. 17, 1798.

V. David Kratz, born May 1, 1801; died—.

V. Philip Kratz, born Nov. 2, 1802; died July 21, 1855, aged 52 yrs., 8 mos. 19 d. Mrd. Catharine Nunnemaker,—. Farmer. Children: David, Rosanna, Ervin, Emma, Philip, and three died in infancy.

VI. David N. Kratz, born June 23, 1843. Mrd. Annie B. Selner, Feb. 15, 1873. P. O., Doylestown, Pa. Slate roofer and dealer in roofing slate. Lutherans. One child: (VII.) Mary Jane Kratz, age 13 yrs. (1891).

VI. Rosanna Kratz, born , 1844. Mrd. Tobias N. Myers, Jan. 19, 1865. Merchant and Real Estate, at 39 N. Eleventh St., Philadelphia, Pa. Children: Ulysses, Allen, Laura, Lillie, Rosa.

VII. Ulysses S. Grant Myers, born Nov. 23, 1865. Mrd. Jennette Kline, Jan. 1, 1890, a graduate of Doylestown Seminary. Housefurnishing business in Philadelphia, Pa.

VII. S. Allen Myers, born Oct. 24, 1869.

VII. Laura Bertha Myers, born Mar. 1876; died 1878.

VII. Lillie May Myers, born Aug. 25, 1878.

VII. Rosa Pearl Myers, born July 2, 1882.

VI. Erwin N. Kratz, born—. Mrd. Laura Jacoby,—. She died—. No issue.

VI. Philip N. Kratz, born July 19, 1853. Mrd. Emma J. Dudbridge, Feb. 19, 1880. P. O., Doylestown, Pa. Formerly miller and millwright, now a mechanic. Attend Luth. Ch. No issue.

VI. Emma E. Kratz, born   Mrd. Theodore Holcomb.

V. Joseph Kratz, born June 25, 1804.

V. Anna Kratz, born in Bucks Co., Pa., Sept. 28, 1805; died Aug. 3, 1890, aged 84 y., 10 m. 5 d. Mrd. Jonas Stover, Oct. 22, 1829. He died June 9, 1883, aged 81 y., 3 m. 12 d. Oct. 22, 1879, was the golden anniversary day of their married life. He was a miller and lived at Stover's Mill near Church Hill, Bucks Co., Pa. Mrs. Stover was a member of the Ref. Ch. Both buried at the Tohickon Ref. Ch. Children: Oliver, Catharine, Lucinda, Reuben, Annie, Emma.

VI. Oliver K. Stover, born Mar. 27, 1831; died Mar. 20, 1833.

VI. Catharine Stover, born May 23, 1833; died Feb. 24, 1864, aged 30 y., 8 m. 27 d. Mrd. Aaron Kratz (see Index of References No. 13.)

VI. Lucinda Stover, born Nov. 27, 1835, S.

VI. Reuben K. Stover, born Feb. 29, 1844; died July 7, 1878, aged 34 y., 4 m. 8 d. Mrd. Catharine A. Weisel, Jan. 15, 1870. Farmer. Ger. Ref. Children: Henry, Clara, Ella.

VII. Henry Edgar Stover, born June 2, 1870; died Dec. 23, 1874.

VII. Clara Ann Stover, born Sept. 21, 1871. Mrd. Leidy M. Fulmer, son of Jonas D. Fulmer, of Carversville, Pa. Jan. 17, 1891. Cashier at Strewbridge's, and Clothier, Phila., Pa. Ref. Ch.

VII. Ella May Stover, born May 30, 1876.

VI. Annie K. Stover, born in Bucks Co., Apr. 28, 1846. Mrd. Jacob S. Funk. (See index of references No. 14.)

VI. Emma Stover, born in Bucks Co., Oct. 27, 1848. Mrd. Moses F. Rittenhouse, Dec. 1871. He was born in Lincoln Co., Ont., Aug. 12, 1846. Lumber merchant in Chicago, Ill. Presbyterians. Children: (VII.) Edward F. Rittenhouse, born November 3, 1872. (VII.) Charles J. Rittenhouse, born Nov. 13, 1874. (VII.) Walter Rittenhouse, born Mar. 31, 1879.

V. Isaac Kratz, born Sept. 10, 1807; died Jan. 23, 1890. Aged 82 yr., 4 m., 13 d. Mrd. Ann Harley, June

18. 1839. She died Aug. 25, 1875. Farmer. Ger. Baptists. Children: Amanda, John, Isaiah, Louisa, William.

VI. Amanda Kratz, born Jan. 4, 1841; died June 4, 1841.

VI. John H. Kratz, born July 4, 1842. Mrd. Emma Reiff.—.

VI. Isaiah Kratz, born Sept. 22, 1844; died Nov. 11, 1876. Mrd. Emma Shepherd. One child:—.

VI. Louisa S. Kratz, born Oct. 23, 1846. Mrd. Philip Kratz. (See index of references No. 15.)

VI. William Henry Kratz, born Aug. 13, 1850; died Feb. 16, 1861.

V. Catharine Kratz, born May 2, 1809; died Mar. 31, 1890. Mrd. Enos Stout, Nov. 13, 1834. He was born Apr. 17, 1813; died Dec. 6, 1886. Farmer. Ger. Ref. Ch. Children: Lewis, John, Reuben, Allen, Edward, Wilhelmina.

VI. Lewis K. Stout, born Dec. 27, 1835. Mrd. Levina M., daughter of Samuel Althouse, of Bedminster, Oct. 28, 1865. P. O., 2519 N. 7th St., Phila., Pa. Occupation fruit preserving. Ger. Ref. Ch. Children: **(VII.)** Henry Erwin Stout, born Sept. 15, 1866; died Apr. 8, 1874. **(VII.)** Anna A. Stout, born Jan. 14, 1868. Dressmaker. S. **(VII.)** Oliver A. Stout, born Nov. 11, 1869. S. He is a graduate of pharmacy, and medical student at the university of Pennsylvania. **(VII.)** Edward Clayton Stout, born Aug. 12, 1872. Clerk in Phila., Pa. **(VII.)** Charles A. Stout, born July 28, 1875. Clerk in drug store in Phila., Pa. **(VII.)** Philip Samuel Stout, born Aug. 20, 1877. **(VII.)** Benjamin Franklin Stout, born Jan. 18, 1880.

VI. John Henry Stout, born July, 22, 1838. Mrd. Emaline, daughter of Isaac and Lydia Ann Deaterly, Oct. 23, 1863. She was born Nov. 5, 1845; died Mar. 22, 1887. Children:

VII. Clara Stout, born; died in infancy.

VII. Minerva D. Stout, born Jan. 31, 1865. Mrd. Samuel O. Fretz, Feb. 13, 1886. P. O., Bedminster, Pa. Farmer. New. Men. Deep Run. One child: **(VIII.)** Nero Fretz, born May 27, 1888.

VI. Reuben Stout, born Mar. 28, 1841. Mrd. Catharine Anna Werte, Nov. 18, 1871. She was born Nov. 5, 1850; died Nov. 5, 1889. P. O., Perkasie, Pa. Mason and plasterer. Children: **(VII.)** Emma Stout, born Sept. 26, 1872; died Feb. 8, 1888. **(VII.)** Harvey Stout, born Oct. 10, 1875; died Oct. 25, 1889.

VI. Allen K. Stout, born May. 21, 1843. Mrd. Catharine Shearer, July 29, 1871. She died Mar. 24, 1887. P. O., Church Hill, Pa. Miller. Children: **(VII.)** Charles Edgar Stout, born Aug. 19, 1872; died Sept. 29, 1872. **(VII.)** Ella Amanda Stout, born Feb. 17, 1874.

VI. Edward Clayton Stout, born Mar. 3, 1846; died Jan. 28, 1862.

VI. Wilhelmina Stout, born Aug. 31, 1850; died Feb. 10, 1862.

V. Rachel Kratz, born Jan. 6, 1811.

V. John Kratz, Jr., born in Bucks Co., Pa., Feb. 24, 1813; died—. Mrd. Elizabeth Rauch. . Moved west and finally settled in Wheeling, West Va., where descendants of his still live, who, as far as learned are:—Edward A. Kratz; Mrs. Adam Kratz, and Mrs. Caroline Kratz's families.

IV. Elizabeth Kratz, born —, 1768; died—. Mrd. Jacob Fretz, son of Christian and Barbara Fretz, of Bedminster, Bucks Co., Nov. 6, 1787. He was born Jan. 1, 1767; died Jan. 12, 1799. Fuller and dyer. Lived in Solebury Twp., at a place known as Fleecydale, which he purchased of Jonas Ingham in 1788 for 700 pounds. The farm contained 83 acres. Children: Philip, Barbara, Christian, Elizabeth and Mary.

V. Philip Fretz, born Jan. 8, 1789; died in Apr. 1851. Mrd. Elizabeth, daughter of Ralph Stover, of Bedminster, Mar. 20, 1810. She was born Nov. 8, 1790; died June 8, 1870. Fuller, dyer and farmer. Children: Jacob, Catharine, Susan, Magdalena, Elizabeth, Violette, Hannah, Infant, Annie, Rachel, Cornelia, Sarah.

VI. Jacob Fretz, born in Bucks Co., Pa., Oct. 22, 1811. Miller and farmer, now retired. He owned the old homestead at Fleecydale, where he lived for many years. In 1875 he retired from business. About

1880 he sold the homestead at Fleecydale, nearly 100 years after it came into the possession of his grandfather. In 1880 he moved to Lumberville, Pa., where he had previously erected a fine dwelling. He never married.

VI. Catharine Stover Fretz, born in Bucks Co., Pa., Oct. 1, 1813; died Dec. 19, 1877. Mrd. Joseph Cowell Heed, in 1840. Farmer and gunmaker. Children: Emma, William, Joseph, Charles, Elizabeth, Joseph, Clifford, Catharine, Stover.

VII. Emma Augusta Heed, born July 1, 1841; died May 10, 1864. S.

VII. William S. Heed, born Sept. 22, 1842; died Dec. 30, 1880. Mrd. Hannah Moore, July 24, 1867. Lawyer. Episcopalians. Children: Emma, Lillian, Florence.

VIII. Emma A. Heed, born Oct. 30, 1868. Mrd. L. H. Adler, Jr.—, 1610 Arch St., Phila., Pa.

VIII. Lillian M. Heed, born Mar. 21, 1872; died Aug. 24, 72.

VIII. Florence May Heed, born Apr. 3, 1873; died Feb. 11, 1887.

VII. Joseph Clark Heed, born July 20, 1845; died Aug. 21, 1846.

VII. Charles Ernest Heed, born June 30, 1846. Resid s in Phila. Wholesale Grain dealer. Attends Quaker meeting. S. (1889.)

VII. Elizabeth Fretz Heed, born June 15, 1848; died Feb. 24, 1850.

VII. Joseph Bradley Heed, born July 30, 1851. Mrd. Virginia A. Rittenhouse, Feb. 3, 1876. Salesman. Attends Presbyterian Ch. Children: (**VIII.**) Helen Catharine Heed, born Aug. 1, 1877. (**VIII.**) Charles Rittenhouse Heed, born Aug. 20, 1879.

VII. Clifford Harold Heed, born May 3, 1853; died Dec. 31, 1886. Attend Methodist Ch.

VII. Catharine Genette Heed, born May 2, 1854; died Sept. 20, 1854.

VII. Stover Keyser Heed, born Oct. 5, 1856; died Mar. 22, 1861.

VI. Susan Fretz, born in Bucks Co., Pa., Aug. 19, 1815; died Apr. 1, 1847. S.

VI. Magdalena Fretz, born in Bucks Co., July 1. 1817; died Dec. 23, 1840. S.

VI. Elizabeth Fretz, born in Bucks Co., Sept. 4. 1821. Mrd. Charles Ferdinand Keyser, Mar. 4, 1845. Retired. Presbyterians. Res. Phila., Pa. Children: Charles, Harry, Stover.

VII. Charles Eugene Keyser, born Feb. 7, 1846. Mrd. Mary Gill, (daughter of Ralph Stover of Point Pleasant. Pa.,) Sept. 20. 1870. Farmer in Virginia: Children: (**VIII.**) Mary Elizabeth Keyser, born Aug. 5. 1871. (**VIII.**) Ella Augusta Keyser, born Nov. 30, 1872. (**VIII.**) Eliza Mariam Keyser, born August. 27. 1875. (**VIII.**) Edgar Eugene Keyser, born June 23. 1877. (**VIII.**) Charles Henry Keyser, born January 12, 1880. (**VIII.**) Ralph Stover Keyser, born May 10, 1883.

VII. Harry Theodore Keyser, born Jan. 20, 1850.

VII. Stover Fretz Keyser, born July 20, 1853; died Dec. 13, 1855.

VI. Violette Fretz, born May 5, 1820; died June 14. 1842. S.

VI. Hannah Fretz, born Jan. 28, 1822; died Feb. 10, 1844. S.

VI. Infant unnamed, born and died in Mar. 1824.

VI. Annie Fretz, born in Bucks Co., Pa., Apr. 1. 1825. Mrd. Hugh E. Walton (dec'd), Jan. 13, 1846. Miller. Res., Sibley. Iowa. Congregationalists. Children: Cornelia, Eugene, Hugh.

VII. Cornelia Walton, born Aug. 28, 1850. Mrd. Geo. W. Jones, Jan. 14, 1880. One child: (**VIII.**) Leslie Jones, born 1881.

VII. Eugene Walton, born June 22, 1859. Mrd. Annette Berger, July 25, 1888. Furniture and Undertaking business at Sibley, Iowa. Congregationalists.

VII. Hugh E. Walton, born Jan. 22, 1862. Furniture and Undertaking business at Sibley, Iowa. Congregationalists.

VI. Rachel Fretz, born Feb. 1, 1827; died June 19, 1844. S.

VI. Cornelia Fretz, born Jan. 1. 1829; died Oct. 28, 1849. S.

VI. Sarah Ann Fretz, born in Bucks Co., Jan. 17, 1831. Mrd. Morris L. Fell, Nov. 27, 1856. Wholesale Grain merchant in Phila., Pa. One child: (**VII.**) Henry Fell.

V. Barbara Fretz, born in Bucks Co., Pa., Apr. 14, 1791; died —, without issue.

V. Christian Fretz, born Dec. 28, 1792; died Mar. 11, 1799.

V. Elizabeth Fretz, born in Bucks Co., May 6, 1795; died—, without issue.

V. Mary Fretz, born in Bucks Co., Sept. 14, 1797. Mrd. William Rich, of Dyerstown, Pa., about 1815, or 1816; died a year or so later without issue.

IV. Mary Kratz, born.—; died—. Mrd. Joseph Fretz, son of Abraham and Dorothy (Kulp) Fretz. Farmer. Mennonites. Children: Henry, John, Abraham.

V. Henry Fretz, born in Bucks Co., Dec. 13, 1794; died Jan. 14, 1858. Mrd. Mary M. White, Jan. 7, 1824. Farmer in Bedminster Twp. He was accustomed to wear velvet pants, and from that fact he was familiarly known as "Velvet Henry." Children: Maria, Francis, Martha.

VI. Maria Fretz, born Oct. 28, 1824; died Sept. 15, 1876. Mrd. John K. Myers, Sept. 22, 1844. Farmer and miller. Children: David, Amos, Martha, Albert, Minerva, Anthony, Anna.

VII. David F. Myers, born Jan. 25, 1845. Mrd. Lucy A. Campbell, Sept. 10, 1868. Whole shipper and dealer in baled hay and grain, and assistant U. S. Express Ag't at Marion, Kan. Lutherans. Children: (**VIII.**) Mamie A. Myers, born Oct. 2, 1869. (**VIII.**) Willie E. Myers, born Sept 9, 1871. (**VIII.**) Stacy Myers, born May 1, 1875. (**VIII.**) Louie Myers, born June 2, 1883. (**VIII.**) Josie Myers, born Nov. 8, 1888.

VII. Amos F. Myers, born Feb. 23, 1847. Mrd. Sarah E. Fretz, daughter of Drover Abraham Fretz, in 1867. She died Jan. 3, 1871. One child: John. Amos mrd. for second wife Mrs. Lavina Solliday (maiden name Gillmer) Sept. 1, 1874. Grocer in Philadelphia. Children: (**VIII.**) John F. Myers, born in Bucks Co., in 1867. School teacher, at present

REV. A. M. FRETZ.

(See Page 45)

clerk in store at Sellersville, Pa. (Ger. Ref. S. **(VIII.)**
Arthur Myers, born Sept. 9, 1879. **(VIII.)** Raymond
Myers, born May 7, 1881. **(VIII.)** Vernon Myers,
born Nov. 24, 1883.

VII. Martha F. Myers, born June 8, 1848. Mrd.
William S. Swope, Sept. 1, 1866. Children: Emaretta, Frances, Harry, John, Mamie.

VIII. Emaretta Swope, born Jan. 8, 1867. Mrd. Reuben Snyder, Aug. 9, 1888. Farmer.

VIII. Frances M. Swope, born June 1, 1870.

VIII. Harry Edgar Swope, born July 10, 1872.

VIII. John Wesley Swope, born Oct. 24, 1877.

VIII. Mamie Swope, born Nov. 25, 1886.

VII. Albert F. Myers, born May 4, 1850. Mrd. Kate
Moyer, Sept. 22, 1877. P. O., Perkasie, Pa. Butcher.
Ger. Ref. Children: **(VIII.)** Ulysses M. Myers, born
Nov. 18, 1879. **(VIII.** Lillie Viola M. Myers, born
July 24, 1883. **(VIII.)** Wesley M. Myers, born Aug.
13, 1885. **(VIII.)** Flora M. Myers, born Mar. 24, 1888.
(VIII.) Raymond M. Myers, born Jan. 6, 1890. **(VIII.)**
Katie Myers, born Mar. 1, 1891.

VII. Minerva F. Myers, born Jan. 10, 1854. Mrd.
Isaac L. Fretz. (See Index of References No. 16.)

VII. Anthony F. Myers, M. D., born in Plumstead
Twp., Bucks Co., Jan. 6, 1856, was reared on his father's farm and mill property on the Tohickon Creek
in Tinicum Twp., and attended the public schools
during the winter months. At the age of 20 he attended the Mennonite Seminary at Wadsworth, Ohio,
for a year, and began teaching in the public schools
of Tinicum in the fall of 1876. The following two
years he taught the Pipersville school, and during the
summer term attended the Millersville State Normal
School In Sept. 1879, he again entered the Normal
school at Millersville for a year, and while there was
tendered and accepted the position of assistant principal of the Tressler Orphan's Home at Loysville,
Perry Co., Pa. After filling the responsible position
very acceptably to the Board of Trustees for two
years, he resigned, and spent several months traveling, visiting numerous National cemeteries, old bat-
tle-fields, and various places of interest in some of

the southern states. In Sept. 1882, he entered the office of Dr. S. S. Brumbaugh, at Pipersville, Pa., and began the study of medicine. He studied under the efficient supervision of his preceptor Dr. Brumbaugh, until the following year, when he entered the Missouri Medical College, at St. Louis from which institution he graduated as physician and surgeon in Mar. 1885. Returning east, he, in order to become a practicing physician in Pa., passed a creditable examination at the Medico Chirurgical College of Phila.; and since Apr. 1885, has been a practicing physician and surgeon at Blooming Glen, where by good success, and his ambition to become more proficient in his profession, he has gained the confidence of the people, and is enjoying a lucrative practice. Dr. Myers was mrd. Oct. 11, 1888, to Wilhelmina S., daughter of Simon H. and Lydia (Savacool) Snyder. She was born Mar. 21, 1864. Lutherans. The doctor is an active member of the Bucks Co., Medical Society, the Lehigh Valley Medical Association, the Medical Society of the state of Pennsylvania. A charter member of the Perkasie Lodge No. 661, I. O. O. F., and member of the Sellersville Encampment I. O. O. F. No. 252.

VII. Anna Barbara Myers, born in Bucks Co., Jan. 5, 1860. Mrd. Hillary S. Althouse, May 23, 1885. Tailor. Ger. Ref. Children: **(VIII.)** Herbert Althouse, born Oct. 29, 1885. **(VIII.)** Irene Althouse, born Oct. 1, 1891.

VI. Francis Fretz, born about 1826; died   . Mrd. Sarah Myers,—. One child: **(VII.)** Jordan Fretz.

VI. Martha C. Fretz, born Aug. 31, 1828. Mrd. Thomas C. Atherholt, Nov. 24, 1859. Wholesale merchant and importer of Queensware, China and Glassware at 422 Market St., Phila. Ger. Ref. Children: **(VII.)** Samuel F. Atherholt, born Sept. 7, 1860. **(VII.)** Wilson D. Atherholt, born June 23, 1862; died Sept. 7, 1863. **(VII.)** Edgar Frank Atherholt, born Dec. 20, 1864. **(VII.)** Arthur Thomas Atherholt, born Apr. 11, 1867. **(VII.)** Joseph Octavius Atherholt, born July 16, 1870.

V. John Fretz, born in Bucks Co. in 1796; died Oct. 23, 1865; aged 69 y., 1 m. 28 d. Mrd. Catharine Heiny, —. About 1820 he moved to Richland, now Ashland Co., Ohio, where he and wife died. Farmer and weaver. Presbyterians. Children: Sarah, Rachel.

VI. Sarah Fretz, born in Bucks Co., Jan. 29, 1826. Mrd. Robert Walker, Nov. 1, 1845. In 1850 they moved to Illinois, and now live near Clinton, Dewitt Co. Farmer. Presbyterians. Children: Enoch, Kate, Carrie, Charles, Jennie, Anna, Mary.

VII. Enoch Walker, born Aug. 17, 1850. Mrd. Jane Gizar, Nov 25, 1874. Lumberman in Escambia Co., Alabama. Presbyterians. Children: (**VIII.**) Frederick Walker. (**VIII.**) Ernest Walker.

VII. Kate Walker, born Nov. 23, 1855. Mrd. William H. Weller, Nov. 27, 1879. Farmer. Presbyterians. No issue.

VII. Carrie Walker, born Feb. 16, 1858. Mrd. P. K. Willson, Sept. 6, 1882. Farmer. Prot. Methodists. Stock-raiser. Children: (**VIII.**) Charles R. Willson, born June 26, 1883. (**VIII.**) Harry K. Willson, born Sept. 16, 1885. (**VIII.**) Bertha M. Willson, born May 2, 1889.

VII. Charles Walker, born Feb. 14, 1860. Mrd. Kate Capron, Oct. 3, 1889. One child: (**VIII.**) Carl C. Walker, born 1890.

VII. Jennie Walker, born Dec. 27, 1862. S.

VII. Anna Walker, born Oct. 16, 1863. Mrd. George H. Thorp, May 2, 1888. Merchant. Methodists. Children: (**VIII.**) Dwight Thorp, born Sept. 1889. (**VIII.**) "Babe" Thorp, born Oct. 1891.

VII. Mary L. Walker, born Aug. 25, 1866. Mrd. John Tackett, Feb. 22, 1884. Farmer. Methodists. Children: (**VIII.**) Estella Tackett. (**VIII.**) Lulu Tackett. (**VIII.**) Dora Tackett.

VI. Rachel Fretz, born in Bucks Co, Pa., Sept. 6, 1828; died in Ohio Mar. 30, 1866. Mrd. John F. Kilaver, Dec. 20, 1858. Farmer. Lutherans. Children: Catharine, Sarah.

VII. Catharine Kilaver, born Sept. 24, 1859. Mrd. S. E. Copus, of Wood Co., Ohio, Dec. 22, 1888. P. O., Hoytville, Ohio. Farmer. Lutheran. One child: **(VIII.)** Franklin L. Copus, born Apr. 8, 1890.

VII. Sarah Kilaver, born Mar. 4, 1862. P. O., Perryville, Ohio. Lutheran.

V. Abraham Fretz, born in Bucks Co., Feb. 8, 1799; died—. Mrd. Anna Myers, daughter of Henry and Mary Magdalena Myers, of Plumstead Twp., Mar. 10, 1829. Farmer. Mennonites Children: Joseph, Mary, Sarah, John, Abraham.

VI. Joseph M. Fretz, born in Bucks Co., June 12, 1831. Mrd. Hannah Cassel, Feb. 27, 1860. Farmer. Children: Emeline, Amanda, Ada, Clinton, Willis.

VII. Emeline Fretz, born Sept. 14, 1862; died Sept. 11, 1865.

VII. Amanda Fretz, born Sept. 11, 1864. Mrd. Mahlon M. Fretz (see Index of References No. 17).

VII. Ada Fretz, born Aug. 30, 1870.

VII. Clinton E. Fretz, born Feb. 24, 1875.

VII. Willis Fretz, born Oct. 30, 1880; died Aug. 29, 1881.

VI. Mary Ann Fretz, born Jan. 18, 1835. Tailoress. Mennonite.

VI. Sarah Fretz, born May 18, 1837. Mrd. John Groman, Dec. 17, 1861. Railroader. Lutherans. Children: Emma, Annie, Orlando.

VII. Emma Catharine Groman, born Aug. 28, 1863. Mrd. Samuel P. Beggs, Aug. 1883. Children: **(VIII.)** Nellie Beggs, born—; died—. **(VIII.)** Raymond Samuel Beggs.

VII. Annie Elizabeth Groman, born Mar. 12, 1866. Moravian.

VII. Orlando DeForest Groman, born Mar. 26, 1868.

VI. John M. Fretz, born in Plumstead Twp., Bucks Co., Sept. 16, 1839. Mrd. Mary Fretz, of Bedminster, daughter of Christian and Mary Fretz, Mar. 2, 1871. Farmer. Members 2d Mennonite Ch. Children: **(VII.)** Elmer Grant Fretz, born Jan. 25, 1872; died Dec. 12, 1876. **(VII.)** John Clarence Fretz, born Aug. 15, 1878.

VI. Abraham M. Fretz, born in Bucks Co., Pa., Aug. 23, 1843. Mrd. Mary Ann Fryling, in 1870. She died Mar. 3, 1879. Farmer. Children: **(VII.)** Oscar Franklin Fretz, born Oct. 4, 1871; died July 10, 1872.

(**VII.**) Matilda Sabina Fretz, born Jan. 8, 1876. (**VII.**) Catharine Fretz, born Feb. 23, 1879; died Aug. 3, 1879. For his second wife Abraham mrd. Selinda Witmeyer, Nov. 16, 1880. He is a member of New Mennonite, and she of the Moravian Ch. Children: (**VII.**) Esther May Fretz, born Oct. 23, 1882. (**VII.**) Joseph Morris Fretz, born Nov. 25, 1884. (**VII.**) Annie Helen Fretz, born Oct. 17, 1886.

IV. Henry Kratz, born –; died young.

IV. Rachel Kratz, born Sept. 5, 1777; died May 22, 1852, aged 74 yrs., 8 mo. 6 d. Mrd. Abraham Fretz, son of Abraham Fretz, Sr., of Fretz Valley, Apr. 4, 1797. He was born Aug. 17, 1775; died May 20, 1816, aged 40 yrs., 9 mos. 3 d. Farmer, and lived on the farm he purchased about 1797, located in what is known as Fretz Valley, Bedminster Twp., and which is still in the possession of his descendants. Mennonites. Children: Susan, Jacob, Anna, Philip, Elizabeth, Abraham.

V. Susan Fretz, born Feb. 25, 1798; died –. Mrd. George Mitman,—. One child: Rachel.

VI. Rachel Mitman born ; died . Mrd. Joseph Moyer, M. D. (dec'd),– . Children: Susan, Sallie.

VII. Susan Moyer, born—. Mrd. Abel Mathias, M. D. Children: (**VIII.**) Joseph Mathias. (**VIII.**) Howard Mathias.

VII. Sallie Moyer, born—. Mrd. Joel Rosenberger, —. Children: (**VIII.**) Joseph Rosenberger. (**VIII.**) Rachel Rosenberger.

V. Jacob Fretz, born in Bucks Co., Oct. 14, 1803; died—. Mrd. Susannah Beidler, Nov. 19, 1839. Farmer, and owned and lived on a part of the homestead in Bedminster Twp. Mennonites. Children: Emma, Reed, Rachel, Abraham, Lizzie, Philip.

VI. Emma Fretz, born Apr. 1, 1841. Mrd. Abraham M. Leatherman, Nov. 1, 1862. Farmer. Children: (**VII.**) Horace Leatherman, born Feb. 1, 1864; died Apr. 18, 1871. (**VII.**) Jacob Kirk Leatherman, born Jan. 26, 1866. (**VII.**) Henry W. Leatherman, born Aug. 30, 1877. (**VII.**) Erwin Ely Leatherman, born Apr. 21, 1871.

VI. Reed Fretz, born in Bucks Co., Mar. 19, 1844. Mrd. Amanda Loux, of Carversville, Jan. 27, 1870. Farmer. Mrs. Fretz, Presbyterian. Children: **(VII.)** Jacob Franklin Fretz, born Nov. 27, 1870. **(VII.)** Minerva Fretz, born July 21, 1872. **(VII.)** Anna Laura Fretz, born Aug. 18, 1873. **(VII.)** Nelson Oswold Fretz, born Nov. 3, 1875. **(VII.)** Mabel Celia Fretz, born Nov. 3, 1877. **(VII.)** Mary Matilda Fretz, born Dec. 30, 1879.

VI. Rachel Fretz, born in Bucks Co., May—, 1846. Mrd. William H. Slotter, Dec.—, 1882. Mr. and Mrs. Slotter, previous to their marriage, were both engaged in teaching school, and Mr. Slotter is the present (1889) County Superintendent of Bucks Co. He is a member of the Ger. Ref. Mrs. Slotter, Mennonite. One child: **(VII.)** Jacob Fretz Slotter, born Jan. 1885.

VI. Abraham Ely Fretz, born—; died from injuries received by being thrown from a horse.

VI. Lizzie Fretz, born Nov. 5, 1850. Mrd. Nelson K. Leatherman,—.

VI. Philip Kirk Fretz, born Nov. 19, 1858. Mrd. Charlotte, daughter of Hon. L. B. LaBarre, Oct. 23, 1879.

V. Ann Fretz, born in Bucks Co., Oct. 3, 1806; died May 26, 1886. Mrd. John Fretz (see Index of References No. 44.

V. Philip K. Fretz, born in Bucks Co., June 25, 1809. Mrd. Eliza Fretz, granddaughter of Mark Fretz, Sr., of New Britain Twp., Nov. 22, 1836. She died—. Retired farmer. Children: Susan, Ann, Rebecca, Henry, Jacob. Philip mrd. second wife, Magdalena (Myers) Hunsberger. —.

VI. Susan Fretz, born in Bedminster Twp., Bucks Co., Apr. 16, 1838; died—. Mrd. Mahlon Meyers,—. He died-. No issue.

VI. Ann Fretz, born in Bucks Co., Feb. 25, 1840. Methodist. Res. at Wheaton, Ill. Unmrd.

VI. Rebecca Fretz, born in Bucks Co., Aug. 21, 1843. Mrd. James L. Reber, Mar. 23, 1863. In fruit preserving business. Res., Wheaton, Ill. Methodists. Children: **(VII.)** Erwin M. Reber. Mrd. Etta Ruppe.

(VII.) Schuyler Colfax Reber. (VII.) Philip Reber;
died—. (VII.) James Watt Reber. (VII.) Pearl Reber.
born—; died—. (VII.) Etna Myrtle Reber, born— .

VI. Henry Ervin Fretz, born in Bucks Co., Apr. 6,
1847. Mrd. Amanda Moyer, Dec. 1, 1870. Farmer.
Res., on the homestead at Fretz Valley. New Mennonites. Children: (VII.) Edgar M. Fretz, born Oct.
19, 1871; died Feb. 15, 1875. (VII.) James Oscar Fretz,
born Jan. 1, 1873. (VII.) Warren Fretz, born May 3,
1875. (VII.) Philip K. Fretz, Jr., born Sept. 7, 1876.
(VII.) Erwin Clarence Fretz, born Oct. 30, 1878. (VII.)
Lizzie Bertha Fretz, born Mar. 1, 1881. (VII.) Eugene Fretz, born Mar. 23, 1883. (VII.) Herbert Fretz,
born July 12, 1885. (VII.) Florence Fretz, born July
8, 1887.

VI. Jacob Fretz, born Apr. 18, 1852; died . Mrd.
Josephine Berks, July 25, 1877. One child: (VII.)
James Garfield Fretz.

V. Elizabeth Fretz, born about 1812; died—. Mrd.
Christian B. Fretz, son of Henry and Elizabeth (Beidler) Fretz, of New Britain Twp. One child: (VI.) Infant, died unnamed.

V. Abraham F. Fretz, born in Bucks Co., Jan. 20,
1815; died Jan. 4, 1888. Mrd. Catharine Swartzlander, Oct. 18, 1856. She died Dec. 21, 1866. Farmer.
New Mennonites. One child: Clara S.

VI. Clara S. Fretz, born Nov. 5, 1857. Mrd.
Frank W. Rotzell, Mar. 7, 1885. Loan Broker at
Kansas City, Mo. Children: (VII.) Blanche F. Rotzel,
born Mar. 14, 1886. (VII.) Edward F. Rotzel, born
Apr. 1, 1887; died same day.

IV. Susanna Kratz, born— ; died—. "She was a
great favorite in the family," always ready and willing to assist any one, and on occasions of sickness, or
other troubles, she was often sent for. She never
married.

IV. Philip Kratz, Jr., born Apr. 16, 1782; died June
2, 1847. Mrd. Elizabeth, daughter of Jacob and Elizabeth (Swartz) Stover, and granddaughter of Henry
and a Miss Hockman, who were natives of Alsace,
now a province of Germany. They were married June
17, 1802. She died Feb. 12, 1860. Farmer, lived on

the homestead in Plumstead Twp. He was Assessor of Plumstead Township one or two terms. Mennonites. Buried at Deep Run. Children: Jacob, John, Rachel, Anna, Catharine, Susanna, Henry, Leah.

V. Jacob S. Kratz, born Apr. 10, 1803; died Nov. 20, 1885. Mrd. Elizabeth Fretz, daughter of William Fretz, Dec. 16, 1830. She was born Oct. 1, 1810; died Feb. 15, 1873. Farmer, and lived in Plumstead, Bucks Co., on the farm that had been his grandfathers. Members Free Christian Ch. Children: Margaret, Emma, Laura, Harvey, William, Jacob.

VI. Margaret Kratz, born Feb. 14, 1833. Mrd. H. Watson Johnson, Nov. 15, 1855. Farmer near Richlandtown, Bucks Co., Pa. Attend the Reformed Ch. Children: Erwin, Oliver, Charles, Harvey, Mary.

VII. Erwin T. Johnson, M. D., born June 18, 1857. Mrd. E. Martha Sheip, of New Britain, Pa., Mar. 11, 1886. Dr. Johnson graduated from the Jefferson Medical College in the spring of 1883. He located at Hilltown, Pa., where he is practicing his profession. Members of the Reformed Ch. of Hilltown. Children: (**VIII.**) Susanna Johnson, born Nov. 24, 1886. (**VIII.**) Margaret Johnson, born May 25, 1888.

VII. Charles J Johnson, born Nov. 23, 1858; died Aug. 24, 1878.

VII. Oliver K. Johnson, born Nov. 24, 1860.

VII. Harvey E. Johnson, born June 22, 1868.

VII. Mary Jane Johnson, born Aug. 15, 1870.

VI. Emma Kratz, born Dec. 7, 1835. Mrd. John Shelly Weinberger, Oct. 13, 1864. Professor in Ursinus College, at Collegeville, Pa. Members Free Christian Ch. One child: (**VII.**) Minerva Weinberger, born Oct. 1, 1860. S.

VI. Laura Kratz, born Jan. 4, 1837; died Mar. 16, 1866. Mrd. I. S. Moyer, M. D.,—. One child: (**VII.**) Lillian Moyer, born—.

VI. Harvey Kratz, born Sept. 2, 1838. Mrd. Sarah Rinker.—. Practicing physician at New Britain, Pa. Attend the Baptist Ch. Children: (**VII.**) Laura, born; died, aged 8 yrs. (**VII.**) Lizzie. (**VII.**) Bertha. (**VII.**) Virginia. (**VII.**) Mabel Rebecca. (**VII.**) Annie Worley.

New Mennonite Church, Deep Run, Bucks Co., Pa.

THE NEW YORK
PUBLIC LIBRARY

(**VII.**) Charles Sumner. (**VII.**) Sarah. (**VII.**) Margaret. (**VII.**) Hannah. (**VII.**) Esther. (**VII.**) Emma.

VI. William Henry Kratz, born Apr. 2, 1843. Mrd. Alice J. Piatt, Jan. 7, 1875. He is engaged in stock raising in Piatt Co., Ill. Attend M. E. Ch. Children: (**VII.**) Laura Kratz, born Oct. 14, 1875. (**VII.**) James Piatt Kratz, born Dec. 12, 1878.

VI. Jacob Thomas Kratz, born Apr. 27, 1850; died Oct. 5, 1862.

V. John Kratz, born Dec. 25, 1805; died Aug. 19, 1865. Mrd. Dorothy Myers, Dec. 13, 1827. She was born Nov. 28, 1803; died Apr. 14, 1885. Farmer. Mrs. Kratz, Mennonite. Children: Sarah, Lewis, Aaron, Reed, Owen, Allen, Mary, Philip, Oliver.

VI. Sarah Kratz, born Nov. 10, 1828. Mrd. John Bewighouse, May 8, 1858. Farmer in Bedminster Twp. New Mennonites. Children: Sarah, Esther, J. Geary, (Christian and Christina, twins), Ellen.

VII. Sarah Ann Bewighouse, born Sept. 19, 1860.

VII. Esther Bewighouse, born Jan. 14, 1865. Mrd. Ezra Frankenfield, Dec. 24, 1887. Creamery operator. Mr. F., Lutheran; Mrs. F., New Mennonite.

VII. J. Geary Bewighouse, born Sept. 16, 1867. S.

VII. Christian and Christina Bewighouse, twins, born Nov. 9, 1869; both died Feb. 1870.

VII. Ellen Bewighouse, born Aug. 13, 1871.

VI. Lewis Kratz, born Dec. 25, 1830. Mrd. Sarah Ann Bewighouse,—. She was born in 1832; died—. One child: (**VII.**) Laura Kratz, born—; died an infant. Lewis mrd. for his second wife, Esther Bewighouse, Feb. 8, 1862 (sister to his first wife). Farmer. New Mennonites. One child: Curtin B.

VII. Curtin B. Kratz, born Aug. 23, 1863. Mrd. Mary S. Fulmer, Nov. 19, 1887. Farmer. Mrs. Kratz is a member of the Ref. Ch.

VI. Aaron Kratz, born July 9, 1832. Mrd. Catharine Stover, Mar. 1, 1860. Children: (**VII.**) Lincoln Hamlin Kratz, born Dec. 23, 1860. (**VII.**) Elmer Elsworth Kratz, born Aug. 4, 1862; died—. Aaron mrd. for his second wife Lizzie W. Engle, Sept. 26, 1866. She was born Nov. 18, 1842. Reside in Plumsteadville, Bucks Co., where he has Carriage, Wagon and Sleigh

Works on a large scale, and is doing a successful business. Children: (**VII.**) Reuben E. Kratz, born Sept. 1, 1868. (**VII.**) Anna May Kratz, born Dec. 1, 1875; died May 30, 1879.

VI. Reed Kratz, born Nov. 20, 1834. Mrd. Esther Michener, Oct. 12, 1862. Oil merchant. Presbyterians. Children: (**VII.**) Eugene H. Kratz, born Oct. 24, 1868. (**VII.**) Florence Kratz, born July 14, 1871.

VI. Owen Kratz, born July 8, 1837. Mrd. Delia Leatherman.

VI. Allen Kratz, born May 31, 1840; died July 4, 1843.

VI. Mary K. Kratz, born at Plumsteadville, Nov. 29, 1842. Mrd. Zackery T. Leatherman, Sept. 28, 1871. In early life he was carriage and sleigh builder at Danboro. He is now housebuilder in Philadelphia. Attend Presbyterian church. Children: (**VII.**) Della May K. Leatherman, born Apr. 7, 1880. (**VII.**) Edgar Lincoln K. Leatherman, born Oct. 28, 1881.

VI. Philip Kratz, born Apr. 22, 1845. Mrd. Louisa S., daughter of Isaac and Mary Kratz, Oct. 27, 1876. Farmer near Fountainville, Pa. Mrs. Kratz Ger. Baptist. No issue.

VI. Oliver James Kratz, born Nov. 26, 1845. Mrd. Sabina Leatherman. . Two children.

V. Rachel Kratz, born Mar. 24, 1808; died Sept. 3, 1869. Mrd. Michael Myers, Sept. 1827. Moved to Ohio. Children: (**VI.**) B. F. Myers, born . P. O., Mount Cary, Ohio.

V. Anna Kratz, born in Plumstead Twp., Bucks Co., Pa., Feb. 5, 1811; died Sept. 12, 1876, aged 65 y., 7 m. 7 d. Mrd. John M. Detwiler, Oct. 26, 1831. He was born in Bedminster Twp., Bucks Co., Pa., June 26, 1805; died July 17, 1856, aged 51 y. 27 d. They at first lived on a farm a little south of Pipersville, on the Durham road, until the spring of 1839, when, after having sold most of their personal property, they loaded the balance on a two-horse wagon, and with a one-horse market wagon containing the family of four, husband, wife and two daughters, they moved to Fairfield Co., Ohio, known at that time as the far west, and purchased a farm of fifty acres of

Mr. John Beatty, situated near the village of Basil, where they lived until the husband's death. Mennonites. Mr. Detwiler was buried in the Lutheran cemetery, Basil, Ohio, and Mrs. Detwiler in the Mennonite cemetery in Elkhart Co., Ind. Children: Jane, Clementine.

VI. Jane Detwiler, born in Bedminster Twp., Bucks Co., Pa., Oct. 9, 1833. At the age of seventeen she taught school. She was married to Moses B. Weaver, a native of Pennsylvania, Sept. 15, 1853. Soon after marriage they purchased a farm of 72 acres of Mrs. Weaver's father, in Fairfield Co., Ohio. This farm was a part of a tract of land extending through several counties, and had been reserved for some military purposes, was called Refuge, and is so called to this day. In the spring of 1861, having sold this farm, they purchased a farm of about 79 acres in Elkhart Co., Ind., where they have since lived. Mennonites. Children: Infant, Lydia, John, Ann, Emma, Harvey, Henry, Ira, Infant, Frank, Jennie.

VII. Infant son, born Feb. 16, 1855; died same day.

VII. Lydia Weaver, born in Fairfield Co., Ohio, Jan. 8, 1859. Mrd. Samuel M. Weaver, of Elkhart Co., Ind., Dec. 30, 1877. Farmer in Emmett Co., Mich., and reside near the village of Harbor Springs, where they commenced in the solid woods where deer and bear abound. The following incident is related as a fact: One of Mrs. Weaver's little boys and another boy, both about 7 years old, were on their way to school one day, a distance of one mile and a half, most of the way through the woods, when they encountered a bear. One of the boys said to the other, "I heard some one say if you walk up to a bear and look in his eyes he will be ashamed of himself and move off in another direction." This the brave little fellows did, and they said the bear hung his head and retreated. When they related their story it was not believed. However, some of the neighbors went to the place where the boys had seen the bear, and sure enough found the tracks. Children: (**VIII.**) Burdetta Weaver, born Dec. 17, 1878; died Aug. 21, 1880.

(**VIII.**) Irvin Weaver, born July 30, 1881. (**VIII.**) Elmer Weaver, born June 2, 1883.

VII. John D. Weaver, born in Fairfield Co., Ohio, Oct. 4, 1860. Painter. P. O., Goshen, Ind.

VII. Anna Weaver, born in Fairfield Co., Ohio, May 17, 1864. Mrd. Simon P. Detwiler, of Emmet Co., Mich., Mar. 8, 1885. Carpenter at Goshen, Ind. Mennonites. Children: (**VIII.**) Frank Austin Detwiler, born June 7, 1887; died Nov. 4, 1887. (**VIII.**) Ira Detwiler, born Sept. 18, 1888.

VII. Emma Weaver, born Apr. 25, 1866.

VII. Harvey C. Weaver, born Feb. 18, 1868.

VII. Henry W. Weaver, born Sept. 14, 1869.

VII. Ira D. Weaver, born Mar. 29, 1871.

VII. A daughter, born Sept. 15, 1872; died next day.

VII. A son, born Aug. 6, 1873; died same day.

VII. Frank M. Weaver, born May 9, 1875.

VII. Jennie M. Weaver, born Jan. 30, 1879.

VI. Clementine Detwiler, born in Bedminster Twp., Bucks Co., Pa., Mar. 27, 1838; died Oct. 26, 1864. Mrd. Wilbur Wickeizer, in Oct. 1861. Farmer, of Fairfield Co., Ohio. A few days before her death she was converted and baptized by Bishop Jacob Bowman, of the Mennonite church. The issue was one son: John D.

VII. John D. Wickeizer, born Apr. 5, 1860; died Apr. 1, 1888, aged 27 y., 11 m. 27 d. Mrd. Alice M. Furst, July 2, 1884.

V. Catharine Kratz, born Sept. 16, 1813; died Mar. 1, 1830.

V. Susan Kratz, born Sept. 20, 1816. Mrd. Aaron Beidler, June 15, 1841. Lumber merchant. Died in 1875. Mrs. Beidler resides at Champaign, Ill. Baptist. Children: Irene, Minerva, Louis, Lizzie.

VI. Irene Beidler, born May 21, 1842. Mrd. R. M. Eppstein, Mar. 26, 1864. Dealer in pianos and organs. Residence, 95 Dearborn Ave, Chicago, Ill. One child: (**VII.**) Aaron R. Eppstein, born Dec. 29, 1875. At Champaign, Ill.

VI. Minerva Beidler, born at Springfield, Ill., May 31, 1845. Mrd. Wesley T. Pratt, of Essex, Conn., Mar. 1, 1863. Contractor at 347 Gray St., Denver,

Colo. Mr. Pratt Methodist. Children: (**VII.**) Helen Maria Pratt, born in New Orleans, Mar. 14, 1866. She is a teacher in the Denver City Schools. (**VII.**) Louise Irena Pratt, born in New Orleans, Sept. 27, 1867. Is also a teacher in the Denver City Schools. (**VII.**) Anna Isabelle Pratt, born in New Orleans, Jan. 8, 1871.

VI. Louis Henry Beidler, born Apr. 4, 1848; died Sept. 13, 1873, while on a trip south for his health. Mrd. Anna Mary,* daughter of B. C. Bradley, Mar. 19, 1872. She was born in Versailles, Ky, Mar. 7, 1849. Lumber merchant. Baptists. One child: (**VII.**) Gertrude Lois Beidler, born Mar. 6, 1873.

VI. Lizzie Lelia Beidler, born July 26, 1859; died May 15, 1861.

V. Henry Kratz, born May 15, 1820. Mrd. Annie, daughter of Abraham Stover, of Bedminster, in June 1843. She was born in 1815; died Mar. 15, 1887; buried in Doylestown cemetery. He is still living on a small farm at Danboro, Pa. It is said pebbles change the course of mighty streams, so little incidents often change the career of many persons, which is fully illustrated in the career of the subject of this sketch. When a boy attending school in a neighboring village, he did the chores and took care of the horses for a doctor, who took a fancy to him, and gave him a little insight into the profession. When he was about to choose for himself, his desire to study medicine was made known to his father, who unfortunately consulted his elder brother Jacob (Henry's uncle), whose prompt reply was, "It will never do for a farmer's son to become a Doctor." So his young ambition was unceremoniously "nipped in the bud." (However, farmer Jacob's oldest boy never worried him about the propriety of becoming a Doctor, for he lost no time in graduating an M. D., and is now a very successful practitioner at New Britain, Pa.) Mr. Kratz was very fond of debating societies, which flourished before and during the war of the Re-

---

* She is a lineal descendant of Thomas Win of Wales, who founded Thomas Win Castle in 1617.

bellion, and always took an active part on whatever subject was presented. He was an Abolitionist, and has always been a Republican. Some sixteen years ago he was the Republican nominee for the State Legislature. Presbyterians. Children (all raised on a portion of the Kratz homestead): Edwin, Alonzo, Annetta, Emily, Henry, Jourdan, Catharine, Reuben, Albert, Ellen, Anson, Fernando.

VI. Edwin Augustus Kratz M. D., born July 12, 1844. In early life he assisted his father on the farm, and attended school. His patriotic spirit and desire to defend the flag, when it was fired upon, and trampled under foot by scornful rebels and traitors, was as strong as his brothers, and his determination was to go to war; but when the family council decided that only one of them could go, he yielded; however hoping that he might yet have an opportunity of "fighting rebels" before the war closed. When the longed for opportunity came, his choice was the Navy; but no word from his brother Alonzo for thirty days, created considerable alarm in the minds of those at home for his safety. It was suggested that he would have a better chance to meet him, if he was in the army; hence he carried a musket. He enlisted in Philadelphia Aug. 16, 1864, as a private in Co. A, (Captain Stanton), 198 Regt., Penna. Vol., (Col. H. G. Sickel.) It was known as the "Sixth Union League regiment" which that Loyal and patriotic organization recruited. The regiment was mustered into the United States service Sept. 5, 1864, and on the 18th left camp Cadwallader, for the scene of action, arriving at the front on the 23d, and in seven days thereafter was under fire. They were assigned to the 1st Brigade (Gen. Chamberlain), 1st Division (Gen. Griffin), 5th Corps (Gen. Warren), Army of the Potomac (Gen. Meade).

Immediately after arriving at the front, Mr. Kratz was detailed as clerk at Brigade Inspectors headquarters; but when the regiment went into battle, he was sent to his command. When he got back to his company, his bayonet, and accoutrements were missing. He went into the fight without any cart ridges, but soon filled his pockets with those he found scattered about. With this experience he refused any further clerkship. On Oct. 26th he learned that his brother Alonzo had been captured three months previously, and was in Danville, Va. This determined him more than ever, never to be taken alive if possible; so when he was wounded and saw the rebels face to face, it gave him strength to get out of their reach, before he fell exhausted. At the battle of Dinwiddie C. H. (Gravelly Run), Mar. 29, 1865, he was wounded, shot through the chest, in the right arm, and in the left fore-arm. The orderly Sergt. reported him killed, and his letter to the captain a month later was the first knowledge of his condition. He was taken from the field to Mt. Pleasant Hospital, Washington, D. C., where he laid on his back for seven weeks, and was discharged from the service July 13th, an invalid for life. The battles in which he fought were: Preeble's Farm, Va., Sept. 30, 1864; South Side R. R., Va., Oct. 27-8, 1864; Warren's Raid to Welden Railroad, Va., Dec. 6-12, 1864; Hatcher's Run, Va., Feb. 6-9, 1865; recapture of Fort Steedman, Va., Mar. 25, 1865; Dinwiddie C. H., Va., Mar. 29, 1865.

After his return from the war he began the study of medicine, and is at this present time a resident physician of Champaign, Ill. He has occupied many positions of honor and trust. He was supervisor of Champaign Twp., for one year, clerk of Champaign City four years. Director of Champaign public library eighteen years. Director of Champaign Branch, Illinois Humane Society. United States examining surgeon for pensions eighteen years. Captain and Assistant surgeon Illinois National Guards, and a past Post Commander of the Grand Army of the Republic, and is now medical director of the department Illinois G. A. R. He is also member of the orders of Masons and Odd Fellows. In politics he is a Republican, and was unanimously nominated for mayor by the republicans of Champaign City in the spring of 1891, but through rum, boodle and treachery he was with the rest of the ticket defeated. He was married to Anna Mary Bradley. widow of Lewis H. Beidler. May 8. 1884. Children: (VII.) Alonzo Plumsted. Kratz. born June 17. 1885. (VII.) Ethel Gyola Kratz. born Oct. 20. 1887. (VII.) Edwin Valentine Kratz. born Mar. 31. 1890.

VI. Alonzo Philip Kratz. born July 26. 1845: died Feb. 12. 1865. At the age of seventeen he enlisted in Doylestown. Pa.. on Aug. 8. 1862. as a private in Company F. 128 Regiment Pa.. Vol.. for nine months in the United States services. The reg't.. soon went to the front. His first letter was dated at Camp Wells. Va.. Aug. 12. 1862. from which it appears that army life agreed with him. he says: "We don't get victuals like at home. but what we do get is enough and healthy: soft bread comes this way once a week." After the battle of Antietam he wrote, "It was a hard fight. and I do not want to get in another like it. The rebels loaded their guns with a large round ball and three buck shot. these flew around us like hail. We loaded our muskets with a large pointed ball. and it did some execution. A soldier who has once fought for his country. will never forget it. neither should he be forgotten." On Jan. 16. 1863 at Fairfax Station. Va.. he says. "Our winter hut is built: it is of logs two feet high. and our tent is the roof: It is a comfortable house that will keep us dry and warm." On Mar. 25. 1863 he wrote from Brook's Station. Va.. "We have five weeks yet to serve: we have been in several skirmishes besides the great battle Sept. 17 (Antietam). and there may be another big fight this spring. before our time is out. Gen. Hooker is getting impatient at this inaction. There is some talk among the boys of re-enlisting. but I think I will go home. although I don't believe I shall be satisfied with home life as long as the war is going on." The anticipated battle was Chancellorsville. through it he passed without a scratch. and was discharged at the end of his term of service. with the following certificate. "This is to certify that Alonzo Philip Kratz was one of the most patriotic soldiers in Company F, (commanded by C. K. Frankenfield). always at his post performing a soldier's duty cheerfully. and I can

Home of Deacon Abraham and Magdalena (Kratz) Fretz,
in Bedminster Twp., Bucks Co., Pa.

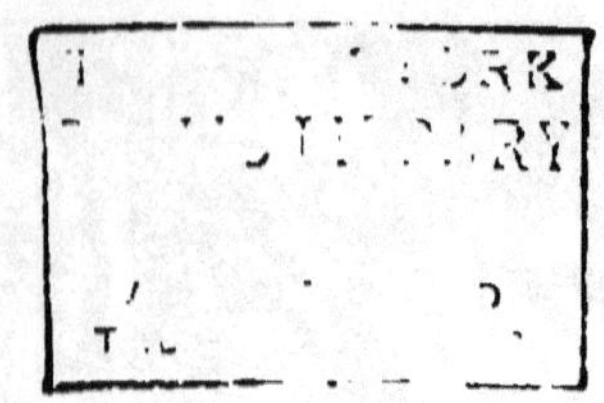
NEW YORK PUBLIC LIBRARY

recommend him as the bravest of the brave, in meeting the foe and daring in battle. T. J. Kline, Orderly Sergt., Co., F. 128 Pa., Vol.

He came home in June 1863, and seemed glad enough to get back to "God's country again: but the outdoor life of a soldier, who so often slept with the blue vault of heaven for a covering, had completely changed his disposition. It was weeks before he could sleep on a soft bed, and enjoy a good meal. His patriotic spirit finally prevailed, to take up arms again: he always spoke of the Artillery service as being the most agreeable, and least dangerous to life and limb: that he would go in the heavy Artillery next. With this object in view, he went to Philadelphia shortly after New Years day, 1864, and enlisted in Battery D, 112 Regt., Penna. H. A. The regt. was, however, supplied with muskets, and served as the "2 Penna. Provisional Volunteers," there being more demand for that branch than Artillery: and he was promoted to Corporal of Company I. The regiment was mustered as "Veteran", and immediately went to the front leaving behind fifty brave and true men, of which number he was one for detached duty in Philadelphia. After guarding various places in the city for three months, he was sent to his regiment in the field, Apr. 24.

A letter dated July 3, 1864, near Petersburg, Va., gives an account of the fierce fighting of the rebels at the Welden R. R., where they charged the Union lines six deep without breaking it: also that they had blown up two rebel forts, and are mining another and a bigger one, and when ready to explode, they will fight day and night if necessary to capture Petersburg, Va. His last letter from the field, is dated July 17, 1864, in which he says, "have been acting as sergeant for two months, and expect to be promoted to that office, as soon as the captain recovers from wounds received in battle." The coveted promotion never came. He was captured July 29, at the explosion referred to (Burnside's mine), and carried away into captivity. He was confined in the famous Libby prison at Richmond, Va., for a while, and then removed to the stockade pen at Danville, Va. The "last letter" received from him was written in the latter place. dated Aug 3d. 1864; it was mailed at Old Point Comfort, and did not reach home until October 19. 1864. It was written with a led pencil in two hand writings. the first half was in his writing. which gave the date and circumstances of his capture. and where he was a prisoner. The last half showed unmistakably. that it was erased and written in another hand; this purported to give the comfortable quarters he had. kind treatment he received at the hands of the rebels. and the quantity and quality of healthy food given him.

After the close of the war it was learned that he was an unwilling guest of rebeldom six months. and died Feb. 12. 1865 of starvation and exposure. He is buried in the National Cemetery at Danville. Va.. grave 130. section A.. division four. A brave and patriotic life sacrificed for country and flag. Battles he was in: Antietam. Va.. Sept. 1862. Chancellorsville. Va.. May 1863. Ream's Station. Va.. June 1864 (Weldon R. R.). and Burnside's Mine. Va.. July 1864.

VI. Annetta Kratz. M. D.. born in Plumstead Twp.. Bucks Co.. Pa. At the age of four years. she attended the public school. After attending school at North Wales. and the Excelsior Normal at Carversville. she commenced teaching at the age of 16. Believing it was best for women patients to be attended by women physicians. she studied medicine in Philadelphia. and occupied the position of interne in the New England Hospital for women in Boston. Mass.. for 18 months. Prejudice against "women doctors." was very fierce at that time (1869) and the students of the university actually collected to mob the women students when dismissed from lecture. The ladies with quiet dignity. however. came off the victors. Miss Kratz also attended the College of Pharmacy. the first year that women were admitted. After graduating in 1871. she began the practice of her profession at Lansdale. Pa.. where she is also managing a drugstore. Attends the Presbyterian church and is unmarried.

VI. Emily Augusta Kratz, born May 15, 1848; died (single) Aug. 31, 1879.

VI. Henry Stover Kratz, born in Plumstead, Pa., June 4, 1849. He is by trade a carriage painter, and for rapidity, delicacy and accuracy of striping and lettering won for himself the name of "Dexter," among the craft. He also has a fine voice for singing, and often delighted his friends with his solos. In 1878 he went to Fort Worth, Texas, where he is engaged as bookseller and publisher. He is unmarried.

VI. Jourdan H. Kratz, born Oct. 12, 1850. Married Margaret C., daughter of William Kerr Bowman, of Philadelphia, Pa. He was a member of the Pa., Military for some time. He is now extensively engaged in farming and fruit culture, near Greenwood Station, Del. Presbyterians. Children: (**VII.**) Edwin Augustus Kratz, born Apr. 28, 1880. (**VII.** Jourdan Homer Kratz, born Dec. 24, 1881. (**VII.**) William Henry Kratz, born Sept. 17, 1884. (**VII.**) Ely Laird Kratz, born Aug. 31, 1889.

VI. Catharine Kratz, born Jan. 25, 1852. She is a successful teacher in the public schools of Bucks and Montgomery counties, Pa. Presbyterian. She is unmarried.

VI. Reuben S. Kratz, born July 7, 1853. Married A. Kate Persey, of Buckingham, Feb. 20, 1889. At the age of 20 he enlisted in the emergency company to quell the rioters at Pittsburg and the West. He afterward enlisted in a military company of state guards. He owns and occupies a part of the old homestead in Plumstead, known as the "Valley Park farm." The house in which he lives was built by his grandfather Philip Jr., in 1819. Mrs. Kratz was born in June 28, 1857. Presbyterians. One child, viz.: (**VII.**) T. Percy Kratz, born Feb. 4, 1890.

VI. Albert Kratz, born Sept. 1, 1854; died Aug. 23, 1856.

VI. Ellen Kratz, born Sept. 25, 1855; died Nov. 10, 1856.

VI. Anson Burlingame Kratz, born Nov. 22, 1856; died Oct. 20, 1859.

VI. Fernando Kratz, born—, painter by trade, but is now engaged in farming at Danboro. He is a member of the Pennsylvania military, and participated in the Divisional Encampment at Mt. Gretna in 1887 and 1890, and Norristown in 1889, also all the military parades at West Chester, Pa., Philadelphia, Washington, D. C. and New York. He is a Royal Mason, and received his first degree in 1885. Presbyterian. He is unmarried.

V. Leah Kratz, born Dec. 6, 1824. In early life she taught school in various parts of Plumstead Twp., Pa., for a number of years. In 1860, after the death of her mother she moved to a sister in Ohio; and in 1870 to Champaign, Ill., where she devotes a great deal of her time to the Baptist church and charities.

IV. There were three or four children born whose names and sex are unknown. Two of them died the same day and were buried in one grave.

DESCENDANTS OF ABRAHAM KRATZ, SON OF JOHN VALENTINE KRATZ.

III. Abraham Kratz, born in Montg., Co., 1741; died in 1717. Mrd. Barbara, daughter of Christian Moyer. They lived in New Britain Twp., about one-fourth of a mile east from the Upper Hilltown Baptist church, and a few hundred yards from the stump road, where Frederick Steeb now lives, where in 1767 he purchased the Williams' Homestead with 188 acres. The buildings are a well built stone house two stories high, and a stone barn. These buildings were, no doubt erected by a Welsh settler of colonial times named William Williams (a descendant of the notable Rodger Williams, founder of Rhode Island) who in 1747 purchased 307 acres, and lived thereon just twenty years, when he sold as above stated to Abraham Kratz. This homestead remained in the possession of Abraham Kratz, during the remainder of his life, and of his son Valentine, who inherited the homestead and 110 acres, and Simeon, who inherited it from his father Valentine. Abraham Kratz and wife were members of the Mennonite church at Deep Run, and are buried there. Children: Anna, Mary, Valentine, Susanna, Barbara, Veronica, Magdalena, Elizabeth, Abraham, Catharine.

IV. Anna Kratz, born in Bucks Co., Sept. 11, 1768; died June 24, 1816. Mrd. Martin Fretz, son of Christian and Barbara Fretz, of Bedminster. He was born Aug. 9, 1764; died Sept. 26, 1835. Farmer and Linseed oil manufacturer. He lived in Hilltown Twp., near Yost's Mill, on the farm now occupied by Jacob Smith. He was an honest, upright man, and held in high esteem. As a Christian, he endeavored faithfully to discharge his religious duties, in all of which he was conscientiously strict. He never allowed any member of his family to leave the church before the benediction was pronounced. An adage of his was: "Wer naus geht vor dem Segen, geht dem Fluch entgegen." Though, at times taking a smoke, it was a saying of his, "that he never wanted to be a slave to tobacco or whisky." In the time of the subject of this sketch, many of the luxuries of the present day were not enjoyed. There were no carpets and no parlor matches in those days. Sometimes they had to go to neighbors for fire, and on one occasion the Fretz meadow was set on fire by borrowed fire.

For the married girls in those days the dry goods outfit was mostly homemade. The spinning wheel was one of the fixtures of the family, and in this family of ten girls there were six spinning wheels going at one time, commencing at 5 o'clock in the morning and continuing until 10 and 11 P. M. One of the daughters, Mrs. Susanna Funk, generally spun eighteen cuts of flax per day, and one day she spun twenty cuts. The reel and the shaving bench were in the same room. Martin Fretz was one of the first to get a Dearborn pleasure wagon. Bows and cover were taken along and if wanted in case of rain they were put up. Among the relics of this home is a bar of soap made by his wife in 1846, one of her last acts, now in the possession of a granddaughter, Esther Hunsberger, of Dublin, Pa. They were members of the Mennonite church at Blooming Glen, where he and wife lie buried. Children: Barbara, Mary, Agnes, Betsy, Betsy, Nancy, Veronica, Martin, Martin, Susanna, Silas, Veronica, Catharine, Leah, Rachel.

V. Barbara Fretz, born Sept. 11, 1787; died in 1879, from the effects of a broken limb occasioned by a fall. Mrd. Rudolph Moyer, in the spring of 1807. He died in 1871. Farmer. Mennonites. Children: Mary, Martin, Nancy, Catharine, Enos, Christian, Abraham.

VI. Mary Moyer, born Feb. 11, 1808. Mrd. Abraham O Alderfer, Nov. 14, 1826. He died Apr. 19, 1868. Farmer in Lower Salford, Montgomery Co., Pa. Mennonites. Children: Isaac, Rudolph, Abraham, Elizabeth, Henry, Mary.

VII. Isaac Alderfer, born Oct. 19, 1828; died Feb. 14, 1830.

VII. Rudolph Alderfer, born Nov. 16, 1830; died Oct. 2, 1859. Mrd. Catharine Bean, Sept. 17, 1853. Farmer. Children: Abraham, Jeremiah, Lizzie.

VIII. Abraham B. Alderfer, born Aug. 11, 1854. Mrd. Maggie Reiff, Dec. 31, 1881. Engineer. Children: (**IX.**) Jacob Linwood Alderfer, born Sept. 4, 1884. (**IX.**) Mary Lizzie Alderfer, born Oct. 17, 1885.

VIII. Jeremiah B. Alderfer, born May 31, 1858. Mrd. Amanda H. Price, Jan. 7, 1882. Dealer in pianos and organs. Children: (**IX.**) Henry P. Alderfer, born Jan. 14, 1884. (**IX.**) Susan P. Alderfer, born Feb. 11, 1886.

VIII. Lizzie B. Alderfer, born Mar. 14, 1860. Mrd. Newton P. Kern, Mar. 28, 1885. Knitter by trade, and farmer near Greensborough, Md. One child: (**IX.**) Clarence Joseph Kern, born Sept. 7, 1889.

VII. Abraham Alderfer, born Oct. 22, 1832; died Feb. 16, 1838.

VII. Elizabeth Alderfer, born Jan. 29, 1838. Mrd. Jacob H. Allebach, in 1855. Farmer in Lower Salford, Montgomery Co., Pa. Mennonites. Children: Mary, Romanus.

VIII. Mary Allebach, born Sept. 27, 1863. Mrd. James D. Swartley, in 1883. Laborer. Mennonites. One child: (**IX.**) Lizzie Swartley, born Aug. 15, 188 .

VIII. Romanus Allebach, born Aug. 14, 1869.

VII. Henry M. Alderfer, born Feb. 26, 1839. Mrd. Barbara H. Tyson, Mar. 1, 1863. Proprietor of the Perkiomen Bridge Hotel, at Collegeville, Montgomery Co., Pa. Mennonites. No issue.

VII. Mary Alderfer, born Jan. 26, 1841. Mrd. Samuel K. Cassel, Jan. 20, 1866. Farmer in Montgomery Co. Mennonites. Children: (**VIII.**) Lizzie Ann Cassel, born Aug. 24, 1868. (**VIII.**) Rachel Cassel, born Apr. 23, 1871. (**VIII.**) Isaiah Cassel, born July 31, 1875.

VI. Martin Moyer, born Oct. 3, 1809; died —. Mrd. Catharine Hunsicker, Sept. 27, 1835. Farmer. Mennonites. They had one son: Rudolph H. Mrs. Moyer died Jan. 9, 1839. Mr. Moyer mrd. for his second wife, Elizabeth Moyer, Nov. 26, 1839. Children: Catharine, Hannah, Barbara, Jacob, Enos, Abraham, William, Isaiah.

VII. Rudolph H. Moyer, born Dec. 25, 1836. Mrd. Anna Kulp, Dec. 25, 1862. She died Mar. 11, 1875. He mrd. for his second wife, Mary Ann Kulp, Oct. 31, 1875. Farmer. Mennonites. Children, all by the first wife: Emma, Allen, Elizabeth, Ellen, Leidy.

VIII. Emma Moyer, born Mar. 9, 1866; died Feb. 11, 1889. Mrd. Milton Stover,—. Children: **(IX.)** Katie M. Stover, born   : died in infancy. **(IX.)** Arthur M. Stover, born   .

VIII. Allen K. Moyer, born Jan. 25, 1868; died June 20, 1884.

VIII. Elizabeth Moyer, born Aug. 4, 1869. Mrd. Samuel Rohr, June 15, 1889.

VIII. Ellen Moyer, born Dec. 9, 1870.

VIII. Leidy K. Moyer, born July 26, 1872, died July 8, 1873.

VII. Catharine Moyer, born in New Britain Twp., Bucks Co., Dec. 14, 1840. Mrd. Isaiah Summers, Dec. 22, 1861. Liveryman. Lutherans. Children: **(VIII.)** Lizzie Summers, born Sept. 2, 1864; died Mar. 19, 1865. **(VIII.)** Harvey M. Summers, born Mar. 2, 1867. Employed in sawmill at Mt. Tabor, in Columbia Co., N. C. Lutheran. **(VIII.)** Edwin Summers, born Nov. 30, 1868. Employed in brass foundry. Lutheran. **(VIII.)** Willie Summers, born Mar. 18, 1870; died Aug. 24, 1870. **(VIII.)** Ellie Summers, born Apr. 1, 1871. Lutheran. **(VIII.)** Martha Summers, born Jan. 11, 1879.

VII. Hannah Moyer, born in Bucks Co., May 12, 1843. Mrd. John W. Lapp, Sept. 2, 1871. He died Sept. 27, 1873. Mrs. Lapp mrd. David L. Gehman, Nov. 30, 1878. Farmer. Mennonites. One child: **(VIII.)** Abraham Gehman, born Mar. 14, 1883.

VII. Barbara Moyer, born Mar. 10, 1845; died 1863.

VII. Jacob Moyer, born Aug. 24, 1847; died—.

VII. Enos Moyer, born Aug. 9, 1849; died—.

VII. Abraham M. Moyer, born Aug. 6, 1861. Mrd. Mary Fly, Sept. 21, 1872. She died Feb. 16, 1875. Butcher. Mennonites. Children: **(VIII.)** Jannetta

OLD MENNONITE MEETINGHOUSE, DEEP RUN, PA.

Moyer, born June 5, 1873. (**VIII.**) Mary Moyer, born Feb. 16, 1875. Abraham mrd. for his second wife, Anna Fly, . Children: (**VIII.**) Magdalena Moyer, born Dec. 21, 1877. (**VIII.**) Henry Rodman Moyer, born July 28, 1881. (**VIII.**) Theodore Moyer, born Oct. 9, 1883.

VII. William Moyer, born Nov. 1, 1853; died –.

VII. Isaiah M. Moyer, born June 2, 1856. Mrd. Mary Ida Fisher, of Doylestown, Sept. 1, 1877. Salesman of the Singer M'f'g Co., of Phila, Pa. Baptists. Children: (**VIII.**) William Henry Moyer, born May 27, 1878. (**VIII.**) Cyrenus Moyer, born Oct. 14, 1880; died Apr. 8, 1884.

VI. Anna Moyer, born in Montgomery Co., Pa., Oct. 11, 1811. Mrd. Henry O. Alderfer, Mar. 17, 1833. Turner and spinning-wheel maker, in Upper Salford, Montg'y Co. Mennonites. Children: Isaac, Abraham, Barbara.

VII. Isaac M. Alderfer, born Feb. 18, 1834; died Mar. 20, 1873. Mrd. Catharine Souder, of Montgomery Co., Oct. 29, 1859. Farmer. Mennonites. Children: Elizabeth, Anna, Malinda, Henry, Samuel, Emaline.

VIII. Elizabeth Alderfer, born Nov. 10, 1860; died June 22, 1866.

VIII. Anna Alderfer, born June 21, 1862. Mrd. Jonas M. Horning, Feb. 2, 1884. Butcher. Mennonites. Children: (**IX.**) Ella Horning, born in 1885. (**IX.**) Kate Horning, born July 12, 1886; died June 1, 1887.

VIII. Malinda Alderfer, born Aug. 28, 1864; died June 17, 1866.

VIII. Henry S. Alderfer, born Jan. 5, 1867. Tinsmith in California. S.

VIII. Samuel S. Alderfer, born June 23, 1868. Carpenter. S.

VIII. Emaline Alderfer, born—. S.

VII. Abraham M. Alderfer, born in Montgomery Co., Pa., Nov. 29, 1839. Mrd. Mary C. Godshall, of Franconia, Nov. 21, 1863. P. O., Telford, Pa. Dealer in Feed, Hay, Coal, etc. Children: Anna, Kate, Mahlon, Mary, Barbara.

8

VIII. Anna Alderfer, born Feb. 1. 1865; died July 15, 1865.

VIII. Kate Alderfer, born Mar. 17, 1866. Mrd. Abraham O. Roth, June 16, 1886. Two days after their marriage, June 18, Mr. Roth took his newly made wife back to her parents from the Roth homestead, and as he was returning to his home, with a friend, Peter Roth, in the carriage with him, they were caught by a wreck train at Clymer's Crossing, and the newly-made husband was instantly killed, while Peter Roth escaped serious injury. Thus the young couple were married only two days when they were separated by death. Kate married for her second husband, Tobias K. Moyer, of Franconia. (See Index of References No. 18.)

VIII. Mahlon G. Alderfer, born July 12, 1867. Mrd. Mary Amelia, daughter of the late Abraham Slotter, Jan. 4, 1890. She was born Oct. 3, 1868. Salesman at Telford, Pa. One child: (**IX.**) Wilmer Alderfer, born Sept. 27, 1890.

VIII. Mary Ann Alderfer, born Mar. 30, 1871. Mrd. Noah B., son of Noah G. Derstine, of Rockhill Twp., Bucks Co., Pa., Sept. 7, 1889. Teamster at his father-in-law's feed store. One child: (**IX.**) Stella Derstine, born Mar. 5, 1890.

VIII. Barbara Alderfer, born Aug. 25, 1876; died Dec. 12, 1878.

VII. Barbara M. Alderfer, born in Montgomery Co., Pa., Dec. 7, 1850; died Mar. 28, 1888. Mrd. Jacob M. Price, Dec. 23, 1871. He died Apr. 7, 1874. One child: (**VIII.**) Anna Price, born May 11, 1873. Barbara mrd. for her second husband, Enos Z. Wambold, Sept. 25, 1880. Farmer. Mennonite. Children: (**VIII.**) Katie Wambold, born July 2, 1881. (**VIII.**) Abraham Wambold, born Apr. 23, 1883. (**VIII.**) Enos Wambold, born Jan. 7, 1885. (**VIII.**) Henry Wambold, born Apr. 25, 1887.

VI. Catharine Moyer, born Dec. 3, 1813. Mrd. Simeon Kratz. (See Index of References No. 19.)

VI. Enos F. Moyer, born Mar. 8, 1816; died Mar. 15, 1883. Mrd. Leah Hunsicker, Jan. 23, 1842. Farmer. Mennonites. Children: Barbara, Lydia, Mary, Elizabeth, Isaac, Rudolph, Leah, Annie.

VII. Barbara Moyer, born Aug. 10, 1841. Mrd. Jacob Godshall.

VII. Lydia Moyer, born Aug. 17, 1846; died Sept. 4, 1846.

VII. Mary H. Moyer, born May 28, 1848. Mrd. Samuel M. Moyer, Nov. 9, 1866. Farmer. Mennonites. Children: **(VIII.)** Allen Moyer, born Sept. 1, 1868. **(VIII.)** Leanna Moyer, born Mar. 8, 1871. **(VIII.)** Enos Moyer, born Sept. 14, 1872. **(VIII.)** William Moyer, born Oct. 15, 1874. **(VIII.)** Jacob Moyer, born Nov. 23, 1876. **(VIII.)** Samuel Moyer, born Mar. 12, 1879. **(VIII.)** Mamie Stella Moyer, born July 19, 1882. **(VIII.)** Henry Clayton Moyer, born Mar. 2, 1887.

VII. Lizzie Moyer, born Dec. 9, 1851. Mrd. Jacob Yoder.

VII. Isaac Moyer, born June 4, 1856; died in infancy.

VII. Rudolph Moyer (twin), born June 4, 1856; died in infancy.

VII. Leah Moyer, born Mar. 4, 1857; died Oct. 10, 1862.

VII. Annie Moyer, born Nov. 26, 1859. Mrd. John Anglemover. (See Index of References No. 20.)

VI. Christian F. Moyer, born in Franconia Twp., Montgomery Co., Pa., Dec. 2, 1818. Mrd. Mary Clymer, Jan. 15, 1844. Farmer. Mennonites. Twelve children: six died in infancy. The living, born in Hilltown Twp., are: William, Abraham, Henry, John, Enos, Christian.

VII. William C. Moyer, born Mar. 5, 1854. Mrd. Mary Moyer, Mar. 9, 1876. Farmer. Mennonites. Children: **(VIII.)** Elmer Moyer, born Dec. 19, 1876. **(VIII.)** Della Moyer, born Mar. 7, 1879. **(VIII.)** Eugene Moyer, born Apr. 2, 1880. **(VIII.)** Clara Moyer, born May 22, 1884. **(VIII.)** Celina Moyer, born Aug. 11, 1886.

VII. Abraham C. Moyer, born Apr. 28, 1856. Mrd. Saloma Fulmer, Jan. 25, 1879. Machine Agent. Mennonites. Children: **(VIII.)** Lilly Moyer, born Apr.

20, 1880. (**VIII.**) Mary Jane Moyer, born Aug. 6, 1887.

VII. Henry C. Moyer, born Mar. 20, 1858. Mrd. Celina Toon, Feb. 17, 1880. Has a bakery. Lutherans. Children: (**VIII.**) Alfred (deceased). (**VIII.**) Mary. (**VIII.**) Elizabeth. (**VIII.**) Florence.

VII. John C. Moyer, born Dec. 31, 1860; died Apr. 26, 1888. Mrd. Lizzie Herman, of Kutztown, Pa., Nov. 20, 1883. Creameryman. Reformed. No issue.

VII. Enos C. Moyer, born July 10, 1862. Mrd. Mary Keeler, of Upper Providence, Montgomery Co., Dec. 24, 1885. Owns and operates a creamery. Lutherans. One child: (**VIII.**) Worman K. Moyer, born Feb. 3, 1887.

VII. Christian C. Moyer, born Mar. 28, 1867. Mrd. Alice Deily, of Perkasie, Mar. 20, 1887. Station agent at Downingtown, Chester Co., Pa. One child: (**VIII.**) Elva D. Moyer, born Nov. 1887.

VI. Abraham F. Moyer, born in Franconia Twp., Montg. Co., Oct. 24, 1820. Mrd. Elizabeth Kolb, Mar. 16, 1847. She died July 28, 1864. Farmer. Mennonites. Children: Tobias, Mary, William, Abraham, Elizabeth, Emaline, Kate. Mr. Moyer mrd. for his second wife, Elizabeth Alderfer, Aug. 19, 1865.

VII. Tobias K. Moyer, born Nov. 1, 1849. Mrd. Kate G. Roth (nee Alderfer), Apr. 7, 1888. Farmer. Mennonites. One child: (**VIII.**) Abraham A. Moyer, born Apr. 5, 1889.

VII. Mary K. Moyer, born June 9, 1851. Mrd. George H. Ruth, in 1873. He was born June 10, 1851. Mennonites. Children: (**VIII.**) Elizabeth Ruth, born May 26, 1875; died Mar. 26, 1876. (**VIII.**) Henry Ruth, born Feb. 26, 1877. (**VIII.**) Abraham Ruth, born Dec. 27, 1879. (**VIII.**) Vincent Ruth, born Apr. 17, 1885. (**VIII.**) Emma Ruth, born Sept. 3, 1886.

VII. William K. Moyer, born Jan. 11, 1853. Mrd. Mary T. Moyer, Jan. 1, 1876. Farmer. Mennonites. Children: (**VIII.**) Sallie M. Moyer, born Feb. 4, 1878. (**VIII.**) Lizzie M. Moyer, born Feb. 10, 1882.

VII. Abraham K. Moyer, born Dec. 1, 1854. Mrd. Mary, daughter of Daniel G. Nice, Nov. 11, 1876.

Farmer. Mennonites. One child: (VIII.) Lizzie Moyer, born Sept. 25, 1877.

VII. Elizabeth K. Moyer, born Sept. 1, 1857. Mrd. Henry M. Nice, Jan. 20, 1877. Farmer. Mennonites. Children: (VIII.) Ellen M. Nice, born Apr. 21, 1878. (VIII.) Abraham M. Nice, born Apr. 7, 1881. (VIII.) Katie M. Nice, born Oct. 23, 1886.

VII. Emaline K. Moyer, born Feb. 23, 1860. Mrd. Hiram Clemmer, Jan. 23, 1880. Farmer. Mennonites. Children: (VIII.) Lizzie Clemmer, born Jan. 29, 1881. (VIII.) Abraham Clemmer, born Nov. 22, 1883; died Dec. 3, 1883. (VIII.) Laadan Clemmer, born Dec. 15, 1886. (VIII.) Hiram Clemmer, born Mar. 10, 1889.

VII. Catharine K. Moyer, born Oct. 9, 1861. Mrd. Abraham A. Groff, Dec. 8, 1883. Miller. Mennonites. Children: (VIII.) Annie Groff, born June 6 1885. (VIII.) Alice Groff, born Sept. 2, 1887.

V. Mary Fretz, born in Bucks Co., Feb. 9, 1788; died—. Mrd. Henry Anglemoyer, Oct. 1807. Farmer. Mennonites. Children: Ann, Elizabeth, Mary, Susan, Leah, Martin, Rachel, Barbara, Catharine, Henry, Samuel.

VI. Ann Anglemoyer, born Sept. 2, 1809; died –. Mrd. Joseph Freed, in 1829. Farmer and merchant. Mennonites. Children: John, Annie, Mary, Henry, Joseph, Jacob.

VII. John Freed, born Dec. 27, 1829; died June 15, 1857.

VII. Annie Freed, born Dec. 25, 1831; died Jan. 11, 1857. Mrd. Franklin Hendricks, in Oct. 1852. Merchant. One child: (VIII.) Louisa Hendricks, born— ; died in infancy.

VII. Mary Freed, born July 3, 1834. Mrd. Philip N. Hartman, Oct. 26, 1851. Farmer and merchant. Ger. Ref. Children: Franklin, Emma.

VIII. Franklin F. Hartman, born July 31, 1855. Mrd. Josie Robinson, Mar. 24, 1880. Children: (IX.) Harry Hartman, born Oct. 28, 1882. (IX.) Mary Emma Hartman, born Oct. 22, 1884.

VIII. Emma Hartman, born June 21, 1865. Mrd. Harry G. Gotwals, June 23, 1888. Machinist in Phila., Pa. Mrs. Gotwals, Ger. Ref.

VII. Henry A. Freed, born Mar. 29, 1838; died Sept. 28, 1846.

VII. Joseph Freed, born Oct. 29, 1842; died Sept. 11, 1847.

VII. Jacob A. Freed, born July 5, 1851. Mrd. Lydia Lewis, Jan. 4, 1873. Farmer. Member of the Mennonite church, of which he is a deacon. Children: (**VIII.** Joseph Freed, born Nov. 8, 1874. (**VIII.**) Lizzie Freed, born Jan. 29, 1876. (**VIII.**) Annie Freed, born Aug. 28, 1877. (**VIII.**) Mary Freed, born Apr. 9, 1879; died Sept. 14, 1879. (**VIII.**) Emma Freed, born Aug. 22, 1881. (**VIII.**) Lydia Freed, born May 3, 1883. (**VIII.**) Susan Freed, born May 6, 1885.

VI. Elizabeth Anglemoyer, born Oct. 26, 1811; died . Mrd. Michael Oberholtzer,—. Farmer. Mennonites. Children: Abraham, Henry, John, Jacob, Michael, Jonas, Lizzie, William, Mary.

VII. Abraham Oberholtzer lives at Bangor, Pa.

VII. Henry A. Oberholtzer lives in Philadelphia, Pa.

VII. John A. Oberholtzer lives in Philadelphia, Pa.

VII. Jacob A. Oberholtzer, born : died .

VII. Michael A. Oberholtzer, born Aug. 31, 1846; died July 28, 1884. Mrd. Mary Ann D. Alderfer, Dec. 24, 1870. Blacksmith. New Mennonites. Children: (**VIII.**) Quintin A. Oberholtzer, born Sept. 31, 1871; died Oct. 21, 1871. (**VIII.**) William Henry A. Oberholtzer, born June 18, 1873; died Mar. 15, 1874. (**VIII.**) Lizzie A. Oberholtzer, born Dec. 8, 1874. (**VIII.**) Abraham A. Oberholtzer, born Mar. 9, 1879; died Sept. 20, 1879.

VII. Jonas Oberholtzer, born : died .

VII. Lizzie Oberholtzer, born : died .

VII. William Oberholtzer, born : died .

VII. Mary Oberholtzer, born : died .

VI. Mary Anglemoyer, born July 4, 1814; died—. Mrd. Michael Ruth. . Carpenter and farmer. Mennonites. Children: Jacob, Eliza, Mary.

VII. Jacob A. Ruth, born . Mrd. Maria Wismer. . She died . Shoemaker. Moravian. Children:

(VIII.) Infant. (VIII.) Malinda. (VIII.) Ambrose. (VIII.) Michael. Jacob mrd. for his second wife, Anna Hoekman. Children: (VIII.) Elmer. (VIII.) Flora.

VII. Eliza Ruth, born   . Mrd. David Zimmerman, -. Carpenter. Children: Lena, Susanna, Frank, two died.

VIII. Lena Zimmerman, born   Mrd Joseph Souder,—.

VIII. Susanna Zimmerman, born

VIII. Frank Zimmerman, born   .

VII. Mary Ruth, born -. Mrd. Abraham Godshall, —. Children: (VIII.) Lizzie. (VIII.) Michael. (VIII.) Anna (deceased). (VIII.) Mary Ann. (VIII.) Emma. (VIII.) Clara.

VI. Susan Anglemoyer, born Oct. 12, 1817; died in 1882. Mrd. John Kauffman, in 1839. He died in 1863. Farmer. River Brethren. Children: Mary, Henry.

VII. Mary A. Kauffman, born Aug. 27, 1841. Mrd. Rev. Henry A. Landis, in 1860. Farmer and minister. He was ordained to the ministry of the River Brethren church at Grater's Ford, Montgomery Co., Pa., in 1877, where he has preached since ordination. Children: Abraham, John, Susan, Magdalena, Elizabeth, Henry, Mary, Martha, Sallie, Wilhelmina, Joseph, Eliza, Andrew, Jane, Kate, Emma.

VIII. Abraham K. Landis, born Apr. 4, 1861. Mrd. Susan A. Wismer, in 1882. Farmer. River Brethren. Children: (IX.) Franie W. Landis, born Jan. 7, 1883. (IX.) Mary W. Landis, born Mar. 14, 1885. (IX.) Henry W. Landis, born Oct. 16, 1887.

VIII. John K. Landis, born Mar. 2, 1862.

VIII. Susan K. Landis, born Jan. 15, 1864.

VIII. Magdalena K. Landis, born Feb. 1, 1865.

VIII. Elizabeth K. Landis, born Apr. 19, 1866; died Jan. 22, 1867.

VIII. Henry K. Landis, born May 2, 1867.

VIII. Mary K. Landis, born Aug. 24, 1868.

VIII. Martha K. Landis, born Oct. 5, 1869.

VIII. Sallie K. Landis, born Nov. 25, 1870.

VIII. Wilhelmina K. Landis, born Aug. 13, 1872.

VIII. Joseph K. Landis, born Oct. 8, 1873.

VIII. Eliza K. Landis, born Jan. 17, 1877.

VIII. Andrew K. Landis, born Aug. 6, 1878; died Ap. 30, 1887.

VIII. Jane K. Landis, born Mar. 17, 1881.

VIII. Katie Ann K. Landis, born Mar. 23, 1882.

VIII. Emma K. Landis, born July 18, 1884 Of the above children the eight oldest are members of the River Brethren church.

VII. Henry Kaufman, born at Lawndale, Bucks Co., in 1846. Mrd. Martha Graybill, June 12, 1869. Merchant at Zeiglersville, Montgomery Co. River Brethren. Children: (**VIII.**) William G. Kaufman, born June 22, 1870. (**VIII.**) Henry G. Kaufman, born Dec. 24, 1874. (**VIII.**) Sallie G. Kaufman, born Mar. 10, 1877; died Jan. 10, 1878. (**VIII.**) Christopher Kaufman, born June 22, 1888.

VI. Leah Anglemoyer, born in Bucks Co., Nov. 20, 1819. Mrd. Joseph D. Detwiler, Feb. 29, 1841. Farmer. Mennonites. Children: Mary, Anna, John, Henry, Garret, Lizzie, Sallie.

VII. Mary Ann Detwiler, born Feb. 11, 1843. Mrd. Rev. Amos K. Bean, Jan. 10, 1864. Farmer and minister of the Mennonite Ch. He was ordained to the ministry in Skippack Twp., Montg. Co., Pa., in 1873, and where he has ever since preached the Gospel. Children: John, Joseph, Leah, Henry, Irwin, Amos, Garret, Lizzie, Isaac, Clement, Mary, William, Alvin, Sallie.

VIII. John D. Bean, born Nov. 23, 1864. Mrd. Emma D. Cassel, Dec. 7, 1889. She was born Mar. 29, 1869. One child: (**IX.**) Newton C. Bean, born Apr. 4, 1891.

VIII. Joseph D. Bean, born July 6, 1866. Mrd. Sallie R. Hunsicker, Feb. 21, 1891. She was born June 5, 1866.

VIII. Leah D. Bean, born Dec. 21, 1868.

VIII. Henry D. Bean, born Dec. 29, 1870.

VIII. Irwin D. Bean, born, Sept. 25, 1872; died June 12, 1873.

VIII. Amos D. Bean, born Dec. 19, 1873.

VIII. Garret D. Bean, born July 10, 1875; died Aug. 9, 1875.

(See Page 49)

VIII. Lizzie D. Bean, born Aug. 7, 1876; died Aug. 20, 1877.

VIII. Isaac D. Bean, born Sept. 23, 1877.

VIII. Clement D. Bean, born Aug. 11, 1879.

VIII. Mary D. Bean, born July 25, 1881.

VIII. William D. Bean, born Apr. 21, 1883; died Sept. 19, 1883.

VIII. Alvin D. Bean, born Oct. 25, 1884; died Apr. 30, 1885.

VIII. Sallie D. Bean, born Sept. 6, 1886.

VII. Anna A. Detwiler, born Mar. 24, 1845. Mrd. George R. Detwiler, Nov. 25, 1865. Farmer. Mennonites. Children: Leanna, Garret, Joseph, Fannie, Harry, Abraham, Jacob, Annie, Mary, Katie.

VIII. Leanna D. Detwiler, born Sept. 3d, 1866. Mrd. John B. Bergey, Oct. 9, 1886. Farmer. Mem. Trinity Christian Ch.

VIII. Garrett D. Detwiler, born Aug. 21, 1868; died Sept. 1, 1868.

VIII. Joseph D. Detwiler, born Nov. 5, 1869.

VIII. Fannie D. Detwiler, born June 22, 1872; died Feb. 25, 1886.

VIII. Harry D. Detwiler, born Sept. 5, 1874.

VIII. Abraham D. Detwiler, born Feb. 9, 1877.

VIII. Jacob D. Detwiler born Mar. 20, 1879.

VIII. Annie D. Detwiler born Sept. 6, 1881.

VIII. Mary D. Detwiler, born Mar. 24, 1884.

VIII. Katie Lizzie Detwiler, born Nov. 17, 1886.

VII. John A. Detwiler, born Dec. 9, 1846. Mrd. Eliza Yoder, Nov. 13, 1869. Farmer. Mennonites. Children: (VIII.) Elemina Y. Detwiler, born Aug. 7, 1870; died Apr. 18, 1871. (VIII.) Irvin Y. Detwiler, born Feb. 16, 1873. (VIII.) Horace Y. Detweiler, born Mar. 16, 1877; died Apr. 11, 1878. (VIII.) Maurice Y. Detwiler, born May 23, 1880; died Jan. 7, 1881. (VIII.) Elmer Y. Detwiler, born Aug. 24, 1882.

VII. Henry A. Detwiler, born Apr. 10, 1849. Mrd. Ellen A. Moyer, Dec. 10, 1872. Farmer. Presbyterians. Children: (VIII.) Martha M. Detwiler, born Nov. 5, 1874. (VIII.) Ephraim M. Detwiler, born Aug. 28, 1877.

VII. Garret A. Detwiler, born Mar. 3, 1853; died Feb. 6, 1887. Mrd. Sadie B. Benner, Oct. 16, 1875. Farmer. Mennonites. Children: (VIII.) Lizzie B. Detweiler, born Sept. 2, 1876; died May 11, 1879. (VIII.) Ellen B. Detwiler, born Sept. 25, 1877. (VIII.) Anna Mary B. Detwiler, born Feb. 10, 1880. (VIII.) Ira B. Detwiler, born Sept. 10, 1882. (VIII.) Leah B. Detwiler, born Aug. 29, 1884; died Jan. 29, 1887 .

VII. Lizzie A. Detwiler, born Aug. 14, 1856. Mrd. David Gehman, Feb. 5, 1876. Shoemaker. Mennonites. Children: (VIII.) Sallie D. Gehman, born Nov. 13, 1877. (VIII.) Laura D. Gehman, born Jan. 16, 1882.

VII. Sallie A. Detwiler, born Apr. 18, 1860. Mrd. Abraham Swartley, Mar. 3, 1877. Farmer. Mennonites. Children: (VIII.) Mary D. Swartley, born Nov. 19, 1878. (VIII.) Martha D. Swartley, born Jan. 12, 1882. (VIII.) Leah D. Swartley, born Jan. 25, 1885.

VI. Martin F. Anglemoyer, born July 5, 1821. Mrd. Eliza Landis, Oct. 27, 1844. She was born Oct. 23, 1823. Farmer. Ger. Baptists. Children: Emma, Henry, Jairus, Samuel.

VII. Emma Anglemoyer, born Aug. 31, 1852; died Aug. 16, 1862.

VII. Henry Anglemoyer, born Jan. 5, 1854. Mrd. Kate L. Deetz, Aug. 27, 1874. She was born Feb. 11, 1854. Policeman. Residence, 605 Vincent St., Phila.. Children: (VIII.) Alice Anglemoyer, born Aug. 20, 1875; died Dec. 26, 1878. (VIII.) Ida Anglemoyer, born Nov. 16, 1876; died Feb. 22, 1878. (VIII.) Laura Anglemoyer, born Nov. 16, 1878. (VIII.) George Anglemoyer, born May 16, 1880. (VIII.) Florence Anglemoyer, born Jan. 31, 1883; died June 9, 1885. (VIII.) Lizzie Anglemoyer, born Apr. 4, 1885. (VIII.) Emma Anglemoyer, born Sept. 28, 1889.

VII. Jairus Anglemoyer, born May 30, 1862. Mrd. Amanda Groff, Apr. 22, 1882. She was born Dec. 22, 1857. Farmer near Benjamin, Pa. Children: (VIII.) Allen K. Anglemoyer, born July 1882. (VIII.) Raymond K. Anglemoyer, born Oct. 8, 1883. (VIII.) Samuel K. Anglemoyer, born Jan. 16, 1886. (VIII.) Clara K. Anglemoyer, born Sept. 1, 1888.

(VIII.) Howard K. Anglemoyer, born Dec. 18, 1889.

VII. Samuel Anglemoyer, born Aug. 24, 1876.

VI. Rachel Anglemoyer, born Oct. 5, 1821. Mrd. John Snovel. Farmer. Children. (VII.) Mary. (VII.) Malinda. (VII.) Emma.

VI. Barbara Anglemoyer, born March 21, 1827; died —. Mrd. Amos Baringer. One child: (VII.) Ephraim Baringer, born —; died —; no issue.

VI. Catharine Anglemoyer, born Jan. 28, 1829; died young.

VI. Henry F. Anglemoyer, born Mar. 28, 1831. Mrd. Elizabeth George, Jan. 23, 1853. She died Mar. 25, 1860. Farmer, and lives on the farm where his grandfather Martin Fretz, once lived 80 years ago. Brethren in Christ. Children: Frank, Joseph, Mary, Henry, James. Mr. Anglemoyer, married for his second wife, Annie Moyer, Jan. 26, 1861. Children: Mary, Ellen, Samuel, Emma, Sallie, Anna, William, Jacob, Lizzie.

VII. Frank Anglemoyer, born 1854; died 1854.

VII. Joseph Anglemoyer, born 1856; died 1856.

VII. Mary Ann Anglemoyer, born 1857; died 1857.

VII. Henry G. Anglemoyer, born Jan. 26, 1859. Mrd. Kate C., daughter of Jacob and Elizabeth Kratz of Franconia Twp., Montg. Co., Nov. 29, 1879. Shoemaker. Mennonites.

VII. James Anglemoyer, born Mar. 10, 1860; died in 1860.

VII. Mary Jane Anglemoyer, born Jan. 27, 1862. Mrd. John M. Fulmer, Oct. 20, 1883. Farmer. One child: (VIII.) Stella A. Fulmer, born Jan. 15, 1885.

VII. Ellen Anglemoyer, born Dec. 28, 1863. Mrd. John Bilger, Jan. 12, 1884. One child: (VIII.) Walter Bilger, born in 1885.

VII. Samuel M. Anglemoyer, born June 28, 1866. Mrd. Martha B., daughter of Moses and Mary Ann Stout, Apr. 23, 1887. Laborer. One child: (VIII.) Arnon Anglemoyer.

VII. Emma Anglemoyer, born Oct. 22, 1868.

VII. Sallie Anglemoyer, born Nov. 22, 1870. Mrd. Howard B. Stout. One child: (VIII.) Raymond Stout.

VII. Anna Anglemoyer, born Jan. 18, 1873; died July 14, 1886.

VII. William M. Anglemoyer, born May 8, 1875.

VII. Jacob M. Anglemoyer, born Feb. 11, 1878; died Oct. 10, 1879.

VII. Lizzie Anglemoyer, born Nov. 28, 1880; died Aug. 16, 1883.

VI. Samuel F. Anglemoyer, born Oct. 28, 1834. Mrd. Lucy Ann Hangey, Feb. 5, 1857. Carpenter. Mennonites. Children: John, Lavina, Hannah, Allen.

VII. John H. Anglemoyer, born June 14, 1858. Mrd. Annie Moyer, Jan. 1, 1880. Carpenter and farmer. Mennonites. Children: (VIII.) Leanna Anglemoyer, born Sept. 8, 1881. (VIII.) Samuel Arthur Anglemoyer, born Jan. 31, 1884.

VII. Lavina Anglemoyer, born June 10, 1861 Mrd. William M. Moyer, May 30, 1879. Farmer. Mennonites. Children: (VIII.) Alice Moyer, born Jan. 24, 1880. (VIII.) Lucy Moyer, born Sept. 5th, 1883. (VIII.) Mamie Moyer, born Sept. 12, 1885. (VIII.) Quilla Moyer, born June 29, 1887.

VI. Hannah Anglemoyer, born Aug. 31, 1865; died June 29, 1882.

VII. Allen Anglemoyer, born Dec. 16, 1867. S.

V. Agnes Fretz, born Aug. 10, 1790; died Sept. 21, 1862. Mrd. Peter Loux, Nov. 28, 1811. He died July 22, 1855. Farmer and oil manufacturer at Fretz's oil mill in Hilltown Twp., Mennonites. Children: Mary, Martin, Jacob, Enos, Silas, Aaron, Samuel.

VI. Mary Loux, born in Hilltown Twp., about 1813. Mrd. Michael Oberholtzer,—. She died Dec. 4, 1873. No issue.

VI. Martin Loux, born Dec. 18, 1814; died Feb. 1, 1832

VI. Jacob Loux, born Feb. 7, 1817; died June 18, 1886. Mrd. Rachel, daughter of Jacob and Anna Bishop, . Farmer. Lost a hand in the cylinder of a threshing machine while threshing. Mennonites. Children: Peter, Anna, Mary, Jacob, Enos, Isaac, Samuel.

VII. Peter B. Loux, born Dec. 29, 1847. Mrd. Eliza Hunsberger, Dec. 24, 1871. Carpenter and farmer. Mennonites. No issue.

VII. Anna Loux, born Apr. 13, 1850. Mrd. Abraham L. Detwiler, May 4, 1869. Farmer and tailor. Mennonites. Children: (**VIII.**) Samuel L. Detwiler, born June 2, 1871; died Feb. 5, 1883. (**VIII.**) Ella May Detwiler, born May 28, 1885.

VII. Mary Loux, born July 8, 1852; died Mar. 1, 1858.

VII. Jacob B. Loux, born in Bucks Co., Pa., Sept. 14, 1854. Mrd. Emeline Yoder, Dec. 22, 1877. Farmer. Mennonites. Children: (**VIII.**) Susan Loux, born Jan. 5, 1880. (**VIII.**) Samuel Y. Loux, born Jan. 5, 1881. (**VIII.**) Annie Loux, born June 20, 1883; died Sept. 13, 1885. (**VIII.**) Jacob Y. Loux, born May 15, 1885 (**VIII.**) Lizzie Loux, born Feb. 15, 1887.

VII. Enos B. Loux, born Jan. 13, 1856. Mrd. Anna Yoder, Dec. 6, 1879. Farmer. Mennonites. One child: (**VIII.**) Levi Y. Loux, born Dec. 20, 1886; died Mar. 13, 1888.

VII. Isaac Loux, born Dec. 15, 1859; died May 12, 1860.

VII. Samuel F. Loux, born Aug. 12, 1862; died May 24, 1863.

VI. Enos F. Loux, born June 20, 1819. Mrd. Anna Rickert, Aug. 28, 1842. She died Dec. 12, 1859. Miller. He was ordained to the ministry of the New Mennonite Church at Deep Run, Pa., where he preached for some years, and of which he is still a member. Children: Isaac, Peter, Amanda, Minerva, Catharine, Menno, David. Enos mrd. for his second wife Anna Beidler, Dec. 28, 1862.

VII. Isaac R. Loux, born July 11, 1843. Mrd. Catharine Yoder, Aug. 29, 1868. Designer and pattern maker at Wadsworth, O. New Mennonites. Children: (**VIII.**) David Franklin Loux, born Oct. 22, 1869; died May 1, 1871. (**VIII.**) Cora Loux, born Feb. 17, 1872; died Jan. 2, 1873. (**VIII.**) Ella Loux, born July 20, 1873. Ger. Reformed. (**VIII.**) Charles Loux, born Aug. 15, 1875. (**VIII.**) Susie Loux, born July 5, 1877. (**VIII.**) Ada May Loux, born Oct. 7,

1882; died Oct. 25, 1882. **(VIII.)** Beulah Loux, born Feb. 7, 1884.

VII. Peter Loux, born Apr. 11, 1845. Mrd. Sarah A. Miller Sept. 10, 1865. Engineer at the Quakertown, Pa., stone works. Mennonite. Children: **(VIII.)** Abigail Loux, born Mar. 7, 1866; died—. **(VIII.)** Hannah Loux, born Mar. 14, 1867; died—. **(VIII.)** Anna M. Loux, born Aug. 22, 1869. **(VIII.)** Amanda Loux, born Aug. 22, 1872; died—. **(VIII.)** Jeremiah Loux, born Nov. 1, 1874; died—. **(VIII.)** Enos Loux, born Apr. 20, 1879; died—. **(VIII.)** Sanford Loux, born June 22, 1881. **(VIII.)** Edith Loux, born June 6, 1884.

VII. Amanda Loux, born Sept. 26, 1846. Mrd. John S. Fretz. (See Index of References No. 21.)

VII. Minerva Loux, born in Hilltown Twp., Bucks Co., Pa., Aug. 8, 1849. Mrd. Jacob B. Zepp, Jan. 15, 1880. Cigar manufacturer at Wadsworth, Medina Co., Ohio. Mennonite. Their children are: **(VIII.)** Alice Zepp, born Jan. 21, 1871. **(VIII.)** Annie Zepp, born Oct. 7, 1872. **(VIII.)** Katie Zepp (twin), born Oct. 7, 1872; died July 24, 1876. **(VIII.)** Irvin Zepp, born Apr. 8, 1874. **(VIII.)** Elmer Zepp, born Jan. 8, 1876. **(VIII.)** Ida May Zepp, born May 25, 1878. **(VIII.)** Eddie Zepp, born Mar. 12, 1880; died Dec. 30, 1881. **(VIII.)** Amanda Elida Zepp, born Sept. 26, 1884. **(VIII.)** Walter Zepp, born Apr. 19, 1886.

VII. Catharine Loux, born in Bucks Co., Pa., Jan. 1, 1853. Mrd. Daniel G. Koppes, July 10, 1875. Painter at Newton, Harvey Co., Kansas. He also owns a farm of 240 acres near Newton, Kan. Children: **(VIII.)** Lloyd Koppes, born Nov. 23, 1876; died Dec. 18, 1876. **(VIII.)** Elno Koppes, born July 2, 1878; died Mar. 15, 1888. **(VIII.)** Olivid Koppes, born Aug. 16, 1881. **(VIII.)** Leonard Koppes, born May 5, 1884. **(VIII.)** Daisy Koppes, born Feb. 18, 1888.

VII. Menno Loux, born May 25, 1856; died Dec. 12, 1859.

VII. David R. Loux, born Feb. 1, 1858; died Jan 4, 1875.

VI. Silas Loux, born Apr. 24, 1821; died Jan. 15, 1841.

VI. Aaron Loux, born Apr. 18, 1823; died Aug. 1, 1830.

VI. Samuel F. Loux, born Apr. 20, 1825. Mrd. Matilda Farley, 1850. Carpenter. No issue.

V. Elizabeth Fretz, born Aug. 10, 1790 (twin to Agnes), died in infancy.

V. Elizabeth Fretz, born May 20, 1792; died Sept. 17, 1872. Mrd. Abraham Kratz. (See Index of References No. 42.)

V. Nancy Fretz, born Jan. 8, 1794; died Sept. 14, 1863. Mrd. Abraham Hunsberger about 1815. He died . Farmer. Mennonites. Children: Esther, Anna, Martin, Susanna, Isaac, Elizabeth, John, Abraham, Enos.

VI. Esther Hunsberger born in 1817. S.

VI. Anna Hunsberger, born in 1818. S.

VI. Martin F. Hunsberger, born Jan. 25, 1821; died Oct. 27, 1852. Mrd. Anna Maria Loux, Sept. 20, 1846. Farmer. Mennonites. Children: Sarah Ann, Remandes, Emeline.

VII. Sarah Ann Hunsberger, born in 1847; died in infancy.

VII. Remandes Hunsberger, born in 1849; died Dec. 31, 1862.

VII. Emeline Hunsberger, born May 20, 1851. Mrd. Charles S. Kachline, Dec. 3, 1870. Farmer. Ger. Ref. Children: (**VIII.**) Jennie H. Kachline, born Feb. 14, 1872, died Aug. 24, 1872. (**VIII.**) Edward H. Kachline, born June 26, 1873. (**VIII.**) Ida May Kachline, born Jan. 28, 1876. (**VIII.**) Minnie H. Kachline, born May 13, 1878. (**VIII.**) Ella Nora Kachline, born Apr. 15, 1884. (**VIII.**) Allen H. Kachline, born July 19, 1887.

VI. Susanna Hunsberger, born in 1823; died June 1823.

VI. Isaac Hunsberger, born in 1825; died Apr. 17, 1848. S.

VI. Elizabeth Hunsberger, born in 1827; died Nov. 14, 1845. S.

V. John S. Hunsberger, born Feb. 25, 1828; died Apr. 10, 1871. Mrd. Mary Magdalena Snyder, Oct. 6, 1852. She died –. Wheelwright and carpenter. Lutherans. Children: Hartwell, Hannah, Alfred, Fremont, Harry. John mrd. for his second wife, Sarah Jane Weeks, Feb. 11, 1864. Presbyterian. Children: Anna, Esther.

VII. Hartwell Hunsberger, born Oct. 31, 1853; died Dec. 5, 1853.

VII. Hannah Hunsberger, born Oct. 29, 1854. Mrd. William Carn, Oct. 15, 1874. Blacksmith. Attend Ger. Ref. Ch. Children: (**VIII.**) Edith May Carn, born May 13, 1876. (**VIII.**) John Henry Carn, born Feb. 16, 1880.

VII. Alfred W. Hunsberger, born Dec. 12, 1855; died Dec. 26, 1877. S.

VII. Fremont S. Hunsberger, born Apr. 25, 1857; Mrd. Lauratine B. Richards, Oct. 13, 1879. Drives an express wagon. One child: (**VIII.**) Flora Mabel Hunsberger, born Oct. 30, 1882.

VII. Harry Clifton Hunsberger, born Aug. 7, 1858; died Jan. 9, 1863.

VII. Anna Martha Hunsberger, born Nov. 17, 1864. Presbyterian. S.

VII. Esther Estella Hunsberger, born Oct. 31, 1866. died May 16, 1882.

VI. Abraham F. Hunsberger, born in 1831. Mrd. Catharine Angeny of Bedminster Twp., Dec. 9, 1858. Farmer. Mennonites. Children: (**VII.**) Mary Ann Hunsberger, born in 1860. S. (**VII.**) Remandes Hunsberger, born in 1863. (**VII.**) Jacob Hunsberger, born in 1867. (**VII.**) Leidy and Edwin Hunsberger (twins), born in 1877.

VI. Enos F. Hunsberger, born Jan. 4, 1835. Mrd. Mary Loux, Nov. 5, 1859. Farmer. Mennonites. Children: Anna, Sarah, Emma, Peter, Harvey.

VII. Anna L. Hunsberger, born Feb. 26, 1860; died Mar. 29, 1863.

VII. Sarah L. Hunsberger, born Nov. 11, 1862; died Apr. 8, 1863.

CORP. JOHN K. FRETZ.
(See Page 42.)
51.

VII. Emma L. Hunsbreger, born June 12, 1864. Mrd. Samuel W. Gross.

VII. Peter L. Hunsberger, born Nov. 9, 1869.

VII. Harvey D. Hunsberger, born Oct. 8, 1873.

V. Veronica Fretz, born about 1796; died young.

V. Martin Fretz, born about 1798; died young.

V. Martin Fretz, born about 1800; died young.

V. Susanna Fretz, born in Bucks Co., Pa., Mar. 23, 1802; died Feb. 4, 1890, aged 87 yr. 10 m. 11 d. Mrd. Jacob Funk, Dec. 9, 1830. He was born near Springtown, in Springfield Twp., Bucks Co., on the 16th of Dec. 1796; died Sept. 4, 1875. Mason, bricklayer and farmer. Mennonites. Children: Margaret, Esther, John, Sarah, Abraham, Jacob, Susan.

VI. Margaret Funk, born Oct. 15, 1831, died Nov. 22, 1857. Mrd. Benjamin Frick in 1853. Mennonites. One child.

VII. Samuel F. Frick, born July 27, 1856. Book-binder and general workman in Chicago, Ill. Married Lizzie Thierolf, June 13, 1891. In March 1892 he removed to his grandfather's farm in Frick's, Bucks Co., Pa., where he now resides.

VI. Esther Funk, born July 1, 1833. Mrd. John L. Frick in 1854. He died in 1880. Merchant and builder. Methodists. Children: (**VII.**) Elizabeth (deceased). (**VII.**) Jacob F., printer with Mennonite Pub'g Co., Elkhart, Ind., died at his home in Philadelphia, Apr. 15, 1882. (**VII.**) Joel, printer in Philadelphia, died at his home July 6, 1881. (**VII.**) Edward (dec'd). (**VII.**) Emma E. (**VII.**) Charles E.

VI. John Fretz Funk, born in Hilltown Twp., Bucks Co., Pa., Apr. 6, 1835. He worked on the farm as soon as he was old enough, going to school in the winter season until he was in his nineteenth year (1854), when he commenced teaching in his native township, and taught during the winter for three successive winters. He also attended school at Freeland Seminary three months during summer of 1855, and again in 1856. In the spring of 1857, after closing his school at Chestnut Ridge S. H., in Hilltown Twp., he went to Chicago, Ill., and engaged in the lumber business, in which he continued nine years.

In the winter of 1859/60 he became a member of the Mennonite church at Line Lexington, Bucks Co., Pa. In January of 1864 he commenced the publication of the *Herald of Truth* and *Der Herold der Wahrheit*, and on the 19th of the same month was married to Salome Kratz, daughter of Jacob Kratz of Hilltown, Bucks Co., Pa. On the 28th of May 1865, he was ordained to the ministry in the Mennonite church near Gardner, Grundy Co., Ill. In April 1867 he removed to Elkhart, Ind., and established there the business house now known as the "Mennonite Publishing Company", first under his own name, and afterwards under the firm name of John F. Funk and Brother, after having associated with himself his brother Abraham K. Funk, and continued the business under this firm name until May 14, 1875, when the Mennonite Publishing Co., was organized. Children: (**VII.**) Martha. (**VII.**) Susan Mary (dec'd). (**VII.**) Phoebe. (**VII.**) Rebecca (dec'd). (**VII.**) Grace Anna (dec'd). (**VII.**) John Edwin (dec'd).

VI. Sarah Funk, born in Hilltown Twp., Bucks Co., Apr. 24, 1837; died Aug. 20, 1839.

VI. Abraham Kratz Funk, born in Hilltown, Bucks Co., Jan. 20, 1840. His early years were spent on his father's farm. He attended school about four months usually in the winter, and a month or two during the summer. He commenced teaching in the public schools of the county, at the age of 18, under the county superintendency of Wm. H. Johnson. He attended school at Freeland Seminary, at Freeland, now Collegeville, Montgomery Co., in 1859, and the Excelsior Normal Institute, at Carversville, Bucks Co., in 1861. After spending five years in farming during the summer and teaching in winter, he went to Chicago, Ill., in the spring of 1863 and engaged in the Lumber business. After a residence of five years in Chicago, he went to Elkhart, and there entered into a co-partnership with his brother, under the firm name of John F. Funk and Brother, as publishers and booksellers. They continued the publication of the *Herald of Truth* and *Der Herold der Wahrheit*, and also issued during the continuance of this co-partner-

ship a number of religious works, the most important
of which was the great book of martyrs, in the german language, containing over 1100 quarto pages,
and the complete works of Menno Simon, which was
translated from the Holland and printed in English.
In 1875 he became one of the principal stockholders
in the Mennonite Publishing Co., which was then organized, and has since held the position of secretary
and treasurer of that institution. He married Annie
M. Landis, daughter of Joseph and Mary (Geil) Landis, of Greer's Corner, near Dublin, Bucks Co., Pa.,
Mar. 11, 1872. Mennonites. Children: (VII.) Mary
Maude. (VII.) Edna Josephine. (VII.) Esther Wini-
fred.

VI. Jacob Silas Funk was born in Hilltown Twp.,
Bucks Co., Pa., Apr. 13, 1842. He spent his early
days on his father's farm, and received, as was cus-
tomary in those days, a fair, common school education. He afterwards, during the early part of 1862
and the summer of 1863, spent two terms at the Excelsior Normal Institute, at Carversville, Bucks Co.
He taught in the schools of his native county, from
1862 to 1865. In the spring of 1865 he gave up that
vocation and went to Chicago, Ill., and engaged in
the lumber business. On the 28th of Sept., of the
same year he purchased a scholarship in the Eastman
Business College of that city, and took a commercial
course, attending evenings only. After four years
residence in Chicago, he determined to engage in
business for himself, and accordingly, in the spring of
1869, located at Chillicothe, Mo., where he opened a
lumber yard and commenced business on his own account. On the 15th of January following (1870), he
was married to Annie K. Stover, daughter of Jonas
Stover, of E. Rockhill Twp., Bucks Co., Pa. He afterwards became connected with the North Western
Lumber Co., who had their mills at Eau Claire, Wis-
consin, and extensive yards at Hannibal, Mo.; and
on the 20th of April 1880 moved with his family from
Chillicothe to Hannibal. Afterwards when the duties
of his position required him to be mostly in the neigh-
borhood where the mills of the company were located,

he found it more economical and convenient to have his family in that vicinity also, and accordingly, on the 20th of July 1885, he removed to Minneapolis, Minn. He continued with the above firm eleven years, during which time he gained with them the highest esteem and respect, both for his conscientious business integrity and his excellent qualifications for the work in which he was engaged. In the spring of 1890 he severed his relations with the N. W. Lumber Co., but the warm feeling of esteem and respect which he had won for himself during these extended business relations continued to the end of his life.

He took an active part in the various civil, social and religious movements of the day, and was always ready and willing to assist in all enterprises of public interest, and held continuously positions of responsibility and honor. Soon after his removal to Chillicothe, in 1869, he was elected superintendent of the Sunday-school of the Presbyterian church of that city, which position he held until his removal to Hannibal in 1880. He was converted and united with the Third Presbyterian church of Chicago during the time of his residence there. In 1871 or 72 he was elected elder of the First Presbyterian church of Chillicothe. He was secretary of the school board of that city, and through his influence was built the beautiful new school building, costing from $45,000 to $50,000. In 1875 he was also member of the city council. During the last three years of his residence in Chillicothe he was correspondent of the "Globe Democrat," a republican paper of St. Louis. During the summer of 1890, after severing his connection with the N. W. L. Co., he, with A. Fiero, was appointed, by the lumber manufacturers of the N. W., to inspect the system of grading employed by the leading manufacturers of the north-west, and their report was received with much favor and satisfaction. After the completion of this commission, he became connected with the T. B. Scott Lumber Co., of Merrill, Wis., and during a business trip through Illinois and Indiana, he was taken sick with a severe bilious attack, and after nearly a week of suffering in hotels, in Terre

Haute, Ind., Chicago, Ill., and on the road, he reached his home in Minneapolis, Minn., on the 22d of September. The disease assumed a complicated form which resulted in blood poisoning, and after three weeks more of intense suffering, which he bore with patience, he died on the 15th of Oct. 1890, aged 48 yr., 6 m. 2 d. Presbyterians. Children: (VII.) Emma Laura Funk, born Mar. 30, 1871; died Oct. 16, 1872. (VII.) Frederick Stover Funk, born Jan. 26, 1873; died Mar. 20, 1877. (VII.) Gertrude Elizabeth Funk, born Feb. 25, 1877. (VII.) Susan Anna Funk, born Jan. 29, 1885.

VI. Susan Elizabeth Funk, born May 4, 1846. Mrd. Henry W. Gross, June 17, 1875, son of Joseph N. Gross. Mr. Gross is a graduate of the Millersville, Pa., State Normal school, having graduated in June 1873. At the time of his marriage he was principal of the public schools of Etna, Allegheny Co., Pa. His present occupation is farmer and creamery business. Members of the Presbyterian church of Doylestown, Pa., of which he was ordained elder in Jan. 1890. Children: (VII.) Sarah Ella Gross. (VII.) Emma Laura Gross. (VII.) Esther Gross. (VII.) Walter Gross, born in 1889; died Mar. 8, 1890.

VI Silas Fretz, born about 1804; died in infancy.

V. Veronica Fretz, born Aug. 8, 1806; died Nov. 1, 1885. Mrd. Jonas Meyers, Apr. 1, 1828. Farmer. Mennonites. Children: Mary, Catharine, Leah.

VI. Mary Ann Meyers, born 1833; died Aug. 10, 1852.

VI. Catharine F. Meyers, born—. Married Tobias Overholt, Jan. 13, 1865. Children: Fannie, Joseph, Erwin, Mary, Lucinda.

VII. Fannie M. Overholt, born Sept. 6, 1866; died July 15, 1887. Mrd. William Mitman, Jan. 1, 1887. One child: (VIII.) Cora Mitman, born July 11, 1887.

VII. Joseph M. Overholt, born Apr. 22, 1868.

VII. Erwin M. Overholt, born Aug. 23, 1873.

VII. Mary Ann M. Overholt, born Feb. 27, 1875.

VII. Lucinda M. Overholt, born Feb. 10, 1880.

VI. Leah Meyers, born Nov. 24, 1839; died— , 1890. Mrd. Henry B. Kratz. (See Index of References No. 22.)

V. Catharine Fretz, born Sept. 9, 1808, died—. Mrd. Abraham Kratz. (See Index of References No. 45.)

V. Leah Fretz, born Oct. 1, 1810. Mrd. Abraham Angeny, Oct. 21, 1828. They lived on the property known as Angeny's Mill, in Bedminster Twp., until the spring of 1848, when they moved to New Columbia, Union Co., Pa. In 1859 they moved to Milton, Northumberland Co., Pa., where Mr. Angeny perished in the great fire May 14, 1880 in his 78th year. Carpenter and cabinet maker. Mennonites. Children: Anna, Barbara, Eva, Martin, Leah, Rachel, Abbie, Katharine, Minerva.

VI. Anna Eliza Angeny, born Dec. 21, 1829; died Jan. 13, 1850. S.

VI. Barbara Angeny, born Aug. 29, 1831, at the old Deep Run mill, in Bedminster, Bucks Co., Pa. Mrd. Jacob Gehman, of Springfield, Bucks Co., Oct. 2, 1849. Farmer in Gage Co., Nebraska. Mennonites. Children: Abraham, Jacob, Elizabeth, Fannie, Rachel, Sarah, Lillie, Emma, Benjamin, Samuel, Mary.

VII. Abraham A. Gehman, born in Bucks Co., Pa., Aug. 26, 1850. Resides at Hutchinson, Kan. Music teacher. S. (1888.)

VII. Jacob Gehman, born in Bucks Co., Pa., Mar. 24, 1852; died Oct. 26, 1860.

VII. Elizabeth Gehman, born in Bucks Co., Pa., Jan. 19, 1854; died Oct. 20, 1860.

VII. Menno S. Gehman, born in Bucks Co., Pa., May 17, 1856. Running a stock-range in Wyo.

VI. Fannie Gehman, born in Bucks Co., Pa., Feb. 19, 1858. Mrd. Samuel Horning, of Clarinda, Page Co., Iowa, Oct. 31, 1878. Farmer. Disciples. Resides at Pickrell, Neb. Children: (**VIII.**) Benjamin F. Horning, born Apr. 19, 1880. (**VIII.**) Jacob Lee Horning, born Apr. 12, 1881. (**VIII.**) Edwin G. Horning, born Aug. 2, 1882 (**VIII.**) Jennie Agatha Horning, born Jan. 5, 1884. **(VIII.)** Alice Horning, born Jan. 19, 1888.

VII. Rachel A. Gehman, born in Bucks Co., Pa., Feb. 17, 1860. Mrd. Henry Wm. Smith, of Rockport, Mo., Oct. 21, 1886. Mrs. Smith, Baptist. Mr. Smith, Lutheran. Children: **(VIII.)** Arthur Raymond Smith, born July 23, 1887. **(VIII.)** — Smith, born—.

VII. Sarah Gehman, born Aug. 10, 1862 in Fayette Co., Iowa. Mrd. William G. Grebe, Dec. 25, 1883. Farmer in Atchison Co., Mo. Methodists. Children: **(VIII.)** Elsie Grebe, born Sept. 27, 1884. **(VIII.)** Guy Grebe, born Mar. 28, 1886. **(VIII.)** Herbert Grebe, born June 12, 1888. **(VIII.)** A daughter, born—.

VII. Samuel Gehman, born in Fayette Co., Iowa, July 6, 1864. Running a stock ranch in Wyo. S.

VII. Lillie A. Gehman, born in Fayette Co., Iowa, Apr. 15, 1868. Teacher. S.

VII. Emma B. Gehman, born in Fayette Co., Iowa, Sept. 27, 1870. Mrd. Rev. H. R. Murphy, Sept. 1, 1891. P. O., Beatrice, Gage Co., Nebr. Minister of Free Baptist Ch.

VII. Benjamin F. Gehman, born in Fayette Co., Iowa, Aug. 1, 1873.

VII. Mary Anna Gehman, born Aug. 6, 1876.

VI. Eva Angeny, born in Bucks Co., Pa., Oct. 25, 1833. Mrd. Reuben L. Hatfield, Dec. 4, 1851, in Union Co. P. O., Milton, Pa. Tinner. Baptists. Children: Annetta, Ella, Lillian, Carroll, Edgar, William, Minnie, Grace, Mabel.

VII. Annetta V. Hatfield, born May 29, 1853. Mrd. William I. Webb, Apr. 27, 1880. Clerk and bookkeeper at Milton, Pa. Methodists. Children: **(VIII.)** John Webb, born Mar. 10, 1881; died Sept. 7, 1881. **(VIII.)** Fannie B. Webb, born July 18, 1883.

VII. Ella E. Hatfield, born Aug. 9, 1855.

VII. Lillian V. Hatfield, born Dec. 1, 1857. Mrd. John H. Krauser, Mar. 27, 1879. Traveling salesman. Res., Milton, Pa. Ger. Ref. Children: **(VIII.)** Webb Guy Krauser, born May 31, 1880. **(VIII.)** James B. Krauser, born July 5, 1883.

VII. Carroll D. Hatfield, born Dec. 1, 1859. Mrd. Laura Quick, Mar. 29, 1881. P. O., Huntsville, Randolph Co., Mo. Carriage maker. Baptists. Children: (VIII.) Walter Hatfield, born Dec. 14, 1882. (VIII.) Annetta Jennie Hatfield, born Jan. 25, 1885.

VII. Edgar A. Hatfield, born Feb. 16, 1862. Mrd. Anna M. Brigg, Nov. 30, 1886. P. O., La Junta, Bent Co., Colo. Machinist.

VII. William S. Hatfield, born Sept. 2, 1864. Painter and paper hanger.

VII. Minnie E. Hatfield, born Feb. 7, 1869.

VII. Grace C. Hatfield, born Jan. 24, 1872.

VII. M. Mabel Hatfield, born Jan. 17, 1877.

VI. Martin F. Angeny, born Nov. 27, 1835; died Oct. 31, 1865. Mrd. Clara F. Hagner, Mar. 3, 1864. Carpenter. Baptists. One child: (VII.) Harry R. Angeny; died Oct. 5, 1865, aged 7 mo.

VI. Leah Angeny, born Dec. 9, 1837; died Jan. 13, 1866. S.

VI. Rachel Angeny, born Feb. 24, 1840. Mrd. Seth Comly Hill, Oct. 3, 1861. Farmer and dairyman. Baptists. P. O., Milton, Pa. Children: (VII.) Raymond C. Hill, born Aug. 31, 1862; died Aug. 11, 1864. (VII.) Clara R. Hill, born May 29, 1864. (VII.) Kate E. Hill, born Aug. 21, 1866. (VII.) Alice Hill, born June 19, 1869. (VII.) Bessie Hill, born Oct. 24, 1872. (VII.) Herbert Hill, born Apr. 16, 1874. (VII.) Harry M. Hill, born Apr. 30, 1878.

VI. Abbie C. Angeny, born in Bucks Co., Pa., June 26, 1842. Mrd. Thomas Shuler, May 24, 1866. Machinist at Grand Junction, Iowa. Methodists. Children: (VII.) Elmer E. Shuler, born Nov. 26, 1867. Druggist in Omaha, Nebr. (VII.) Charles C. Shuler, born July 2, 1869. Groceryman at Grand Junction, Iowa. (VII.) J. Eugene Shuler, born Mar. 28, 1871. Clerk in Chicago. (VII.) Martin A. Shuler, born May 27, 1872. Painter. (VII.) Bessie M. Shuler, born Oct. 3, 1875. (VII.) Willie T. Shuler, born Jan. 16, 1878. (VII.) Robert A. Shuler, born Aug. 14, 1880. (VII.) David O. Shuler, born Oct. 8, 1883; died Nov. 28, 1886. (VII.) Forest Shuler, born Feb. 25, 1886. (VII.) Ben Harrison Shuler, born July 18, 1888.

VI. Katharina Angeny, born Sept. 18, 1844. Mrd. William Shields, Dec. 26, 1867. Wheelwright at

MRS. M. BELLA BARANDON.
See Page ~~54~~
53

JOHN W. BARANDON.
See Page ~~54~~

MRS. FLORENCE E. THOMPSON.
See Page ~~54~~
53.

Kelly Point, Union Co., Pa. Mrs. Shields, Baptist. Children: (**VII.**) Esther Lucas Shields, born Dec. 26, 1868. Presbyterian. (**VII.**) Lillian Angeny Shields, born Dec. 12, 1870. Baptist. (**VII.**) Ellen Harris Shields, born Jan. 31, 1873. Presbyterian. (**VII.**) William Scott Shields, born Apr. 11, 1875. (**VII.**) Edgar Thomson Shields, born Sept. 24, 1877. (**VII.**) Charlotte Elliott Shields, born May 4, 1880. (**VII.**) James Leigh Shields, born Jan. 27, 1885.

VI. Minerva Angeny, born at New Columbia, Union Co., Pa., June 26, 1852. S.

V. Rachel Fretz, born in Hilltown Twp., Bucks Co., Pa., Jan. 1, 1814; died Dec. 11, 1858. At an early age she lost her mother, and the only remembrances she had of her fond parent were the recollections of early childhood. It is related that on the day of her mother's funeral she stood beside her casket, calling her mamma to listen to her childlike questions. She received such educational advantages as the public schools of that early period afforded. She read both German and English well, and in later years the reading of German poetry afforded her especial pleasure. She was a constant reader of the Bible, and delighted to call the attention of her own family to the beauty of its precepts. She was married to Henry S. Krout, of Bedminster, Nov. 2, 1835. He was born Apr. 10, 1810; died May 30, 1888. They lived near Line Lexington for eight years. Then moved to the homestead of the Krout family, on the Deep Run, where six more years of their busy lives were spent in tilling the soil that had been cultivated for more than a century by the paternal ancestral line. While residing here they determined to own a home of their own, and purchased and occupied the Kramer farm, on the east branch of Perkiomen Creek. While living here the family ties were broken. The mother having contracted consumption, was called to precede the rest of the family circle and join the great majority in the eternal world, beyond the shadowy vale. She was a truly pious mother, and her chief care was to bring up her children in the nurture and admonition of the Lord. Above all she loved her family, her church, her Savior and her God. They were members of the Mennonite church at Deep Run. Children: Jacob, Martin, Abraham, John.

VI. Jacob F. Krout, born in Bucks Co., Pa., Oct. 29, 1836. He always lived under the parental roof, and after the decease of his father, came into possession of the homestead in Bedminster, where he is the proprietor of the farm and the Bedminster Nursery of Fruit and Ornamental Trees. By industry and frugality he has acquired much success as a farmer and nurseryman. He is unmarried, and a member of the Mennonite church at Deep Run.

VI. Martin F. Krout, born in Bucks Co., Pa., Nov. 3, 1838; died Apr. 20, 1876. He lived with his parents and worked on the farm until he was twenty-one years of age. He then took a position in a mercantile house in Philadelphia, where, during his four years of service, he became thoroughly conversant with the business and enjoyed the confidence of all. In 1862 he went to River Styx, Ohio, and engaged in farming, in which business he continued for a time. He then purchased a farm near that town, and settled upon it, where he remained until his death. He married Rebecca, daughter of Dr. William Andrews, of River Styx, Ohio, Oct. 2, 1864. Children: (**VII.**) James H. Krout, born Apr. 30, 1866. (**VII.**) William Arthur Krout, born Apr. 20, 1871.

VI. Abraham F. K. Krout, born in Bucks Co., Pa., Feb. 2, 1843. He lived at home until he was nineteen years of age. He then entered the North Wales Institute to obtain a more thorough education than the public schools afforded. Here he remained about a year. In the fall of 1862 he commenced teaching, and until 1868 taught successively in the Deep Run, Rocky Ridge, Algard, Sellersville and Plumsteadville schools. In 1868 he took charge of the West Bethlehem schools, Lehigh Co., and in 1869 accepted the Principalship of Coplay schools, in the same County. Here he remained from Sept. '69 to June '83, when he asked to be relieved to become the accountant and cashier for Coplay Iron Co. This position he held from July '83 to Oct. '88. In the fall of 1889 he took charge of the Borough schools of Emlenton, Venango Co., Pa., where as Principal he re-organized the school system and introduced a number of important changes for the improvement of the public schools in that municipality. Having been offered still better inducements by the Board of Education of the Lehighton Borough Schools, he will in the future have the Principalship and supervision of the schools of that growing town on the Lehigh.

Through all these years of teaching there is one idea that has never been lost sight of, namely, that of self-improvement. The schooling at the academy was only the beginning of a life of study. In 1876 he appeared before the State Board of Examiners, passed the examination, and was granted a Normal Certificate as Teacher of Didactics. He found much pleasure in pursuing a course of general studies in science and language, and in 1877 Franklin and Marshall College recognized his industry as a student and conferred on him the honorary degree of A. M. He has been a member of Pa. State Teachers' Association since 1877, and an active member of the Touvey Botanical Club of Columbia College, New York City, since Oct. 1881.

Having the confidence of the people at his permanent home in Coplay, he was frequently called upon to fill positions of honor and responsibility. He was the first commissioned Justice of the Peace for this Borough, and has continuously held this office from 1869 to 1890. He was Secretary of Town Council for thirteen years, and a School Director while serving the Coplay Iron Co. The Judges the Courts frequently appointed him to serve on Road Juries and Commissions, and there are few Townships in Lehigh County in which he has not been called to execute these appointments. Being a member of the Ref. Ch. he took an active interest in the founding of Trinity Congregation, at Coplay, in 1872. He served as deacon and was for many years the Secretary of the Consistory. He was the Superintendent of the Sabbath-schools of this congregation for eighteen years. He married Mary C. Moyer, of Skippack, Montgomery

Co., Pa., Oct. 1, 1868. Children: **(VII.)** Mabel Olivia Krout, born Dec. 25, 1871. **(VII.)** Jacob Henry Krout, born May 16, 1874. **(VII.)** Clarence A. Krout, born May 3, 1883; died Sept. 12, 1883. **(VII.)** Helen Rachel Krout, born Nov. 5, 1885.

VI. John H. Krout, born in Bucks Co., Pa., June 26, 1845; died Mar. 22, 1888. He worked on the farm until of age. After having taught one term of school he went to Philadelphia and engaged as clerk, and afterwards followed the mercantile business in Montgomery and Lancaster Counties. He was a member of the Roman Catholic Church.

IV. Mary Kratz, born in Bucks Co., Mar. 7, 1770; died July 9, 1849. Mrd. John Fretz, son of Jacob and Catharine (Nash) Fretz, Apr. 15, 1792. He was born Aug. 28, 1763; died Feb. 24, 1842. Farmer in Hilltown Twp. Mennonites. Children: Magdalena, Rachel, Elizabeth, Abraham, Barbara, John, Mary, Susan, Lydia.

V. Magdalena Fretz, born in Bucks Co., Mar. 20, 1794; died —. Mrd. Christian S. Loux, Dec. 19, 1815. Farmer in Hilltown Twp. Mr. Loux, Ger. Ref.; Mrs. Loux, Mennonite. Children: Maria, Jeremiah, Eli, Jacob, John, Ephraim, Barbara.

VI. Maria Loux, born in Bucks Co., Nov. 2, 1816. Mrd. Henry Weisel, Nov. 18, 1847. He died June 3, 1885. Farmer. Ger. Ref. Children: John, Lydia, Oliver, Louis, Mary.

VII. John G. Weisel, born May 29, 1850; died Feb. 23, 1853.

VII. Lydia A. Weisel, born in Bucks Co., Pa., July 13, 1852; died Mar. 11, 1879. Mrd. Henry G. Funk, Dec. 17, 1874. Children: **(VIII.)** Lauretta M. Funk, born Nov. 1875. **(VIII.)** H. Norman Funk, born Mar. 4, 1879.

VII. II. Oliver Weisel, born in Bucks Co., Pa., Feb. 21, 1855. Mrd. Sallie Clymer, Oct. 26, 1878. Agent in the Freight Dept. of the Reading R. R. at 2d and Berks St. depot, Phila. Mem. of Ref. Ch. Children: **(VIII.)** Florence Weisel, born Jan. 31, 1880. **(VIII.)** Winfield Weisel, born July 31, 1881.

VII. M. Louis Weisel, born Nov. 26, 1857. Mrd. Mary A. Wilgus, Apr. 18, 1882. Mem. Ref. Ch. Children: (**VIII.**) Olive Weisel. (**VIII.**) Susan Weisel.

VII. Mary L. and M. Louis Weisel (twins), born Nov. 26, 1857; died Sept. 1858.

VI. Jeremiah Loux, born in 1848; died in infancy.

VI. Eli Loux, born in Bucks Co., Pa., Aug. 12, 1819. Mrd. Hannah Krupp, Nov. 5, 1843. She died June 12, 1848. Carpenter and builder. Mem. of the Dutch Ref. Ch. One child: (**VII.**) Elizabeth Loux, born Jan. 3, 1846; died Jan. 27, 1850. Eli mrd. second wife, Margaret Ambers, Oct. 8, 1853. She died Feb. 3, 1885. Children: William, Sarah, Charles, Mary, Emma, Anna.

VII. William H. Loux, born Apr. 1, 1855. Assistant Teller in National Bank of the Northern Liberties, Philadelphia, Pa. (S. 1889.)

VII. Sarah Virginia Loux, born Oct. 26, 1856.

VII. Charles Wesley Loux, born Jan. 26, 1859. Carpenter in Philadelphia, Pa. (S. 1889.)

VII. Mary Ellen Loux, born Jan. 5, 1860. Mrd. George D. Bradley, Sept. 12, 1889. Dentist.

VII. Emma Jane Loux, born Oct. 3, 1864; died Nov. 17, 1864.

VII. Anna Margaret Loux, born Mar. 13, 1867.

VI. Rev. Jacob Loux, born Oct. 5, 1822. Mrd. Hannah Rittenhouse, Nov. 21, 1847. Retired farmer and minister. He was ordained to the ministry May 21, 1867, at the Plain's meeting-house in Hatfield Twp., one of the first Mennonite churches in Montgomery Co., and where he still preaches. Children: Samuel, Mary, Jacob, Hiram, Abraham.

VII. Samuel R. Loux, born Jan. 24, 1849, in Montg. Co., Pa. Mrd. Ellen M. Benjamin, in St. Paul, Minn., May 1882. Book keeper. Children: (**VIII.**) Llewellyn R. Loux, born Dec. 4, 1884; died same day. (**VIII.**) Ina Jeanette Loux, born Dec. 23, 1887.

VII. Mary Ellen Loux, born Aug. 7, 1852, in Montg. Co.; died Mar. 8, 1882. Mrd. Franklin Metz (dec'd), Jan. 12, 1878. Children: (**VIII.**) Emma L. Metz, born July 10, 1879. (**VIII.**) Hiram L. Metz, born Nov. 27, 1880.

142

VII. Jacob R. Loux, born in Bucks Co., Pa., July 11, 1856. Mrd. Henrietta D., daughter of Abraham and Elizabeth Clemmer, Jan. 4, 1879. Farmer. Mennonites. Children: (**VIII.**) Lizzie C. Loux, born Jan. 1, 1782. (**VIII.**) Abraham C. Loux, born Feb. 17, 1888.

VII. Hiram R. Loux, M. D., born in Bucks Co., July 16, 1859. Mrd. Lillian Lake, Sept. 13, 1885. Physician at Souderton, Pa. No issue.

VII. Abraham R. Loux, born in Hatfield Twp., July 16, 1870. Painter. (S. 1889.)

VI. John F. Loux, born Oct. 1, 1824; died at 17 yr.

VI. Ephraim Loux, born in Bucks Co., Pa., Oct. 22, 1826. Mrd. Susannah H. Oberholtzer, Dec. 8, 1850. Carpenter. Lutherans. Children: Ephraim, Elizabeth, Comly, Frank, Anna, Laura, Susie, Ida.

VII. Ephraim Loux, born Jan. 8, 1852; died same day.

VII. Elizabeth A. Loux, born Aug. 13, 1853.

VII. Comly Loux, born May 9, 1855; died Feb. 24, 1875.

VII. W. Frank Loux, born June 25, 1857. Mrd. Marcella Egee, Oct. 18, 1882. Merchant. Children: (**VIII.**) Edna Loux, still-born Mar. 19, 1884. (**VII..**) Ada Marcella Loux, born Nov. 19, 1885. (**VIII.**) Edith Loux, born Aug. 6, 1888.

VII. Anna M. Loux, born in Bucks Co., Pa., Mar. 26, 1859. Mrd. John B. S. Egee, M. D., Sept. 15, 1880. Practicing physician in Philadelphia, Pa. Lutherans. Children: (**VIII.**) Edgar G. Egee, born July 6, 1881. (**VIII.**) Marcella Egee, born Mar. 20, 1883. (**VIII.**) Anna M. Egee, born Mar. 19, 1885; died next day. (**VIII.**) George Benton Egee, born May 6, 1888.

VII. Laura N. Loux, born Feb. 7, 1866; died Aug. 5, 1866.

VII. Susie N. Loux, born Sept. 14, 1867.

VII. Ida N. Loux, born Feb. 26, 1872.

VI. Barbara Loux, born in Bucks Co., Pa., Oct. 24, 1828. Mrd. Joseph Davis, Dec. 12, 1850. Bricklayer and farmer. Mem. Ref. Ch. Children: Eliam, Elmira.

VII. Eliam L. Davis, born—. Farmer in Minnesota. Baptist. (S. 1889.)

VII. Elmira Davis, born—. Mrd. Reuben D. Rosenberger, Jan. 1, 1876. Farmer in Woodson Co., Kan. Mrs. Rosenberger, Baptist. Children: (**VIII.**) Melvin and (**VIII.**) Viola Vincent Rosenberger, twins. (**VIII.**) Lillian Rosenberger (**VIII.**) George Rosenberger.

V. Rachel Fretz, born in Bucks Co., Pa., Apr. 22, 1796; died July 7, 1877. Mrd. Isaac Delp, Feb. 28, 1829. Farmer. Mrs. Delp was a Mennonite. One child: Ephraim.

VI. Ephraim Delp, born Jan. 7, 1834. Mrd. Angelina W. Baker, Jan. 15, 1859. Farmer. Children: Henry, Elizabeth, Jacob, William, Emma, Amanda, Charles, Ada, Angelina, Ephraim.

VII. Henry B. Delp, born Aug. 31, 1860. Mrd. Annie H. Bower, Dec. 6, 1884. Teacher in the public schools. Children: (**VIII.**) Emma B. Delp, born Jan. 31, 1886. (**VIII.**) Alvin B. Delp, born Aug. 1, 1888.

VII. Elizabeth Delp, born Sept. 22, 1862; died Aug. 30, 1863.

VII. Jacob B. Delp, born Aug. 26, 1864. Mrd. Sallie D. Moyer, Mar. 2, 1889. Carpenter.

VII. William B. Delp, born Sept. 9, 1866; died Oct. 17, 1867.

VII. Emma B. Delp, born Jan. 23, 1868; died Aug. 31, 1869.

VII. Amanda B. Delp, born May 10, 1869.

VII. Charles B. Delp, born Feb. 5, 1872.

VII. Ada B. Delp, born Dec. 7, 1874.

VII. Angelina B. Delp, born June 7, 1876.

VII. Ephraim B. Delp, Jr., born May 9, 1878.

V. Elizabeth Fretz, born in Bucks Co., Pa., July 15, 1798; died Mar. 26, 1880. Mrd. Abraham Hiestand, Apr. 20, 1820. He died Jan. 8, 1862. Farmer. Mennonites. Children: Catharine, Mary, Susanna, Herman, Elizabeth.

VI. Catharine Hiestand, born in Bucks Co., Pa., Nov. 25, 1822; died May 5, 1868. Mrd. Henry Detweiler, Oct. 1, 1843. Blacksmith. Mennonites. Children: Elizabeth, Catharine.

VII. Elizabeth Detweiler, born in Bucks Co., Pa., Nov. 20, 1845. Mrd. Tobias Lapp, Apr. 21, 1866;

died . Farmer. Mennonites. Children: Ellen, William, Martha, A—.

VIII. Ellen Lapp, born—. Mrd. Harry Rosenberger,—. Farmer. Mennonites.

VII. Catharine Detweiler, born Sept. 19, 1849. Mrd. Allen Sampey, May 3, 1879. Farmer. Mennonites. One child: (VIII.) Harvey Sampey.

VI. Mary Hiestand, born Mar. 10, 1824; died Sept. 25, 1824.

VI. Susanna Hiestand, born in Bucks Co., Apr. 25, 1826; died Jan. 6, 1882. Mrd. Jesse Kratz. (See Index of References No. 23.)

VI. Herman Hiestand, born Mar. 12, 1828; died May 22, 1838.

VI. Elizabeth Hiestand, born Apr. 14, 1830. Mrd. John S. Kratz. (See Index of References No. 24.)

V. Abraham Fretz, born in Bucks Co., Pa., June 23, 1800; died June 16, 1872. Mrd. Sarah Haldeman, Nov. 30, 1826. In 1849 they moved to Medina Co., Ohio, where he died. Farmer. Mennonites. Children: Mary, Eli, Eliza, Gideon, Sarah, Abraham.

VI. Mary Ann Fretz, born in Bucks Co., Pa., Mar. 26, 1827. Mrd. Abraham Rickert, Sept. 19, 1847. P. O., River Styx, Ohio. Farmer. Mennonites. Children: Allen, Catharine, Sarah, Henry, Levi, David, Mary, Abraham, Barbara, Amelia.

VII. Allen Rickert, born Dec. 21, 1848. Farmer in Columbiana Co., Ohio. Mrd. Sarah Lehman, Jan. 4, 1873. Mennonites. Children: (VIII.) Edwin Rickert, born Nov. 12, 1874. (VIII.) Lizzie Rickert, born Jan. 26, 1877. (VIII.) Edith Rickert, born Aug. 19, 1879. (VIII.) Harry Rickert, born Sept. 23, 1881. (VIII.) Margaret Rickert, born Mar. 11, 1884. (VIII.) Isaiah Allen Rickert, born Oct. 17, 1889.

VII. Catharine Rickert, born in Medina Co., Ohio, May 7, 1850.

VII. Sarah Rickert, born Nov. 24, 1851.

VII. Henry F. Rickert, born Sept. 10, 1853. Mrd. Sarah Markley, Nov. 13, 1875. Farmer in Medina Co., Ohio. Children: (VIII.) Uriah Rickert, born Oct. 22, 1877. (VIII.) Rilla Rickert, born Sept. 7, 1879.

(**VIII.**) Clarence B. Rickert, born July 28, 1884. (**VIII.**) Mary A. Rickert, born Aug. 16, 1888.

VII. Levi F. Rickert, born in Medina Co., O., May 29, 1856. Mrd. Alice C. Curtis, Oct. 2, 1886. Farmer in Medina Co., O. One child: (**VIII.**) Mabel Rickert, born Mar. 20, 1888.

VII. David Rickert, born in Medina Co., Ohio, Aug. 19, 1858. Mrd. Eva M. Heath, Jan. 13, 1883. Mr. Rickert was a carpenter and was considered one of the best mechanics in Medina Co. While engaged building a new barn for John Morrell, near Weymouth, Ohio, June 12, 1891, he fell from the end beam backwards into the basement, striking his head on the corner of a scantling, fracturing his skull, from which injuries he died next morning. Children: (**VIII.**) Dick Rickert, born Apr. 13, 1885. (**VIII.**) Nellie A. Rickert, born Sept.—, 1890.

VII. Mary Rickert, born Jan. 8, 1861. Mrd. David Gable, Dec. 21, 1882. Reside in Cleveland, O. One child: (**VIII.**) Charles Gable, born Sept. 18, 1887.

VII. Abraham Rickert, born Apr. 3, 1863.

VII. Barbara Rickert, born Apr. 3, 1870. Mrd. A. H. Rohrer, May 20, 1891. Farmer.

VII. Amelia Rickert, born Apr. 8, 1872.

VI. Eli H. Fretz, born in Bucks Co., P., Aug. 3, 1829; died Jan. 23, 1881. Mrd. Esther Koppes, Sept. 28, 1851. He was a sawyer for fifteen years, then carpenter, and lastly farmer. Near the close of his life he moved with his family from Ohio to Kansas, and died there. Mennonites. Children: Nelson, Rebecca, Nathaniel, Abraham, Jacob, Jeremiah, John, Sarah, David, Isaac.

VII. Nelson K. Fretz, born Aug. 16, 1852; died Oct. 21, 1853.

VII. Rebecca Fretz, born Mar. 20, 1854; died Oct. 1, 1863.

VII. Nathaniel K. Fretz, born in Medina Co., Ohio, May 18, 1856. Mrd. Nancy Krieble, Dec. 29, 1886. Carpenter and builder; also dealer in house plants and cut flowers at Pratt, Kan. Children: (**VIII.**) Earl H. Fretz, born Dec. 5, 1887; died Apr. 11, 1890. (**VIII.**)

Daisy Fretz, born Aug. 31, 1889. (**VIII.**) Glen E. Fretz, born Nov. 26, 1890.

VII. Abraham K. Fretz, born in Medina Co., Ohio, Nov. 19, 1858. Sadler. S.

VII. Jacob K. Fretz, born July 20, 1861; died Mar. 28, 1863.

VII. Jeremiah K. Fretz, born in Medina Co., Ohio, Jan. 1, 1864. Mrd. Mary, daughter of Noah and Mary M. Basenger, Apr. 11, 1885. Carpenter at Newton, Kan. Children: (**VIII.**) Warren Elmer Fretz, born July 8, 1886. (**VIII.**) Nettie Estella Fretz, born July 13, 1887. (**VIII.**) Homer Earl Fretz, born Mar. 5, 1890.

VII. John K. Fretz, born in Medina Co., Ohio, Mar. 12, 1867. Farmer. S.

VII. Sarah K. Fretz, born in Medina Co., Ohio, July 5, 1868. Mrd. Henry H. Rodgers, Aug. 5, 1885. Reside in Harvey Co., Kan. Children: (**VIII.**) Cora E. Rodgers, born Sept. 13, 1886. (**VIII.**) Charles S. Rodgers, born Jan. 25, 1888. (**VIII.**) John Samuel Rodgers, born Dec. 21, 1889.

VII. David K. Fretz, born July 4, 1871.

VII. Isaac K. Fretz, born April 28, 1876.

VI. Eliza Fretz, born in Bucks Co., Pa., July 3, 1833. Mrd. John Rickert, Nov. 9, 1851. Farmer in Medina Co., Ohio. Children: Sarah, Valentine, Mary, Abraham, Sarah, John, Ella, Ida.

VII. Sarah Rickert, born June 30, 1853; died July 2, 1853.

VII. Valentine Rickert, born in Medina Co., Ohio, Sept. 17, 1854. Mrd. Lewie Henry, Dec. 12, 1879. She died—. Farmer in Medina Co., Ohio. Children: (**VIII.**) James Rickert, born June 15, 1880. (**VIII.**) Clare Rickert, born May 3, 1882; died Mar. 1883. (**VIII.**) Hiram Carl Rickert, born November 26, 1883. (**VIII.**) Lewie Belle Rickert, born Oct. 19, 1886; died Feb. 24, 1887. Valentine mrd. second wife, Minnie Thompson, Apr. 8, 1891.

VII. Mary Susan Rickert, born in Medina Co., Ohio, Oct. 13, 1857. Mrd. Reuben Yoder, Feb. 25, 1882. Farmer in Whiteside Co., Ill. One child: (**VIII.**) Id. Yoder, born Mar. 2, 1884.

VII. Abraham Rickert, born Oct. 18, 1859. Mrd. Addie Reese, Sept. 26, 1889.

VII. Sarah F. Rickert, born Apr. 18, 1862.

VII. John Rickert, born May 10, 1864; died July 2, 1888.

VII. Ella K. Rickert born Sept. 30, 1867.

VII. Ida Eliza Rickert, born Mar. 11, 1871.

VI. Gideon H. Fretz, born in Bucks Co., Pa., Dec. 29, 1836. Mrd. Amanda Weimer, of Cressonia, Pa., Apr. 20, 1865. She died Aug. 4, 1888. Carpenter and builder in Philadelphia. Methodists. Children: (**VII.**) Sallie E. Fretz, born July 8, 1866. (**VII.**) William F. Fretz, born Aug. 4, 1867. (**VII.**) Milton W. Fretz, born Nov. 19, 1869. (**VII.**) Harry A. Fretz, born Aug. 27, 1871.

VI. Sarah C. Fretz, born in Bucks Co., Pa., July 2, 1847. Mrd. Cosam H. Kindig, Dec. 14, 1866. Carpenter and joiner at Union City, Mich. Ger. Ref. Children: Ella, Ephraim, Mary, Rodney, Eddie, Gertie.

VII. Ella Kindig, born Aug. 8, 1866; died Oct. 2, 1888. Mrd. Charles B. Howe, Aug. 13, 1883. Children: (**VIII.**) Roy Howe, born July 4, 1884; died Oct. 10, 1884. (**VIII.**) D. O. Howe, born June 3, 1885.

VII. Ephraim F. Kindig, born Sept. 13, 1868.

VII. Mary Kindig, born Oct. 23, 1870. Mrd. Ralph Woodruff, May 29, 1888. He was born in Calhoun, Co., Mich. P. O., Pine Creek, Mich. Farmer. One child: (**VIII.**) —— Woodruff, born July 21, 1891.

VII. Rodney F. Kindig, born July 22, 1872.

VII. Eddie F. Kindig, born July 22, 1875.

VII. Gertie Kindig, born Feb. 14, 1877.

VI. Abraham Fretz, born Mar. 23, 1852; died Sept. 18, 1856.

V. Barbara Fretz, born Sept. 1, 1802; died——. Mrd. Abraham K. Moyer, Nov. 13, 1842, his second wife. No issue.

VI. John Fretz, born in Bucks Co., Pa., May 9, 1804. Mrd. Sarah Delp, May 14, 1829. She died Oct. 26, 1829. He mrd. second wife Elizabeth Kline, July 10, 1830. She was born June 10, 1811. Ev. Assoc.

Children: Ephraim, Mary, Sarah, Susanna, William, Elizabeth, John, Emeline, Amanda, Jeremiah.

VI. Ephraim H. Fretz, born in Bucks Co., Pa., Oct. 16, 1832. Mrd. Jane E. Ferry, Jan. 8, 1857. Farmer. Ev. Assoc. Children: Dewitt, John, Frank, Isaac, Kate.

VII. R. DeWitt Clinton Fretz, born Oct. 30, 1857; died Oct. 10, 1858.

VII. John Wesley Fretz, born in Bucks Co., Pa., Aug. 12, 1859. Mrd. Clara M. Stover, Mar. 31, 1886. Carpenter in Philadelphia, Pa. Baptist. One child: **(VIII.)** Walter S. Fretz, born Sept. 14, 1888.

VII. Frank Ellsworth Fretz, born Nov. 17, 1861. Mrd. Laura M. Good, Mar. 31, 1888. Farmer in Bucks Co., Pa. Baptist.

VII. Isaac Newton Fretz, born Mar. 15, 1864. Mrd. Carrie Jones, Sept. 12, 1888. Carpenter in Philadelphia. Presbyterian.

VII. Kate C. Fretz, born Sept. 11, 1866. Baptist church. Unmrd. 1889.

VI. Mary Fretz, born in Bucks Co., Pa., Aug. 29, 1834. Mrd. George Stahr, Sept. 15, 1859. He was born Nov. 28, 1824. Farmer in Bucks Co., Pa. Mem. Ev. Assoc. Ch. Children: Ella, Sallie, John, Harvey.

VII. Ella Elizabeth Stahr, born July 15, 1860; died Feb. 5, 1864.

VII. Sallie Stahr, born July 3, 1863; died Dec. 3, 1885. Mrd. Lewis F. Fretz. (See Index of References No. 25.)

VII. John Clinton Stahr, born Aug. 20, 1867.

VII. Harvey S. Stahr, born Sept. 2, 1874.

VI. Sarah Ann Fretz, born in Bucks Co., Nov. 9, 1836. Mrd. Gilbert Sellers, Dec. 23, 1857. Corporal in Co. A. 104 Reg't. Pa., Vol. Died at Rose Cottage Hospital, Virginia. Ger. Reformed. One son: J. Clinton. Sarah mrd. second husband Robert Reeder, Mar. 19, 1874. Grocer in Phila. Ger. Reformed. Children: Clara, Florence.

VII. J. Clinton Sellers, born in Bucks Co., Jan 25, 1861. He attended the schools of Hilltown Twp., and when about fifteen years of age he attended the high school at Quakertown, and subsequently the high school at Doylestown. Through the kindly assistance of his guardian Jonas D. Moyer, of Dublin, Pa., the subject of this sketch was enabled to attend the State Normal school at Millersville, beginning with the winter session of '78 and '79, and the spring term of '79 and '80. Beginning with the winter term of '79 he taught school for three successive winters in Hilltown Twp. In June of 1882 he was offered and accepted a position in the Car Record Department of the Phila. and Reading R. R., Company in Philadelphia. He remained here until Nov. 3, 1885. During these three years he was the accredited Philadelphia correspondent of the Norristown (Pa.) "Daily and Weekly Times." The work being done principally at night, or during spare hours of the day. This connection eventually resulted in the offer of a position on the staff of the Times at Noristown. On Nov. 3d, '85, he resigned his position with the R. R. Co., and went to Norristown, where he was installed in the position of associate editor of the "Daily and Weekly Times." This position he occupied for something over a year, and on the retirement of the then editor, Mr. Sellers was advanced to managing editor. Mr. S. also represents several metropolitan newspapers: among them the Philadelphia Press, the New York World, and other journals of less importance. He was instrumental in bringing about the organization of the Norristown Board of Trade, and has been its secretary since its organization in 1887.

VII. Clara Reeder, born Apr. 1. 1876.

VII. Florence Reeder, born June 1, 1878.

VI. Susan F. Fretz, born in Bucks Co., Pa., Mar. 13. 1839. Married Jonas Shelly, March 30. 1861. Farmer in Jefferson Co., Neb. Methodists. Children: Charles. John, Elmer, Amanda. Henry, Milton, Anna.

VII. Charles Dayton Shelly, born Mar. 24, 1862; died Feb. 1. 1864.

VII. John Shelly, born Dec. 24, 1863; died Feb. 18, 1864.

VII. Elmer E. Shelly, born Feb. 9, 1865; died July 18. 1865.

VII. Amanda Elizabeth Shelly, born in Bucks Co., Pa., Mar. 10, 1868. Mrd. Herman Zeigenhain, in 1885 in Jefferson Co., Neb. Children: **(VIII.)** William Henry Zeigenhain, born Jan. 6, 1887. **(VIII.)** Albert Zeigenhain, born Apr. 8, 1889.

VII. Henry Shelly, born Apr. 26, 1874.

VII. Milton Shelly, born Jan. 20, 1876.

VII. Anna Mary Shelly, born Apr. 13, 1879; died Aug. 18, 1880.

VI. William K. Fretz, born in Bucks Co., Pa., Jan. 15, 1841. Mrd. Ruth Ann Burns, in Denver City, Col., June 7, 1874. She was born in Gentry Co., Mo., Oct. 3, 1852. Mr. Fretz went West in 1866— to Nebraska in 1880, and in 1887 he settled on a homestead in Brewster, Thomas Co., Neb. Painter. Methodist No issue.

VI. Elizabeth Fretz, born in Bucks Co., Pa., July 14, 1843; died Feb. 2, 1866. Unmarried

VI. John S. Fretz, born in Bucks Co., Pa., Oct. 30, 1845. Mrd. Emma Koch, of Bridgetown, Pa., Feb. 24, 1877. She was born in Lehigh Co., Pa., Dec. 8, 1857. Laborer. Presbyterians. One child: **(VII.)** Dora Fretz, born Jan. 6, 1886.

VI. Emeline Fretz, born May 10, 1848. Single.

VI. Amanda Louisa Fretz, born May 8, 1852; died Feb. 19, 1864.

VI. Jeremiah Fretz, born Nov. 30, 1855; died Dec. 11, 1855.

V. Mary Fretz, born Apr. 21, 1807, in Bucks Co., Pa., died Mar. 11, 1865. Mrd. Samuel Funk, Apr. 22, 1829. He was born July 22, 1805; died Mar. 1878. Mennonites. Children: John, Mary, Ann, Abraham, Samuel, Milton.

VI. John Funk Sr., born Jan. 19, 1830. Mrd. Elizabeth Detterer, in 1856. She was born Nov. 12, 1826. In early life followed teaching, and later laborer. Mennonite. Children: W. W., Mary, J. C. M.

VII. W. W. Funk, born July 12, 1860; died at birth.

VII. Mary Amanda Funk, born Feb. 12, 1862. Mrd. F. L. Strasser (deceased), Oct. 6, 1883.

VII. J. C. M. Funk, born Nov. 8, 1866; died Aug. 12, 1884.

VI. Mary Funk. born Nov. 27, 1832. Mrd. Henry Gross, Dec. 2, 1854. Harness-maker at Doylestown, Pa. Presbyterians. Children: Milton, Samuel H. Ida, Anna, A. Lincoln, Emma, Ella, J. Asher.

VII. Milton H. Gross, born,—; died Mar. 16, 1859.

VII. Samuel H. Gross, born,—; died Sept. 4, 1877.

VII. M. Ida Gross, born,—.

VII. Anna M. Gross, born,—. Mrd. Isaiah H. Godshall, Jan. 13, 1885. Operator in a creamery. Mrs. Godshall Presbyterian.

VII. A. Lincoln Gross, born, —; died Mar. 25, 1863.

VII. Emma L. Gross, born Mar. 5, 1864. Mrd. Jacob Bissey, Mar. 5, 1887. Farmer. Presbyterians. No children.

VII. Ella E. Gross, born —.

VII. J. Asher Gross, born—.

VI. Anna Elizabeth Funk, born June 15, 1835. Mrd. Amandus B. F. Cope, in 1857. Farmer. Children: Mary, Benjamin, Samuel, Amandus, Edwardene, Clinton, James, John, Daniel.

VII. Mary Jane Cope, born Nov. 29, 1857. Mrd. Samuel Eckstine, Apr. 29, 1879. Superintendent of a stock farm. One child: **(VIII.)** Samuel Eckstine, Jr., born Jan. 10, 1883.

VII. Benjamin Franklin Cope, born Aug. 14, 1859. Mrd. Rose Ella Barton, Feb. 22, 1883. Foreman in a creamery. Children: **(VIII.)** Linford W. Cope, born Aug. 19, 1884; died Dec. 5, 1884. **(VIII.)** Edmund B. Cope, born June 15, 1886.

VII. Samuel Ellsworth Cope, born Mar. 29, 1861. Mrd. Lizzie Wood, Jan. 12, 1889.

VII. Amandus Cope, born Jan. 3, 1863; died Jan. 6, 1863.

VII. Edwardene M. Cope, born Dec. 28, 1864. Mrd. Harry L. Riley, Nov. 14, 1881. Baggage-master in the Reading Depot at Atlantic City, N. J. Children: **(VIII.)** Florence Virginia Riley, born Apr. 20, 1883. **(VIII.)** Stella Cushman Riley, born Mar. 6, 1885.

VII. Clinton B. Cope, born May 3, 1867. Farmer.

VII. James R. Cope, born Sept. 18, 1869. Clerk.

VII. John A. Cope, born May 12, 1872. Clerk.

VII. Daniel Cope, born Oct. 30, 1874.

VI. Abraham Funk, born June 27, 1838. Mrd. Martha Kotfel, Nov. 25, 1884. Slate-roofer. Children: **(VII.)** Ida Jane Funk, born Apr. 1, 1886. **(VII.)** Tobias K. Funk, born May 23, 1887. **(VII.)** Abraham Fretz Funk, born June 10, 1888.

VI. Samuel Funk, born Aug. 2, 1842; died Nov. 18, 1845.

VI. Milton Funk, born July 29, 1846; died Feb. 7, 1864.

V. Susanna Fretz, born Nov. 18, 1810; died Dec. 18, 1840. Mrd. Abraham K. Moyer, Jan. 26, 1883. Two children: **(VI.)** John H. Moyer, born Dec. 26, 1833; died July 18, 1858. School teacher. Unmrd. **(VI.)** Mary Ann Moyer, born Mar. 17, 1837; died Apr. 16, 1883. Unmarried.

V. Lydia Fretz, born Nov. 14, 1813; died Dec. 28, 1871. Mrd. Jonas Nace, Dec. 21, 1834. Tailor. Mennites. Children: Francis, Sarah, Levi.

VI. Francis Nace, born about 1839. Mrd. Mary Fretz (daughter of the late Henry Fretz of Amboy, N. J.), Oct. 26, 1861. Children: **(VII.)** Milton Harvey Nace, born Aug. 27, 1862. **(VII.** Jonas Henry Nace, born Feb. 29, 1864; died Nov. 9, 1867. **(VII.)** Emma J. Nace, born Nov. 9, 1866. **(VII.)** Matilda Nace, born October 12, 1871; died same day. **(VII.)** Leidy Nace, born July, 25, 1874. **(VII.)** Erwin Nace, born Nov. 19, 1877.

VI. Sarah Ann Nace, born Jan. 14, 1841; died Oct. 19, 1883. Mrd. Isaac B. Kratz. (See Index of References No. 34.)

VI. Levi F. Nace, born Apr. 8, 1848. Mrd. Lydia B. Nace, Jan. 1, 1872. Printer in Philadelphia, Pa. Lutherans. Children: **(VII.)** Preston Nace, born Dec. 13, 1877. **(VII.)** Robert Nace, born Nov. 11, 1886; did Mar. 24, 1887.

IV. Valentine Kratz*, born Apr. 22, 1773; died Sept. 18, 1830, aged 57 yr., 4 m. 26 d. Mrd. Anna Overholt.—. Farmer in New Britain Twp. Mennonites at Blooming Glen. Children: Simeon, Elizabeth, Jacob, Abraham, Barbara, Mary.

---

* Died while on a visit to his brother-in-law Isaac Fretz.

(See Page 54)

V. Simeon Kratz, born Feb. 22, 1807; died Mar. 5, 1865. Mrd. Catharine Moyer, Nov. 23, 1834. She was born Dec. 3, 1813. Farmer. Old Mennonites. Children: Enos, William, Mary, Barbara, Ephraim, Mahlon, Catharine, Aaron, Emma.

VI. Enos M. Kratz, born in 1836; died Apr. 1890. Mrd. Hannah, daughter of Rev. Henry B. Moyer of Blooming Glen, in 1865. Farmer. Mennonites. Children: Henry, Harvey, Mary, Katie, Frank, Lizzie, Daniel, Oliver, Emma.

VII. Henry Kratz, born in 1866. Mrd. Emma Treffinger, Oct. 3, 1891. Res. Philadelphia, Pa.

VII. Harvey Kratz, born in 1869. S.

VII. Mary Kratz, born in 1874.

VII. Katie Kratz (twin to Mary), born in 1874; died 1883.

VII. Frank Kratz, born in 1877.

VII. Lizzie Kratz, born in 1879.

VII. Daniel Kratz, born in 1882.

VII. Oliver Kratz, born in 1884.

VII. Emma Kratz, born in 1887.

VI. William M. Kratz, born Nov. 24, 1837. Mrd. Mary E. Shaddinger, of Plumstead, Nov. 19, 1864. She died Apr. 25, 1882. No issue. William, mrd. for his second wife, Elizabeth Hunsberger, Dec. 26, 1885. Farmer. P. O. Dublin, Pa. Mennonites. Children: (**VII.**) Ida May Kratz, born October 12, 1886. (**VII.**) Laura Kratz, born July 14, 1889. (**VII.**) Katie Kratz, born Feb. 1891.

VI. Mary Ann Kratz, born Feb. 8, 1842. Mrd. Joseph G. Moyer, of Hilltown Twp., Dec. 23, 1862. Wholesale and retail lumber and coal merchant at Perkasie, Pa. Ger. Ref. Children: Madora, Irwin, Elmer, Mary, Dyre, Gertie.

VII. S. Madora Moyer, born Apr. 3, 1864. Mrd. B. Frank Hartzell, Feb. 23, 1883. Merchant miller. Ger. Ref. Children: (**VIII.**) Russell M. Hartzell, born Mar. 11, 1885. (**VIII.**) Percy M. Hartzell, born Mar. 15, 1887.

VII. H. Irvin Moyer, born Aug. 2, 1865. Mrd. Eliza, daughter of David K. Moyer, of Hilltown, Sept. 29, 1887. Clerk. Ger. Ref.

VII. Elmer K. Moyer, born July 22, 1867. Mrd.
Laura, daughter of Tilghman Wickert, of Milford
Square. Telegraph operator at Perkasie. Ger. Ref.

VII. Mary Delilah Moyer, born Nov. 2, 1872. Ger.
Ref.

VII. J. Dyre Moyer, born Sept. 14, 1875.

VII. Gertie K. Moyer, born Mar. 4, 1882.

VI. Barbara Kratz, born in Bucks Co., Oct. 4, 1843.
Mrd. Christian D. Moyer,—. He was born Mar. 13,
1839. Farmer. Mennonites. Children: Edwin, Anna,
Emma, Catharine, Abraham, Alice.

VII. Edwin K. Moyer, born May 16, 1863. Mrd.
Anna S. Moyer, of Franconia, Montg. Co., Nov. 6,
1886. Farmer. Children: (**VIII.**) Lizzie Moyer, born
May 10, 1888. (**VIII.**) Miriam Moyer, born Feb. 1891.

VII. Anna K. Moyer, born Mar. 4, 1865.

VII. Emma K. Moyer, born Sept. 15, 1867. Mrd.
Abraham H. Kratz, Sept. 1890. Farmer.

VII. Catharine K. Moyer, born Mar. 19, 1869. Mrd.
Jonas C. Cressman, Dec. 24, 1887. Harness maker.
One child: (**VIII.**) Ida Bedella Cressman, born Apr.
1891.

VII. Abraham K. Moyer, born Jan. 1878.

VII. Alice K. Moyer, born Jan. 3, 1880.

VI. Ephraim M. Kratz, born Mar. 26, 1845. Mrd.
Catharine Clymer, daughter of Henry Clymer, of
Warrington, Bucks Co., Pa.,—. School-teacher.
Methodists. Children: (**VII.**) Norman C. Kratz, born
Mar. 9, 1874. (**VII.**) Mary Kratz, born Oct. 16, 1875.
(**VII.**) Estella Kratz, born Feb. 23, 1877. (**VII.**) Eu-
gene Kratz, born Dec. 21, 1878. (**VII.**) Mabel Kratz,
born May 8, 1882. (**VII.**) Ephraim LeRoy Kratz, born
May 12, 1888.

VI. Mahlon Kratz, born Feb. 22, 1847. Mrd. Mary
Ella Cohill, Apr. 28, 1886. Dispensing chemist at
Manheim St. and Germantown Ave., Phila., Pa. One
child: (**VII.**) Raymond Cohill Kratz, born Oct. 12,
1887.

VI. Catharine Kratz, born Nov. 15, 1848. Mrd.
Isaac George, Nov. 16, 1867. Carpenter. Mennonites. Children: Wilson K., Emma Jennette.

VII. Wilson K. George, born Nov. 13, 1868. Mrd. Rosa Glassmyer, Oct. 1890. Manufacturer of clothing. Wife, Lutheran. One child: (**VIII.**) Robert Clark George, born – .

VII. Emma Jennette George, born Nov. 30, 1876.

VI. Aaron M. Kratz, born Nov. 13, 1855. Mrd. Mary Clymer, Jan. 8, 1878. Baker. Ger. Ref. One child: (**VII.**) A. Wesley Kratz, born May 16, 1880.

VI. Emeline Kratz, born Feb. 2, 1859. Mrd. Nero Button, Nov. 25, 1875. P. O., Blooming Glen, Pa. Artesian well driller and general agent for wind mills and force pumps. Ger. Ref. No issue.

V. Elizabeth Kratz, born May 4, 1809; died June 26, 1836. Unmrd.

V. Jacob Kratz, born in Bucks Co., Pa., June 3, 1814. Mrd. Mary Myers, Nov. 28, 1838. She was born Mar. 7, 1818. Farmer. Members of the Mennonite church, Blooming Glen. Children: Salome, Henry, Annie, Isaiah.

VI. Salome Kratz, born in Bucks Co., Pa., Aug. 30, 1839. Mrd. John F. Funk, Jan. 19, 1864. (See Index of References No. 26.)

VI. Henry M. Kratz, born in Bucks Co., Pa., July 23, 1845. Mrd. Sophia L. Shaddinger, Jan. 4, 1868. She was born Apr. 12, 1844. Farmer. Member Mennonite church of Blooming Glen. One child: (**VII.**) Mary Emma Kratz, born Sept. 23, 1868.

VI. Anna Kratz, born in Bucks Co., Pa., July 22, 1850. S.

VI. Isaiah Kratz, born May 7, 1856; died Aug. 31, 1856.

V. Abraham Kratz, born Mar. 25, 1817; died May 9, 1889. Mrd. Sarah Swartley, Nov. 25, 1839 (prob). Farmer. Mennonites. Children: John, William, Mary, Henry, Levi, Abraham, Oliver, Jacob.

VI. John S. Kratz, born Feb. 1, 1841. Mrd. Angelina R. Godshalk, Nov. 18, 1869. P. O., Chalfont, Pa. Farmer. Mennonites. Children: (**VII.**) Abraham Kratz, born Dec. 24, 1870; died Aug. 31, 1871. (**VII.**) Jennetta Kratz, born Apr. 6, 1872. (**VII.**) Harvey Kratz, born Mar. 29, 1874. (**VII.**) William Kratz, born Oct. 1, 1875. (**VII.**) Mary A. Kratz, born Mar.

29, 1877. **(VII.)** Sarah Emma Kratz, born Sept. 16, 1879. **(VII.)** Ella Kratz, born Oct. 16, 1880. **(VII.)** Howard Kratz, born Nov. 22, 1883. **(VII.)** Ida Kratz, born Sept. 28, 1885; died Feb. 28, 1887. **(VII.)** Franklin Kratz, born Apr. 9, 1889.

VI. William S. Kratz, born Oct. 28, 1846. Mrd. Sallie Clymer,—. Res., Philadelphia. Children: **(VII.)** Flora Kratz. **(VII.)** Della Kratz. **(VII.)** Wellington Kratz, dec'd. **(VII.)** Howard Kratz, dec'd. **(VII.)** Frank Kratz, dec'd. **(VII.)** Irene Kratz, dec'd. **(VII.)** George Kratz. **(VII.)** Edwin and Abel Kratz, twins, both deceased.

VI. Mary A. Kratz, born May 15, 1847; died Feb. 14, 1887. Mrd. Levi Clymer,—. He died—. Farmer. Children: **(VII.)** Wilmer Clymer. **(VII.)** Mattie Clymer. **(VII.)** Arthur Clymer. All living.

VI. Henry S. Kratz, born Oct. 19, 1849. Mrd. Anna Bishop, in 1877. She died Aug. 29, 1878. They had one child: **(VII.)** Oliver B. Kratz, born Aug. 24, 1878. Henry mrd. for his second wife, Annie Fehnel, of Northampton Co., Pa., in 1881. P. O., Petersville, Pa. Creameryman. Ger. Ref. Children: **(VII.)** Clara May Kratz, born June 18, 1883. **(VII.)** Charles Kratz, born Sept. 27, 1885. **(VII.)** Jennie Kratz, born Jan. 6, 1887. **(VII.)** Elsie Kratz, born Feb. 3, 1888. **(VII.)** Lillian Kratz, born June 8, 1889.

VI. Levi Kratz, born June 12, 1851; died April 14, 1865.

VI. Abraham Kratz, born Jan. 15, 1853. Mrd. Jennie Markley. P. O., Chalfont, Pa. Book-keeper in Phila. Ger. Ref. One child: **(VII.)** Clarence Kratz.

VI. Oliver Kratz, born June 12, 1855. He was a student at Cornell University, Ithica, N. Y., and was drowned while out bathing, June 3, 1877. S.

VI. Jacob Kratz, born Aug. 10, 1859; died Sept. 12, 1859.

V. Barbara Kratz, born July 1, 1818; died Apr. —, 1891. Mrd. William Clymer, Oct. 14, 1837. Carpenter by trade and farmer. Mennonites. Children: Isaiah, Ephraim.

VI. Isaiah K. Clymer, born Jan. 30, 1841. Mrd. Emma C. Moore, of Phila., Pa., June 5, 1877. P. O.,

Chalfont, Pa. Teacher in the public schools. Ger. Ref. No issue.

VI. Ephraim K. Clymer, born July 5, 1845. Mrd. Annie Little, in St. Paul, Minn., Sept. 30, 1885. Printer and publisher of the firm of Rich, Clymer, at 108 East Fifth St., St. Paul, Minn. Ger. Ref. One child: **(VII.)** William Raymond Clymer, born July 4, 1887.

V. Mary Kratz, born Sept. —, 1826. Mrd. Charles Haldeman, Feb. 9, 1851. P. O., Chalfont, Pa. Retired farmer. Mennonites. Children: Sarah, Daniel, Emma, Edwin, William.

VI. Sarah Ann Haldeman, born Oct. 26, 1851. Mrd. Henry M. Fretz, Sept. 26, 1874. P. O., Dublin, Pa. Farmer. Mr. Fretz is a member of the Presbyterian, and wife, of the Mennonite Ch. No issue.

VI. Daniel Haldeman, born Mar. —, 1854. Married Ella Haldeman, . P. O. Chalfont, Pa. Farmer. She Baptist. Children: **(VII.)** —— Haldeman, born —, died. **(VII.)** Charles Haldeman. **(VII.)** Edgar Haldeman.

VI. Emma Haldeman, born Apr. —, 1858; died Mar. —, 1888. Mrd. Abraham G. Ruth, —. Children: **(VII.)** Mary Ruth, born Feb. 28, 1884. **(VII.)** Sadie Ruth—; died—.

VI. Edwin Haldeman, born May 11, 1862. Married Emma Wilgus,—. P. O. Chalfont, Pa. She Ger. Ref. One child: **(VII.)** Mabel Haldeman.

VI. William Haldeman, born in 1866; died aged 4 months.

IV. Susanna Kratz, born Sept. 3, 1775; died Mar. 20, 1798. Mrd. Isaac Fretz, son of Christian and Barbara Fretz, of Bedminster, May 28, 1793. He was born Feb. 12, 1771; died Nov. 1, 1843. In early life Isaac Fretz followed the vocation of farmer. He owned and lived on the farm in Tinicum Twp., now owned and occupied by Henry F. Myers. He also had teams on the road freighting goods from Philadelphia to Easton, Bethlehem, and Nazareth, and an occasional visit to Pittsburg and other points west. In 1815 he built what is now known as the Fretz Valley Mill, on the Tohickon Creek, and in addition to farming operated the mill. During his busy life he succeeded to competency, and accumulated nearly 300 acres of land. Mennonites. Children: Abraham, Enos, Susanna.

V. Abraham K. Fretz, born in Bucks Co., Pa., Feb. 13, 1794; died Nov. 7, 1875. Mrd. Hannah Groff, of Salford, Montg. Co., June 20, 1820. She was born Sept. 3, 1803; died Mar. 20, 1873. At the age of 18 he commenced to learn the shoemaking trade, and as was the custom of that time, went from house to house carrying his "kit" with him. At the age of twenty-one, he apprenticed himself to the milling trade which he followed many years. About 1818, he in company with Samuel, son of "lame" Anthony Fretz, "velvet" Henry Fretz, made a trip to Canada, to visit friends and relatives there. The entire trip was made on foot, and was attended with the usual amount of adventures. At an early age he connected himself with the Mennonite church, but on marrying a Ger. Ref. lady, he was excluded from membership, and so remained until the division, twenty-six years later, when he and wife connected themselves with the new Mennonites. He was at one time nominated for deacon, but not elected. He served as trustee for some time, and was the second sexton of the church, which position he held for over twenty-two years. Children: Susanna, Catharine, Josephus, Elizabeth, Reuben, Amanda, Henry.

VI. Susannah Fretz, born in Philadelphia Co., Pa., Apr. 7, 1830; died Nov. 22, 1873. Mrd. Enos Kulp, of Bedminster, May 20, 1853. Farmer. Ger. Ref. Children: Martha, Andrew, George, Mary, Frank, Sarah, Hannah, Barbara.

VII. Martha Kulp born and died May 6, 1855.

VII. Andrew Kulp, born July 19, 1857; died July 26, 1873.

VII. George Kulp, born Mar. 26, 1860. Resides in Sabetha, Nemaha Co., Kansas.

VII. Mary Etta Kulp, born Sept. 23, 1861. Mrd. Charles Swope of Phila., 1880. Mrs. Swope Reformed. Children: (**VIII.**) Sophia Swope, born Apl. 15, 1881. (**VIII.**) Sarah Elizabeth Swope, born Jan. 26, 1884;

died May 26, 1885. (**VIII.**) Mary Bertha Swope, born June 26, 1886. (**VIII.**) George Swope, born Jan. 6, 1889.

VII. Frank Kulp, born Jan. 4, 1864. Farmer in Nemaha Co., Kansas.

VII. Sarah Elizabeth Kulp, born June 18, 1866. Mrd. Frank Diehl, of Rockhill, Pa., in 1886. Ger. Ref. Children: (**VIII.**) William Diehl, born Jan. 9, 1887. (**VIII.**) Bertha Florence Diehl, born 28, 1889.

VII. Hannah Kulp, born Dec. 23, 1868; died Feb. 17, 1873.

VII. Barbara Kulp, born Aug. 10, 1870.

VI. Catharine Fretz, born in Phila., Co., Pa., June 5, 1833; died, aged 3 years.

VI. Josephus Fretz, born in Phila. Co., Pa. Mrd. ——, 23, 1835; died Sept. 19, 1854.

VI. Elizabeth Ann Fretz, born in Bucks Co., Nov. 16, 1837. Mrd. Harvey G. Shaddinger, of Plumstead township. He was born January 7, 1843. On the 6th of Sept. 1861, he enlisted in Co. A, 104 Penna. Vol., for three years, and served in the following engagements: Lee's Mills, Williamsburg, Chickahominy, Seven Pines, Fair Oaks, Bottom Bridge, White Oak Swamp, Carter's Hill, James Island, siege of Fort Wagner and siege of Charleston. He was appointed Corporal Apr. 1, 1863, discharged on expiration of enlistment Sept. 30, 1864. Re-enlisted as sergeant in Company I., 213 Pa., Vol., the 16th of Feb. 1865, for one year, or during the war, and was discharged at the close of the war, Nov. 18, 1865. New Mennonites. Children: (**VII.**) A. Wesley Shaddinger, born Aug. 5, 1866. (**VII.**) Elmer F. Shaddinger, born Apr. 12, 1869; died Aug. 24, 1869. (**VII.**) Anna Charlotta Shaddinger, born Sept. 6, 1870. New Mennonite. (**VII.**) Jonas Moyer Shaddinger, born Apr. 21, 1873. (**VII.**) M. Magdalena Shaddinger, born Oct. 4, 1875. (**VII.**) Dora May Shaddinger, born May 3, 1878.

VI. Reuben G. Fretz, born in Bucks Co., Pa., July 16, 1841. Mrd. Henrietta B. Carter, of Doylestown, July 14, 1866. She was born Nov. 26, 1833; died July 18, 1884, without issue. He mrd. for his second wife Ella Butterworth, of Hatboro, Pa., Mar. 1, 1886. She was born Sept. 4, 1844. At the age of sixteen years he apprenticed himself to the wheelwright trade, and in Mar. 1861, began to learn the milling trade with his father, which he followed for thirteen years. His present occupation is wheelwright. In 1863 and 64 he enlisted to drive the invaders from the state, and served two months in the 45th Regt., Penna. V. M. Baptists.

VI. Amanda Fretz, born Oct. 6, 1844. Mrd. Joseph Holden, Oct. 1866. He was born May 13, 1841; died Mar. 10, 1873. Children: (**VII.**) Edward Holden, born Feb. 24, 1870. (**VII.**) Ellwood Holden, born July 29, 1872; died Sept. 6, 1873. (**VII.**) Ella Nora Opdyke, born Apr. 8, 1874. Amanda married her second husband Daniel Nusbickel, Apr. 11, 1875. Lutherans. Children: (**VII.**) Anna Laura Nusbickel, born July 7, 1876. (**VII.**) Thomas Nusbickel, born Jan. 9, 1881. (**VII.**) Sallie Nusbickel, born Dec. 23, 1884. (**VII.**) Milton H. Nusbickel, born May 19, 1887.

VI. Henry Fretz, born in 1848; died same day.

V. Enos Fretz, born in Bucks Co., Feb. 14, 1796; died Aug. 15, 1860. Mrd. Mary Leatherman, May 6, 1821. She was born Sept. 8, 1803; died without issue, Oct. 12, 1875. Farmer. Owned and lived on the Esquire Stover farm on the Tohickon. New Mennonites at Deep Run Ch., of which he was a trustee for a number of years. He presented the church with a part of the new burying-ground, and was among the first to be buried there.

V. Susannah Fretz, born in Bucks Co., Jan. 1, 1798; died Jan. 14, 1872. Mrd. Samuel G. Myers, Dec. 27, 1825. He was born Nov. 14, 1802; died Nov. 8, 1877. Farmer, and run a commission wagon for many years, after which he engaged in the milling business at Doylestown Borough. Mennonites. Children: Catharine, Isaac, John

VI. Catharine Myers, born Dec. 5, 1826; died Dec. 30, 1851. Mrd. Joshua Histand, Feb. 4, 1851. Mennonites. One child: Catharine.

VII. Catharine Histand, born Dec. 20, 1851. Mrd. Frank Heaton, Jan. 28, 1879. Farmer of Doyles-

J. Freeman Hendricks, M. A.

(See Page 55.

THE NEW YORK
PUBLIC LIBRARY

town, Pa. Presbyterians. One child: (VIII.) Edwin
Mathias Heaton, born Dec. 10, 1880.

VI. Isaac F. Myers, born Feb. 23, 1832. Mrd. Catharine Bewighouse, Mar. 7, 1868. Farmer and merchant. Also in the milling business for some years,
at present merchant. Mennonites. Children: (VII.)
Susan B. Myers, born Mar. 2, 1869. (VII.) Elwood
B. Myers, born Aug. 13, 1872.

VI. John Myers, born Apr. 17, 1833. Mrd. Annie
E. Beidler, Mar. 15, 1883. He was engineer for some
years, now farming. Attend Presbyterian church.

IV. Barbara Kratz, born in 1777; died in 1850. Mrd.
John Godshalk, —. He died in 1858. Farmer. Men-
nonites. Children: Christiann, Enos, Samuel, Anna,
Mary, Frances, Abraham, Margaret, Barbara.

V. Christiann Godshalk, born Aug. 13, 1799; died
Oct. 10, 1883, aged 84 yrs., 1 m. 27 d. Mrd. Isaac
Myers, —. Children: John, Isaac, Magdalena, Barbara, Eliza, Christiann, Mary. Christiann mrd. second husband, Rev. John Gross, Oct. 19, 1836. He
was ordained to the ministry of Mennonite church at
Doylestown Meeting-house, where he preached until
his death. Children: Sarah, William, Samuel.

VI. John G. Myers, born—. Mrd. Sarah Franken-
field,—. Retired farmer and carpenter. P. O.,
Blooming Glen, Pa. Mennonites. Children: Maria,
William.

VII. Maria Myers, born —. Mrd. Jacob N. Myers,
—. Farmer. Children: John, Damon.

VIII. John Myers, born—. Mrd. —— Rosenberger,
daughter of Rev. John Rosenberger.—. Farmer.

VIII. Damon Myers, born—.

VII. William F. Myers, born Jan. 1, 1844. Mrd.
Maria Moyer, Jan. 21, 1865. P. O., Blooming Glen,
Pa. Farmer. Children: Levi, Sarah, Daniel, Anna.

VIII. Levi Myers, born Dec. 6, 1866; died Sept. 15,
1868.

VIII. Sarah M. Myers, born Sept. 11, 1869. Mrd.
Enos F. Mood, Sept. 29, 1888. P. O., Perkasie, Pa.
Farmer. Mennonites. Children: (IX.) Ella Nora M.
Mood, born Nov. 11, 1889. (IX.) Annie Valeria M.
Mood, born Feb. 23, 1890.

11

VIII. Daniel M. Myers, born Oct. 7, 1872.

VIII. Annie M. Myers, born Oct. 17, 1875.

VI. Isaac Myers, born—. P. O. Lattasburg, Ohio.

VI. Magdalena Myers born—. Mrd. John Hunsberger—. He died—. Shoemaker and farmer. Mennonites. Children: Esther, Christiana, Sarah, Emma. Magdalena mrd. second husband, Philip K. Fretz (See Index of References No. 27.)

VII. Esther Hunsberger, born—. Mrd. Jacob M. Bishop,—. P. O.. Hilltown. Pa. Farmer. Mennonites. Children: (**VIII.**) Harvey. (**VIII.**) Rosa. (**VIII.**) Maggie S. (**VIII.**) John H. dee'd. (**VIII.**) Erwin H. (**VIII.**) Mary. (**VIII.**) Emma. (**VIII.**) Elmer S. (**VIII.**) Minnie. (**VIII.**) Hattie. (**VIII.**) Sallie.

VII. Christiana Hunsberger, born March 15, 1853. Mrd. Reuben Albright, son of Henry Albright, Esq. of Hilltown, October 29, 1870. P. O. Dublin, Pa. Farmer. Presbyterians. Children: (**VIII.**) Oliver H. Albright, born Aug. 17, 1871. (**VIII.**) Maggie Albright, born Aug. 24, 1873. (**VIII.**) Reuben H. Albright, born Aug. 4, 1875. (**VIII.**) Sadie Albright, born Aug. 1, 1877. (**VIII.**) Philip H. Albright, born Jan. 1, 1880: died Mar. 14, 1882. (**VIII.**) Howard H. Albright, born Mar. 24, 1882. (**VIII.**) Grover Cleveland Albright, born Mar. 28, 1885. (**VIII.**) Katie Albright, born Feb. 24, 1888. (**VIII.**) Walter Albright, born Feb. 27, 1891.

VII. Sarah Hunsberger, born—. Mrd. Jacob C. Scholl. P. O.. Fricks, Pa. Paper-hanger. Ger. Ref. No issue.

VII. Emma Hunsberger, born—. Mrd. Leidy Aker, —. P. O.. Fricks, Pa. Commission merchant. Ger. Reformed. One child: (**VIII.**) Grace Aker.

VI. Barbara Myers, born—. Mrd. Jacob Overholt. He died in 1865. Farmer. Mennonites. Children: (**VII.**) Tobias. (**VII.**) Eli. (**VII.**) Ephraim, dee'd. (**VII.**) Isaiah. (**VII.**) John. (**VII.**) Christian. (**VII.**) Barbara. (**VII.**) Hannah.

VI. Elizabeth Meyers, born June 7, 1833. Mrd. William S. Meyers, Jan. 16, 1853. P. O., Dublin, Pa. Farmer. Mennonites. Children: Isaac, John,

Christiana, William, Ida, Sallie, Lizzie, Allen, Maggie, Irwin.

VII. Isaac M. Meyers, born Feb. 23, 1854. Married Emma Weize, Nov. 8, 1879. P. O., Chatham Centre, Ohio. Farmer. Ger. Baptists. Children: (**VIII.**) Ida May Meyers, born October 29, 1880. (**VIII.**) Lizzie Grace Meyers, born Oct. 8, 1889.

VII. John M. Meyers, born Jan. 5, 1857. Mrd. Anna Kuth,—. She died—. Children: (**VIII.**) William Meyers. (**VIII.**) Eddie Myers, dec'd. John mrd. second wife Carrie Bergey—. One child: (**VIII.**) Stella Meyers.

VII. Christiana M. Myers, born Aug. 21, 1858. Mrd. John Rickert,—. P. O., Dublin, Pa. Ger. Ref. Children: (**VIII.**) William Henry Rickert. (**VIII.**) Valentine Austin Rickert. (**VIII.**) Quincy Rickert.

VII. William Henry Meyers, born Nov. 13, 1860. Mrd. Kate Rickert,—. P. O., Dublin, Pa. Mennonites. Children: (**VIII.**) Valentine Meyers. (**VIII.**) S. Lincoln Meyers. (**VIII.**) Isaac Meyers, dec'd. (**VIII.**) Katie Meyers.

VII. Ida Meyers, born Oct. 24, 1863. Mrd. Enos Gehman,—. P. O., Dublin, Pa. Children: (**VIII.**) Lizzie Gehman. (**VIII.**) Emma Verdia Gehman. (**VIII.**) William Asher Gehman.

VII. Sallie M. Meyers, born May 12, 1866. Mrd. Lincoln S. Godshall, Sept. 27, 1888. P. O., Dublin, Pa. Reformed. One child: (**VIII.**) Arthur Stanley Godshall, born July 4, 1890.

VII. Lizzie M. Meyers, born Oct. 30, 1868. Married Isaiah M. Fretz,—. P. O., Blooming Glen, Pa.

VII. Allen M. Meyers, born Feb. 15, 1871.

VII. Maggie Meyers, born Mar. 21, 1873; died July 24, 1875.

VII. Irwin F. Meyers, born Aug. 2, 1876.

VI. Christiann Myers, born—. Mrd. John Clymer, —. P. O., Line Lexington, Pa. Children: Mary, Sallie, Malinda, Harry, Christiann.

VII. Mary Ann Clymer, born—. Mrd. Garret Detweiler,—. He died—.

VII. Sallie Clymer, born—.

VII. Malinda Clymer, born—.

VII. Harry Clymer, born.

VII. Christiann Clymer, born- ; died- . Mrd.—

VI. Mary Myers, born . Mrd. John Geisinger—. P. O., Chatham Centre, Ohio.

VII. Sarah Gross, born July 26, 1837. Mrd. Samuel W. Lapp, Oct. 16, 1856. P. O., Ayr, Neb. Farmer. Deacon of Mennonite Ch. Children: John, Amanda, Anna, Emma, William, Daniel, Samuel, Mahlon, Abraham, Sarah, George.

VII. John Lapp, born Oct. 31, 1857; died Mar. 18, 1860.

VII. Amanda Lapp, born Aug. 4, 1859; died Aug. 18, 1860.

VII. Anna Lapp, born May 17, 1861. Mrd. John T. Hill, Feb. 9, 1879. Children: (VIII.) Altie Hill, born Jan. 29, 1880. (VIII.) Charles Hill, born Apr. 29, 1882. (VIII.) Hazel Hill, born Feb. 6, 1887.

VII. Emma Lapp, born Oct. 15, 1763, died May 4, 1865.

VII. William Lapp, born Feb. 11, 1866; died Mar. 11, 1866.

VII. Daniel Lapp, born Apr. 29, 1867.

VII. Samuel Lapp, born Oct. 23, 1869.

VII. Mahlon Lapp, born Feb. 4, 1872.

VII. Abraham Lapp, born Oct. 18, 1874; died Jan. -, 1878.

VII. Sarah Lapp, born Apr. 18, 1876, died Sept. 1, 1880.

VII. George Lapp, born May 26, 1879.

VI. William G. Gross, born Mar. 2, 1839. Mrd. Annie, daughter of Rev. Samuel Godshall, Nov. 1863. P. O., Fountainville, Pa. Farmer. Mennonites. Children: Samuel, Infant, William, Abraham, John, Jacob, Martha, Sarah, Harvey.

VII. Samuel G. Gross Jr., born Oct. 26, 1864. Mrd. Salome R. Myers, Sept. 16, 1885.

VII. Infant, born Dec. 1865; died—.

VII. William G. Gross, Jr., born Jan. 26, 1868. Mrd. Hannah P. Overholt, Nov. 14, 1890.

VII. Abraham G. Gross, born- .

VII. John G. Gross, born ; died—.

VII. Jacob G. Gross, born ; died .

VII. Martha G. Gross, born—; died .

VII. Sarah G. Gross, born—.

VII. Harvey G. Gross, born Aug. 18, 1883.

VI. Samuel G. Gross (twin to William), born Mar. 2, 1839. Mrd. Lydia Myers, Oct. 10, 1863. She died March 23, 1881. Retired farmer. P. O., Fountainville, Pa. Mr. Gross was ordained to the ministry of the Mennonite Church at Doylestown meeting-house, Nov. 13, 1866, and Bishop, Nov. 3, 1883, at Blooming Glen. Children: Christiana, Joseph, Emanuel, Christian, Lydia, Isaac, Henry, John.

VII. Christiana Gross, born Nov. 7, 1864. Mrd. William H. H. Swartley, Jan. 22, 1887. P. O., Fountainville, Pa. Farmer. Mennonites. Children: (**VIII.**) Harvey G. Swartley, born Mar. 14, 1888. (**VIII.**) Mahlon G. Swartley, born Sept. 8, 1890.

VII. Joseph Gross, born June 28, 1866. Mrd. Maria Moyer of Canada, Aug. 2, 1890. P. O., Dublin, Pa. School teacher.

VII. Emanuel Gross, born Jan. 16, 1868; died Sept. 22, 1868.

VII. Christian Gross, born Aug. 3, 1869. Mrd. Ella D. Landes, Jan. 12, 1891. P. O., Dublin, Pa. Carpenter. One child: (**VIII.**) Hiram L. Gross, born May 8, 1891.

VII. Lydia Gross, born Mar. 3, 1872.

VII. Isaac Gross, born May 13, 1874.

VII. Henry Gross, born Apr. 20, 1876.

VII. John Gross, born Apr. 14, 1878.

V. Enos Godshall, born in 1802; died in 1830. S.

V. Samuel Godshall, born in 1804; died in 1858. S.

V. Anna Godshall, born Sept. 14, 1806; died Mar. 16, 1850. Mrd. John Detwiler.- -. He was born Mar. 7, 1799; died Mar. 12, 1872. Farmer. Mennonites. Children: Elizabeth, Mariah, Sarah, Enos, Magdalena, John, William.

VI. Elizabeth Detwiler, born June 3, 1825; died Mar. 7, 1850. Mrd. Cornelius Bergy. Had two children, both dead.

VI. Mariah Detwiler, born Mar. 16, 1827; died June 16, 1852. Mrd. Henry Benner, dec'd. One child;

(VII.) Maria D. Benner, born — . Mrd. Michael Hershey.—. P. O., Cherry Box, Shelby Co., Mo.

VI. Sarah Detwiler, born Aug. 27, 1832. Mrd. Joseph S. Angeny, Feb. 15, 1851. P. O., New Britain, Pa. Farmer. Children: Josephine, Mary, Leidy, Wilson, Emma, John, Edwin, Joseph, Ida, Sarah, Granville, Ferdinand.

VII. Josephine Angeny, born—; died Nov. 14, 1881.

VII. Mary Angeny, born Aug. 21, 1854. Mrd. Benevil F. Markley, Oct. 22, 1890. Resides at 2854 Germantown Ave., Phil'a., Pa. Produce dealer. Mrs. Markley Baptist. No children. (1891.)

VII. Leidy Angeny, born ; died Apr. 17, 1862.

VII. Wilson H. Angeny, born—. Mrd. Amanda Brunner—. Resides at 1725 Diamond St., Phil'a., Pa.

VI. Enos G. Detweiler, born Jan. 5, 1834. Mrd. Sarah Sherm, Oct. 18, 1860. P. O., Chalfont, Pa. Farmer. Mennonites. Children: John, William, Anna, Enos, Irwin, Alfred, Phares, Emma, Elizabeth, Edwin.

VII. John F. Detweiler, born June 16, 1863. Mrd. Anna Eliza Lapp, Mar. 26, 1885. She was born Dec. 22, 1862. P. O., New Britain, Pa. Farmer. Ger. Refor. Children: (VIII.) Clarence L. Detweiler, born Sept. 9, 1886. (VIII.) Uriah L. Detweiler, born Oct. 26, 1887. (VIII.) John R. Detweiler, born Apr. 1, 1889; died Aug. 17, 1889. (VIII.) Sarah L. Detweiler, born Aug. 18, 1890.

VII. William H. Detweiler, born June 16, 1863. Mrd. Mary A. Weisel, May 6, 1886. P. O., New Britain, Pa. Children: (VIII.) Katie W. Detweiler, born Apr. 30, 1887. (VIII.) Sallie W. Detweiler, born Oct. 21, 1889.

VII. Anna Barbara Detweiler, born July 24, 1865. Mrd. Levi S. Moyer, Feb. 6, 1887. He was born May 22, 1864. P. O., Chalfont, Pa. Children: (VIII.) William D. Moyer, born Dec. 25, 1887. (VIII.) Sarah Amelia D. Moyer, born July 27, 1889.

VII. Enos S. Detweiler, born Oct. 3, 1869; died Apr. 13, 1883.

VII. Irwin S. Detweiler, born Mar. 5, 1872.

VII. Alfred S. Detweiler, born Nov. 5, 1873.

VII. Phares S. Detweiler, born Nov. 26, 1875; died July 11, 1876.

VII. Emma B. Detweiler, born June 30, 1878; died Oct. 30, 1878.

VII. S. Elizabeth Detweiler, born Sept. 7, 1879.

VII. Edwin Detweiler, born Sept. 14, 1880; died May 1, 1882.

VI. Magdalena G. Detweiler, born June 6, 1837. Mrd. H. M. Detweiler, Dec. 21, 1861. P. O., Penrose, Ill. Farmer. Mennonites. Children: William, Eliza, Amelia, Franklin, Maggie, Uriah.

VII. William D. Detweiler, born Oct. 7, 1862. Mrd. Elizabeth Kratz, Nov. 24, 1887. P. O., Penrose, Ill. Merchant. Lutherans. No children.

VII. Eliza J. Detwiler, born June 6, 1864. Mrd. Martin Book, Sept. 7, 1886. P. O., Penrose, Ill. Farmer.

VII. Amelia D. Detwiler, born Oct. 23, 1866. Mrd. Esrom Wade, Feb. 14, 1888. P. O., Penrose, Ill. Farmer.

VII. Franklin D. Detwiler, born May 5, 1870.

VII. Maggie D. Detwiler, born Jan. 4, 1873.

VII. Uriah D. Detwiler, born Nov. 17, 1877.

VI. John G. Detwiler, born Mar. 24, 1842. Mrd. Magdalena Hershey,—. P. O., Cherry Box, Mo.

VI. William Detwiler, born Apr. 22, 1844; died Mar. 1, 1882. Mrd. Anna Tyson, Oct. 15, 1870. She was born July 25, 1848. Merchant. Mrs. Detwiler, Presbyterian. One child: (**VII.**) Mamie Detwiler, born Sept. 7, 1878.

V. Mary Godshalk, born in New Britain Twp., Pa. Aug. 15, 1807; died Feb. 11, 1844, aged 36 years, 3 months and 25 days. Mrd. Abraham F. Freed, May 17, 1829. He was born Feb. 13, 1806; died June 11, 1862. In early life he was a farmer, and later he went into the lumber business. Mennonites. Children: Elizabeth, Enos, Isaac, William, Abraham, Mary, John, Jacob.

VI. Elizabeth Freed, born in Montgomery Co., Apr. 29, 1830; died Oct. 15, 1853. Mrd. Charles Hallman, five weeks before her death.

VI. Enos G. Freed, born in Montgomery Co., May 17, 1832; died Feb. 21, 1854. Mrd. Elizabeth Bealer, 16 days before his death.

VI. Isaac G. Freed, born in Montgomery Co., Jan. 2, 1834. Mrd. Miranda L. Seese, Sept. 14, 1859. P. O., North Wales, Pa. Hardware merchant and a licentiate of the Baptist Ch. One child: **(VII.)** Ida May Freed.

VI. William G. Freed, born in Montgomery Co., Sept. 8, 1835. Mrd. Lydia K. Moyer, daughter of John O. Moyer, Mar. 15, 1862. She was born Dec. 2, 1839. P. O., Cedars, Pa. Farmer. Mennonites. Children: Mary, Jemima, Elizabeth, Anna, Mattie, Lydia, William.

VII. Mary Freed, born Apr. 26, 1863; died Aug. 27, 1863.

VII. Jemima Freed, born May 31, 1864; died Nov. 18, 1864.

VII. Elizabeth Freed, born in Montgomery Co., Pa., Dec. 24, 1865. Mrd. Herman G. Delp, Feb. 26, 1887. P. O., Elroy, Pa.

VII. Anna Freed, born in Montgomery Co., Sept. 17, 1867. Mrd. Abram C. Kulp, Jan. 7, 1888. P. O., Kulpsville, Pa. Children: **(VIII.)** Mattie Kulp, born Nov. 22, 1888. **(VIII.)** Alvin Kulp, born Jan. 12, 1890.

VII. Mattie Freed, born in Montgomery Co., Sept. 29, 1870. Mrd. Henry K. Nyce, Feb. 21, 1891. P. O., Kulpsville, Pa.

VII. Lydia Freed, born Aug. 8, 1872.

VII. William M. Freed, born Oct. 7, 1874.

VI. Abraham G. Freed, born Sept. 16, 1837. Mrd. Catharine Tate.

VI. Mary Freed, born Oct. 24, 1839; died Mar. 26, 1859. Mrd. Geo. Hartzel, Jan. 13, 1858.

VI. John G. Freed, born Oct. 29, 1841. Mrd. Delila Weigner, of Luzerne, Pa., Dec. 23, 1871. She was was born in Luzerne Co., Apr. 25, 1852. P. O., Shickshinny, Pa. Carriage-builder. He enlisted in the 63d Regt., Pa., and served until the close of the war and received an honorable discharge. Children: **(VII.)** Lillie Freed, born in Luzerne Co., Pa., Sept. 17, 1872. Clerk in store. P. O., Shickshinny, Pa.

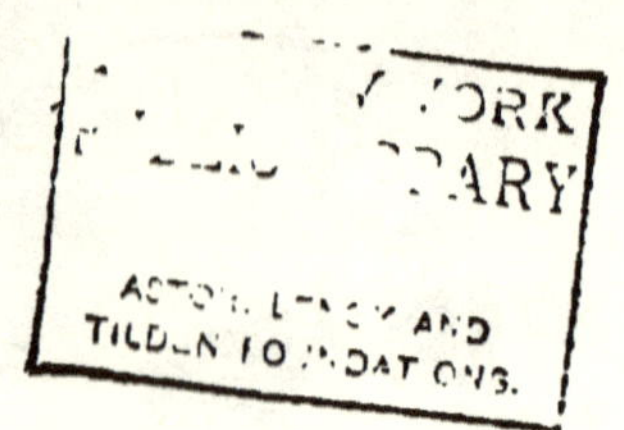
NEW YORK PUBLIC LIBRARY
ASTOR, LENOX AND
TILDEN FOUNDATIONS.

(**VII.**) Anna Freed, born Jan. 14, 1875. (**VII.**) Virgie Freed, born Nov. 14, 1876. (**VII.**) Fannie Freed, born July 17, 1879. (**VII.**) Myrtle Freed, born July 27, 1881. (**VII.**) Charles Freed, born May 5, 1884. (**VII.**) Eva Freed, born Dec. 5, 1886; died July 17, 1887, and (**VII.**) Beulah Freed, born Dec. 5, 1886; died July 19, 1887. Twins, both buried in one coffin. (**VII.**) John Freed, born Aug. 22, 1889.

VI. Jacob G. Freed, born in Montgomery Co., Pa., Feb. 5, 1844. Mrd. Emeline Bauman, Oct. 11, 1864. P. O., Boyertown, Pa. Cigar maker and packer. Lutherans. Children: (**VII.**) Alice Freed, born Sept. 3, 1856; died Nov. 15, 1869. (**VII.**) Sallie Freed, born Oct. 13, 1867; died Sept. 9, 1880. (**VII.**) Vincent Freed, born Nov. 11, 1869. (**VII.**) Emma Freed, born Feb. 16, 1873; died Aug. 3, 1873. (**VII.**) Walter Freed, born Feb. 18, 1875. (**VII.**) Katie Freed, born Feb. 7, 1877; died Dec. 1, 1881. (**VII.**) Rufus Freed, born Mar. 4, 1880; died Aug. 5, 1880. (**VII.**) Mary Freed, born Oct. 3, 1881. (**VII.**) Lottie Freed, born Dec. 24, 1883; died Feb. 18, 1885.

V. Frances Godshalk, born Jan. 3, 1809. Mrd. Daniel Barnes of Berks Co., Jan. 8, 1832. Tailor. Mennonites. Children: Mary, Hannah, Barbara, John.

VI. Mary Barnes, born Jan. 12, 1834. Mrd. William C. Fretz, Jan. 6, 1855. P. O., Chalfont, Pa. Presbyterians. Children: Allen, Daniel, Mary, William, Mahlon, Edwin, Amanda, Anna, Ella, Walter, Mary.

VII. Allen B. Fretz, born Apr. 19, 1856. Mrd. Sue L. Stine, Aug. 30, 1885. P. O., —. Salesman.

VII. Daniel B. Fretz, born Mar. 5, 1859. Farmer in Ill. Lutherans.

VII. Mary E. Fretz, born Oct. 22, 1860. Presbyterian.

VII. William B. Fretz, born Nov. 14, 1862; died Oct. 12, 1888.

VI. Mahlon B. Fretz, born Jan. 14, 1866. Druggist in Philadelphia. Presbyterian.

VII. Rev. Edwin H. Fretz, born Jan. 5, 1867. He was licensed a local preacher of the Methodist Episcopal church, Jan. 14, 1888, and is now (1888) a student at Pennington Seminary, preparing for the ministry.

VII. Amanda Fretz, born Mar. 27, 1869.

VII. Anna Fretz, born Feb. 18, 1872.

VII. Ella Martha Fretz, born Sept. 7, 1875.

VII. Walter Fretz, born Aug. 23, 1879.

VII. Mary Fretz, born,—.

VI. Hannah Barnes, born Dec. 3, 1838. Mrd. Jacob D. Rosenberger, of Bedminster, Oct. 31, 1857. P. O., Dublin, Pa. New Mennonites at Deep Run. Children: (**VII.**) Daniel. (**VII.**) Mary. (**VII.**) Isaiah. (**VII.**) Lizzie. (**VII.**) Emma. (**VII.**) John. (**VII.**) Maggie. (**VII.**) Fanny. (**VII.**) William. (**VII.**) Annetta.

VI. Barbara Barnes, born Apr. 2, 1842; died Apr. 7, 1870. Mrd. John Lapp,—. Children: Anna, Fannie.

VII. Anna Mary Lapp, born—. Mrd. — Clymer.

VII. Fannie Lapp, born—. Mrd. — Clymer.

VI. John H. Barnes, born Mar. 13, 1851; Mrd. Mary Ann Rickert,—. She died —. Children: Lizzie, Bertha, Daniel.

VII. Lizzie Barnes, dec'd.

VII. Bertha May Barnes.

VII. Daniel Warren Barnes, born . Mrd. Laura Renner, Oct. 1890. One child: (**VIII.**) Barnes, born 1891.

V. Abraham Godshall, born Apr. 27, 1811; died Sept. 12, 1865. Mrd. Mary Reiff—. Farmer. Mennonites. Children: Oliver, Daniel, John, Abraham, Angelina, Jacob, Sarah, Enos, William.

VI. Oliver Godshall, born Feb. 8, 1835; died Nov. 23, 1878. Mrd. Sarah Brunner—. She died—. Merchant. Children: (**VII.**) Ida Godshall. (**VII.**) Henry Godshall. (**VII.**) Leon Godshall, dec'd.

VI. Daniel Godshall, born . Mrd. Rebecca McKinley,—. Druggist. Methodists. Children: (**VII.**) William Godshall. (**VII.**) Emma Godshall.

VI. John Godshall, born . Mrd. Kate West.—. Slater, Methodist. No issue.

VI. Abraham Godshall, born -; died Apr. 29, 1863, from effects of service in the army. S.

VI. Angelina R. Godshalk, born Sept. 13, 1844. Mrd. John S. Kratz. (See Index of References No. 28.)

VI. Jacob Godshalk, born Jan. 2, 1846; died Apr. 2, 1854, from effects of service in the army. Unmrd.

VI. Sarah Ann Godshalk, born Aug. 23, 1848; died Feb. 26, 1849.

VI. Enos Godshalk, born —. Mrd. Kate Branson, —. Carpenter. Methodists. Children: (**VII.**) Flora Godshalk. (**VII.**) Edna Godshalk. (**VII.**) Walter Godshalk.

VI. William Godshalk, born—. Mrd. Della Williams, —. Coachmaker. Methodist. Children: (**VII.**) Ola Godshalk. (**VII.**) Carrie Godshalk. (**VII.**) Harold Godshalk. (**VII.**) Irene Godshalk, born ; died, —. (**VII.**) Leon Godshalk.

V. Margaret Godshall, born in 1814; died in 1889. Mrd. Jesse Garner, of Warrington. He died, . Farmer. Mennonites. Children: Samuel, Amos, William, Sarah, Barbara, Isaiah, Abraham.

VI. Samuel Garner, born . Mrd. Eliza Ann Bishop, Oct. 26, 1862. Farmer. Mennonites. Children: (**VII.**) Joseph B. Garner, born Mar. 16, 1868. (**VII.**) Emma Margaret Garner, born Dec. 17, 1869. (**VII.**) Lewis D. Garner, born Oct. 20, 1871. (**VII.**) Marietta Garner, born May 20, 1873.

VI. Amos Garner, born .

VI. William Garner, born —.

VI. Sarah Garner, born —.

VI. Barbara Garner, born ; died—.

VI. Isaiah Garner, born—; died.

VI. Abraham Garner, born —.

V. Barbara Godshall, born in 1816; died in 1889. Mrd. Christian Moyer, Apr. 10, 1836. He was born Mar. 15, 1814; died in 1867. Farmer and miller. He lived first on the lead mine farm in New Britain Twp., which he sold after discovering the lead. A year later he built the new store house at New Galena, where he kept store the last six years of his life. Mennonites. Children: Lydia, Enos, Isaac, Mary, Allen, Amanda, Mahlon, Isaiah.

VI. Lydia Ann Moyer, born Nov. 4, 1836. Mrd. Samuel Leatherman, Sept. 9, 1855. Cattle broker. Mennonites. Res. Doylestown, Pa. Children: William, Marietta, Anna, Mahlon, Franklin.

VII. William Hendrie Leatherman, born May 26, 1857. Mrd. Josie R. Knight, Jan. 26, 1882. Gardener. Methodists. One child: **(VIII.)** Laura W. Leatherman, born Aug. 1, 1883.

VII. Marietta Leatherman, born March 19, 1865. Mrd. Michael F. Bishop, Nov. 3, 1883. Farmer. Attends Mennonite church. Children: **(VIII.)** Bertha Bishop, born Feb. 1, 1886. **(VIII.)** Stella Bishop, born Apr. 20, 1888.

VII. Anna Barbara Leatherman, born May 17, 1867. Mrd. Harry F. Webber, Jan. 10, 1888. Farmer and butcher. Ger. Reformed. One child: **(VIII.)** Warren L. Webber.

VII. Mahlon M. Leatherman, born Aug. 1, 1871.

VII. Franklin James Leatherman, born Nov. 7, 1874.

VI. Enos G. Moyer, born June 7, 1840. Mrd. Mary Harrer, in 1863. She died Sept. 5, 1879. Miller by trade. Ger. Reformed. Children: **(VII.)** Ellanore Moyer, born June 20, 1864; died Mar. 1886. **(VII.)** Jennie Moyer, born Mar. 31, 1865; died Aug. 4, 1865. **(VII.)** Georgie Ann Moyer, born June 12, 1866. **(VII.)** Josiah Rich Moyer, born Sept. 27, 1867; died July 24, 1868. **(VII.)** James Ellwood Moyer, born July 22, 1869. **(VII.)** Josephine Moyer, born Feb. 20, 1872. **(VII.)** Anderson Moyer, born Feb. 12, 1874; died May 29, 1874. **(VII.)** Charles V. Moyer, born May 31, 1875; died Dec. 18, 1877. **(VII.)** Cora Moyer, born Sept. 12, 1877. **(VII.)** Ervin Moyer, born Sept. 1, 1879; died Sept. 10, 1879.

VI. Rev. Isaac G. Moyer, born in Bucks Co., Pa., July 10, 1843. Mrd. Kate, daughter of Eli Leatherman, Dec. 21, 1867. At the January Quarterly Conference of 1888, at Doylestown, Pa., he was licensed a local preacher of the M. E. Ch. P. O., Dover, N. J. Children: **(VII.)** Edmund H. Moyer born June 17, 1869. Methodist. **(VII.)** Mary Emma Moyer, born Aug. 18, 1870. Methodist. **(VII.)** Sada L. Moyer, born Dec. 2, 1875. Methodist. (**VII.**) Bertha Moyer, born Nov. 22, 1879.

VI. Mary Moyer, drowned when 3 or 4 years old.

VI. Allen G. Moyer, born, Aug. 5, 1848. Mrd. Mary A. Brand, June 22, 1870. Butcher. Presbyterians. Children: (**VII.**) Wauneta Moyer, born Jan. 6, 1871. (**VII.**) J. Arthur Moyer, born Mar. 9, 1872. (**VII.**) Purdy Moyer, born Dec. 27, 1873. (**VII.**) Allen Moyer, born Apr. 23, 1875; died —. (**VII.**) Carey Moyer, born Jan. 10, 1877. (**VII.**) Harvey K. Moyer, born Apr. 28, 1878. (**VII.**) Margaretta B. Moyer, born Feb. 8, 1880. (**VII.**) Jesse Moyer, born June 1, 1882. (**VII.**) William Warren Moyer, born Nov. 23, 1884; died —. (**VII.**) Elsie Moyer, born Apr. 9, 1885. (**VII.**) Nellie Moyer, born Dec. 1, 1887.

VI. Amanda Moyer, born in Bucks Co., Feb. 16, 1851. Mrd. H. Erwin Fretz. (See Index of References No. 29.)

VI. Mahlon G. Moyer, born in Bucks Co., Aug. 30, 1853. Mrd. Lizzie Keller, Jan. 28, 1875. Telegraph operator at North Wales, Pa. Presbyterians. Children: (**VII.**) Alberta Virginia Moyer, born Oct. 8, 1876. (**VII.**) Laura Parsons Moyer, born June 23, 1883.

VI. Isaiah G. Moyer, born —; died aged 6 years.

IV. Veronica Kratz, born in Bucks Co., Mar. 1, 1770; died Mar. 9, 1859. Mrd. John Hunsberger, Dec. 12, 1802. He was born Aug. 12, 1771; died—. Farmer. Mennonites. Children: Elizabeth, Enos, Barbara, Abraham, Anna.

V. Elizabeth Hunsberger, born—; died—. Mrd. Joseph Moyer, dec'd, —. Farmer. Mennonites. Children: Barbara, John, Elizabeth.

VI. Barbara Moyer, born—. Mrd. Francis Gerhart, —. P. O., Dublin, Pa. Tailor and Farmer. Children: Maria, Abraham, Emma, Joseph, Samuel.

VII. Maria Gerhart, born —; died—.

VII. Abraham M. Gerhart, born—. Mrd. Amanda Springer, —. Carpenter in Philadelphia.

VII. Emma Gerhart, born—. Mrd. Harry Leatherman, —.

VII. Joseph Gerhart, born—. Mrd. Adda Derr, —. Res., Broad St., Philadelphia.

VII. Samuel Gerhart, born —. Mrd. Mattie Swartz,—.

VI. John Moyer, born—; died—. Mrd. — Benner. One child: (**VII.**) Milton Moyer.

VI. Elizabeth Moyer, born—; died—. Mrd. Abraham Landis,—. He died—. Children: (**VII.**) John and two others, all single.

V. Enos Hunsberger, born—; died—. Mrd. Mary Moyer, about 1829. She was born Sept. 28, 1810; died —. Farmer. Mennonites. Children: John, Elizabeth, Mahlon, Abraham, Reuben, Edwin, Isaac, Enos.

VI. John M. Hunsberger, born Dec. 14, 1830; died Mar. 4, 1871. Mrd. Barbara Moyer,—. Farmer. Mennonites. Children: (**VII.**) Mary Hunsberger, dec'd. (**VII.**) Emma Hunsberger, dec'd. (**VII.**) Harry and Enos Hunsberger, twins, dec'd. (**VII.**) Wilson Hunsberger. (**VII.**) Elmer Hunsberger, dec'd.

VI. Elizabeth Hunsberger, born Dec. 6, 1883; died Dec. 18, 1888. Mrd. Henry Rickert, Mar. 27, 1853. He was born Dec. 22, 1829. Children: Mary, Catharine, Levi, Enos, Reuben, Rosa, Mahlon, Magdalena, Salome.

VII. Mary Ann Rickert, born Jun. 6, 1854; died Apr. 1886. Mrd. John H. Barnes, . (See Index of References No. 30.)

VII. Catharine Rickert, born Sept. 21, 1855; died Feb. 20, 1858.

VII. Levi Rickert, born July 18, 1857; died Mar. 10, 1866.

VII. Enos Rickert, born Feb. 2, 1859; died Apr. 3, 1862.

VII. Reuben Rickert, born June 11, 1863. Resides in Kansas.

VII. Rose Emma Rickert, born Sept. 2, 1866. Mrd. Samuel Yoder,—. One child: (**VIII.**) Anna Valeria Yoder.

VII. Mahlon Rickert, born Mar. 10, 1870. Res., Philadelphia, Pa.

VII. Magdalena Rickert, born Apr. 8, 1873.

VII. Salome Rickert, born Nov. 21, 1875.

VI. Mahlon Hunsberger, born in Bucks Co., Feb. 22, 1835; died Feb. 1889. Mrd. Elizabeth Hunsberger,

Huckster. Ger. Ref. One child: (**VII.**) Annie Hunsberger, dec'd.

VI. Abraham Hunsberger, born Mar. 3, 1837; died June 30, 1877. Mrd. Emeline Rosenberger. Farmer. Mennonites. No issue.

VI. Reuben Hunsberger, born Sept. 17, 1841; died July, 1884. He enlisted in the army in which he served three years. In 1876 he moved to Wimar, Texas, where he died. Hardware merchant. Children: Clara, Fremont, Oscar, Robert, Henry, Walter, Jessie, James.

VII. Clara Hunsberger, born—. Mrd. Harry White.

VI. Edmund Hunsberger, born Oct. 11, 1843. Mrd. Mary Lang,—. Huckster. One child: (**VII.**) Margaretta Hunsberger, dec'd.

VI. Isaac Hunsberger, born May 22, 1847; died July 13; 1881. Mrd. Margaret Brand. —. Merchant. Presbyterians. Children: (**VII.**) Gardette Hunsberger. (**VII.**) Mamie Valeria Hunsberger.

VI. Enos Hunsberger, born in Bucks Co., Sept. 27, 1849; died June 16, 1879. Farmer. Ger. Ref. S.

V. Barbara Hunsberger, born—. Mrd. Jacob Kulp, —. He died—. Farmer. Mennonites. Children: Anna, John, Veronica, Elizabeth.

VI. Anna Kulp, born Sept. 22, 1838. Mrd. Henry Smith, May 4, 1867. P. O., Blooming Glen, Pa. Farmer. Mennonites. Children: (**VII.**) Mary Ann Smith, born Feb. 2, 1868. (**VII.**) Lizzie Smith, born Sept. 20, 1869. (**VII.**) Harvey Smith, born Apr. 17, 1872. (**VII.**) Jacob Smith, born Aug. 26, 1875. (**VII.**) Henry Smith, born Oct. 7, 1884.

VI. John H. Kulp, born in Bucks Co., Oct. 28, 1840. Mrd. Catharine S. Kulp, Mar. 16, 1867. Farmer in Hilltown Twp. Mennonites. Children: (**VII.**) Jacob Kulp, born Oct. 31, 1868. (**VII.**) Abraham K. Kulp, born May 10, 1871. (**VII.**) Sallie K. Kulp, born Aug. 21, 1873. (**VII.**) Mary K. Kulp, born Feb. 11, 1876; died June 7, 1880. (**VII.**) John K. Kulp, born Mar. 4, 1879.

VI. Veronica Kulp, born about 1843; died young.

VI. Elizabeth Kulp, born Oct. 9, 1845. Lives with her brother, John H. Kulp. Unmrd.

V. Abraham K. Hunsberger, born Mar. 1, 1811; died Aug. 23, 1865. Mrd. Mary Moyer, Apr. 11, 1833. Farmer. Mennonites. Children: Barbara, Joseph, Veronica, Maria, Lucy, Eliza, Isaiah, Lydia.

VI. Barbara Hunsberger, born Apr. 5, 1834. Mrd. Levi Loux, Dec. 1, 1855. He died Mar. 15, 1863. Wheelwright. Children: **(VII.)** Abraham F. Loux, born May 14, 1856; died Mar. 8, 1863. **(VII.)** Oliver S. Loux and Alfred H. Loux, twins, born Sept. 6, 1857; died Mar. 8, 1863. **(VII.)** William M. Loux, born Sept. 17, 1859; died Mar. 3, 1863. **(VII.)** H. Erwin Loux, born Feb. 4, 1862; died Apr. 22, 1863. Barbara married for her second husband, Samuel T. Morris, Oct. 14, 1865. P. O., Dublin, Pa. Farmer. Ref.

VI. Joseph Hunsberger, born Feb. 15, 1836; died aged about 3 years.

VI. Veronica Hunsberger, born Dec. 31, 1837; died aged about 2 years.

VI. Maria Hunsberger, born Feb. 15, 1840. Mrd. William H. Fretz, Dec. 25, 1873. He was born Nov. 24, 1826; died May 13, 1888. Carpenter. Mennonites. Children: **(VII.)** Edmund Fretz, born Oct. 19, 1874. **(VII.)** Mary Lizzie Fretz, born July 16, 1876. **(VII.)** Leah Anna Fretz, born Mar. 17, 1879.

VI. Lucy A. Hunsberger, born Mar. 23, 1843. Mrd. Joseph Loux, Aug. 14, 1869. P. O., Plumsteadville, Pa. Carriage trimmer. Ger. Ref. Children: **(VII.)** Ulysses G. Loux, born Nov. 5, 1872. **(VII.)** Abraham W. Loux, born Feb. 26, 1877.

VI. Eliza Hunsberger, born July 1, 1846. Mrd. Peter B. Loux. (See Index of References No. 31.)

VI. Isaiah Hunsberger, born Apr. 5, 1850. Mrd. Emily Gick; died May 31, 1877. No issue.

VI. Lydia A. Hunsberger, born Nov. 1, 1853; died Mar. 24, 1863.

V. Anna Hunsberger, born Mar. 17, 1817; died in 1826.

IV. Magdalena Kratz, born Apr. 17, 1782; died Jan. 25, 1868, aged 85 years, 9 months and 8 days. Mrd. William Godshall, Dec. 20, 1803. He was born July 16, 1781; died Dec. 12, 1837, aged 56 years, 4 months 8 days. They were both born in New Britain Twp.,

PHILIP K. FRETZ.

See Page ~~151~~.
65.

Bucks Co. Farmer in Plumstead Twp. Mennonites. Children: Barbara, Jonas, Leah, Rachel, Aaron, Catharine, Veronica, Christiana, Mary, Magdalena.

V. Barbara Godshall, born Oct. 21, 1804; died Dec. 10, 1888. Mrd. Samuel Overholt, Nov. 9, 1826. He was born Sept. 2, 1804; died July 9, 1880. Barbara, Mennonite. Children: Jonas, David, Mary, William, Aaron, Charles, Simeon.

VI. Jonas G. Overholt, born Jan. 3, 1828. Mrd. Lavina Lapp, May 23, 1855. She was born Dec. 25, 1835. P. O., Manito, Ill. Attend Methodist Ch. Children: (**VII.**) Thomas Grippy Overholt, born June 7, 1856; died Sept. 4, 1862. (**VII.**) Samuel John Overholt, born Mar. 29, 1858; died Jan. 8, 1859. (**VII.**) Mary Margaret Overholt, born July 18, 1859; died Nov. 12, 1859. (**VII.**) Lewis C. W. Overholt, born Jan. 31, 1861; died Sept. 20, 1862. (**VII.**) Sidney M. Overholt, born Mar. 21, 1864. P. O., Manito, Ill. Farmer. Christian. S. (**VII.**) William C. Overholt, born Mar. 18, 1867. P. O., Manito, Ill. Farmer. Methodist. S. (**VII.**) John H. Overholt, born Nov. 4, 1869. P. O., Manito, Ill. Farmer. Lutheran. S.

VI. David Godshalk Overholt, born in Bucks Co., Pa., Aug. 15, 1830. At the age of fifteen years he apprenticed himself to the wheelwright trade, serving 3 years and 3 months. In the spring of 1849 he went to Ohio with relatives, and there continued his trade until the spring of 1852, when he crossed the plains with an ox team to California, and worked at his trade until the spring of 1863. He then settled in Canyon City, Oregon, where mining was extensively carried on, and engaged in wagon making and carpentering. In the fall of 1868 he returned to Bucks Co., Pa., on a visit, and while there married Sybilla Tyson. She was born Dec. 17, 1840. He returned with his wife to Canyon City, Oregon, where he has since been engaged in the mercantile business. Children: (**VII.**) Mary E. Overholt, born Nov. 2, 1869. (**VII.**) Lillie Jane Overholt, born Nov. 15, 1871. (**VII.**) William E. Overholt, born July 27, 1874.

VI. Mary Ann Overholt, born in Bucks Co., Pa., June 8, 1832. P. O., Fountainville, Pa. Single.

12

VI. William G. Overholt, born in Bucks Co., Pa., June 20, 1834. Mrd. Elizabeth Whitton, in Napa Co., Cal., Jan. 26, 1860. She was born Feb. 24, 1845. P. O., Monument, Oregon. Wheelwright by trade, which he followed until about 1880, since which time he has been engaged in stock raising and farming. Children: William, George, Mary.

VII. William H. Overholt, born Oct. 18, 1861.

VII. George W. Overholt, born Aug. 9, 1863; died Oct. 8, 1864.

VII. Mary A. Overholt, born Jan. 4, 1865. Mrd. John Robertson, at Canyon City, Oregon, Sept. 27, 1884. P. O., Drewsey, Oregon. Children: (**VIII.**) Joseph William Robertson, born Nov. 19, 1885. (**VIII.**) Lillie Aileen Robertson, born Dec. 6, 1886. (**VIII.**) Lena May Robertson, born July 8, 1889.

VI. Aaron G. Overholt, born Aug. 12, 1836. P. O., Vernal, Uintah Co., Utah. Stockraiser and rancher. Unmrd.

VI. Charles Overholt, born Nov. 9, 1839.

VI. Simeon Overholt, born Dec. 1, 1840.

V. Jonas Godshall, born Nov. 7, 1806. Mrd. Catharine Kreider, –. Farmer. Lived at Wadsworth, Ohio. Children: (**VI.**) Aaron. (**VI.**) David. (**VI.**) Eli. (**VI.**) William. (**VI.**) Mary. (**VI.**) Addie, are living; others dead.

V. Leah Godshall, born Aug. 24, 1808. Mrd. Jacob King,—. No living issue.

V. Rachel Godshall, born May 7, 1812. Mrd. William Overholt,—. Both dec'd. Children: Magdalena, William, James, Isaac, Mary, Samuel, Emma, Rachel.

VI. Magdalena Overholt, born—. Mrd. Henry B. Culp,—. P. O., South West, Ind.

VI. William G. Overholt, born—. P. O, South West, Ind.

VI. James Overholt, born —. P. O., Wakarusa, Ind.

VI. Isaac Overholt, born—. P. O., La Paz, Ind.

VI. Mary Ann Overholt, born—. Mrd. — Lechlithner.

VI. Samuel Overholt, born —. P. O., Mulhall, I. T.

VI. Emma Overholt, born—; died young.

VI. Rachel Overholt, born in Ashland Co., Ohio, July 21, 1844. Mrd. Solomon B. Culp, Feb. 12, 1861. He was born in Columbiana Co., Ohio, Nov. 18, 1829. P. O., New Paris, Ind. Farmer. Mennonites. Had three boys and two girls. All died unnamed.

V. Aaron Godshall, born Nov. 28, 1813; died Mar. 2, 1879. Mrd. Mary Detweiler, July 16, 1843. Farmer. Mennonites. Children: Jonas, Elizabeth, Reuben.

VI. Jonas Godshall, born Nov. 12, 1843. Mrd. Amanda Schlifer, Nov. 18, 1866. She died Feb. 12, 1868. One child: **(VII.)** Alvin, died Aug. 12, 1868. For his second wife Jonas mrd. Amanda Moyer, Mar. 29, 1873. P. O., Perkasie, Pa. Cigar manufacturer. Reformed. Children: **(VII.)** Eugene. **(VII.)** Addie. **(VII.)** Ulysses. **(VII.)** Edward, dec'd. **(VII.)** Howard. **(VII.)** Calvin.

VI. Elizabeth Godshall, born D. 24, 1844. Mrd. Jacob Beidler, Nov. 25, 1867. P. O., Blooming Glen, Pa. She is Mennonite. Children: **(VII.)** Mary. **(VII.)** Nathan. **(VII.)** Clara.

VI. Reuben Godshall, born Nov. 11, 1850; died Feb. 10, 1857.

V. Catharine Godshall, born Nov. 11, 1815; died Mar. 10, 1880. Married Martin Cassel, Dec. 3, 1843. He was born Dec. 6, 1816. Farmer. Mennonites. Children: Joseph, Mary, Sarah, Catharine, Charles.

VI. Joseph M. Cassel, born Mar. 9, 1845. Married Lizzie Jane Landes, May 19, 1870. She died—. Repairer of watches and clocks, etc., at 1633 Ridge Ave., Philadelphia, Pa. Member of " The church of the brethren. One child: **(VII.)** Louis Cassel, born Feb. 10, 1875. Joseph mrd. for his second wife Mrs. Louressa A. Adolph, Sept. 23, 1880. Children: **(VII.)** Joseph Cassel, twin, born Aug. 23, 1881; died July 23, 1882. **(VII.)** Howard Cassel, twin, born Aug. 23, 1881; died July 25, 1882. **(VII.)** Ann Cassel, born Mar. 13, 1883. **(VII.)** Emma Cassel, born Oct. 20, 1885. **(VII.)** Martin Cassel, born Aug. 26, 1887; died Apr. 7, 1889.

VI. Mary Cassel. born Sept. 3, 1846; died July 30, 1878. Mrd. George Sentman,—. He died Apr. 5, 1887. Children: Sarah. Charles, Martin.

VII. Sarah, Catharine Sentman. born Apr. 23, 1867. Mrd. John Johnson. Nov. 26, 1886. Farmer. Mennonites. Children: **(VIII.)** Harvey Johnson, born Sept. 20, 1887. **(VIII.)** Mary Johnson, born Dec. 22, 1889. **(VIII.)** Lydia Johnson. born Apr. 16, 1891.

VII. Charles Sentman. born Sept. 7, 1869.

VII. Martin Sentman. born Oct. 15, 1871.

VII. George Sentman. born May 1, 1873.

VII. Joseph Sentman, born Oct. 20, 1874.

VI. Sarah Cassel. born Aug. 25, 1848; died Sept. 29. —. Mrd. Isaac Hunsicker.—. Children: **(VII.)** Harry Hunsicker. **(VII.)** Jacob Hunsicker, born—; died,—. **(VII.)** Martin Hunsicker. **(VII.)** Allen Hunsicker,—; died—.

VI. Catharine Cassel. born Apr. 29. 1852. Married Albert L. Beck. Jan. 2, 1875. P. O.. Hilltown, Pa. Children: **(VII.)** Laura C. Beck. born Oct. 24, 1875; died Mar. 24, 1876. **(VII.)** Lydia Ann C. Beck, born Dec. 19. 1876. **(VII.)** Henry C. Beck, born Oct. 24, 1878. **(VII.)** Sarah Elizabeth Beck. born Mar. 3. 1882; died Oct. 8. 1883. **(VII.)** Albert C. Beck, born Jan. 6. 1885. **(VII.)** Mary C. Beck. born May 9, 1887. **(VII.)** Erwin C. Beck. born Feb. 25. 1889.

VI. Charles Cassel. born Jan. 26, 1854; died Sept. 7, 1854.

V. Veronica Godshall. born in Bucks Co.. May 6. 1817; died Dec. 17. 1866. Mrd. John Krupp, Feb. 24. 1839. Mennonites. Children: Magdalena, Hannah, Mary. Christiana. Sarah. Elizabeth. Samuel R., Jacob.

VI. Magdalena Krupp. born in Bucks Co.. Dec. 29. 1839; died June 20, 1872. Married Jacob H. Moyer, S. S.. Sept. 10. 1859. P. O.. Dublin. Pa. Farmer. Mennonites. Children: Samuel. Mary, Rosanna.

VII. Samuel K. Moyer. born Oct. 16. 1860. Mrd. Masura Barndt, Jan. 5. 1884. P. O.. Blooming Glen. Penna.

VII. Mary Malinda Moyer. born July 13. 1864; died July 22. 1865.

VII. Rosanna Moyer, born May 29, 1868. S.

VI. Hannah Krupp, born Sept. 29, 1841; died July 5, 1844.

VI. Mary Krupp, born May 4, 1843; died July 6, 1844.

VI. Christiana Krupp, born in Bucks Co., Pa., Feb. —, 1845. Mrd. David Yoder,—, 1868. P. O., Blake, Ont. Children: **(VII.)** Pearson Yoder, born Sept.—, 1869; died June 29, 1887. **(VII.)** Sadie Yoder. **(VII.)** Eli Yoder. **(VII.)** Isaac Yoder. **(VII.)** Emma Yoder. **(VII.)** George Yoder.

VI. Sarah Krupp, born in Bucks Co., Pa., June 27, 1846. Mrd. Henry B. Yoder, Dec. 20, 1868. P. O., Mendon, Mich. Farmer. Reformed. Children: **(VII.)** Elmira Yoder, born Sept. 19, 1869. S. **(VII.)** Osvin Yoder, born May 1, 1872. **(VII.)** Milton Yoder, born Apr. 12, 1874. **(VII.)** Elmer Yoder, born July 29, 1877. **(VII.)** Susie Yoder, born Sept. 15, 1883. **(VII.)** Ines Yoder, born Dec. 15, 1886.

VI. Elizabeth Krupp, born in Bucks Co., Pa.,—; died—. Mrd. Abraham Drumboer,—. Reformed Ch. No issue.

VI. Samuel R Krupp, born in Bucks Co., Oct. 19, 1852. Mrd. Amanda Hunsberger, Oct. 19, 1877. P. O., Wadsworth, Ohio. Carpenter. Reformed Ch. Children: **(VII.)** Nina Krupp. **(VII.)** Mattie Krupp.

VI. Jacob S. Krupp, born Bucks Co., Pa., Mar. 6, 1857. Mrd. Mary Kreider, Nov. 10, 1877. P. O., Mendon, Mich. Farmer. Mrs. Krupp is a Mennonite. Children: **(VII.)** Della May Krupp, born Feb. 8, 1879, in Ohio. **(VII.)** Elam High Krupp, born Jan. 23, 1880, in Ohio. **(VII.)** Lizzie Josephine Krupp, born Jan. 5, 1882, in Ohio. **(VII.)** Hattie Louisa Krupp, born Jan. 6, 1884 in Michigan. **(VII.)** Mary Lavina Krupp, born Oct. 29, 1886; died Sept. 1, 1887. **(VII.)** Elva E. Krupp, born May 24, 1888.

V. Christiana Godshall, born Feb. 14, 1819. Mrd. David Newcomer. Children: **(VI.)** Mathias—etc.

V. Mary Godshall, born Mar. 20, 1821. Mrd. John F. King, Jan. 28, 1849. Carpenter and farmer, now retired, resides near Fountainville, Pa. Mennonites. Children: Isaiah, John.

VI. Isaiah G. King, born Jan. 25, 1850; died Feb. 7, 1862.

VI. John G. King, born Dec. 6, 1857. Mrd. Belle M. Worthington, Dec. 26, 1882. Farmer. P. O., Fountainville. No living issue.

V. Magdalena Godshall, born—; died young.

IV. Elizabeth Kratz, born—; died—. Mrd. Joseph Fretz, son of Abraham and Dorothy Fretz,—his second wife. He was born about 1770, and died in October 1843. Farmer, lived in Bedminster Twp. Mennonites. Children: Mary, Joseph, Elizabeth.

V. Mary Fretz, born Apr. 22, 1802. Mrd. Jacob Hockman, Oct. 9, 1821. Miller and farmer. Members of 2d Mennonite Ch. Children: Joseph, Elizabeth, Stephen, Mary, Jacob, Samuel, Moses.

VI. Joseph Hockman, born May 3, 1823; died —. Mrd. Mary Baringer, of Richland Twp., Oct. 25, 1846. Farmer. New Mennonites. Children: Amanda, Louisa.

VII. Amanda Hockman, born Feb. 6, 1854. Mrd, Reuben Miller, Sept. 19, 1874. Farmer. Lives on a part of the original Old "Fretz" Homestead, of Bedminster, formerly owned by Martin Fretz. Mem. 2d. Mennonite Church. Children: (**VIII.**) Estella Miller, born Oct. 26, 1879. (**VIII.**) Mary Amanda Miller, born Oct. 10, 1881. (**VIII.**) Jonas Warren Miller, born Sept. 20, 1884.

VII. Louisa Hockman, born Dec. 14, 1859. Mrd. Mahlon K. Shearer, Jan. 13, 1883. Shoemaker. New Mennonites. Children: (**VIII.**) Arabella Shearer, born Jan. 11, 1884. (**VIII.**) Huldah Shearer, born Nov. 30, 1885.

VI. Elizabeth Hockman, born Nov. 16, 1824; died Nov. 3, 1878. Mrd. William Gable, Sept. 19, 1824. He was born July 26, 1823. Farmer and blacksmith. Lutherans. Children: Amanda, Jacob, Sarah, Albert, William, Charles, Edward, Simon, Ann.

VII. Amanda Gable, born June 15, 1848. Mrd. Franklin B. King, Oct. 29, 1870. He was born Feb. 9, 1848. Shoemaker by trade, at present farmer. Lutherans. Children: (**VIII.**) Alice King, born Jan. 2, 1874. (**VIII.**) Simon King, born Jan. 5, 1876. (**VIII.**)

Sallie A. King, born Nov. 4, 1879. **(VIII.)** Franklin King, born Sept. 9, 1882. **(VIII.)** Infant: died small.

VII. Jacob Gable, born Feb. 1, 1850; died May 23, 1862.

VII. Sarah Gable, born Dec. 3, 1851. Mrd. Lewis Fulmer, Nov. 23, 1868. He was born July 1, 1842. Farmer. Lutherans. No issue.

VII. Albert H. Gable, born Nov. 19, 1853; died Oct. 6, 1888. Mrd. Catharine Kramer, Mar. 25, 1876. She was born Nov. 3, 1854. Farmer. Lutherans. Children: **(VIII.)** Cora Ellen K. Gable, born Sept. 16, 1876. **(VIII.)** Aurilla K. Gable, born Mar. 1, 1878. **(VIII.)** Horace K. Gable, born July 19, 1880. **(VIII.)** Mary Catharine K. Gable, born Mar. 4, 1883. **(VIII.)** Elizabeth K. Gable, born May 6, 1885; died Dec. 12, 1886. **(VIII.)** Auilla K. Gable, born Jan. 22, 1887; died Dec. 27, 1887. **(VIII.)** Albert K. Gable, born Feb. 8, 1889.

VII. William N. Gable, born Aug. 30, 1855. Mrd. Mary F. Deaterly, Aug. 22, 1874. Farmer in Bucks Co., Pa. Lutherans. Children: **(VIII.)** Lewis D. Gable, born Dec. 4, 1874. **(VIII.)** Wilson D. Gable, born Mar. 14, 1880. **(VIII.)** Estella D. Gable, born Oct. 28, 1881. **(VIII.)** Mary D. Gable, born June 14, 1884. **(VIII.)** Harvey D. Gable, born Jan. 6, 1889.

VII. Charles H. Gable, born Aug. 6, 1857. Mrd. Hannah Eliza, daughter of Jacob Sames, Nov. 4, 1886. Farmer near Richland Centre, Pa. Lutherans. No issue.

VII. Edward Gable, born Apr. 14, 1860; died May 25, 1862.

VII. Simon H. Gable, born Jan. 10, 1863. Mrd. Jennie, daughter of George Unangst, Oct. 25, 1884. Farmer near Hagersville, Pa. Lutherans. Children: **(VIII.)** Charles U. Gable, born June 15, 1885. **(VIII.)** Saidy Florence Gable, born Aug. 10, 1886. **(VIII.)** Annie U. Gable, born Apr. 1, 1888.

VII. Ann Elizabeth Gable, born Apr. 17, 1865. Mrd. Jacob L. Swenk, Mar. 14, 1886. Miller. Feed and Flour merchant. Lutherans. One child: **(VIII.)** Willie Swenk, born Feb. 2, 1887.

VI. Mary Hockman, born   . Mrd. William Baringer.

VI. Stephen F. Hockman. born Aug. 28, 1828; died Oct. 3, 1862. Mrd. Caroline Yerger, Jan. 25, 1855. Farmer. Lutherans. Children: Clayton, Salome.

VII. Clayton Y. Hockman. born Feb. 11, 1855. Mrd. Ellamand Kilmer. Feb. 13, 1886. Carpenter at Sellersville. Pa. Mr. Hockman, Lutheran. Mrs. Hackman. Ger. Ref. No issue.

VII. Salome Hockman. born July 14, 1856. Mrd. Manasseh S. Snyder, Nov. 16, 1878. Farmer. Lutherans.

VI. Moses F. Hockman. born Apr. 5, 1830; died Nov. 14, 1885. Mrd. Rebecca Wagner. . She died -. Farmer. Ger. Ref. Children: Newton, Sarah. Jonas, Sevilla.

VII. Newton Hockman. born Dec. 8, 1860. Mrd. Cora Belle Gruver. in 1886. Farmer. Ger. Ref. One child: **(VIII.)** Lloyd Hockman. born Nov. 22, 1887.

VII. Sarah Ada Hockman. born .

VII. Jonas Hockman. born : died.

VII. Sevilla Hockman. born : died. Moses mrd. 2d. wife Leanna Wagner, Feb. 23, 1867. Children:

VII. Allen Hockman. born Oct. 17, 1868.

VII. Simeon Hockman. born Oct. 15, 1869.

VII. Mary Alice Hockman. born Dec. 15, 1870. Mrd. Thomas Walters. Feb. 23, 1887.

VII. Joseph Hockman. born Mar. 24, 1872.

VII. Moses Hockman. born July 4, 1875.

VII. Leanna Hockman. born Oct. 18, 1876.

VI. Jacob F. Hockman. born May 4, 1832. Mrd. Matilda, daughter of Jacob Deaterly of Bedminster. May 9, 1852. Farmer. Lutherans. Children: Levi, Leidy, Malinda.

VII. Levi Hockman, born Mar. 2, 1853. Mrd. Catharine, daughter of Reading Snyder, of Bedminster Twp.. Aug. 1, 1874. Carpenter and farmer. In 1875 he purchased the farm he now occupies, from his grandfather. Jacob Hockman. Lutherans. Children: **(VIII.)** Laura Louisa Hockman, born May 28, 1875. **(VIII.)** Ida Hockman. born Sept. 18, 1876.

VII. Leidy Hockman. born Aug. 22, 1854. Mrd. Lucinda, daughter of Charles M. Deaterly, of Bedminster. Nov. 8, 1879. Farmer. Res. with his father.

Theo. P. Austin.

See Page ~~155~~ 65.

Lutherans. Children: (VIII.) Clara Hockman, born Aug. 4, 1882. (VIII.) Sallie Hockman, born Aug. 5, 1884.

VII. Malinda Hockman, born Mar. 7, 1856; died Jan. 24, 1887. Mrd. John O. Snyder, May 23, 1875. Merchant at Souderton, Pa. Lutherans. Children: (VIII.) Nora Snyder, born Nov. 1, 1876. (VIII.) Carrie Snyder, born Mar. 18, 1879; died young. (VIII.) Lottie Snyder, born Sept. 7, 1881. (VIII.) Alice Snyder, born Oct. 12, 1884; died young.

VI. Samuel Hockman, born in Bucks Co., May 2, 1834; died at the house of his brother Joseph, near Bedminsterville, Pa., Sept. 23, 1878. Mrd. Jane E. Jardine, in Omaha, Neb., Mar. 12, 1866. Farmer and stockraiser. Children: (VII.) Gippie A. Hockman, born at Hamlin Grove, Iowa, Mar. 18, 1867; died at Salt Lake City, Utah, Jan. 22, 1888. (VII.) Delbert I. Hockman, born in Weld Co., Col., Nov. 30, 1868. (VII.) Brick P. Hockman, born at Snake Valley, Utah, Nov. 22, 1870. (VII.) Clara B. Hockman, born in Utah, Jan. 15, 1873. (VII.) Minnie M. Hockman, born in Utah, Aug. 23, 1875. (VII.) Kittie E. Hockman, born July 8, 1878.

VI. Sarah Hockman, born in Bucks Co., May 29, 1835. Mrd. William R. Strohm, July 7, 1854. Stonemason. In 1876 he purchased a farm in Milford Twp., on which he now resides. Ger. Ref. Children: James, Mary, Edward, Laura, Wilson, Hulda, Julia, Sarah, William, Amanda, Alice.

VII. James Monroe Strohm, born July 22, 1855. Mrd. Sophia S. Nicholas, Nov. 8, 1885; she died in 1889. Painter. Lutherans. No issue.

VII. Mary Ann Strohm, born Mar. 22, 1857. Mrd. Frank Erney, Feb. 24, 1877. Cigar-maker at Quakertown, Pa. Lutherans. Children: (VIII.) Flora Virginia Erney, born Apr. 2, 1877. (VIII.) Howard Solomon Erney, born June 9, 1880; died June 24, 1886. (VIII.) Carrie Irene Erney, born Feb. 15, 1882. (VIII.) Norman Erney, born June 2, 1885. (VIII.) Fredrick Erney, born Feb. 7, 1888; died Sept. 19, 1888.

VII. Edward H. Strohm, born in Plumstead Twp., Aug. 11, 1858. Mrd. Addie Shup, Sept. 20, 1883.

Creameryman. Ger. Ref. One child: (VIII.) Elsie May Strohm, born May 29, 1889.

VII. Laura Strohm, born Apr. 26, 1860. Ger. Reformed. S.

VII. Wilson H. Strohm, born Dec. 19, 1861. Mrd. Elizabeth Roth, Oct. 10, 1888. Farmer. Ger. Ref.

VII. Huldah Strohm, born July 15, 1863. Mrd. Henry J. Bossert, Sept. 26, 1885. Creameryman. Ger. Ref. Children: (VIII.) William S. Bossert, born Aug. 15, 1886. (VIII.) Laura S. Bossert, born Oct. 13, 1887.

VII. Julia Etta Strohm, born Jan. 30, 1866. Ger. Ref.

VII. Sarah Jane Strohm, born Aug. 4, 1873.

VII. William Franklin Strohm, born Dec. 23, 1875.

VII. Amanda Strohm, born Mar. 13, 1877; died Aug. 16, 1877.

VII. Alice Strohm, born Aug. 13, 1878.

V. Joseph Fretz, born in Bucks Co., Pa., Dec. 11, 1803; died Dec. 4, 1880. Mrd. Catharine Rickert, July 15, 1845. She was born—; died—. Joseph Fretz was a farmer, owned and lived all his life time on a part of the homestead purchased by his grandfather Abraham Fretz, in Bedminster Twp., and now owned and occupied by his sons Anthony R., and Quincy A. Fretz. Mr. Fretz was a man of perhaps more than ordinary intelligence, a very observing man and a great reader. He and his wife were members of the New Mennonites at Deep Run. Children: Allen, Quincy, Joseph, Susan, Anthony, Ella.

VI. Allen W. Fretz, born Mar. 5, 1846. Mrd. Mary E. McFarland, of Coshocton Co., Ohio, July 3, 1870. She was born Dec. 8, 1845, in Montreal, Canada. Mrs. Fretz is a member of the 2d Mennonite Church at Deep Run. Children: (VII.) Rilla Alice Fretz, born in Bedminster Twp., Pa., Apr. 9, 1871. S. (VII.) J. Titus Fretz, born Feb. 2, 1873. (VII.) Wilson Shurtz Fretz, born June 19, 1875. (VII.) Charles J. Fretz, born Mar. 22, 1877. (VII.) Delbert B. Fretz, born Dec. 28, 1879. (VII.) Merrill Linn Fretz, born Dec. 17, 1881. (VII.) Robert A. Fretz, born May 26, 1883. (VII.) Mamie Fretz, born Feb. 15, 1886; died May 8, 1887.

VI. Quincy A. Fretz, born July 18, 1847. He lived with his parents until a few years after his marriage, after which he lived in Hilltown one year, and at Souderton four years, engaged in manufacturing force pumps. In 1879 he returned to the farm where he now lives, and which, as a portion of the old homestead, he purchased after his father's death. He was mrd. Oct. 10, 1873 to Catharine Yeakel, of Hilltown. She is a descendant of the Schwenkfelders and was born May 27, 1847. Members of the 2d Mennonite Ch., at Deep Run. One child: (**VII.**) Alice Y. Fretz: died an infant.

VI. Joseph Titus Fretz, born May 5, 1849; died Apr. 27, 1870: aged 20 yr., 11 m. 22 d.

VI. Susan Fretz, born June 7, 1852. Mrd. Mahlon Essig, of Arcadia, Hamilton Co., Ind., June 22, 1884. Farmer in Hamilton Co., Ind. Mrs. Essig, New Mennonite. Children: (**VII.**) Infant daughter born and died Apr. 11, 1886. (**VII.**) Emma Mabel Essig, born July 8, 1887.

VI. Anthony R. Fretz, born Feb. 19, 1856. Mrd. Ella Barron, of Springfield, —. She was born Jan. 27, 1862. Farmer, and lives on the old homestead, which he purchased in 1881. Children: (**VII.**) Morris Dillwyn Fretz, born Mar. 5, 1883. (**VII.**) Chester Arthur Fretz, born Mar. 26, 1885. (**VII.**) Joseph Edgar Fretz, born Aug. 6, 1886. (**VII.**) Ida May Fretz, born Oct. 8, 1888.

VI. Ella R. Fretz, born Oct. 22, 1862. Mem. of 2d Mennonite Church of Deep Run. S.

V. Elizabeth Fretz, born—; died –.

IV. Abraham Kratz, born Jan. 14, 1788; died Sept. 14, 1852. Aged 64 years, 8 months. Mrd. Elizabeth Wismer, daughter of Abraham and Veronica Wismer, –. She was born July 26, 1794; died Aug. 12, 1852. Farmer in Plumstead Twp. Mennonites. Buried at Blooming Glen. Children: Henry, Levi, Frances, Barbara, Abraham, William, Valentine, Catharine, Christian, Elizabeth, Reuben.

V. Henry Kratz, born Feb. 27, 1815; died Feb. 15, 1873, buried at Deep Run Presbyterian church yard. Mrd. Mary Jane Harris, . She died,—. Children:

(**VI.**) Josiah Kratz, born—: died young. (**VI.**) John Kratz, born—. Mysteriously disappeared.

V. Levi Kratz, born in Bucks Co., Pa., Feb. 28, 1817. Mrd. Lydia A. Clark, Mar. 21, 1885. Farmer and gardener in Clay Co., Ill. Mr. Kratz, Mennonite. Mrs. Kratz, Christian Ch. No issue.

V. Frances Kratz, born in Bucks Co., Pa., Jan. 17, 1819. Mrd. William E. Fretz, about 1840. He was born Sept. 28, 1817. Carpenter by trade and farmer. Reside near Lawndale, Pa. Ev. Assoc. Children: Samuel, Elizabeth, Reuben, Abraham, Mary,

VI. Samuel K. Fretz, born in Bucks Co., Pa., June 14, 1841. Mrd. Mary E. Boyer, of Hatfield Twp., Pa., Jan. 7, 1865. Farmer near Clayton, Kent Co., Delaware. Methodists. Children: (**VII.**) Ervin B. Fretz, born June 20, 1866. S. (**VII.**) Abraham B. Fretz, born Oct 25, 1867. S. (**VII.**) Hannah E. Fretz, born May 5, 1871; died in 1872. (**VII.**) Fannie B. Fretz, born Feb. 11, 1873. (**VII.**) Horace B. Fretz, born Oct. 19, 1876. (**VII.**) Peter B. Fretz, born Sept. 6, 1878. (**VII.**) William B. Fretz, born Sept. 9, 1880. (**VII.**) Emma B. Fretz, born Sept. 16, 1882.

VI. Elizabeth Fretz, born Dec. 27, 1843. Mrd. Charles George,—. Children: (**VII.**) William George, born—: died in infancy. (**VII.**) Jacob George, born Mar. 30, 1883.

VI. Reuben K. Fretz, born in Bucks Co., Pa., Dec. 2, 1846. Mrd. Mary R. Detwiler, Nov. 21, 1868. She was born Dec. 5, 1847. Farmer near Lucon, Montgomery Co., Pa. Old Mennonites. Children: (**VII.**) Garret D. Fretz, born Sept. 28, 1869. (**VII.**) Fannie D. Fretz, born Dec. 8, 1871. (**VII.**) Annie D. Fretz, born Feb. 25, 1875. (**VII.**) William D. Fretz, born Mar. 13, 1877; died Oct. 11, 1879. (**VII.**) Henry D. Fretz, born July 21, 1879. (**VII.**) Wilson D. Fretz, born May 8, 1882. (**VII.**) Reuben D. Fretz, born Sept. 3, 1884. (**VII.**) Abraham D. Fretz, born Apr. 27, 1887.

VI. Abraham K. Fretz, born in Bucks Co., Pa., May 9, 1851. Mrd. Anna Amanda Hechler, Oct. 15, 1881. She was born Aug. 25, 1860. Reside near Hatfield, Pa. Ev. Assoc. Chidren: (**VII.**) Mary Alice Fretz, born Sept. 3, 1882. (VII.) Aaron Melrose Fretz, born Feb. 15, 1887.

VI. Mary B. Fretz (twin to Abraham), born May 9, 1851. S.

V. Barbara Kratz, born June 29, 1821; died Oct. 12, 1890. Mrd. Henry K. Myers, in 1842. He was born in 1817. Farmer. Mennonites. Children: Levi, Huldah, Elias.

VI. Levi Myers, born in 1843; died in 1887. S.

VI. Huldah Myers, born in 1848. Mrd. Amos Myers, in 1868. Farmer. Mennonites. Children: (VII.) Clara Myers, born in 1869. (VII.) Henry Myers, born 1870; died 1870. (VII.) Horace Watson Myers, born 1871. (VII.) Edward M. Myers, born 1874. (VII.) Annetta Myers, born 1876. (VII.) Samuel Myers, born 1878; died 1878. (VII.) Alice Myers, born 1881. (VII.) Susanna Myers, born 1885; died 1885. (VII.) Charles Elmer Myers born 1886. (VII.) Howard Myers, born 1889.

VI. Elias Myers, born in 1854; died in 1862.

V. Abraham Kratz, born Feb. 25, 1823. Mrd. Elizabeth Dateman,—. P. O., Dublin, Pa. Wagonmaker. Mr. Kratz, Mennonite; Mrs. Kratz, Lutheran. Children: Menan, Abraham, Amanda.

VI. Menan Kratz, born Oct. 11, 1850. Mrd. Catharine Aker, Dec. 22, 1875. She was born Nov. 5, 1851. Wheelwright. Mrs. Kratz, Ger. Ref. One child: (VII.) Elva Kratz, born Oct. 5, 1887.

VI. Abraham D. Kratz, Jr., born Sept. 6, 1856. Mrd. Sarah Derstine, Feb. 19, 1881. She was born Apr. 3, 1860. P. O., Dublin, Pa. Farmer. Mennonites. Children: (VII.) Lizzie Kratz, born Jan. 31, 1882. (VII.) Sallie Kratz, born Mar. 15, 1883. (VII.) Leidy Kratz, born Jan. 17, 1886. (VII.) A. Linford Kratz, born June 22, 1890.

VI. Amanda Kratz, born June 9, 1860. Mrd. Jeremiah W. Fillman, Oct. 12, 1880. He was born Dec. 2, 1857. P. O., Dublin, Pa. Farmer. Mrs. Fillman, Mennonite. Children: (VII.) Ella Fillman, born Aug. 15, 1881. (VII.) Stella Fillman, born Aug. 5, 1884. (VII.) Ida May Fillman, born Feb. 27, 1887. (VII.) Lizzie Fillman, born Nov. 22, 1889.

V. William Henry Kratz, born July 26, 1825; died May 7, 1871, aged 45 yrs., 9 m. 11 days. Mrd. Martha I. Kennedy, at New Britain, Pa., Oct. 18, 1849. She was born Sept. 12, 1824; died Jan. 12, 1876, aged 51 yrs., 4 mo. Farmer. Children: Emily, Joseph, William, Janet, Horace, James, Martha.

VI. Emily E. Kratz, born May 26, 1851; died Sept. 21, 1862.

VI. Joseph Kratz, born May 11, 1853; died Sept. 28, 1862.

VI. William Henry Kratz, born Sept. 21, 1855; died Sept. 24, 1862.

VI. Janet Fairies Kratz, born Mar. 19, 1857. Mrd. Mahlon Clymer Haldeman, July 11, 1878. P. O., 454 Jackson St., St. Paul, Minn. Druggist. Baptists. Children: **(VII.)** Eva Ferris Haldeman, born July 14, 1879. **(VII.)** Grace Anna Haldeman, born Dec. 28, 1881. **(VII.)** Horace Kratz Haldeman, born May 27, 1886.

VI. Horace Greeley Kratz, born in New Britain, Bucks Co., Aug. 4, 1859. Mrd. Anna Apel, Oct. 22, 1889. Milk dealer in Philadelphia. Baptist; wife, Ger. Ref. One child: **(VII.)** Horace Harry Kratz, born Aug. 12, 1891.

VI. James Monroe Kratz, born Jan. 6, 1862; died Apr. 12, 1878.

VI. Martha Isabelle Kratz, born July 13, 1865. S. Attends Presbyterian Ch.

V. Valentine Kratz, born Feb. 24, 1828. Mrd. Sarah, daughter of William and Mary Kratz, in 1852. P. O., Plumsteadville, Pa. Farmer. Mennonites. Children: Mary, Allen, William, Abraham, Valentine, Tobias, Henry, Sarah, Emma, Laura.

VI. Mary Ann Kratz, born Nov. 23, 1853; died—.

VI. Allen Kratz, born June 28, 1855. Lives in Franklin Co., Kans.

VI. William Kratz, born May 8, 1858; died aged 10 months.

VI. Abraham L. Kratz, born Dec. 24, 1859. Mrd. Anna, daughter of Daniel Myers, of Souderton, Pa., Dec. 26, 1886.

VI. Valentine Kratz. born Mar. 31. 1862; died aged
2 years.

VI. Tobias Kratz. born June 13. 1864; died aged 2
years.

VI. II. Ervin Kratz. born in Hilltown Twp.. Bucks
Co.. Mar. 8. 1867. He attended the public schools
from the age of six until he was eleven years old.
when his mother died. He was then hired to his Uncle Henry K. Myers. where he remained three years,
and then hired to William and Amos Myers for two
years. going to school in winter. after which he returned to his Uncle Henry K. Myers. where he remained four years. On March 1. 1890. he arrived at
Pomona. Kansas. where he has since been employed
by the month. S.

VI. Sarah Kratz. born Sept. 3. 1869; died . 1891.
Mrd. Oliver J. Mills. of Tinicum. Oct. 5. 1889. P. O..
Lansdale. Pa. One child: **(VII.)** Clara Mills. born Nov.
17, 1890.

VI. Emma E. Kratz. born June 8. 1871; died aged 9
months.

VI. Laura Kratz. born Feb. 1. 1875.

V. Catharine Ann Kratz. born in Bucks Co.. Pa..
Feb. 24. 1830; died Nov. 29. 1863. aged 33 yrs.. 9 m.
3d. Mrd. Rev. Abraham F. Detweiler. May 27.
1855. He was born Apr. 6. 1829. Moved to Illinois
in 1856. Farmer and minister. Resides in Clay Co..
Ill. Mennonites. Children: Roseana. Catharine.
Mary, Abraham.

VI. Roseana K. Detweiler, born Oct. 2, 1858. Mrd.
Frank Clark. No issue.

VI. Catharine Ann Detweiler. born Oct. 15. 1859. S.

VI. Mary Elizabeth Detweiler. born June 29. 1861.
Mrd. Charles Shroder. Oct. 20. 1885. Farmer. Children: **(VII.)** Estella Catharine Shroder. born Oct. 8.
1885. **(VII.)** Caroline Shroder. born Feb. 2. 1887.
(VII.) William Augustus Shroder. born Dec. 8. 1889.

VI. Abraham Lincoln Detweiler. born May 17, 1863.
Single.

V. Christian Kratz. born Mar. 22. 1832; died July
31, 1834, aged 2 yrs.. 4 m. 8 d.

V. Elizabeth Kratz, born May 24, 1835; died Sept. 15, 1840, aged 5 yrs., 3 m. 21 d.

V. Reuben W. Kratz, born in New Britain, Bucks Co., Pa., Feb. 23, 1838. In the fall of 1852 his father and mother died in the space of five weeks. Left an orphan at the early age of 14 years, he went to Plumstead, Pa., where he attended one winter term of school. In the following spring he hired to H. K. Myers for eight months at farm work. Then apprenticed to his brother Abraham at wagon-making, serving one year and nine months. In the spring of 1856, he faced towards the West, believing there were better things in store for the young than in the densely inhabited East; went to Whiteside Co., Ill., and worked at wagon-making, breaking prairie with an ox team, threshing, etc. In the spring of 1860, he married Emeline A. Swena, of Sterling, Ill. In the spring of 1863 they loaded their goods and effects in an old wagon and started for Kansas. Their whole wealth consisted of a team, wagon, bed, stove, a few minor articles of household goods, and $21 in cash. They started for a point in eastern Kansas to find a home for themselves, and on May 10, 1863, located where they now reside, in Appanoose Twp. (P. O., Pomona), Franklin Co., Kansas. Here they lived in a log cabin with puncheon floor and clapboard roof. In August Mr. Kratz joined the State Militia, and served in Kansas and Missouri 18 months. While on such duty the family remained without a protector, and he had permission to go home at times and get supplies for their maintenance. The nearest mill was 20 miles away and run only one day in a week. The nearest trading store was at Lawrence, 32 miles distant. The Militia was disbanded in 1864, and from that time Mr. Kratz was able to be at home and care for his family. Neighbors were a long distance apart. No settlement except along the streams, and it was common to visit neighbors 10 or 12 miles distant. The Sac and Fox reserve was near by and Indians were plenty, but always peaceable and friendly. Mrs. Kratz was left alone one night, and, sleeping with the doors open, several Indians entered to inquire for

Mrs. Mary C. Austin.
See Page ~~155~~.
65.

whisky. She informed them the whisky, if there was any, was at the wakeup, about three miles distant, and they retired.

In the winter of 1865, through the kindness of two of their old neighbors in Illinois, Messrs. C. C. Alexander and John Benjamin, who advanced the money, they were able to buy a stock farm of 152 acres; 37 acres of this was afterwards sold to assist in paying for the balance. In 1878 Mr. Kratz purchased 240 acres, making a farm at this date of 355 acres. In the spring of 1866 he erected a log cabin 16x16 feet foundation. This the family occupied until the fall of 1873, when a more commodious house was built, but this the family soon outgrew, and in the spring of 1886 a house costing over $3,000 was erected. In an early day Mr. Kratz determined to give strict attention to raising stock, and he has never allowed himself to lose sight of this idea. He has at times 150 head of cattle, 40 head of horses, and 200 hogs feeding, making a specialty of fattening beef cattle. The business has not always been prosperous, owing to grasshoppers, chinch bugs and dry weather. School facilities have always been good, probably as good as many in the older states. Mr. Kratz has served on the School Board in his district 24 years. He and wife are members of the Congregational Ch. Children: Frances, William, Horace, Lemuel, Amy, Harriet, Esther.

VI. Frances R. Kratz, born Dec. 26, 1860. Mrd. Watson Beaman, Mar. 11, 1884. P. O., Coronado, Kans. Children: (**VII.**) Chancy Ray Beaman,* born Feb. 3, 1885; died Aug. 23, 1890. (**VII.**) Ava Charlottie Beaman, born Apr. 29, 1886. (**VII.**) Infant son, born Mar. 21, 1888; died Mar. 31, 1888. (**VII.**) Effie Catharine Beaman, born July 8, 1889.

---

* While out herding stock he rode his horse onto an old well covered over with boards and dirt, and which, breaking through, precipitated him down 108 feet to the bottom and the horse on top of him. His mother was the first to go down into the well by a hastily-improvised windlass and rope to rescue the mangled remains of her first born.

VI. William Henry Kratz, born June 26, 1867. Unmarried.

VI. Horace Clement Kratz, born Aug. 22, 1870. Unmarried.

VI. Lemuel Abraham Kratz, born Feb. 7, 1872.

VI. Amy Elizabeth Kratz, born Aug. 18, 1876.

VI. Harriet Emeline Kratz, born Mar. 29, 1878.

VI. Esther Amelia Kratz, born Nov. 23, 1882.

IV. Catharine Kratz, born   : died . Mrd. Joseph Krout. . No issue.

III. Isaac Kratz, born in 1742: died young.

III. Michael Kratz, born in 1734. Probably left no issue.

III. Gerhart Kratz, born in 1736. It is thought that he also died without issue.

Note.—(III.) Isaac, (III.) Michael, (III.) Gerhart Kratz were not born in the order in which they are mentioned above. Isaac is the sixth-born, and appears here in the right order, while Michael and Gerhart were born second and third. The three are placed together here as neither of them shows any issue.

DESCENDANTS OF ANN KRATZ, DAUGHTER OF JOHN VALENTINE KRATZ.

III. Anna Kratz, born Oct. 1, 1743; died Nov. 8, 1806. Mrd. Lewis Sweitzer,—. He was born Aug. 10, 1740; died Oct. 21, 1795. Farmer, lived at or near Doylestown, Pa. Mennonites. Children: Valentine, Anna, Mary, Lewis, Conrad, Elizabeth, Henry, Barbara, Simon, John.

IV. Valentine Sweitzer, born Sept. 27, 1765; died —. Mrd. Mary Armstrong. He died without issue.

IV. Anna Sweitzer, born Sept. 27, 1766; died at Springtown, Pa., Aug. 28, 1838. Mrd. Jacob Funk, in 1797. He was born —; died —. Farmer and merchant. Mennonites. One child: Henry.

V. Henry Funk, born in Bucks Co., Pa., Feb. 20, 1798; died June 25, 1852. Mrd. Catharine Stover, Aug. 26, 1819. She was born Aug. 12, 1799; died Sept. 29, 1871. They removed to Northumberland Co., Pa., in 1839 and located on a farm three miles from Milton, Pa. Baptists. Children: Anna, William, Benjamin, Emeline, George, Clementine, Lewis, Catharine.

VI. Anna Maria Funk, born Oct. 28, 1820; died Apr. 11, 1885. Mrd. William Heinen, Sept. 7, 1841. He was born in York Co., Pa., May 3, 1817; died July 19, 1879. He was a son of Doctor Heinen, who emigrated from Germany and mrd. Elizabeth Etzler of York Co., Pa., and practiced medicine in said county before removing to Milton, Pa. William Heinen was engaged in the mercantile business of the firm Heinen, Schreyer & Co., Milton, Pa. He was a member of the Lutheran, and Mrs. Heinen of the Baptist Ch.

Children: Henry. Melanchton. Catharine. William, Sallie. Anna, Thomas. Eddie.

VII. Henry Jacob Heinen, born May 24, 1843; died Mar. 19, 1887. Mrd. Anna Rebecca, daughter of John G. and Lydia A. (James.) Mann, of Bucks Co., Sept. 1, 1870. She was born Oct. 1, 1844. Succeeded his father in the mercantile business. Presbyterians. Children: **(VIII.)** Edna Heinen, born June 22, 1871. **(VIII.)** Anna Maria Heinen, born December 16, 1872. **(VIII.)** Grace James Heinen, born Sept. 29, 1875. **(VIII.)** Florence Greir Heinen, born June 22, 1880. **(VIII.)** Elizabeth Mann Heinen, born Apr. 9, 1884.

VII. Melanchton Etzler Heinen, born Feb. 15, 1846; died Nov. 21, 1868.

VII. Catharine Elizabeth Heinen, born Mar. 26, 1848. Mrd. Daniel Krauser, Oct. 18, 1886. He was born May 31, 1845. P. O., Milton, Pa. Druggist. Mr. Krauser. Presbyterian. Mrs. Krauser, Baptist. One child: **(VIII.)** William Heinen Krauser, born Dec. 31, 1889.

VII. William Augustus Heinen, born Oct. 16, 1850. Mrd. Mary Catharine Shimer, daughter of Samuel J. and Catharine A. (Stout.) Shimer, Oct. 8, 1889. She was born near Bethlehem, Pa., Dec. 9, 1864. Moved to Milton, Pa., with her parents in 1871. P. O., Milton, Pa. Dairy farmer. Mrs. Heinen, Presbyterian.

VII. Sallie A. Heinen, born May. 12, 1854; died May 4, 1855.

VII. Anna M. Heinen, born Feb. 22, 1856; died Sept. 19, 1858.

VII. Thomas Curtis Heinen, born Mar. 11, 1859. Mrd. Carrie Virginia, daughter of David and Maria (Wiley) Belford, Oct. 22, 1885. She was born July 27, 1860. Member of the firm Heinen, Schreyer & Co., Milton, Pa. One child: **(VIII.)** Katharine Elizabeth Heinen, born Jan. 20, 1888.

VII. Eddie E. Heinen, born Sept. 8, 1862; died Mar. 11, 1864.

VI. William Funk, born Nov. 27, 1822; died in infancy.

VI. Benjamin, Franklin Funk, born Feb. 20, 1825. Mrd. Sarah M. Lloyd, Dec. 5, 1854. She was born

Sept. 7, 1832. She was the daughter of David and Mary (Quinn) Lloyd, of Bucks Co., and later of Muncy, Pa. Mr. Funk is a clerk in the grocery department of Heinen, Schreyer & Co., of Milton, Pa. Baptists. Children: David, William, Henry, Mary, Anna.

VII. David Lloyd Funk, born Dec. 31, 1855. Mrd. Rebecca M. Righter, Nov. 23, 1882. P. O., Ridge Ave., and Hermit St., Roxborough, Philadelphia, Pa. Clerk. Baptist. One child: (**VIII.**) Franklin Lloyd Funk, born Aug. 23, 1886; died Oct. 10, 1886.

VII. William Heinen Funk, born Oct. 9, 1858; died in infancy.

VII. Henry Stover Funk, born Sept. 21, 1860. Mrd. Hattie Stephens, of Wellington, Kansas, Jan. 18, 1889. P. O., 3004 Main St., Kansas City, Mo. Pacific Express Messenger through Kansas and Colorado. Mrs. Funk, Methodist. One child: **VIII.**) Frank Lane Funk born and died Jan. 9, 1890.

VII. Mary Catharine Funk, born Jan. 6, 1863; died in infancy.

VII. Anna Heinen Funk, born Dec. 1, 1865.

VI. Emeline Funk, born Oct. 15, 1829; died in infancy.

VI. George Washington Funk, born July 27, 1831. Mrd. Rebecca Gauly, (daughter of Geo. L. and Catharine (Martin) Gauly, natives of Berks county, who removed to Milton, Pa., in 1840. Farmer, resides on the old homestead three miles from Milton, Pa. Baptists. No issue.

VI. Clementine Stover Funk, born Dec. 21, 1833. Mrd. Samuel F. Hoffa, Nov. 11, 1856, son of Jacob and Ragina (Follmer) Hoffa. He was born Oct. 27, 1832. P. O., Milton, Pa. Farmer. Mrs. Hoffa, Baptist. Mr. Hoffa, Lutheran. No issue.

VI. Lewis Henry Funk, born Aug. 22, 1836; died Aug. 13, 1869. He was in the three months' service of the first call of President Lincoln for 75,000 men. He was also state printer for two sessions under Gov. Curtin. Mrd. Eliza Groff, of Harrisburg, Pa., in Sept. 1861. Mr. Funk Baptist. Mrs. Funk Methodist. Children: **(VII.)** Franklin. **(VII.)** Harry E. **(VII.)** Eddie, died infant.

VI Catharine Amanda Funk, born June 24, 1839. Mrd. Michael, son of Jacob and Elizabeth (Dehl) Rissel, Jan. 1, 1863. He was born May 5, 1833. Dealer in furniture, Pianos, Organs, etc., of the firm J. R. Smith & Co., Milton, Pa. Mrs. Rissel, Baptist. No issue.

IV. Mary Sweitzer born in Bucks Co., June 20, 1772; died Dec. 3, 1849. Mrd. Christian Clemens, Oct. 7, 1792. He was born May 7, 1766. Farmer. Mennonites. Children: Ann, Eliza, Catharine, George, Elizabeth, Leah, Lewis, Jacob, Henry, John.

V. Ann Clemens, born Jan. 22, 1794. Mrd. Mathias Stover. Children: Leah.

VI. Leah Stover, born in Bucks Co., Pa. Mrd. Levi Yost.—. He died—. Children: **(VII.)** Reuben. **(VII.)** Emma.

V. Eliza Clemens, born Dec. 28, 1795; died Aug. 4, 1796.

V. Catharine Clemens, born in Warwick Twp., Bucks Co., Pa., June 19, 1797, died July 1885. Mrd. Isaac Stout, Apr. 20, 1815. He was born in Northampton Co., Mar. 24, 1787; died Jan. 5, 1857. He was a farmer and afterward Justice of the Peace for about thirty years. They were members of the Lutheran church of which Mr. Stout was an elder for a number of years. Children: Frederica, Mary, Barbara, Elizabeth, Anna, Louisa, Abraham, Lewis, Catharine.

VI. Frederica Amelia Stout, born Jan. 29, 1816. Mrd. Charles Christman, May 5, 1858. He died—. Farmer. Lutherans. Mrs. Christman resides in Bethlehem, Pa. No issue.

VI. Mary Stout, born June 29, 1818; died Dec. 23, 1853. Mrd. Samuel Riegel. Merchant. Reformed. Children: Emma, Elizabeth, Isaac, Anna, Dorsey, George.

VII. Emma Riegel, born –. Mrd. Stephen Laubach, M. D. One child: **(VIII.)** Lida.

VII. Elizabeth Riegel, born ; died . Mrd. Stephen Laubach, M. D., . One child: **(VIII.)** Minnie Laubach.

This Photo was taken in September, 1894, at the age of 83 years.

VII. Isaac Mathias Riegel, born   . Mrd.   .

VII. Anna Mary Riegel, born —. Mrd. Marcus Beidleman.

VII. George S. Riegel, born Dec. 6, 1853. Mrd. Ellamina Weaver, Mar. 16, 1882. Miller. Reformed. P. O., Bethlehem, Pa. No issue.

VI. Barbara Stout, born Mar. 13, 1821; died Oct. 5, 1822.

VI. Elizabeth Stout, born July 31, 1823. Mrd. William Steckel, Dec. 30, 1840. He died Aug.—, 1884. Merchant. Presbyterians. Mrs. Steckel resides in Bethlehem, Pa. Children: Emma, Jacob, Clara, Anna, Laura.

VII. Emma Steckel, born Aug. 16, 1843. Mrd. John M. Knisely, Oct. 19, 1871. P. O., Bethlehem. Lutherans. Children: (**VIII.**) Edward Steckel Knisely, born Oct. 15, 1873. (**VIII.**) Clara Amelia Knisely, born Mar. 27, 1877.

VII. Jacob Stover Steckel, born Nov. 6, 1847; died Oct. 22, 1849.

VII. Clara Hammer Steckel, born Mar. 8, 1850. Mrd. James M. Schnabel, Feb. 27, 1878. P. O., Bethlehem, Pa. Merchant. Lutherans. One child: (**VIII.**) William Russel Schnabel, born Nov. 28, 1882.

VII. Anna Elizabeth Steckel, born July 31, 1853. Mrd. David Wambold, Jan. 10, 1874. Children: (**VIII.**) Warren S. Wambold. (**VIII.**) Lillie May Wambold. (**VIII.**) Elizabeth Steckel Wambold. (**VIII.**) William Henry Wambold. (**VIII.**) Mary L. Wambold. (**VIII.**) Frank R. Wambold. (**VIII.**) Robert L. Wambold. (**VIII.**) George W. Wambold. (**VIII.**) Arthur S. Wambold. (**VIII.**) John R. Wambold. (**VIII.**) Walter S. Wambold. (**VIII.**) Viola Wambold.

VII. Laura Steckel, born Dec. 27, 1858. Mrd. A. Halsey Gibbs, Nov. 12, 1884. No issue.

VI. Anna Melinda Stout, born Dec. 14, 1826; died—. Mrd. Jacob Lily. Children: Lewis, Henry.

VII. Lewis Stout Lily, born—. Mrd. Anna Yost. Farmer.

VII. Henry Lily, born—. Mrd. Clara—.

VI. Louisa Emily Stout, born Dec. 19, 1828; died Dec. 27, 1858. S.

VI. Abraham Stout, M. D., born Aug. 22, 1831. Mrd. Mary L. Cartright, Feb.—, 1856. She died Aug. 26, 1887. Practicing Physician in Bethlehem, Pa. Children: Ira, George, Edward.

VII. Ira Stout, born Apr. 1, 1859. Mrd. Mary Himelright,—. Children:
VII. George C. Stout, M. D., born June 29, 1862.
VII. C. Edward Stout, M. D., born Jan. 2, 1866. Mrd. Nellie Storm,—, 1888. Practicing in S. Bethlehem, Pa. One child:

VI. Lewis Henry Stout, born Jan. 27, 1834; died May 3, 1884. Lawyer, practiced in Easton, afterwards in Bethlehem. S.
VI. Catharine Amanda Stout, born Mar. 26, 1837. Mrd. Samuel J. Shimer, Sept. 27, 1860. He was born Dec. 3, 1837. P. O., Milton, Pa. Manufacturer. Presbyterians. Children: Elmer, Mary, George.

VII. Elmer Stout Shimer, born Sept. 19, 1862. Mrd. Margaretta Sinclair Lawson, Sept. 19, 1888. She was born Mar. 2, 1862. P. O., Milton, Pa. Member of the firm S. J. Shimer & Sons, and Milton Manufacturing Company. Presbyterians. One child: (**VIII.**) Elizabeth Shimer, born June 1, 1891.
VII. Mary Catharine Shimer, born Dec. 9, 1864. Mrd. William A. Heinen. (See Index of References No. 32.)
VII. George S. Shimer, born Mar. 26, 1865. Mrd. Libba Stewart Moore, May 12, 1887. She was born Dec. 2, 1867. P. O., Milton, Pa. Member of the firm of S. J. Shimer & Sons, and Milton Manufacturing Company. Presbyterians. Children: (**VIII.**) Miriam Catharine Shimer, born Apr. 29, 1889. (**VIII.**) Florence Elizabeth Shimer, born Nov. 27, 1890.

V. George Clemens, born Sept. 27, 1799; died—. Mrd. – Rickabach,—. Children: David, Jacob, Carrie, Lizzie.

VI. David Clemens, born-. Lives in Kansas.
VI. Jacob Clemens, born—.
VI. Carrie Clemens, born   Mrd. John Aikens.
VI. Lizzie Clemens, born . Mrd.   .

(See Page 102)

V. Elizabeth Clemens, born Mar. 12, 1802; died -. Mrd. James Lovett.—. Children: Mary, Elmina, Emily, Henry, John.

VI. Mary Matilda Lovett, born Aug. 10, 1825. Mrd. Lucius Clavill. . Children: Evelyn P., Elmina E., J. Harry, John K., Theo. A.

VII. Evelyn Putnam Clavill, born July 9, 1853. Mrd. .

VII. Elmina Emily Clavill, born Mar. 23, 1855. Mrd. .

VII. J. Harry Lovett Clavill, born Oct. 3, 1857.

VII. John Kinsey Clavill, born June 20, 1863; died July 6, 1863.

VII. Theo. Atkins Clavill, born Feb. 13, 1866; died Dec. 30, 1866.

VI. Elmina Andry Lovett, born Sept. 12, 1829; died Jan. 18, 1874. Mrd. Jeremiah Larzelere. .

VI. Emily Ann Lovett, born Oct. 19, 1833; died Dec. 2, 1887. Mrd. Frank Tackett. . No issue.

VI. Henry Switzer Lovett, born Oct. 19, 1837. Mrd. Martha E. Hand, Feb. 22, 1870. P. O., Doylestown, Pa. Retired farmer. Presbyterians. Children: (**VII.**) George Hand Lovett, born Nov. 7, 1871; died Aug. 31, 1877. (**VII.**) J. Warren Lovett, born Jan. 29, 1873. Res., 1010 Green St., Phila., Pa. Telegraph operator. S.

VI. John Lovett, born . Mrd. . P. O., Doylestown, Pa.

V. Leah Clemens, born June 16, 1804; died Aug. 21, 1822. Mrd. Aaron Townsend,—. One child: Mary.

VI. Mary Leah Townsend, born Aug. 8, 1822; died Sept. 18, 1880. Her mother dying when she was only a few days old, her grandfather Christian Clemens took her into his family and raised her. She was married to Israel Worthington,—. Farmer. He was a member of the Quaker, and she of the Presbyterian church. Children: Edward, Aaron, Henry, John, Walter.

VII. Edward H. Worthington, born Feb. 3, 1843. Mrd. Emaline Miller, Mar. 4, 1869. P. O., Rising Sun, Md.

VII. Aaron T. Worthington, born Dec. 2, 1845. Mrd. Elizabeth W. Green, Feb. 17, 1870. P. O., Edison, Pa. Children: **(VIII.)** H. Watson Worthington, born May 28, 1873; died Aug. 18, 1878. **(VIII.)** Susie F. Worthington, born July 22, 1878.

V. Lewis Clemens, born Sept. 12, 1806; died June 3, 1883. Mrd. Eliza Kulp.—. She died Feb. 22, 1848. Farmer. Presbyterian. Mrs. Clemens, Mennonite. Children: Jacob, John, Lewis.

VI. Jacob Clemens, born Oct. 8, 1840. Mrd. Mary C. Meyers.—. Farmer near Doylestown, Pa. Presbyterians. Children: **(VII.)** Harry M. Clemens, S. **(VII.)** Margaret Elizabeth Clemens, S. **(VII.)** Anna Clemens, S.

VI. John Clemens, born Jan. 1, 1842. Mrd. Hannah Johnson.—. P. O., Doylestown, Pa. Farmer. Presbyterian. Children: **(VII.)** Eliza Clemens, dec'd. **(VII.)** Mary Clemens, dec'd. **(VII.)** Katie Clemens, dec'd. **(VII.)** Emma Clemens.

VI. Lewis H. Clemens, born Nov. 22, 1843. Mrd. Ida M. Palmer.—. P. O., Doylestown, Pa. Florist, and Justice of the Peace. Children: **(VII.)** George Clemens, born Apr. 23, 1881. **(VII.)** Lizzie Clemens, born Apr. 13, 1883. **(VII.)** Anna Clemens, born Apr. 1, 1885.

V. Jacob Clemens, born Dec. 29, 1808; died June 10, 1872. Mrd. Catharine Ott, Feb. 13, 1834. Farmer and Tanner. Ev. Assoc. Children: Anna, Emma, Addie, Carrie, Eliza, Henry, Charles, Kate, Alonzo. *Mother Clemens was born at Pleasant Valley, Pa., Nov. 21, 1811; died Mar. 10, 1890. They lived on a farm and tannery at Springtown, until 1868, they moved to Bethlehem, where, four years later, the King of kings whom he faithfully served received Father Clemens into the mansions not made with hands eternal in the heavens. Mother Clemens survived her husband 18 long years in the home at Bethlehem, where she also died. She reared an interesting family of nine children, who with 19 grandchildren, and 7 great-grand-

* Extracts from published obituary of Mrs. Catharine Clemens.

children remain to mourn their loss. Mother Clemens was a bright, intelligent, and well informed woman. Above all she was a good, devoted, noble-hearted Christian, and an excellent Bible student. At the age of 23 she gave her heart to Jesus, and joined the Evangelical Association and remained faithful to God and the church until called from labor to reward. A liberal supporter, an earnest worker in the church, she also did much for the itinerant preachers of her church, and her home was usually their stopping place.

She was a good mother to all, giving good advice and counsel to all with whom she came in contact. One young man plucked as a brand from the eternal burning, who said he never heeded any minister of the gospel, was a drunkard, atheist, and a very profane man. By the constant admonition of mother Clemens, he finally amended his ways. This young man was her last class-leader on earth, and has since become a minister of the gospel. In her last hours she said, "Christ is still my stay and staff. We must all be sanctified. I can die in peace." Mother Clemens took great delight in speaking about the battles and victories in Christ's service, in hearing old choruses sung, and the word of God read, and prayer, during which, even in the midst of all her sufferings she would clap her hands and shout for joy. Her's was indeed the death of the righteous, and precious in the sight of the Lord. To her children, grandchildren, and great-grandchildren, how sweet, how impressive, and how inviting are her last words *"Good-bye, meet me in heaven."*

VI. Anna M. Clemens, born, ; died—. Mrd. John Eakins,—; died—.

VI. Emma B. Clemens, born—. Mrd. Solomon Frey —. He died,—. P. O., Bethlehem, Pa.

VI. Addie L. Clemens, born—. Mrd. John Lewis,—. P. O., Allentown, Pa.

VI. Carrie Clemens, born—. Mrd. Sylvanus Frey,—. P. O., Center Valley, Pa.

VI. Eliza B. Clemens, born . Mrd. Albert Romig —. Res. Phila., Pa.

VI. Henry S. Clemens, M. D., born—. Mrd. Emily Hartman,—. Physician in Allentown, Pa.

VI. Charles O. Clemens, born May 4, 1843. Mrd. Emily Rennard, Dec. 26, 1865. P. O., Bethlehem, Pa. Traveling salesman. Methodists. Children: Bertha, Hattie, Charles, Rosa, Alonzo.

VII. Bertha E. Clemens, born Mar. 17, 1867. Mrd. Benjamin E. Cohen, —. P. O., West Chester, Pa. One child: (VIII.) Charles Grey Cohen.

VII. Hattie R. Clemens, born June 16, 1868. Teacher in the High School at Bethlehem, Pa.

VII. Charles W. Clemens, born July 1, 1873. Draftsman in Bethlehem Iron Works.

VII. Rosa E. Clemens, born Oct. 29, 1875; died Aug. 25, 1886.

VII. Alonzo W. Clemens, born Sept. 24, 1879.

VI. Kate Clemens, born at Springtown, Bucks Co., Dec. 14, 1856. Mrd. Oliver H. Sterner, M. D., May 6, 1879. Dr. Sterner is the oldest son of Charles Sterner of Allentown, Pa., where he was born, May 29, 1858. When 17 years of age he entered the drug business, and graduated from the Philadelphia College of Pharmacy, Apr. 1879, after which he started in the drug business for himself in Frankford, Philadelphia, which he has carried on ever since. In the spring of 1886 he began the study of medicine and graduated from Jefferson Medical College in the spring of 1889. Since then he has been practicing medicine in connection with his drug store. Methodists. One child: (VII.) Clarence P. Sterner, born Jan. 10, 1883.

VI. Alonzo W. Clemens, born , died . Married Amanda Spinner. . She died .

V. Henry Clemens, born Dec. 20, 1810; died July 14, 1833. S.

V. John Clemens, born Feb. 6, 1814; died —. Mrd. Emma Heiss. Stove and hardware merchant. Presbyterian. Children: William, Crissie.

VI. William H. Clemens, born at Doylestown, Pa., Oct. 7, 1850. Mrd. Mary E. Campbell, of Leesburgh, Va., Nov. 15, 1871. P. O., Leesburgh, Va. Has served as road commissioner of Leesburgh District, at present farmer. Presbyterians. Children: (VII.) Two children, still-born. (VII.) John R. Clemens, born July 20, 1876. (VII.) Christian H. Clemens, born Aug. 20, 1887.

VI. Crissie H. Clemens, born ―. Mrd. William H. Kirk, M. D. P. O., Doylestown, Pa.

IV. Lewis Sweitzer, born Mar. 21, 1774; died ―. Mrd. ―Bell. Descendants if any, not found.

IV. Conrad Sweitzer, born June 15, 1776; died― Mrd.―. Descendants not found.

IV. Elizabeth Sweitzer, born Sept. 29, 1778; died at Newville, Herkimer Co., N. Y., Jan. 9, 1848. Mrd. Samuel Haupt, at Doylestown, Pa.,―. He was born Sept. 22, 1773; died Jan. 9, 1851. After marriage they moved to Newville, Herkimer Co., N. Y., where he carried on farming and owned several mills, a flouring mill, saw mill, fulling, carding and dying mills, and had an interest in a furnace for casting stoves, and ware of different kinds. Lutherans. Children: Henry, Nancy, Lewis, Chauney, Eliza, Catharine.

V. Henry Houpt, born Dec.―, 1804; died―. Mrd. ―. Children: Chauney.

VI. Chauney Houpt, etc.

V. Nancy Houpt, born May 29, 1806. Married John Dysslin, at Newville, N. Y., Apr, 9, 1825. He was born May 27, 1799; died Oct. 23, 1877. Cabinet maker. Lutherans. Children: Eliza, Ann, John, Sarah, Franklin, Lewis, Morris, Clark.

VI. Eliza Dysslin, born Dec. 31, 1826; died Jan. 6, 1832.

VI. Ann Alida Dysslin, born Aug. 22, 1828. She died Mar. 7, 1865. Mrd. George A. Bellinger,―. Architect and builder. Baptist. Children: Henry, Charles, Ida.

VII. Henry F. Bellinger, born Mar. 4, 1850.

VII. Ida Ann Bellinger, born June 7, 1854; died Nov. 14, 1856.

VII. Charles G. Bellinger, born July 1, 1852. Mrd. Louisa E. Evans, May 13, 1875. Residence 421 W. 44th St., New York City. Carpenter. No issue.

VI. John Henry Dysslin, born Nov. 15, 1830; died Dec. 16, 1830.

VI. Sarah C. Dysslin, born Oct. 28, 1831. Mrd. Charles H. Little, in Springfield, Mass., Mar. 2, 1857. P. O., Freeport, Ill. Wholesale and retail crockery merchant. Mrs. Little is a "Christian Scientist." No issue.

VI. Franklin Dyslin, born July 26, 1834. Mrd. Ursula Maria Cison, Jan. 10, 1856, in Herkimer Co., N. Y. Formerly architect and builder, last 30 years farmer. P. O., Lanark, Ill. Methodist Episcopal. Children: Nancy, Mattie, Frankie, Roy.

VII. Nancy J. Dyslin, born Oct. 3, 1856. Mrd. William C. Babcock, Dec. 25, 1878. He was born in Herkimer Co., N. Y., Nov. 21, 1850. P. O., Shannon, Carroll Co., Ill. Children: (**VIII.**) Fannie E. Babcock, born Sept. 29, 1879. (**VIII.**) Ursula H. Babcock, born Feb. 25, 1881.

VII. Mattie E. Dyslin, born Jan. 25, 1861; died Apr. 6, 1862.

VII. Frankie B. Dyslyn, born Feb. 17, 1867. Mrd. O. J. Aurand, June 25, 1890. P. O., Loran, Stephenson Co., Ill. Physician. Methodist Episcopal.

VII. Roy Dyslin, born Feb. 17, 1872; died Mar. 6, 1888, aged 16 years, 18 days.

VI. Lewis H. Dyslin, born Dec. 25, 1836 or 7. Mrd. Arminda Wilcox, of Little Falls, N. Y., in 1861. She was born Oct. 16, 1842. P. O., Lanark, Ill. Farmer. Children: Nettie, John William, Sarah, Frank, Morris, George.

VII. Nettie Dyslin, born Feb. 19, 1862; died Nov. 17, 1873.

VII. John N. Dyslin, born May 30, 1864.

VII. William H. Dyslin, born July 13, 1866. Mrd. Lizzie Grasseck, Nov. 27, 1890.

VII. Sarah E. Dyslin, born Nov. 19, 1868. Mrd. Thede Wilkins, Sept. 8, 1886. P. O., Lanark, Ill.

VII. Frank B. Dyslin, born Feb. 19, 1869.

VII. Morris E. Dyslin, born May 6, 1870.

VII. George Dyslin, born Oct. 6, 1872.

VI. Morris Dysslin, born in Herkimer Co., N. Y., Mar. 10, 1838. Mrd. Frances Fralick, of Little Falls,

Corporal Alonzo F. Kratz.

(See Page 104.)

THE NEW YORK
PUBLIC LIBRARY

N. Y., Jan. 23. 1861. Farmer. Children: Charles, Clark, Philo. Addie.

VII. Charles M. Dysslin. born Dec. 8. 1861. Mrd. Delia Higley, Feb. 27. 1888. No children (1891).

VII. Clark H. Dysslin. born Aug. 15. 1863.

VII. Philo R. Dysslin. born Aug. 2. 1865.

VII. Addie A. Dysslin. born. Oct. 15. 1867.

VI. Clark Dyslin. born Nov. 23. 1841. Mrd. Eugenia Wilcox, Mar. 6. 1864. P. O., Lanark. Ill. Farmer. Children: (**VII.**) Lewis Dyslin. born Nov. 20. 1865. P. O., Amelia. Iowa. (**VII.**) Lulie Dyslin. born Dec. 12. 1867. (**VII.**) Walter Dyslin. born Oct. 20. 1869. P. O., Sherburn. Minn.

V. Lewis Houpt. born Apr. 11. 1810; died July 21. 1853. Mrd. Caroline F. Benedict. May 26. 1844. Farmer. Children: Sarah. Annie. Lewis.

VI. Sarah E. Houpt. born at Ephratah. Fulton Co.. N. Y.. July 30. 1846. Mrd. Frank E. Spencer. Jan. 29. 1880. P. O.. New Haven. Conn. Merchant. No issue.

VI. Annie Houpt. born in Newville. Herkimer Co.. N. Y.. Aug. 2. 1848. Mrd. Rev. I. N. Elwood. May 26. 1868. He died—. P. O.. Flint. Mich. Methodist Episcopal. Children: (**VII.**) Carrie F. Elwood. born June 18. 1870. (**VII.**) Alice M Elwood. born Sept. 23. 1873.

VI. W. Lewis Houpt. born in Herkimer Co., N. Y.. Feb. 11, 1851. P. O., Lisbon. N. Dakota. S.

V. Eliza Houpt. born Mar. 25. 1818. Mrd. Jefferson Church. M. D., of Springfield. Mass., in 1850. He died in 1885. Physician. Children: (**VI.**) Eliza Church. born—; died aged 9 months. (**VI.**) Martha Church. born—; died aged 3 years and 6 months.

V. Catharine Houpt. born in Newville. Herkimer Co., N. Y., Dec. 18, 1818. Mrd. William Morris, Mar. 19, 1839. Physician. Children: William. Charles. Samuel.

VI. William H. H. Morris. born in Utica, N. Y., Ap. 29. 1840; died Oct. 8, 1876. at High Point. Mo. Physician.

VI. Charles Morris. born in Utica, N. Y.. Apr. 1, 1842: died Apr. 1, 1844.

VI. Samuel H. Morris, born in Utica, N. Y., Apr. 13, 1845; died Apr. 20, 1888. Mrd. Emily C. Stevens, in Danube, Herkimer Co., N. Y., June 28, 1870. Physician. Children: **(VII.)** Julia Catharine Morris, born May 21, 1876. **(VII.)** Susan H. Morris, born Sept. 27, 1882.

IV. Henry Sweitzer, born Oct. 27, 1780.

IV. Barbara Caroline Sweitzer, born in Bucks Co., Oct. 14, 1784; died Nov. 26, 1867. Mrd. John S. Dugan, in 1811. He was born in 1780; died in 1825. Mail Contractor. Catholics. One child: Lewis H.

V. Lewis H. Dugan, born July 10, 1812. Mrd. Sarah Ann Culbertson, Apr. 26, 1836. She died Aug. 16, 1840. P. O., Zanesville, Ohio. Farmer. Catholic. Children: James T., John S., Carrie.

VI. James T. Dugan, born Feb. 25, 1837; died June 18, 1851. S.

VI. John S. Dugan, born Oct. 12, 1838; died Oct. 2, 1841.

VI. Carrie Dugan, born Sept. 5, 1840. Mrd. William A. Fillmore, Oct. 13, 1863. P. O., Zanesville, Ohio. Stockholder and President of Zanesville Hardware Co., Mrs. Fillmore, Catholic. Children: Annie, Arthur, Harry, Willie, Ralph.

VII. Annie S. Fillmore, born July 6, 1864. Mrd. Douglas C. Blandy,—. P. O., Zanesville, Ohio.

VII. Arthur E. Fillmore, born Oct. 31, 1865. S.

VII. Harry L. Fillmore, born June 1, 1867. Mrd. Ida Marshall,—. P. O., Zanesville, Ohio.

VII. Willie H. Fillmore, born Mar. 4, 1871.

VII. Ralph D. Fillmore, born Feb. 5, 1880.

IV. Simon Sweitzer, born Oct. 12, 1787; died unmarried.

IV. John Sweitzer, born—; died young.

III. A daughter, born 1746; died young.

PK
RY

DESCENDANTS OF VALENTINE KRATZ, SON OF JOHN VALENTINE KRATZ.

III. Valentine Kratz, born in Montg. Co., May 16, 1747; died July 28, 1834, aged 87 yrs., 2 m. 12 d. Mrd. Mary Rosenberger, —. She died Jan. 23, 1805, aged 47 years. Children: Ann, Daniel, Valentine, Abraham, John, Isaac, David, William, Jacob. His second wife was Widow Margaret King, born—. She died Apr. 4, 1835, aged 75 yrs., 2 m. 5 d. Farmer. Mennonites. Lived in Upper Salford, on the 150 acre farm he inherited from his father, where Henry Weber now lives, and where he died. It is related that when he was old he had men threshing grain. During the day he asked them how much they would charge per day. They replied, 45 cents. In the evening he asked again, and received the same reply. Then he said, "Forty-five cents is *too* much, and is too much, and is too much!"

IV. Ann Kratz, born Nov. 17, 1778; died (single) Oct. 24, 1822, aged 44 yrs., 11 mo. 7 d.

IV. Daniel Kratz, born—. Mrd. a Miss Geist,—. Lived near Rochester, N. Y., where he died without issue. It is said that when he came to receive his share of his father's estate, and was ready to return home to Rochester, N. Y., he was afraid he might get robbed, and persuaded Samuel K. Smith and Jonas Boyer to go with him. They got a horse and wagon, and took a load of harness along, and peddled it out, and saw him safe home.

IV. Valentine Kratz, born Feb. 5, 1783; died Oct. 29, 1865, aged 82 yrs., 8 mo. 24 d. Mrd. a widow Boyer, maiden name Christman. She died Oct. 24, 1822. Children: Jonas, Valentine, Mary, Ann,

George. Valentine mrd. second wife, widow Mary Detweiler,—. She died Mar. 6, 1866. Farmer. Lived in Frederick Twp.. Montg. Co. He was lame and was known as "lame Felty." Mennonites. Children: Jacob, Rebecca, Daniel, Sarah, Esther, Hannah.

V. Jonas Kratz, born in Montg. Co., Oct. 30, 1807; died Feb. 25, 1882. Mrd. Susanna Bechtel,—. She was born Aug. 26, 1808; died Nov. 1, 1850. Farmer. Mennonites. Children. Abraham, Harrison, Mary Ann.

VI. Abraham Kratz; died July 20, 1845, aged 11 yr., 5 m. 16 d.

VI. Harrison Kratz; died July 22, 1845, aged 5 yr., 4 m. 14 d.

VI. Mary Ann Kratz; died July 29, 1845, aged 14 yr., 5 m. 9 d.

Jonas mrd. second wife, Elanora B. Fryer,—. She was born May 5, 1823; died Aug. 4, 1889. Children: Amos, Saloma, Ida, Elanora, Infant.

VI. Amos F. Kratz, born in Upper Providence Twp., Montg. Co., July 9, 1852. Mrd. Annie Matilda Spare, Nov. 22, 1889. P. O. Collegeville, Pa. Farmer. Lutherans. No children.

VI. Salome F. Kratz (twin), born July 9, 1852; died June 23, 1876. Mrd. George W. Zimmerman, Feb. 18, 1874. One child: (**VII.**) Frank Ernest Zimmerman, born June 16, 1875.

VI. Ida F. Kratz, born in Montg. Co., May 6, 1856. Mrd. J. Warren Rosenberger, Feb. 9, 1876. P. O., Yerkes, Pa. Farmer. One child: (**VII.**) Katie K. Rosenberger, born June 15, 1881.

VI. Elanora F. Kratz, born in Montg. Co., May 26, 1866. Mrd. Allen Bard, Sept. 24, 1888. P. O.. Yerkes, Pa. Farmer. One child: (**VII.**) Samuel Leroy Bard, born Feb. 18, 1889.

VI. Infant, died— .

V. Valentine Kratz, born Aug. 23, 1809; died Mar. 25, 1887. Mrd. Rhoda Bush, Nov. 16, 1834. Moved to Cattaraugus Co., N. Y., in 1833. Farmer. Baptists. Children: Peter, Henry, Lucy, Lucinda, Isaac.

VI. Peter S. Kratz, born Feb. 28, 1837. Mrd. Lorinda Knight, Jan. 1, 1861. P. O., Olean, N. Y.

Farmer. Baptists. Children: (VII.) Henry Kratz, born July 22. 1862: died Feb. 11. 1868. (VII.) Hattie D. Kratz, born Aug. 28. 1864. (VII.) Eddie V. Kratz, born Jan. 21. 1869. (VII.) Wilbur J. Kratz, born Sept. 5. 1871. (VII.) Clarence E. Kratz. born July 10. 1874. (VII.) Samuel Kratz. born May 1. 1878; died Feb. 27. 1890. (VII.) Charles Kratz. born Feb. 17. 1880.

VI. Henry W. Kratz. born Mar. 25. 1839; died Aug. 10. 1841.

VI. Lucy Kratz. born Dec. 25. 1844. Mrd. P. O. Cleveland. Dec. 25. 1876. P. O., Olean. N. Y. Farmer. Wife, Baptist. Children: (VII.) Dora Cleveland. born Sept. 26. 1877. (VII.) Salome Cleveland. born Mar. 10. 1879. (VII.) Arthur Cleveland. born Nov. 18. 1880. (VII.) Mabel Cleveland. born Mar. 18. 1882. (VII.) Marcella Cleveland. born Oct. 8. 1884 (VII.) Mildred Cleveland. born May 22. 1885.

VI. Lucinda A. Kratz. born Mar. 30. 1847. Mrd. George W. Barnes. Oct. 15. 1874. P. O.. Olean. N. Y. Farmer. Baptists. Children: (VII.) Lewis D. Barnes, born July 10. 1875: died Mar. 9. 1876. (VII.) Loren S. Barnes. born June 20. 1878. (VII.) Valentine K. Barnes. born Feb. 28. 1882.

VI. Isaac N. Kratz. born Dec. 9. 1849. Mrd. Sarah Gowen. Oct. 10. 1874. P. O., Olean. N. Y. Farmer.

V. Mary Kratz. born Oct. 16. 1811: died Dec. 20. 1890. Mrd. Joseph D. Gotwals. Mar. 1. 1840. Children: Matilda. Abraham. Hannah. Benjamin, Mary. Anna, Sarah.

VI. Matilda Gotwals. born Jan. 2. 1840. Mrd. Israel H. Heips. July 1. 1869. Special officer in Philadelphia. Pa. Methodists. Children: (VII.) Elmer Franklin Heips. born Feb. 10. 1872. (VII.) Ida Matilda Heips, born Dec. 24. 1875.

VI. Abraham K. Gotwals, born June 4. 1841. P. O., Hyattville. Wyoming. Farmer and stock raiser. S.

VI. Hannah Gotwals, born Oct. 23. 1844. Mrd. John Grigg Johnson. Sept.—. 1869. No issue.

VI. Benjamin Franklin Gotwals, born Oct. 30. 1846. Mrd. C. Emma Oberholtzer. July 5, 1879. P. O.. Rockford. Ill. Employed in Stocking Factory. Baptists. Children: (**VII.**) Harriet N. Gotwals, born Apr. 17, 1880. (**VII.**) Jacob Walter Gotwals, born Mar. 27, 1883.

VI. Mary Jane Gotwals, born Oct. 3, 1851; died June 1878. Mrd. James E. Carlisle, Dec. 1874. One child: (**VII.**) Olive May Carlisle, born —; died —.

VI. Annie C. Gotwals, born Sept. 23, 1853. Mrd. Rev. Henry A. Hunsicker (his second wife), May 11, 1876. P. O., Mount Bethel, Pa. Mr. Hunsicker was born near Trappe, Montg. Co., Nov. 10, 1825. Spent his boyhood days on his father's farm, and had only the limited advantages of the country schools of that time. In 1835 Henry Prizer opened a Boarding School in the village of Trappe. He died in 1838 and was succeeded in the school by Rev. Henry S. Rodenbough. This was Mr. Hunsicker's Alma Mater. In 1848, he and his father founded "Freeland Seminary," an educational institution designed for young men and boys. He at once became the principal of the school, and three years later the proprietor. He continued as Principal of this school until 1865, when he leased the school and property to A. N. Fetterolf, one of his assistants for five years. During the time of his lease to Prof. F. he sold the school property to Rev. J. H. A. Bombroger, D. D., of Philadelphia, who, in connection with other enterprising persons, obtained a charter and founded Ursinus College. In 1850 Mr. Hunsicker was ordained to the ministry of the New (Oberholtzer) Mennonite church. On account of the liberal and progressive ideas in church work, a chism took place in 1851, which resulted in establishing an independent church, known as Trinity Christians, of which Mr. Hunsicker was one of the founders, and for which he continued to preach until 1875. Children: (**VII.**) Mary Anna Hunsicker, born Sept. 25, 1879. (**VII.**) Edna E. Hunsicker, born July 6, 1882.

VI. Sarah Emma Gotwals, born June 19, 1826. Mrd. James Carlisle, Nov. 18, 1880. He died Feb. 9, 1883. No issue.

V. Ann Kratz, born Feb. 12, 1814. Single.

V. George Kratz, born in Frederick Twp., Montg. Co., Pa., June 15, 1815; died Oct. 31, 1863. Mrd. Elizabeth, widow of Joseph Johnson (maiden name Bechtel), Jan. 11, 1845. Farmer. Children: Henry, Jacob, George.

VI. Henry B. Kratz, born at Trappe, Montg. Co., Feb. 7, 1846. Mrd. Catharine High, Jan. 4, 1868. P. O., Allentown, Pa. Railway Postal Clerk. Children: **(VII.)** Sallie Kratz, born June 28, 1869. **(VII.)** Lizzie Kratz, born Aug. 7, 1874.

VI. Jacob B. Kratz (twin), born Feb. 7, 1846; died 1849.

VI. George B. Kratz, born at Trappe, Montg. Co., Oct. 9, 1849. Mrd. —.

V. Jacob J. Kratz, born in Frederick Twp., Montg. Co., Nov. 15, 1820; died Nov. 24, 1885. Mrd. Elizabeth, daughter of George Wambold, of Franconia Twp., June 5, 1842. Farmer. Lutherans. Children: Mary, Catharine, George, Daniel, Samuel, Frank.

VI. Mary Kratz, born Aug. 15, 1843; died Aug. 10, 1845.

VI. Catharine Kratz, born in Montgomery Co., Oct. 16, 1845. Mrd. Henry Frederick. P. O., Earlington, Pa. One child: **(VII.)** Lizzie Frederick, born—.

VI. George W. Kratz, born in Montg. Co., June 26, 1847. Mrd. Emma A. Stout, daughter of Jacob Stout, of Rockhill, Twp., Bucks Co., Pa., Nov. 26, 1870. P. O., Earlington, Pa. Lutherans. No issue.

VI. Daniel W. Kratz, born Aug. 17, 1849. Mrd. Lizzie Souder, daughter of Henry Souder of Franconia Twp., Nov. 8, 1873. P. O., Telford, Pa. Lutherans. Children: **(VII.)** Katie Kratz. **(VII.)** Harry Kratz. **(VII.)** Ervin Kratz.

VI. Samuel W. Kratz, born Aug. 28, 1851. Mrd. Lizzie Kober, daughter of John Kober, Dec. 4, 1875. Lives on his father's farm in Franconia Twp. P. O., Earlington, Pa. Lutheran. Children: **(VII.)** Sallie Kratz, born Sept. 25, 1876. **(VII.)** George Kratz, born Sept. 27, 1878.

VI. Frank W. Kratz, born in Montg. Co., Feb. 27, 1854. Mrd. Susanna Rahn, daughter of Elias Rahn,

of Perkiomen Twp., Dec. 15, 1877. P. O., Schwenksville, Pa. Lutheran. No issue.

V. Rebecca Kratz, born Nov. 12, 1822. Mrd. Francis
Zepp, Jan. 19, 1851. He was born Aug. 16, 1814.
Lutherans. Children: Mary, Rebecca, Jacob, Frank,
Sarah.

VI. Mary Zepp, born Oct. 28, 1851; died May 5,
1871.

VI. Rebecca Zepp, born Jan. 27, 1853. Mrd. John
Borneman,—. P. O., Lucon, Pa. Lutherans. Children:

VI. Jacob K. Zepp, born Jan. 4, 1855. Mrd. Kate
K. Gebart, Sept. 23, 1882. P. O., Hendricks, Pa.
Lutherans. Children: (**VII.**) Frank G. Zepp, born
May 4, 1884. (**VII.**) John G. Zepp, born Aug. 24,
1886. (**VII.**) George G. Zepp, born Sept. 11, 1887.

VI. Frank K. K. Zepp, born Nov. 4, 1856. Mrd.
Mary D. Nace, of Rockhill, Bucks Co., Dec. 11,
1886. Lutherans. Children: (**VII.**) Elmer N. Zepp,
born May 11, 1888. (**VII.**) Jonas N. Zepp, born May
12, 1889.

VI. Sarah K. Zepp, born Dec. 11, 1858. Mrd. Eli
Geisinger—.

V. Daniel K. Kratz, born in Frederick Twp., Montg.
Co., Pa., Nov. 15, 1826; died either from a fall
through a trap door at the residence of Abraham F.
Kratz, or from heart failure which produced the fall,
Jan. 30, 1885; aged 58 yrs. Mrd. Hannah B. Boorse,
of Worcester Twp., Montg. Co., Jan. 23, 1853. She
died after untold sufferings for a number of years,
from tumors on lower jaw and neck, Sept. 13, 1889;
aged 55 years. Children: Amanda, Mary, Hannah,
Henry, Franklin, Emma, Ellen, Horace, Daniel,
John, Jacob.

V. Amanda Kratz, born Apr. 21, 1854; died Aug.
10, 1886. Mrd. John B. Wismer, Mar. 2, 1876.
P. O., Linfield, Pa. Miller. Children: (**VII.**) Irvin
Wismer. (**VII.**) Warrel Wismer. (**VII.**) Hannah Wismer.

VI. Mary Kratz, born July 18, 1855. Mrd. Samuel
Hiestand, Jan. 20, 1877. Farmer. Children: (**VII.**)

Laura Hiestand. **(VII.)** Daniel Hiestand. **(VII.)** John Hiestand. **(VII.)** Mary Hiestand.

VI. Hannah Kratz, born July 22, 1857. Mrd. Nathaniel C. Hiestand, Jan. 1, 1881. He was born Dec. 9, 1857. P. O., Corning, Pa. Farmer. Mennonites. Children: **(VII.)** Hannah H. Hiestand, born Nov. 26, 1883. **(VII.)** Horace K. Hiestand, born May 1, 1885. **(VII.)** Katie K. Hiestand, born May 25, 1887; died Sept. 12, 1888. **(VII.)** Sallie K. Hiestand, born Jan. 25, 1889. **(VII.)** Lizzie K. Hiestand, born July 1, 1891.

VI. Henry B. Kratz, born Nov. 15, 1858; died aged 4 years.

VI. Franklin B. Kratz, born Sept. 8, 1860. Mrd. Maggie Heiner. . Farmer. Children: **(VII.)** Warren Kratz. **(VII.)** Lizzie Kratz. **(VII.)** Hannah Kratz.

VI. Emma Kratz, born Apr. 18, 1863; died aged 4 years.

VI. Ellen B. Kratz, born Oct. 26, 1864; died aged 5 years.

VI. Horace B. Kratz, born Oct. 19, 1866. Mrd. Sallie Longaker, July 27, 1889. P. O., Schwenksville, Pa. Merchant, miller.

VI. Daniel B. Kratz, born Sept. 8, 1868; died Sept. 29, 1888. At the time of his death he was a medical student with Dr. Hiram Loux, of Souderton, Pa.

VI. John B. Kratz, born Aug. 28, 1872.

VI. Jacob B. Kratz, born Jan. 27, 1878.

V. Sarah Kratz, born—. Single.

V. Esther Kratz, born—; died young.

V. Hannah Kratz, born—. died young.

IV. Abraham Kratz, born Aug. 25, 1785; died Feb. 11, 1870, aged 80 yrs., 5 m. 7 d. Mrd. Elizabeth Cassel, daughter of Jacob and Susanna Cassel. She died Nov. 9, 1861. Farmer, and lived in Skippack Twp., on the farm now belonging to their son Daniel. Buried at Salford Mennonite Meeting-house. Children: Mary, John, Jacob, Lydia, Abraham, Daniel, Elizabeth, Catharine.

V. Mary Kratz, born Apr. 13, 1808. Mrd. Samuel Gehman—. He died in 1878. No issue.

V. John C. Kratz, born Oct. 23, 1814; died July 7, 1875. Mrd. Catharine Z. Gotwals, Dec. 15, 1839.

Farmer. Mr. Kratz, Trinity Christian. Mrs. Kratz, Methodist. Children: Abraham, John, Lizzie, Mary, Kate, Cornelius, Sally, Henry.

VI. Abraham G. Kratz, born in 1840; died (single). Enlisted in 1861, and was killed at Resaca, Georgia, in 1864.

VI. John G. Kratz, born Oct. 28, 1842. Married Eleanor Elizabeth Deeds, March 9, 1871. Farmer. P. O., Yerkes, Montg. Co., Pa. Member Trinity Christian, and his wife of the St. James Episcopal. Children: **(VII.)** Mary Kate Kratz, born Apr. 24, 1872. **(VII.)** Chester Arthur Kratz, born Nov. 20, 1873. **(VII.)** John D. Kratz, born April 19, 1875. **(VII.)** Harry Thomas Kratz, born Aug. 26, 1876. **(VII.)** Albert Kratz, born July 18, 1878; died July 24, 1878. **(VII.)** Ella May Kratz, born June 8, 1884.

VI. Lizzie G. Kratz, born —, 1845. S.

VI. Mary A. Kratz, born —, 1846. S.

VI. Catharine G. Kratz, born Jan. 20, 1849. Mrd. George Otto Kunkle, May 26, 1877. He died Sept. 5, 1884. Carpenter. No issue. Catharine mrd. for her second husband, Jacob Steiver Springer, Jan. 8, 1887. P. O., Royer's Ford, Pa. Carpenter by trade, now farmer. Mrs. Springer is a member of the Reformed church. No issue.

VI. Cornelius Tyson Kratz, born in Montg. Co., Pa, Aug. 11, 1850. Mrd. Annie W., daughter of Joseph S. Siddall, Esq., of Phila., Nov. 5, 1874. In early life he worked on his father's farm, and attended school during the winter until he was sixteen years of age, when he began teaching. He taught school off and on until he was 23; part of the time he spent at Freeland Seminary and Lafayette College. He taught in Upper and Lower Providence, Montg. Co., Pa., Camden Co., N. J., Lorimer Co., Col., and Washington Hall Institute, Trappe, Pa.

At the age of 22 he entered the office of Carroll Brewster, Esq., of Phila., and began the study of law, remaining about two years. He was admitted to the Philadelphia Bar in 1874. In 1876 he was admitted to the Norristown Bar. Most of his time for some years past has been devoted to the business of Titles

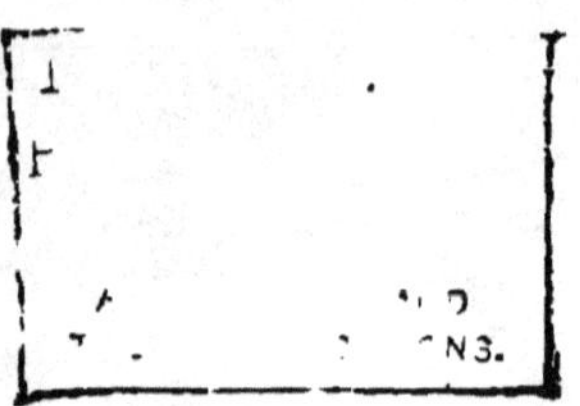

to Real Estate and Title Insurance. He has been connected with the Real Estate Title Insurance and Trust Company of 10th and Chestnut Streets, Phila., Pa., since 1881; and is now their resident attorney for the counties of Chester, Bucks and Montgomery, with headquarters at Norristown, Pa. Mr. Kratz was elected to the Legislature of Pa., by the Republicans of Montgomery Co., Pa., in Nov. 1888, and served in the session of 1889. He is at present living in Lower Providence Twp., Montg. Co., Pa., on the farm his father owned for many years, and carries on the farming in connection with his duties as Attorney. Children: (VII.) Annie May Kratz, born Aug. 22, 1875. (VII.) Joseph Stancliffe Kratz, born Aug. 4, 1878. (VII.) Edwin Cornelius Kratz, born Jan. 28, 1882.

VI. Sallie K. Kratz, born Apr. 19, 1854. Married Thomas Long, May 31, 1883. Farmer, at King of Prussia, Montg., Co., Pa. Presbyterian. Children: (VII.) James B. Long, born Mar. 8, 1884. (VII.) Bessie K. Long, born Sept. 23, 1888. .

VI. Henry H. Kratz, born in 1860; died in 1862.

V. Jacob Kratz, born —; died aged 2 years.

V. Lydia Kratz, born —; died aged 6 years.

V. Abraham C. Kratz, born Sept. 1, 1820. Mrd. Fannie Coal. Weaver at Grater's Ford, Montg. Co., Pa. Old Mennonite. Children: Benjamin, Abraham, Noah, Daniel, John, Lizzie, Catharine, Mary, Fannie, Henry.

VI. Benjamin C. Kratz, born Dec. 7, 1844. Mrd. Sarah S. Kulp, Nov. 30, 1867. She was born Dec. 4, 1846. Farmer and huckster. P. O., Bergey, Pa. Mennonites. Children: (VII.) Ulysses K. Kratz, born July 9, 1869. (VII.) Katie K. Kratz, born July 27, 1873. (VII.) John K. Kratz, born May 4, 1875; died Sept. 14, 1875. (VII.) Abraham K. Kratz, born July 21, 1876. (VII.) Sallie K. Kratz, born June 22, 1878.

VI. Abraham C. Kratz, born Aug. 18, 1846. Mrd. Mary F. Hawk, Mar. 4, 1871. She was born Jan. 1, 1847. Farmer, and saddler. P. O., Creamery, Montgomery Co., Pa. Mennonites. Children: (VII.) Ellen H. Kratz, born Nov. 4, 1872; died Feb. 16, 1879.

(VII.) Clara H. Kratz, born Feb. 6, 1874. (VII.) Sarah H. Kratz, born Aug. 25, 1875; died Feb. 11, 1884. (VII.) Abraham H. Kratz, born Aug. 31, 1877. (VII.) Henry H. Kratz, born Sept. 1, 1882.

VI. Noah C. Kratz, born Nov. 14, 1849; died June 9, 1883. Mrd. Mary K. Kieble of Skippack Twp., Jan. 20, 1872. Engineer on the Perkiomen R. R. Wife, member of Dunkard Ch. Children: (VII.) Alice K. Kratz, born Jan. 25, 1873. Dunkard. (VII.) Harvey K. Kratz, born Apr. 27, 1874; died Aug. 15, 1874.

VI. Daniel C. Kratz, born Nov. 3, 1851. Mrd. Elizabeth S. Kulp, Sept. 2, 1875. She was born Oct. 18, 1854. Farmer, miller. P. O., Hendricks, Pa. Mennonites. Children: (VII.) Harvey K. Kratz, born Feb. 14, 1879. (VII.) Katie K. Kratz, born Apr. 29, 1884.

VI. John C. Kratz, born May 27, 1853. Mrd. Kate M. Stauffer,—. Farmer. P. O., Saint Peters, Pa. Mennonites. Children: (VII.) Emma Jane S. Kratz, born Apr. 20, 1877; died Aug. 17, 1878. (VII.) Idella S. Kratz, born June 15, 1878. (VII.) Flora S. Kratz, born Oct. 17, 1880. (VII.) Dillman Oscar Kratz, born Dec. 19, 1882. (VII.) Mary S. Kratz, born Dec. 5, 1884. (VII.) John Clayton Kratz, born July 17, 1886. (VII.) Katie Augusta S. Kratz, born Mar. 17, 1888. (VII.) Fannie Ada S. Kratz, born Dec. 29, 1890.

VI. Lizzie C. Kratz, born May 15, 1858. Mrd. Daniel Anderson, Oct. 20, 1877. Carpenter and mason. P. O., Lucon, Pa. One child: (VII.) Ida K. Anderson, born Aug. 3, 1888.

VI. Kate C. Kratz, born May 27, 1863. Mrd. William D. Fitzgerald, Feb. 11, 1887. Employed in the American Cash Register Company of Philadelphia, Pa. One child: (VII.) Bertha May Fitzgerald, born May 27, 1887; died May 1887.

VI. Mamie C. Kratz, born Aug. 30, 1864. S.

VI. Fannie C. Kratz, born   ; died in infancy.

VI. Henry C. Kratz, born   ; died in infancy.

V. Daniel C. Kratz, born Apr. 13, 1829. Married Amanda Boorse, Oct. 1860. She died Feb. 17, 1861. Mrd. second wife Hettie B. Funk, Feb. 14, 1862. P. O., Lucon, Pa. Farmer, and lives on his father's farm. Mennonites. Children: Anna, Abraham, Amanda, Maria, Esther, Sylvanus, Araminda, Elizabeth, Emma, Harry.

VI. Anna F. Kratz, born Jan. 13, 1863. Mrd. Peter Hunsberger, Sept. 8, 1888. P. O., Lucon, Pa. Farmer. Children: **(VII.)** Elmer K. Hunsberger, born Mar. 23, 1889. **(VII.)** Edwin K. Hunsberger, born Aug. 16, 1890.

VI. Abraham F. Kratz, born Mar. 31, 1865; died Apr. 24, 1885.

VI. Amanda F. Kratz, born Nov. 20, 1866. Mrd. Abraham L. Alderfer, Jan. 5, 1889. P. O., Lucon, Pa. Laborer. One child: **(VII.)** Bertha K. Alderfer, born Feb. 15, 1890.

VI. Mary F. Kratz, born Jan. 1, 1867. Mrd. Joseph L. Wismer. P. O., Harleysville, Pa.

VI. Esther F. Kratz, born June 27, 1871.

VI. Sylvanus F. Kratz, born Jan. 10, 1873.

VI. Mintie F. Kratz, born Nov. 19, 1874.

VI. Elizabeth F. Kratz, born Sept. 19, 1876; died Feb. 1877.

VI. Emma F. Kratz, born Dec. 24, 1877.

VI. Harry F. Kratz, born Mar. 13, 1880.

V. Elizabeth Kratz, born—; died aged 1 yr., 10 m.

V. Catharine Kratz, born –. Mrd. Heubert Boorse. Children: (Eliza Fretz) Abraham, William, Amanda, Annie.

VI. Eliza Fretz, born in 1849. Mrd. Schumacher,—.

VI. Abraham Boorse, born 1861; died aged 10 mo.

VI. William Henry Boorse, born 1863.

VI. Amanda Mary Ann Boorse, born 1865; died aged 3 yrs., 5 mo.

VI. Annie Maria Boorse, born 1869.

IV. John Kratz, born Apr. 27, 1788; died Oct. 21, 1820. Mrd. Catharine Detweiler,—. She died Mar. 8, 1864. Lived in Skippack Twp. Children: Henry, Jacob.

V. Henry D. Kratz, born Mar. 9, 1817; died Oct. 13, 1889. Mrd. Mary K. Kratz, Feb. 11, 1844. In early life he taught school for several winters, afterwards, and until his death he followed farming. They are members of the Mennonite church. Children: Michael, Isaac, William, Henry.

VI. Michael Kratz, born Nov. 17, 1845; died in infancy.

VI. Isaac Kratz, born Mar. 24, 1847; died in infancy.

VI. William K. Kratz, born Oct. 23, 1848. Mrd. Mary Ann Kinsey, Nov. 4, 1875. She died Feb. 10, 1887. Farmer; Children: (VII.) Harvey G. Kratz, born July 27, 1879. (VII.) Anna G. Kratz, born Apr. 9, 1883. (VII.) Ida G. Kratz, born Feb. 9, 1886.

VI. Henry K. Kratz, born May 20, 1855. Mrd. — Delp, daughter of Henry Delp.

V. Jacob D. Kratz, born Mar. 22, 1819. Mrd. Elizabeth Clemens, daughter of Geo. Clemens, Feb. 22, 1841. P. O., Harleysville, Pa. Children: Henry, John, Jacob, Daniel, Catharine, Mary, Amanda, Anna.

VI. Henry C. Kratz, born July 2, 1842. Mrd. Mary Ann, daughter of Isaac Kline, Aug. 13, 1866. P. O., Harleysville, Pa. Farmer. Member of the Dunker church. Children: Lizzie, Susan, Harry, Emma.

VII. Lizzie Ann K. Kratz, born May 9, 1867. Mrd. John Landis, Oct. 13, 1887. One child: (VIII.) Estella Landis, born Feb. 9, 1890.

VII. Susan K. Kratz, born Apr. 3, 1871.

VII. Harry K. Kratz, born July 7, 1872; died.

VII. Emma K. Kratz, born Sept. 16, 1877.

VI. John C. Kratz, born Sept. 18, 1844. Mrd. Lavina Weidenmoyer, of West Rockhill, in 1875. She died in 1877. P. O., Harleysville, Pa. Laborer. One child: (VII.) Lizzie W. Kratz, born Oct. 5, 1877.

VI. Amanda C. Kratz, born Aug. 2, 1859. Mrd. Mahlon B. Moyer, of Hilltown, Bucks Co., in 1881. Children: (VII.) Lizzie J. Moyer, born Jan. 20, 188 . (VII.) Susie K. Moyer, born Sept. 17, 1887. (VII.) Annie K. Moyer, born Aug. 7. .

VI. Annie C. Moyer, born July 7, 1862. Mrd. John Alebaugh, of Hilltown, Bucks Co., in 1891. Plasterer.

VI. Jacob C. Kratz, born Nov. 7, 1846; died about 12 years ago. Mrd. Mary, daughter of Abraham M. Hagey, in 1868. She was born in 1845. Farmer.

Mennonites. Children: Abraham, Jacob, Jonas, Wilson, Henry.

VII. Abraham H. Kratz, born May 29, 1869. Mrd. Emma, daughter of Christian Moyer, Sept. 20, 1890. P. O., Elroy, Pa. Farmer.

VII. Jacob H. Kratz, born Oct. 5, 1872.

VII. Jonas H. Kratz, born Oct. 13, 1874.

VII. Wilson H. Kratz, born Sept. 25, 1876.

VII. Henry H. Kratz, born Sept. 12, 1878.

VI. Daniel C. Kratz, born July -, 1850; died about 1882. Mrd. Amanda, daughter of Geo. Snyder. Children: (**VII.**) George Kratz, aged about 14 years. (**VII.**) Harvey Kratz. (**VII.**) Anna Kratz. (**VII.**) Ella Kratz.

VI. Catharine C. Kratz, born May 21, 1853. Mrd. Henry G. Anglemoyer, Nov. 29, 1879. P. O., Lawndale, Pa. Shoemaker. Mennonites. (See Index of References No. 18.)

VI. Mary C. Kratz, born Dec. 28, 1856; died Apr. 1863.

IV. Isaac Kratz, born Nov. 13, 1790; died July 13, 1868, aged 77 years 8 months. Mrd. Catharine, daughter of Valentine Hunsicker, —. She died Aug. 24, 1864, aged 77 years, 6 months 11 days. Farmer. Mennonites. Died in Upper Providence, Montg. Co., and buried at the Mennonite meeting-house at Skippack. Children: Valentine, William, Ann, Margaret, Elizabeth, Catharine, Mary, Isaac.

V. Valentine Kratz, born in Perkiomen Twp., Oct. 10, 1810; died Oct. 30, 1891. Mrd. Mary Weikel, May 2, 1833. She was born Nov. 9, 1809. Children: Henry, Catharine, Sarah, Andora, Elizabeth.

VI. Henry W. Kratz, born in Perkiomen Twp., Montg. Co., Pa., July 31, 1834. At the age of five years he removed with his parents to the village of Trappe, Montg. Co., where at first he had the benefit of common school instruction, but later on received a thorough academic training at Washington Hall Collegiate Institute, under Joseph Hunsicker, Esq., and Professor Abel Rambo, where he was also prepared to enter the Sophomore class in College. Instead of taking a regular Collegiate course, however, as at first contemplated, he engaged in teaching and pursued that calling for eighteen years. During two years of that period he was tutor at his Alma Mater, under Prof. Rambo, teaching the English language and Mathematics.

In 1862 he was elected Justice of the Peace by the citizens of Upper Providence Twp., and was continued in that position for twenty years; during which time he devoted much of his attention to surveying, conveyancing, settling estates, and selling real estate; all of which resulted in a large and remunerative business. In 1866, through the efforts of Senator Horace Royer, he was appointed a transcribing clerk of the Senate of Pennsylvania at Harrisburg; and the year following was promoted to the double position of bill cook and message clerkships, which places he served with credit to himself and the satisfaction of the Senate.

In 1880 Mr. Kratz was nominated by acclamation for Recorder of Deeds by the Republican County Convention, and was elected by nearly five hundred majority. In serving that office he not only performed his duties faithfully and well, but was courteous and obliging in his official relations with the people. He was also one of the original number who organized the National Bank of Schwenksville, served as Director until January 1890, when he was elected President to succeed Jacob G. Schwenk, dec'd. He devotes much time and attention to that flourishing institution. He is prominently connected with Ursinus College at Collegeville, Montg. Co., being President of the Board of Directors, and a member of the Building Committee, which is superintending the erection of that massive and commodious structure known as "Bomberger Memorial Hall," on the College Campus. He is a member of the State Board of Agriculture; and while not a farmer, he has rendered valuable service to that body. He has been selected essayest upon several important occasions. He delivered two well-prepared essays on the road question which were well received and highly praised. He is manager and auditor of the Perkiomen and

Reading Turnpike Company, and treasurer of the Times Publishing Company of Norristown. He was married to Myra Bean, May 26, 1857. She was born Nov. 30, 1828; died Oct. 17, 1887. After the death of his wife Mr. Kratz sold his beautiful residence at Trappe and moved to Norristown, where he now resides. His business career has been useful and valuable to himself and to the community in which he lived. He advanced the profession of teaching, acquired distinction as surveyor and accountant, and displayed executive ability in the management and settlement of estates. He has proved himself to be a man of integrity in the many positions of responsibility which he has occupied among his fellow-citizens. Children: Mary, Irwin, Kate, Jane, Henry.

VII. Mary Kratz, born Feb. 8, 1858. Mrd. Augustus W. Bomberger, July 3, 1888. Children: **(VIII.)** Helen Bomberger. **(VIII.)** Julia Bomberger.

VII. Irwin Kratz, born Jan. 25, 1859; died Feb. 25, 1863.

VII. Kate B. Kratz, born Aug. 30, 1860. Mrd. Horace T. Royer, Oct. 5, 1881. Children: **(VIII.)** Donald Royer. **(VIII.)** Henry Royer. **(VIII.)** Jacob Royer. **(VIII.)** Lewis Royer.

VII. Jane Kratz, born Sept. 23, 1864; died Aug. 23, 1865.

VII. Henry E. Kratz, born Nov. 28, 1870.

VI. Catharine Kratz, born Mar. 16, 1837; died Sept. 7, 1841.

VI. Sarah Kratz, born May 3, 1840; died Aug. 24, 1841.

VI. Andora Kratz, born Sept. 27, 1841; died Mar. 16, 1845.

VI. Elizabeth Kratz, born Apr. 2, 1846; died Feb. 8, 1859.

V. William Kratz, born Mar. 27, 1812, died Nov. 20, 1873. Mrd. Elizabeth Custer, Nov. 6, 1836. She was born July 25, 1814; died June 8, 1890. Children: Isaac, Kate, Magdalena, Anna, Josiah, Catharine, Lavina, Elizabeth.

VI. Isaac C. Kratz, born Sept. 29, 1837. Mrd. Anna H., daughter of George and Catharine (Halteman) Shoemaker, Jan. 5, 1861. She was born July 31, 1835. P. O., Trappe, Pa. Children: Mary, William, Francis, Sallie.

VII. Mary Lizzie Kratz, born Oct. 25, 1861. Mrd. Oliver L. Grimley, Jan. 12, 1884. Four children:

VII. William H. Kratz, born June 15, 1863. Mrd. Hettie Whitby, Dec. 19, 1885. One child: (**VIII.**) — Kratz.

VII. Francis S. Kratz, born Dec. 25, 1865; died Sept. 24, 1866.

VII. Sallie S. Kratz, born Dec. 30, 1866; died Feb. 10, 1890. Mrd. Walter Cauffman, Jan. 1, 1889. One child: (**VIII.**) — Cauffman.

VI. Kate Kratz, born Sept. 6, 1839; died—.

VI. Magdalena Kratz, born Apr. 16, 1841; died—. Mrd. Jacob Stearley.—.

VI. Anna Kratz, born Sept. 4, 1843; died—. Mrd. Milton Smith.—.

VI. Josiah Kratz, born Apr. 19, 1846. Mrd. Annie Jane Zollers.—. P. O., Norristown, Pa. Three children.

VI. Catharine Kratz, born Oct. 26, 1848; died Oct. 8, 1852.

VI. Lavina Kratz, born July 23, 1851; died Sept. 25, 1852.

VI. Elizabeth Kratz, born Aug. 19, 1853. Mrd. Allen Miller.—. P. O., Limerick, Pa. Three children:

V. Ann Kratz, born Aug. 12, 1815; died Mar. 1890. Mrd. — Cassel.

V. Margaret Kratz, born Dec. 27, 1817; died Apr. 5, 1884. Mrd. William H. Gottshall, Nov. 3, 1835. He was born Oct. 8, 1812 (still living, 1891). Farmer. Old Mennonites. Children: Catharine, Isaac, William, Henry, Moses, Sarah, Margaret, Emaline, Amanda, Mary, Hannah.

VI. Catharine Gotshall, born Apr. 10, 1837; died Aug. 21, 1837.

VI. Isaac K. Gottshall, born July 8, 1838. Mrd. Sarah Kolb, Jan. 4, 1862. Farmer. Old Mennonites. No issue. P. O., Creamery, Pa.

VI. William K. Gottshall, born Feb. 11, 1840. Mrd. Sarah M. Detweiler, Nov. 7, 1861. She died Mar. 24,

THE NEW YORK
PUBLIC LIBRARY

1891. P. O., Lederachville, Pa. Farmer. Old Mennonites. Children: Benjamin, Mary, Amanda, Irwin, Maggie, Enos.

VII. Benjamin D. Gottshall, born Nov. 19, 1862; died May 3, 1864.

VII. Mary Ann D. Gottshall, born Jan. 29, 1865. Mrd. Henry S. Detweiler, Dec. 12, 1885. P. O., Creamery, Pa. Farmer. Old Mennonites. Children: (**VIII.**) William G. Detweiler, born Dec. 17, 1886. (**VIII.**) Vincent G. Detweiler, born July 18, 1887.

VII. Amanda D. Gottshall, born Sept. 19, 1867. Mrd. Allen S. Nice, Jan. 1, 1887. P. O., Lederach-ville, Pa. Farmer. Old Mennonites. Children: (**VIII.**) Abraham G. Nice, born Jan. 23, 1888. (**VIII.**) Maggie G. Nice, born Mar. 27, 1890.

VII. Irwin, D. Gottshall, born Aug. 30, 1872; died Mar. 30, 1873.

VII. Maggie D. Gottshall, born Mar. 30, 1875.

VII. Enos D. Gottshall, born Mar. 9, 1878.

VI. Henry K. Gottshall, born Nov. 18, 1841. Mrd. Anna Clemens, Apr. 8, 1865. She died . Children: Lizzie, William. Henry mrd. for his second wife, Barbara Gotwals, Aug. 14, 1875. P. O., Lederach-ville, Pa. Farmer. Old Mennonite. Children: Henry, Harvey, Jacob.

VII. Lizzie C. Godshall, born Dec. 22, 1865. Mrd. Henry M. Musselman, Jan. 3, 1885. P. O., Harleys-ville, Pa. Farmer. Old Mennonites. Children: (**VIII.**) Sallie G. Musselman, born Mar. 19, 1887. (**VIII.**) Emma G. Musselman, born May 11, 1888.

VII. William C. Gottshall, born Aug. 6, 1869. Mrd. Amanda Hechler, Sept. 7, 1889. P. O., Lederach-ville, Pa. Farmer. One child: (**VIII.**) Sallie H. Gott-shall, born Sept. 7, 1890; died Sept. 17, 1890.

VII. Henry G. Gottshall, born May 16, 1877.

VII. Harvey G. Gottshall, born Sept. 2, 1880.

VII. Jacob G. Gottshall, born Dec. 26, 1883.

VI. Moses K. Gottshall, born Sept. 8, 1843. Mrd. Mary C. Freed, Apr. 21, 1866. P. O., Harleysville, Pa. Farmer. Dunkards. Children: William, Samuel, Michael, Isaac, Henry, Sarah, Mary, Emma, Rein-hart.

VII. William F. Gottshall, born Apr. 10, 1868. Mrd. Lizzie P. Kern. P. O., Royer's Ford, Pa. Farmer. Dunkards. One child: (VIII.) Reinhart Gottshall.

VII. Samuel F. Gottshall, born Feb. 21, 1869.

VII. Michael F. Gottshall, born May 2, 1870.

VII. Isaac F. Gottshall, born Feb. 27, 1873.

VII. Henry F. Gottshall, born Nov. 17, 1873.

VII. Sarah F. Gottshall, born Dec. 26, 1874.

VII. Mary F. Gottshall, born Feb. 6, 1876.

VII. Emma F. Gottshall, born May 3, 1878.

VII. Reinhart F. Gottshall, born Dec. 30, 1880.

VI. Sarah K. Gottshall, born Sept. 7, 1845. Mrd. Isaac Hunsberger, May 14, 1870. P. O., Perkiomenville, Pa. Farmer. New Mennonites. Children: Henry, Lizzie, William, Ephraim, Franklin, Maggie, John, Bertha.

VII. Henry G. Hunsberger, born Nov. 16, 1870; died Mar. 18, 1871.

VII. Lizzie G. Hunsberger, born Jan. 11, 1873. Mrd. James Calvin Wood, Aug. 16, 1890. P. O., Perkiomenville, Pa. Bricklayer. Reformed church. One child: (VIII.) Rufus H. Wood, born Jan. 5, 1891.

VII. William G. Hunsberger, born July 1, 1875.

VII. Ephraim G. Hunsberger, born Mar. 31, 1877.

VII. Franklin G. Hunsberger, born Nov. 7, 1878.

VII. Maggie G. Hunsberger, born June 26, 1881.

VII. John G. Hunsberger, born Feb. 26, 1883.

VII. Bertha G. Hunsberger, born June 30, 1885.

VI. Margaret K. Gottshall, born Apr. 13, 1847. Mrd. Oliver Hendricks, Sept. 23, 1871. He died May 10, 1889. P. O., Green Lane, Pa. Farmer. Lutherans. Children: (VII.) Ephraim G. Hendricks, born Dec. 13, 1872. (VII.) Oliver G. Hendricks, born Feb. 6, 1874. (VII.) Amanda G. Hendricks, born Dec. 23, 1875. (VII.) William G. Hendricks, born Apr. 24, 1877; died Aug. 25, 1877. (VII.) Emaline G. Hendricks, born Apr. 23, 1878. (VII.) Ambrose G. Hendricks, born July 28, 1879. (VII.) Elmer G. Hendricks, born Apr. 15, 1881. (VII.) Margaret G. Hendricks, born Sept. 4, 1882; died Dec. 11, 1886. (VII.) Morgan G. Hendricks, born Dec. 21, 1883.

VI. Emaline K. Gottshall, born Mar. 25, 1849. Mrd. Benivil H. Kolb, Dec. 6, 1870. P. O. Salford, Pa. Farmer. New Mennonites. Children: (VII.) Henry G. Kolb, born Apr. 6, 1871. (VII.) John G. Kolb, born Oct. 2, 1874. (VII.) Maggie G. Kolb, born Jan. 10, 1877. (VII.) Webster G. Kolb, born Oct. 24, 1878. (VII.) Alice G. Kolb, born July 21, 1881. (VII.) Elizabeth G. Kolb, born June 26, 1883. (VII.) William G. Kolb, born Apr. 13, 1887.

VI. Amanda K. Gottshall, born Feb. 15, 1851; died Jan. 4, 1856.

VI. Mary K. Gottshall, born July 18, 1852; died Apr. 3, 1864.

VI. Hannah K. Gottshall, born Apr. 25, 1854. Mrd. Henry Nace, Mar. 27, 1875. P. O., Salford, Pa. Children: (VII.) Amanda G. Nace, born June 13, 1875; died June 24, 1875. (VII.) Harrison G. Nace, born Mar. 1, 1878. (VII.) Elmer G. Nace, born Feb. 24, 1881. (VII.) Bertha G. Nace, born Mar. 4, 1883; died July 14, 1890. (VII.) Irwin G. Nace, born May 22, 1889.

V. Elizabeth Kratz, born Mar. 14, 1821. Mrd. Isaac Young, —. He died—. Have issue.

V. Catharine Kratz, born July 28, 1823. Mrd. Jacob Rittenhouse, —. No issue.

V. Isaac Kratz, born July 1, 1826; died July 14, 1868. S.

V. Mary Kratz, born Sept. 9, 1829. Mrd. John Bean,—. Have issue.

IV. David Kratz, born Mar. 14, 1792; died Jan. 27, 1872, aged 79 yrs., 9 m. 24 d. Mrd. Ann, daughter of Henry Lederach, of Worcester, Pa. She died Sept. 6, 1868. Buried at the Lower Skippack meetinghouse. Farmer. Children: Henry, William.

V. Henry Kratz, born about 1820; died about 1880. Mrd.—Zilling.—. Children: (VI.) Amos, etc.

V. William Kratz, born about 1822. Mrd.—Krause, —. Children: (VI.) David. (VI.) Milton. (VI.) Jura. (VI.) Ida.

IV. William Kratz, born in 1793; died in 1834. Mrd. Mary, daughter of Henry Rosenberger, of Hilltown, in 1820. She died in 1866. Lived for a time in Upper

Salford, Montg. Co., and afterwards moved to Hill-
town, Bucks Co. Weaver. Mennonites. Buried at
Blooming Glen. Children: Jesse, Samuel, Henry,
David, Sarah, Hannah.

V. Jesse Kratz, born Oct. 8, 1821. Mrd. Susanna
Hiestand, Oct. 20, 1844. P. O., Perkasie, Pa. Farmer. Mennonites. Children: Abraham, William,
Mary, Lizzie, Albert, David, Henry, Susan, Jesse,
Annie, Katie, Marcus. Jesse mrd. second wife, Catharine Freed, Nov. 1, 1884. She was born Feb. 28,
1828.

VI. Abraham Kratz, born Sept. 23, 1845; died Mar.
18, 1846.

VI. William J. Kratz, born in Bucks Co., Dec. 5,
1846. Mrd. Josephine Ritter, Sept. 23, 1873. Solic-
itor. Lutheran. Children: (VII.) Cora Kratz. (VII.)
Ruth Kratz.

VI. Mary Kratz, born in Bucks Co., Dec. 18, 1848.
Mrd. Samuel K. Moyer, Jan. 1, 1874. He was born
Sept. 26, 1843. Farmer. Mennonites. Children:
(VII.) Christian K. Moyer, born Dec. 17, 1874. (VII.)
Jessie K. Moyer, born Sept. 13, 1876; died Feb. 9,
1878. (VII.) Elmer K. Moyer, born Dec. 25, 1878.
(VII.) Susannah K. Moyer, born Mar. 10, 1881. (VII.)
Edward K. Moyer, born Dec. 6, 1882. (VII.) Mamie K.
Moyer, born Jan. 1, 1885. (VII.) Maggie K. Moyer,
born Oct. 4, 1888.

VI. Lizzie Kratz, born in Bucks Co., Feb. 5, 1851.
Mrd. Jonathan Gulick, of Hilltown, Oct. 9, 1875.
Farmer. Children: (VII.) Merari K. Gulick, born July
9, 1876. (VII.) Jesse K. Gulick, born Dec. 25, 1877.
(VII.) John H. Gulick, born Sept. 24, 1879. (VII.)
Marcus Wilson Gulick, born Dec. 30, 1881. (VII.)
Warren K. Gulick, born Mar. 23, 1884.

VI. Albert P. Kratz, born in Bucks Co., Mar. 5,
1853. Mrd. Malinda S. Bean, of Hilltown, Pa., Oct.
1, 1887. School-teacher. Presbyterians. Children:
(VII.) Luther B. Kratz, born June 11, 1889. (VII.)
Irma B. Kratz, born Aug. 25, 1891.

VI. David H. Kratz, born in Bucks Co., Mar. 31,
1855. Mrd. Ida L., daughter of Rev. J. Fritzinger,
of Allentown, Pa., Jan. 3, 1888. School-teacher.

Mem. Ref. Ch. Children: (**VII.**) Robert Fritzinger Kratz, born May 20, 1889. (**VII.**) Margaret Susan Kratz, born Nov. 13, 1890.

VI. Susan H. Kratz, born May 31, 1857. Mrd. Jacob S. Landis, Mar. 4, 1882. He was born Oct. 16, 1856. Farmer. Children: (**VII.**) Eva K. Landis, born July 10, 1883. (**VII.**) Isaac K. Landis, born June 1, 1886. (**VII.**) Arthur K. Landis, born Jan. 21, 1890; died Jan. 14, 1891.

VI. Harry E. Kratz, born in Bucks Co., Aug. 30, 1859. Formerly taught school, now clerk in store.

VI. Jesse Hiestand Kratz, born in Bucks Co., Dec. 3, 1861. Graduate of Edinburg, Pa., State Normal School, and is teaching.

VI. Annie Kratz, born Jan. 31, 1864; died Nov. 11, 1878.

VI. Katie Kratz, born May 16, 1866; died Oct. 13, 1879.

VI. Marcus Wilson Kratz, born in Bucks Co., July 26, 1868. Graduate of Bloomsburg, Pa., State Normal School, and is teaching.

V. Samuel R. Kratz, born in Upper Salford, Montg. Co., Pa., Oct. 18, 1824. Mrd. Elizabeth Hunsberger, Oct. 16, 1853. P. O., Hebron, Neb. Farmer. Mem. German Baptist Ch. Children: William, Emma, Sarah, George, Mary, Isaiah, Hannah, David, Elmer, Jacob, Amanda, Ephraim, Anna, Samuel, Lydia, Cornelius.

VI. William Henry Kratz, born November 20, 1854. Mrd. Cordelia Crosse, Apr. 13, 1875. She was born Jan. 15, 1853. P. O., North Baltimore, Ohio. Teamster and farmer. Mr. Kratz was elected Marshal of N. Baltimore, Ohio—. In his capacity as Marshal and in self-defense, he shot and instantly killed Frank Archer, for which he was arrested, but the grand jury justified him in the act, and promptly acquitted him, bringing in a verdict of no cause. Mrs. Kratz member of the church of God. Children: (**VII.**) Maud May Kratz, born Oct. 24, 1877; died Mar. 24, 1878. (**VII.**) Harry C. Kratz, born Feb. 23, 1879; died June 8, 1879. (**VII.**) Ray Leuern Kratz, born Aug. 4, 1888.

VI. Emma Sevilla Kratz, born Feb. 2, 1856. Mrd. Levi S. Myers, Aug. 11, 1885. P. O., Hebron, Neb. Farmer. Members of Methodist church. Children: **(VII.)** Shelly Myers, born Aug. 12, 1886. **(VII.)** Bessie Myers, born Oct. 28, 1887.

VI. Sarah Ann Kratz, born in Philadelphia, Pa., Mar. 27, 1857. Mrd. Jacob H. Wismer, Jan. 29, 1876. P. O., Plumsteadville, Pa. Carpenter. Mrs. Wismer, Baptist. Children: **(VII.)** Rosella Wismer, born Nov. 17, 1876. **(VII.)** Elizabeth Wismer, born June 23, 1878. **(VII.)** Franklin K. Wismer, born May 25, 1880. **(VII.)** Wilson K. Wismer, born June 5, 1882. **(VII.)** Samuel K. Wismer, born Sept. 22, 1885. **(VII.)** Bertha May Wismer, born Dec. 7, 1887. **(VII.)** Sarah Wismer, born June 4, 1890.

VI. George Washington and Mary Jane Kratz, born July 4, 1858. George died Mar. 22, and Mary died 20, 1859.

VI. Isaiah F. Kratz, born Dec. 18, 1859; died June 20, 1890, of heart disease. He was a school teacher and taught for about nine years. Member of the Christian Church. S.

VI. Hannah Kratz, born Apr. 13, 1861; died Jan. 21, 1865.

VI. David Christian Kratz, born Sept. 23, 1862. Mrd. Minnie B. Schell, May 1, 1890. P. O., Hebron, Neb. Farmer and minister. Members of the Christian church, of which he was ordained minister.

VI. Elmer Kratz, born Mar. 19, 1864; died Jan. 15, 1865.

VI. Jacob R. Kratz, born in Bucks Co., Pa., May 18, 1865. Mrd. Hannah Elzina Sutton, of Fairbury, Neb., Nov. 3, 1887. P. O., Belvidere, Neb. Farmer. Members of the Christian Church. They have one child: **(VII.)** Gertrude Kratz, born Sept. 6, 1888.

VI. Amanda E. Kratz, born Sept. 2, 1866. Mrd. Paul F. Sandman, Aug. 16, 1883. P. O., Harbine, Neb. Farmer and cheese maker. Mrs. Sandman is a member of the Christian Church. Children: **(VII.)** Henry Sandman, born July 29, 1884; died Aug. 5, 1884. **(VII.)** Minnie Myrtle Sandman, born July 19, 1885. **(VII.)** Elzina Emma Sandman, born Sept. 4,

1887. (**VII.**) Edwin Sandman, born May 7, 1889; died June 13, 1889. (**VII.**) Lizzie Sandman, born May 16, 1890.

VI. Ephraim Kratz, born Nov. 20, 1867, died Apr. 2, 1868.

VI. Anna Jemima Kratz, born Sept. 21, 1869. Mrd. Charles W. Warren, July 28, 1887. Merchant at Auburn, Ohio. Mem. Christian Ch. Children: (**VII.**) Mabel Lottie Warren, born Jan. 15, 1889. (**VII.**) Charles Earl Warren, born Feb. 12, 1891.

VI. Samuel H. Kratz, Jr., born Jan. 11, 1872. Student. Mem. Christian Ch.

VI. Lydia Kratz, born May 11, 1873; died same day.

VI. Cornelius Kratz, born May 9, 1874. Student.

V. Henry R. Kratz, born in Upper Salford Twp., Montg. Co., Pa., Feb. 26, 1827. Mrd. Sarah Delp Dec. 26, 1852. She died in Aug. 1865. Children: Mary, Clayton, William, Catharine. Henry mrd. for his second wife Levina Fluck, Dec. 7, 1869. Farmer. P. O., Hatfield, Pa. Dunkards. Children: Harry, Ella, Martha.

VI. Mary Kratz, born Feb. 12, 1854; died Jan. 17, 1881. Mrd. Daniel Bright in 1879.

VI. Clayton Kratz, born June 13, 1856; died in Aug. 1862.

VI. William D. Kratz, born Nov. 27, 1859. Mrd. Susan S., daughter of J. D. Rosenberger, of Hilltown, Pa., Jan. 2, 1882. Farmer. P. O., Lawndale, Pa. German Baptists. Children: (**VII.**) Lucretia R. Kratz, born May 29, 1882; died June 9, 1882. (**VII.**) Jacob R. Kratz, born Aug. 29, 1884. (**VII.**) Lavina R. Kratz, born Nov. 1, 1886. (**VII.**) Henry Clayton R. Kratz, born Nov. 28, 1888. (**VII.**) Artemas R. Kratz, born Dec. 16, 1890.

VI. Catharine Kratz, born Nov. 2, 1862. Mrd. Levi Fluck in 1890.

VI. Harry F. Kratz, born Apr. 16, 1870. Farmer. P. O., Hatfield, Pa. Single.

VI. Ella Kratz, born Oct. 25, 1872; died next day.

VI. Martha Kratz, born May 31, 1881.

V. David Kratz, born —; died young.

V. Sarah Kratz, born Sept. 25, 1831; died Mar. 29, 1877. Mrd. Valentine Kratz. (See Index of References No. 33.)

V. Hannah Kratz, born   ; died young.

IV. Jacob Kratz, born June 24, 1798; died Aug. 25, 1881, aged 83 yrs., 2 m. 1 day. Mrd. Mary, daughter of John Stover, of Upper Salford. She was born Dec. 24, 1800; died Feb. 13, 1887, aged 83 yrs., 1 m. and a few days. He lived for many years on his father's farm which he owned, on the Skippack Road in Upper Salford, where Henry Weber now lives. Buried at Lower Salford Mennonite church. Children: John, Rachel, Eli, Mary, David, Hannah.

V. John S. Kratz, born about 1826. Mrd. Elizabeth Hiestand, Dec. 1847. P. O., Hatfield, Pa. Farmer. Ger. Baptists, of which he is a deacon. Children: Abraham, Anna, Amanda, Mary, Jacob, Emma, Martha.

VI. Abraham Herman Kratz, born Apr. 28, 1849; died Aug. 18, 1885. Mrd. Anna Oberholtzer, in 1871. Cigar maker. Children. **(VII.)** Lizzie Ann Dora Kratz. **(VII.)** John Tobias Kratz. **(VII.)** Owen Kratz.

VI. Anna Kratz, born Feb. 3, 1852; died Feb. 11, 1852.

VI. Amanda Kratz, born in Bucks Co., Pa., Feb. 7, 1856. Mrd. Jacob Rosenberger, Oct. 13, 1883. Farmer. German Baptists. No issue.

VI. Mary Kratz, born Feb. 22, 1861; died Jan. 13, 1863.

VI. Jacob Kratz, born - . Single.

VI. Emma Kratz, born —. Single.

VI. Martha H. Kratz, born   . Single.

V. Rachel Kratz, born Oct. 28, 1828. Mrd. Samuel K. Ziegler, Oct. 17, 1847. He was born Nov. 8, 1821. Farmer. Dunkards. Children: John and Nathaniel.

VI. John K. Ziegler, born Aug. 9, 1848. Mrd. Elizabeth C. Geyer, Apr. 14, 1870. She was born Oct. 30, 1850. Farmer. Members of Reformed Church. Children: (**VII.**) Sallie G. Ziegler, born Jan. 2, 1871. **(VII.)** Irwin G. Ziegler, born Sept. 9, 1872. **(VII.)** Mary Elizabeth G. Ziegler, born Jan. 26, 1874. **(VII.)** John Harvey G. Ziegler, born Feb. 14, 1877.

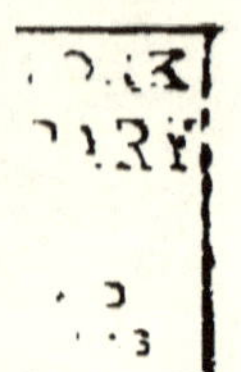

(**VII.**) Alice Amanda G. Ziegler, born Aug. 5, 1878. (**VII.**) William G. Ziegler, born Apr. 19, 1884; died May 14, 1884. (**VII.**) Annie G. Ziegler, born Aug. 30, 1883.

VI. Nathaniel K. Ziegler, born Sept. 4, 1849. Mrd. Elizabeth Karver, Sept. 13, 1879. She was born Apr. 16, 1856. Mail Carrier. Mrs. Ziegler is a member of the Lutheran Church. Children: (**VII.**) William David K. Ziegler, born Dec. 8, 1881; died Mar. 5, 1887. (**VII.**) John Horace Ziegler, born Apr. 10, 1886; died Mar. 12, 1887. (**VII.**) Harry Wilmer Ziegler, born July 2, 1889; died Sept. 21, 1889.

V. Mary Kratz, born Apr. 16, 1836. Mrd. David Tyson, Oct. 4, 1850. P. O., Salfordville, Pa. Farmer. Dunkards. Children: (**VI.**) Mary Ann E. Tyson, born July 26, 1857; died Dec. 28, 1863. (**VI.**) Nathaniel K. Tyson, born Nov. 28, 1863; died Feb. 2, 1864. (**VI.**) Charles K. Tyson, born June 8, 1868. (**VI.**) Emma Lizzie Tyson, born Dec. 21, 1875.

V. David S. Kratz, born Feb. 26, 1842. Mrd. Elizabeth Stearly, Feb. 7, 1863. Farmer in Upper Salford. Dunkards. One Child: (**VI.**) Mary Elizabeth Kratz, born Dec. 27, 1865.

V. Hannah Kratz, born Oct. 5, 1844; died June 24, 1872. Mrd. Abraham B. Trumbauer, Oct. 6, 1866. He was born June 24, 1842. P. O., Spring Mount. Member Dunkard Ch. Carpenter. Children: (**VI.**) Jonathan K. Trumbauer, born Nov. 28, 1867. Carpenter. Single. (**VI.**) Irwin K. Trumbauer, born Sept. 18, 1869. Operator at P. & R. R. Single.

V. Eli Kratz, born—. Mrd. Angelina Beysher. P. O., Hatfield, Pa. One Child: George, mrd.—. P. O., Hatfield.

DESCENDANTS OF ISAAC KRATZ, SON OF JOHN VALENTINE KRATZ.

III. Isaac Kratz, born in Montg. Co., July 15, 1749; died Sept. 15, 1823, aged 74 yrs., 2 mo. Mrd. Mary Yellis—. She was born Mar. 14, 1758; died Jan. 3, 1832, aged 73 yrs., 9 m. 19 d. Isaac Kratz, became the owner of the old homestead in Lower Salford. He built the first house on the farm owned by Jacob K. Freed, deceased, and occupied by his son-in-law John K. Clemens, in 1811. The farm now owned by Samuel Ziegler, is also a part of the Kratz homestead farm. His last will and testament was dated Dec. 16, 1817, and his son John, and son-in-law Henry Clemens, were the executors. His will was probated Oct. 23, 1823. The farm at that time contained 108 acres, and was released by the heirs to their brother Isaac, Mar. 27, 1824, for $2066.67. Mennonites. Children: Valentine, Fronica, Ann, John Mary, Abraham, Philip, Isaac, Elizabeth

IV. Valentine Kratz, born Nov. 29, 1776; died Aug. 6, 1852, aged 75 yrs., 8 m. 7 d. Mrd. Mary Moyer, of Lower Salford—. She was born Apr. 17, 1785; died Aug. 22, 1820. He was known as "deaf Felty," because he did not hear well. They at first lived in Frederick Twp., but afterward removed to Towamencin. They removed to Towamencin before the bridge near Groff's mill was built over the Branch Creek, and when their moving went through the stream below the mill the water was so high that it nearly swept them away. It is said to have been a very narrow escape. Valentine mrd. for his second wife Elizabeth Young. She was born Dec. 23, 1796; died June 10, 1857. Farmer. Mennonites.

Buried at Delp's graveyard, Franconia. Children all by first wife: Jacob, Isaac, Joseph, Samuel, Elizabeth, Henry, John.

V. Jacob Kratz, born Feb. 20, 1803; died May 23, 1823.

V. Isaac Kratz, born July 15, 1807; died May 4, 1879. Mrd. Elizabeth Beidler, Oct. 20, 1831. She was born Sept. 1, 1811. Farmer, lived in Plumstead Twp. Mennonites. Children: Susanna, Mary, Jacob, Henry, Isaac, John, Abraham, David.

VI. Susanna Kratz, born Aug. 12, 1832. Mrd. Moyer.

VI. Mary B. Kratz, born Nov. 17, 1833; died Mar. 14, 1837.

VI. Jacob B. Kratz, born Dec. 12, 1835, in Montgomery Co. Mrd. Catharine Loux, of Tinicum Twp., Bucks Co., Oct. 21, 1860. She was born Jan. 20, 1834. P. O., Pipersville, Pa. Farmer. Reformed Ch. Children: Isaac, Lizzie.

VII. Isaac L. Kratz, born in Montg. Co., Nov. 19, 1865. Mrd. Minnie Nora Ott, Mar. 4, 1890. Miller at Pipersville, Pa. Ger. Ref. One child: (VIII.) Jacob Kratz, born Jan. 10, 1891.

VII. Lizzie A. Kratz, born Oct. 13, 1868. Married Milton B. Geho, Feb. 2, 1889. Farmer. Mr. G., Lutheran. Mrs. G., Ger. Reformed.

VI. Henry B. Kratz, born Aug. 2, 1838. Mrd. Leah Meyers, Nov. 10, 1860. She died Mar. 1890. P. O., Bedminster, Pa. Farmer. Mennonites. Children: Sylvanus, Emma, Jonas, Leidy, Mary, Harvey, Horace, Henry. Mr. Kratz mrd. second wife Kate (Godshall) Gerhart, Apr. 11, 1891.

VII. Sylvanus Kratz, born Sept. 2, 1861. Mrd. Sarah Meyers,—. Farmer. Mennonites. Children: (VIII.) Infant died unnamed. (VIII.) Aaron Kratz, died in infancy.

VII. Emma Jane Kratz, born Mar. 31, 1864. Mrd. William H. Fulmer, Oct. 1, 1887. P. O., Bedminster, Pa. Farmer. Mrs. Fulmer, Mennonite. One child: (VIII.) Leah Anna Fulmer, born Jan. 8, 1889.

VII. Jonas Kratz, born Feb. 4, 1866. Mrd. Lizzie Sine, in 1886. Farmer. New Mennonite. One child: (**VIII.**) Estella Kratz, born in 1886.

VII. Leidy M. Kratz, born Sept. 11, 1868. Mrd. Lizzie Ott.

VII. Mary Ellen Kratz, born Jan. 6, 1870. Mrd. Daniel Hartzell.

VII. Harvey Kratz, born May 29, 1873.

VII. Horace Kratz, born May 31, 1875.

VII. Henry W. Kratz, born Mar. 5, 1879.

VI. Isaac B. Kratz, born May 4, 1841. Mrd. Sarah Ann Nace, Nov. 4, 1865. She died—. Ger. Reformed. Children: Jonas, Lizzie, Franklin. Isaac mrd. second wife, Mary Fretz, Nov. 21, 1885. Mrs. Kratz Baptist. (**VII.**) Jonas N. Kratz, born Aug. 23, 1866. (**VII.**) Lizzie N. Kratz, born July 28, 1868. (**VII.**) Franklin N. Kratz, born Jan. 14, 1873.

VI. John B. Kratz, born June 25, 1844. Mrd. Annie L. Fretz, Sept. 7, 1876. Saddler by trade, now farmer near Bedminster, Pa. New Mennonites. Children: (**VII.**) Isaac F. Kratz, born Jan. 31, 1881. (**VII.**) Irene F. Kratz, born Sept. 6, 1884.

VI. Abraham B. Kratz, born May 13, 1847; died Apr. 19, 1865.

VI. David B. Kratz, born Aug. 20, 1850; died—. Mrd. Annie Myers,—. No issue.

V. Joseph Kratz, born in Montgomery Co., Dec. 13, 1810; died Oct. 4, 1872. Mrd. Anna Hagy, Oct. 29, 1837. Merchant. New Mennonites. Children: (**VI.**) John.

VI. John Kratz, born Sept. 12, 1838. Mrd. Mary Loux. . P. O., Sterling, Ill. Farmer. Lutherans. Children: Elizabeth, Catharine, Joseph, Mathias, Mary, Noah.

VII. Elizabeth A. Kratz, born Jan. 15, 1862. Mrd. William D. Detweiler. (See Index of References, No. 35).

VII. Catharine E. Kratz, born Apr. 13, 1864. Mrd. J. D. Wolber, Jan. 10, 1889. P. O., Sterling, Ill. General Laborer. Lutheran.

VII. Joseph L. Kratz, born July 23, 1867. Married Adelia B. John, Jan. 14, 1891. P. O., Sterling, Ill.

Bank Clerk, of First Nat. Bank, Sterling, Ill. Lutheran.

VII. Mathias L. Kratz, born Nov. 14, 1869. P. O., Sterling, Ill. Stone mason. Lutheran. Unmarried.

VII. Mary E. Kratz, born July 28, 1872. Mrd. Rev. C. F. Oehler, Sept. 28, 1890. P. O., No. 1410 H. Street, Sacramento, Cal. Minister. Lutheran.

VII. Noah Kratz, born Apr. 22, 1876. Student.

V. Samuel Kratz, born in Montgomery Co., Pa., Mar. 15, 1813. Mrd. Rebecca Garges, of Montgomery Co., Pa. Farmer. P. O., Kappa, Ill. In 1852 they moved to Medina Co., Ohio, and later to Illinois. They are members of the Old Mennonite church. Children: Josiah, Elizabeth, Joseph, Mary.

VI. Josiah G. Kratz, born in Montgomery Co., Pa., Apr. 5, 1838. Mrd. Sybilla Gulick, of Montgomery Co., Pa., May 15, 1870. Farmer. P. O., Kappa, Ill. Mennonites. Children: **(VII.)** John Henry Kratz, born —; died —. **(VII.)** Urie Ellen Kratz, born ; died —. **(VII.)** Catharine Kratz, born —; died . **(VII.)** Charles Kratz, born —.

VI. Elizabeth Kratz, born in Montgomery Co., Pa., Sept. 23, 1841. Mrd. Henry C. Nice, of Medina Co., Ohio, June 7, 1858. He was born in Bucks Co., Pa., July 9, 1831. Stone mason. Farmer. Mennonites. Children: Amanda, Mary, Reuben, Ella, Emma, Vina.

VII. Amanda Fice, born Mar. 23, 1859. Mrd. Abraham Kuhns, in 1876. P. O., Columbus, Kans., Farmer. Members of the Mennonite church, of which Mr. Kuhns is a deacon. Children: **(VIII.)** Orpha E. Kuhns, born Feb. 20, 1877. **(VIII.)** Elijah F. Kuhns, born July 4, 1879. **(VIII.)** Ida B. Kuhns, born July 13, 1881. **(VIII.)** Allen W. Kuhns, born Nov. 18, 1883. **(VIII.)** Harvey E. Kuhns, born Apr. 18, 1886; died July 12, 1886. **(VIII.)** Bertha M. Kuhns, born Sept. 18, 1887; died Apr. 11, 1890.

VII. Mary Ann Nice, born in Medina Co., O., June 7, 1861. Mrd. Charles W. Girton, May 7, 1884. He was born in Luzerne Co., Pa., Oct. 12, 1860. P. O., Neutral, Kans. Farmer. They have one child: **(VIII.)** Percy Girton, born Nov. 9, 1887.

VII. Reuben Nice, born July 9, 1865; died Jan. 21, 1866.

VII. Ella Nice, born May 28, 1867.

VII. Emma Nice, born June 20, 1869.

VII. Vina Nice, born July 24, 1872.

VI. Joseph Kratz, born in Montg. Co., Pa., June 12, 1852. Mrd. Elizabeth Mishler, Aug. 19, 1878. P. O., Kappa, Ill. Farmer. Children: (**VII.**) Fannie Belle Kratz, born Feb. 23, 1881. (**VII.**) Ella May Kratz, born Dec. 22, 1882. (**VII.**) Infant, born May 10, 1885; died unnamed.

VI. Mary Kratz, born in Medina Co., Ohio, Aug. 5, 1856. Mrd. Abraham Kilmer, May 2, 1875. P. O., Fulton, Mich. Mennonites. Children: (**VII.**) Dora Frances Kilmer, born July 2, 1876. (**VII.**) Etta May Kilmer, born Jan. 7, 1879. (**VII.**) Milton Henry Kilmer, born Feb. 28, 1882. (**VII.**) Myrtie Belle Kilmer, born May 22, 1884. (**VII.**) Bertha Alice Kilmer, born Sept. 6, 1886. (**VII.**) Charles Byron Kilmer, born Apr. 7, 1888; died May 22, 1888.

V. Elizabeth Kratz, born July 24, 1815; died Nov. 26, 1872. Mrd. John Kindig,—. He was born Apr. 10, 1817; died July 4, 1872. Farmer. Mennonites. Children: Mary, Henry, Valentine, Jacob, Samuel, Joseph, John, Margaret, Sarah.

VI. Mary Ann Kindig, born in Montg. Co., Dec. 3, 1837. Mrd. Philip R. Swartly, Sept. 19, 1857. P. O., Lansdale, Pa. Mennonites. Children: Mary, Samuel, John, Leidy, Sallie, Margaret, Sophia, Emma.

VII. Mary Elizabeth Swartly, born Jan. 8, 1859. Mrd. Wm. B. Moyer, of Montg. Co. P. O., Lansdale, Pa. Children: (**VIII.**) Rinia Moyer. (**VIII.**) Henry Moyer. (**VIII.**) Mary Ann Moyer. (**VIII.**) Samuel Moyer. (**VIII.**) Walter Moyer. (**VIII.**) William Moyer.

VII. Samuel K. Swartly, born Aug. 28, 1860. Mrd. Jennie B. Moyer, of Montg. Co. P. O., Lansdale, Pa. Children: (**VIII.**) William Swartly. (**VIII.**) Annie Swartly.

VII. John K. Swartly, born Jan. 1, 1862. Married Amanda Hunsberger,—. P. O., Lansdale, Pa. Children: (**VIII.**) Lillie Swartly. (**VIII.**) Bertha Swartly.

VII. Leidy K. Swartly, born Oct. 27, 1863. Mrd. Katie Young, of Montg. Co. P. O., Lansdale, Pa. No children.

VII. Sallie K. Swartly, born July 21, 1865. Mrd. Frank Clymer, of Montg. Co. P. O., Lansdale, Pa. Children: (**VIII.**) Wellington Clymer. (**VIII.**) Howard Clymer. (**VIII.**) Mabel Clymer.

VII. Margaret K. Swartly, born June 6, 1867. Mrd. Edward Blum,——. P. O., Lansdale, Pa. One child: (**VIII.**) Alice Blum.

VII. Sophia K. Swartly, born Mar. 7, 1869. Mrd. Oscar Carver, of Montg. Co. P. O., Lansdale, Pa. One child: (**VIII.**) Henry Carver, dec'd.

VII. Emma K. Swartly, born Jan. 3, 1872. Mrd. Hiram E. Fluck, of Montg. Co. P. O., Lansdale, Pa. One child: (**VIII.**) Philip Fluck, dec'd.

VI. Henry K. Kindig, born Oct. 29, 1839. Mrd. Sophia Anders, Sept. 10, 1859. She was born Aug. 29, 1840; died Jan. 2, 1887. Wholesale grocer in Philadelphia. Presbyterians. Children: Mary, Emma, Annie, John, Katie, Lillie, Marvin, Carrie. Henry mrd. second wife, Annie Maria Wagner, Dec. 31, 1889. She was born Mar. 24, 1848.

VII. Mary Kindig, born June 24, 1860; died Feb. 5, 1861.

VII. Emma Kindig, born Sept. 14, 1862. Mrd. Arthur M. Rowe, Sept. 13, 1882. He was born Aug. 1862. Children: (**VIII.**) Gertrude Rowe, born June 9, 1883. (**VIII.**) Ethel May Kindig, born May 5, 1887.

VII. Annie Kindig, born Sept. 14, 1863. Mrd. William F. Breitenbach, Mar. 1890. He was born Nov. 15, 1863. One child: (**VIII.**) Helen Maria Breitenbach, born Dec. 11, 1890.

VII. John Kindig, born Feb. 20, 1866.

VII. Katie Kindig, born Feb. 23, 1868. Mrd. Martin P. Rively, M. D., Oct. 25, 1888. He died Mar. 3, 1891.

VII. Lillie Kindig, born Jan. 21, 1870

VII. Marvin Kindig, born Aug. 12, 1872.

VII. Carrie Kindig, born June 15, 1875.

VI. Valentine Kratz, born Jan. 1848; died Sept. 1849.

VI. Jacob K. Kindig, born Feb. 2, 1849. Mrd. Angelina Neman, Aug. 17, 1870. Grocer at 2317 Pennsylvania Av., Philadelphia. Attends Baptist church. Children: (VII.) Elizabeth Kindig, born Feb. 18, 1872. (VII.) Jeannette May Kindig, born Mar. 28, 1880.

VI. Samuel K. Kindig, born Sept. 14, 1854. Mrd. Fannie C. Large, June 28, 1880. She was born June 17, 1857. Grocer of firm of Kindig Bros., Philadelphia. Presbyterians. No issue.

VI. John K. Kindig, born Feb. 2, 1854. Mrd. Annie Roops, Feb. 8, 1876. She died Apr. 19, 1879. One child: (VII.) Walter Kindig, born Mar. 1, 1877. John mrd. second wife, Sallie Roops (sister to first wife), Sept. 20, 1883. P. O., Kulpsville, Pa. Merchant. Methodists. Children: (VII.) Ella Kindig, born 1884. (VII.) Leroy Kindig, born 1886. (VII.) Pearl Kindig, born 1888. (VII.) John Kindig, born 1890.

VI. Joseph K. Kindig, born in Lansdale, Pa., Oct. 4, 1857. Mrd. Lillian Rockhill, of Tuckertown, N. J., Feb. 25, 1880. Res. 1904, Mt. Vernon St., Phila. Pa. In Grocery business with Kindig Bros., 2319 25 Penna. Ave. Presbyterians. Children: (VII.) Clarence Olin Kindig, born Sept. 5, 1882. (VII.) Ralph Nelson Kindig, born July 12, 1886.

VI. Margaret Kindig, born —. Mrd. Benjamin Landis, —. P. O., Souderton, Pa.

VI. Sarah Kindig, born —. Mrd. John D. Hunsberger,—. P. O., Souderton, Pa.

V. Henry Kratz, born in Montgomery Co., Pa., Jan. 13, 1818. Mrd. Mary Godshall, Dec. 25, 1845. She was born Dec. 10, 1825. P. O., Kulpsville, Pa. Carpenter. Members of the Methodist Episcopal church. No issue.

V. John M. Kratz, born Feb. 20, 1820. Mrd. Ury Gulick, Sept. 4, 1844. She was born June 11, 1821; died Aug. 6, 1890, aged 67 yrs., 1 m. 15 d. P. O. Telford, Pa. Farmer. Ref. Ch. Children: Marary, John, Mary.

VI. Marary Kratz, born May 5, 1846.

VI. John Kratz, born Mar. 14, 1850. Mrd. Kate, daughter of Henry Stover. She was born Apr. 1846. P. O., Telford, Pa. Children: (VII.) Henry Kratz,

Rev. Henry A. Hunsicker
(See Page 212.)

... ORK
... ... ARY
... ...

born Aug. 17, 1872. (VII.) Lilly Kratz, born Aug. 23, 1875. (VII.) Sarah Kratz, born Oct. 25, 1878. (VII.) Joseph Kratz, born Dec. 18, 1883.

VI. Mary Elizabeth Kratz, born Dec. 5, 1855. Mrd. Milton Benner, May 19, 1877. He was born Aug. 2, 1857. P. O., Souderton, Pa. Cigar maker. He is a member of the Lutheran, and she of the Reformed church. Children: (VII.) Ury Catharine Benner, born Apr. 4, 1878; died Feb. 4, 1881. (VII.) Barnard K. Benner, born Aug. 23, 1882. (VII.) Milton Ernest Benner, born Dec. 15, 1884. (VII.) Jonathan Benner, born Feb. 12, 1886.

IV. Veronica Kratz, born Oct. 27, 1778; died Jan. 13, 1821. Mrd. Isaac Fretz, son of Christian and Barbara Fretz, of Bedminster, Bucks Co., Pa., in 1800. Farmer and miller. Lived in Tinicum Twp., on the farm now owned and occupied by Henry F. Myers. During his absence from home Mar. 4, 1804, his barn was struck by lightning and burned. On this occasion his wife Veronica displayed heroic energy in rescuing horses and cattle from the burning building, and undoubtedly would have perished herself in the flames had she not at least been held back by the neighbors. In spite of all efforts to rescue the cattle from the flames, one horse and fourteen (some say twenty-one) head of cattle perished. In 1815 he built the "Fretz Valley Mill," on the Tohickon Creek, and operated same in addition to farming. Successful in business, he became possessor of nearly 300 acres of land. Mennonites. Children: John, Elizabeth, Jacob, Isaac, William, Mahlon, Mary, Samuel.

V. John Fretz, born in Bucks Co., Aug. 12, 1801; died in Putnam Co., Ohio, July 1, 1881. Mrd. Veronica Shelly, of Milford, Bucks Co., Nov. 15, 1824. She died Apr. 18, 1850. In 1834 they emigrated to Wayne Co., O., and in 1835 to Putnam Co., which was then a dense wilderness. Although he lived on the banks of the Blanchard River, he had to go thirty miles to mill. For some years their bread stuff, which consisted mainly of corn, was all ground on a hand mill. The entire family shoes were made of wood. In 1856 he sold his farm and emigrated to Linn Co.,

Kansas, where he purchased a farm, which he worked
for three years, then sold to his sons Jacob and John,
and returned to Ohio, where he spent the remainder
of his days with his daughters, Elizabeth and Fannie.
He and wife were members of the Mennonite church,
and assisted in building the first Mennonite meeting-
house in Putnam Co., where they worshiped for a
long time. Children: Elizabeth, Fannie, Mary, Lavina, Isaac, Barbara, Shelly, Susan, Jacob, Catharine, John, Hannah.

VI. Elizabeth Fretz, born in Bucks Co., Pa., July
16, 1828. Mrd. Stephen Crow, Oct. 28, 1847. Farmer of Putnam Co., O. Christians. Children: Mary,
Fannie, William, Sarah, James, Isaac, Elias, Thomas.

VII. Mary M. Crow, born Aug. 26, 1848. Mrd.—
Towsley,—. Farmer in Putnam Co., O. Christians.
Children: (**VIII.**) Armina E. (**VIII.**) Electa V. (**VIII.**)
Lavina E. (**VIII.**) Stephen R. (**VIII.**) Nellie F.

VII. Fannie Crow, born Aug. 6, 1850. Christian.
Unmrd.

VII. William Crow, born Oct. 27, 1852. Mrd. Mary
Haskel,—. Children: (**VIII.**) Maud M. (**VIII.**) Fannie.
(**VIII.**) Grace. (**VIII.**) Lucy.

VII. Sarah Crow, born Mar. 7, 1855. Mrd. James
Agner,—. Farmer in Putnam Co., O. Christians.
Children: (**VIII.**) Pratt E. (**VIII.**) Nora B. (**VIII.**) Neva
B. (**VIII.**) Stephen J. (**VIII.**) Everje R.

VII. James Crow, born Apr. 7, 1857. Mrd. Mary C.
Agner,—. Methodists. One child: (**VIII.**) Pet Agner
Crow.

VII. Isaac Crow, born Jan. 5, 1860. Farmer. S.

VII. Elias F. Crow, born Dec. 27, 1862. Mrd. Ren-
nie M. Clymer,—. One child: (**VIII.**) Carl C. Crow.

VII. Thomas Crow, born Mar. 23, 1865. Mrd. Elva
Schib,—.

VI. Fannie Fretz, born in Bucks Co., Pa., in 1825;
died in Putnam Co., O., Nov. 3, 1886. Mrd. Jacob
Ridenour, Mar. 2, 1847. He died Oct. 14, 1888. Farmer in Putnam Co., O. Fannie, member of U. B.
church. Children: William, Jane, John, Albert,
Mary, Elizabeth, George, Emma, Orlando, Clara.

VII. William Ridenour, born Apr. 14, 1848; died Oct. 11, 1849.

VII. Jane E. Ridenour, born Jan. 19, 1850. Mrd. Samuel Wollam, Apr. 19, 1868. Mrs. Wollam and seven of the children are mems. U. B. Ch. Children: **(VIII.)** Frank D. Wollam, born Jan. 18, 1869. **(VIII.)** Alfred L. Wollam, born Oct. 16, 1870. **(VIII.)** Waldo O. Wollam, born Jan. 17, 1874. **(VIII.)** Iden Wollam, born Sept. 16, 1879. **(VIII.)** Leo J. Wollam, born Feb. 3, 1885.

VII. John F. Ridenour, born Sept. 21, 1851. Mrd. Julia Wollam, Jan. 11, 1878. Children: **(VIII.)** Lloyd W. Ridenour, born Nov. 8, 1879. **(VIII.)** Eva P. Ridenour, born Jan. 17, 1884. **(VIII.)** Orlando B. Ridenour, born Aug. 17, 1887.

VII. Albert E. Ridenour, born Feb. 5, 1854.

VII. Mary A. Ridenour, born Jan. 30, 1856. Mrd. Samuel M. Bibler, Sept. 5, 1872. He died Jan. 31, 1887. Mary mem. of U. Br. Ch. Children: **(VIII.)** Iva A. Bibler, born Nov. 20, 1876. **(VIII.)** Blanch M. Bibler; born Aug. 6, 1778. **(VIII.)** Claud C. Bibler, born May 6, 1880. **(VIII.)** Fannie Bibler, born Dec. 31, 1881. **(VIII.)** Charles Bibler, born Dec. 20, 1883. **(VIII.)** Clara Bibler, born Jan. 6, 1886; died Apr. 27, 1887.

VII. Elizabeth L. Ridenour, born July 26, 1858; died Jan. 26, 1889. Mrd. George L. Marriott, Aug. 21, 1883. Farmer in Putnam Co., O. Elizabeth mem. of U. B. Ch. Children: **(VIII.)** Randolph J. Marriott, born Dec. 20, 1884. **(VIII.)** Rosco C. Marriott, born Jan. 16, 1887.

VII. George W. Ridenour, born October 27, 1860. Mrd. Reona Simons, Dec. 1, 1887. One child: **(VIII.)** Lewis J. Ridenour born June 25, 1889.

VII. Emma Ridenour, born Jan. 16, 1863. Mrd. Nathan C. Shirley, Aug. 12, 1888. Clerk of Dupont, Ohio. Mems. of U. B. Ch. One child: **(VIII.)** Ashley R. Shirley, born June 22, 1889.

VII. Orlando E. Ridenour, born Apr. 15. 1865.

VII. Clara E. Ridenour, born Feb. 9, 1869; died July 2, 1886.

VI. Mary Fretz, born in Bucks Co., Pa., July 26, 1831. Mrd. Henry Eyer, Apr. 29, 1849. Farmer in Putnam Co., Ohio. Children: John, George, Sarah, Wesley, Lavina.

VII. John Eyer, born Mar. 24, 1850. Mrd. Nancy Jane Howard, Jan. 1, 1872. Children: (**VIII.**) Clarence E. Eyer, born Oct. 6, 1873; died Sept. 6, 1874. (**VIII.**) LeRoy Howard Eyer, born Sept. 24, 1875; died aged 8 years. (**VIII.**) William Harrison Eyer, born Sept. 29, 1877. (**VIII.**) Florence Delilah Eyer, born Nov. 21, 1880. (**VIII.**) Henry Martin Eyer, born Oct. 30, 1882. (**VIII.**) Mary Grace Eyer, born May 20, 1885. (**VIII.**) Margaret Elizabeth Eyer, born Jan. 3, 1887.

VII. George Washington Eyer, born Feb. 22, 1852. Mrd. Fannie Moyer, of Grand Rapids, Mich., Apr. 1, 1877. Children: (**VIII.**) John Eyer, born in July, 1877. (**VIII.**) Ida Eyer, born Oct. 1879. (**VIII.**) Laura Eyer, born Mar. 1884.

VII. Sarah Eyer, born Sept. 23, 1855. Mrd. Henry Crisman, of Porter Co., Ind., Aug. 15, 1877. Children: (**VIII.**) William Henry Crisman, born Oct. 14, 1878. (**VIII.**) Mabel Crisman, born Mar. 31, 1883. (**VIII.**) Grace Crisman, born Apr. 26, 1885.

VII. Wesley Eyer born May 21, 1859. Mrd. Catharine Moyer, of Kent Co., Mich., Oct. 11, 1882. Children: (**VIII.**) Arthur DeWitt Eyer, born Aug. 26, 1883. (**VIII.**) Bessie Eyer, born Sept. 11, 1885. (**VIII.**) Earle Eyer, born Feb. 16, 1887. (**VIII.**) Harrison Eyer, born Oct. - , 1888.

VII. Lavina Eyer, born July 19, 1862. Married George O. Martin, of Etna Green, Kosciusko Co., Ind., Feb. 22, 1885. No children.

VI. Lavina Fretz, born —. Mrd. Reuben Adams, of Putnam Co., Ohio,—. No issue.

VI. Isaac Fretz, born in Putnam Co., Ohio, in 1834; died June 4, 1865. Mrd. Rosanna Sylvester, June 4, 1860. She was born in Dearborn Co., Ind., Jan. 1839. Occupation: Clerk, teacher, farmer, etc. At the outbreak of the "Border Ruffian War," he enlisted in the Government service and served nine months. During the war of the Rebellion he enlisted and served in Sherman's corps; was wounded in the battle of Goldsboro, and died on the way to the hospital. Methodists. Children: Rose, Lavina.

VII. Rose Fretz, born in Bureau Co., Ill., Feb. 3, 1852. Mrd. John A. Fox, Jan. 26, 1876. Farmer in Dallas Co., Iowa. Children: (**VIII.**) Milton F. Fox, born Mar. 13, 1880. (**VIII.**) Dermott Fox, born Aug. 1, 1881. (**VIII.**) Cross Fox, born Apr. 11, 1883. (**VIII.**) Mary Rosanna Fox, born June 1, 1885. (**VIII.**) Richard L. Fox, born Mar. 26, 1887. (**VIII.**) George Fox, born Feb. 12, 1889; died Mar. 5, 1889.

VII. Lavina Fretz, born Oct. 2, 1864; died Mar. 1865.

VI. Barbara Fretz, born in Putnam Co., O., in 1835; died in 1855.

VI. Shelly Fretz, born in Putnam Co., O., Jan. 14, 1837; died Mar. 17, 1855.

VI. Susan Fretz, born in Putnam Co., O., Mar. 17, 1840. Mrd. Francis M. Sylvester, Feb. 28, 1864. Farmer. In June 1869 they moved to Carroll Co., Mo., where he died Apr. 18, 1877. Baptists. Children: (**VII.**) Andrew J. Sylvester, born in Elkhart Co., Ind., Feb. 5, 1865. (**VII.**) Fannie J. Sylvester, born in Elkhart Co., Ind., Jan. 18, 1867; died Apr. 11, 1871. (**VII.**) Wesley J. Sylvester, born in Carroll Co., Mo., Apr. 12, 1869. (**VII.**) Maggie A. Sylvester, born in Carroll Co., Mo., May 29, 1871. (**VII.**) Joseph Sylvester, born in Carroll Co., Mo., Mar. 2, 1874. (**VII.**) Mary B. Sylvester, born in Carroll Co., Mo., May 1, 1876.

VI. Jacob Fretz, born in Putnam Co., Ohio, June 9, 1841. Mrd. Susan H. Flemming, of Defiance Co., O., Sept. 21, 1861. He enlisted in the war of the Rebellion, in the 26th Regt. Ky. Vol. Went with Gen. Thomas to Nashville, Tenn., and all through the Tennessee campaign; then with the 23d Army Corps through North Carolina, and was discharged at Newbern Hospital, June 16, 1865. He is a member of Avalon Post, No. 146, in Livingston Co., Mo. They attend the M. E. Ch. Children: Sarah, William, Elmer, Stephen, Almon, Cora, Ida, Ervy, Frank, Fannie, Charles, Delmer, Louella.

VII. Sarah A. Fretz, born Mar. 22, 1863. Mrd. William E. Wilson, of Carroll Co., Mo., in 1887. One child: (**VIII.**) Benjamin Jacob Wilson.

VII. William John Fretz, born Nov. 18, 1864.

VII. Elmer Ellsworth Fretz, born Jan. 26, 1867; died Aug. 1, 1869.

VII. Stephen Grant Fretz, born Nov. 14, 1868.

VII. Almon Fretz, born Dec. 20, 1870.

VII. Cora May Fretz, born Mar. 10, 1873.

VII. Ida Elizabeth Fretz, born Jan. 13, 1875.

VII. Ervy Clarence Fretz, born Mar. 6, 1877; died Oct. 11, 1878.

VII. Frank and Fannie Fretz (twins), born Mar. 24, 1879.

VII. Charles Eldon Fretz, born May 12, 1881.

VII. Delmer Ray Fretz, born July 13, 1883; died Sept. 14, 1883.

VII. Louella Belle Fretz, born May 31, 1885.

VI. Catharine Fretz, born Oct. 26, 1844; died Aug. 12, 1855.

VI. John Fretz, born in 1848. Mrd. Lucy Round, of Carroll Co., Mo., Jan. 27, 1887. Lived for a time in Kansas, and at the time of the grasshopper plague lost heavily. He afterwards returned to Ohio. He enlisted in the 5th Ohio Cavalry and served seven months in Sherman's command. He also served in the 199th Ill. 100 days' service. Methodists. One child: (**VII.**) — Fretz, born in 1888.

VI. Hannah Fretz, born Oct. 22, 1849; died Sept. 30, 1855.

V. Elizabeth Fretz, born in Bucks Co., Pa., Dec. 18, 1803; died in Phila., Pa., Feb. 25, 1884. Mrd. George Leffler, about 1835. He was born in Gerling, Germany, Nov. 18, 1802; died Mar. 10, 1876, in Phila., where he was engaged in the carriage building business, and succeeded in accumulating a small fortune. He was Lutheran, and she, Ger. Ref. No issue.

V. Jacob Fretz, born in Bucks Co., Pa., Aug. 18, 1805; died Dec. 29, 1848. Mrd. Rebecca Walters, Dec. 24, 1829. She was born Feb. 2, 1807; died June 2, 1834. Blacksmith. Children: Caroline, Catharine, Mahlon.

VI. Caroline Fretz, born in Bucks Co., Pa., Sept. 21, 1830. Mrd. Andrew P. Schlichter, of Blooming Glen, Pa., Jan. 6, 1850. He has been variously occupied, first in the commission, then in the livery business, in Phila., and finally Flour, Feed and Hay Merchant, at Telford, Pa. Now retired. Dunkards. Children: Enos, Mary.

VII. Enos F. Schlichter, born Sept. 11, 1856. Mrd. Malinda H. Tettemer, of Pipersville, Pa., Feb. 5, 1879. His occupation is carriage builder, at Telford, where he has successfully carried on the business to the present time. Children: (**VIII.**) Harvey T. Schlichter, born Jan. 18, 1882. (**VIII.**) Carrie T. Schlichter, born June 3, 1883. (**VIII.**) Frank Russel Schlichter, born Aug. 11, 1888.

VII. Mary F. Schlichter, born in 1861; died in 1864, aged 3 yrs., 4 m. 6 d.

VI. Catharine Fretz, born July 24, 1832. Mrd. Jacob Fluck, Nov. 29, 1851. He was born June 18, 1827. Members of Union Ch., Dublin, Pa. Children: Mary, Susan, Hiram, Carrie, Samuel, Emma.

VII. Mary Ann Fluck, born July 25, 1852; died Feb. 3, 1857.

VII. Susan Fluck, born Sept. 18, 1854; died Oct. 17, 1884. Mrd. Enos Yost, in 1877. Farmer. One son: (**VIII.**) — F. Yost; died aged about 3 years.

VII. Hiram F. Fluck, born Aug. 28, 1856; died Apr. 17, 1858.

VII. Carrie Fluck, born Feb. 19, 1859. S.

VII. Samuel F. Fluck, born Sept. 7, 1861. Farmer. Resides in Kansas.

VII. Emma Fluck, born Apr. 3, 1868. S.

VI. Mahlon Fretz, born Aug. 12, 1833; died Aug. 11, 1834.

Jacob Fretz married for his second wife, Mary Swartz, Jan. 24, 1836. She was born Mar. 31, 1816; died June 8, 1884. Children: Elizabeth, Rebecca, Isaac, Sarah, Jacob.

VI. Elizabeth Fretz, born Jan. 22, 1837; died Apr. 15, 1837.

VI. Rebecca Fretz, born May 5, 1838; died Sept. 5, 1840.

VI. Isaac S. Fretz, born in Bucks Co., Oct. 23, 1839. Mrd. Mary J. Smith, of Venango Co., Pa., Sept. 28, 1865. His earliest occupation was blacksmith. In 1864 he served the Government as mechanic for seven months. In 1875 he went to the Oil Regions of Venango Co., where he was engaged as engineer and tool dresser. In March 1883, he moved to Valley Co., Neb., where he is engaged in farming. In 1890 his name was brought before the convention for the nomination of State Senator, and received 19 out of 35 votes cast. In the fall of 1890 he was elected County Treasurer of Valley County, Neb., by the People's Independent Party. Mrs. Fretz, member of the Church of God. Children: Mary, Edwin, Annetta, Austin, Millie, George.

VII. Mary Fretz, born Aug. 28, 1866. Mrd. John E. Guthrie, Dec. 27, 1885. Mrs. Guthrie, member of Christian Ch. Children: (**VIII.**) William Edwin Guthrie, born Oct. 5, 1886. (**VIII.**) Rawlin Guthrie, born May 6, 1888. (**VIII.**) Archie Leland Guthrie, born Sept. 18, 1890.

VII. Edwin Fretz, born Apr. 26, 1870.

VII. Annetta Fretz, born Nov. 1, 1872; died Aug. 31, 1873.

VII. Austin Fretz, born July 22, 1874.

VII. Millie Fretz, born Feb. 1, 1877.

VII. George Fretz, born June 1, 1879.

VI. Sarah Fretz, born in Bucks Co., Pa., June 1, 1843. Mrd. Levi Longacre, of Phila., Aug. 21, 1867. He was born June 28, 1836. Stair builder in Phila. Mrs. Longacre, Ger. Ref. Children: (**VII.**) Frank Longacre, born Sept. 9, 1875; died Sept. 18, 1875. (**VII.**) Edward Longacre, born Dec. 17, 1887.

VI. Jacob S. Fretz, born in Bucks Co., Pa., April 5, 1847. Mrd. Emma Brown, Dec. 25, 1873. She was born Sept. 2, 1850. Producer of coal oil at Bradford, Pa. Mrs. Fretz, Baptist. One child: (**VII.**) Flora May Fretz, born May 15, 1876.

V. Isaac Fretz, born in Bucks Co., Aug. 22, 1807; died June 5, 1874. Mrd. Catharine Stover, of Bedminster, Bucks Co., in 1832. He owned and run the mill until 1850, when he sold it and bought the old homestead, where he lived until about 1865; then sold and moved to Bridgetown. New Mennonites at Deep Run, of which he was a trustee for some time, and of which he was twice nominated for the ministry but not elected. Children: Elizabeth, Jemima, Annie, John, Mary, Catharine, Violetta, Hannah, Saloma, Caroline.

VI. Elizabeth Fretz, born in Bucks Co., Mar. 13, 1833. Mrd. Eli Stover, . He died Sept. 16, 1878. Farmer. New Mennonites. Children: Minerva, Newton, Jordan, Jennie, Carrie, Katie.

VII. Minerva Stover, born Dec. 29, 1854. Mrd. Peter D. Harris, May 20, 1878. Farmer. Mr. H., Ger. Ref. Mrs. H., Mennonite. One child: **(VIII.)** Jacob Harris.

VII. Newton F. Stover, born June 26, 1856. Mrd. Catharine Anders in 1881. Farmer. Ger. Reformed. Children: **(VIII.)** Minnie Idella Stover, born—; died Apr. 7, 1883. **(VIII.)** Carrie Stover, born Jan. 5, 1883. **(VIII.)** Sadie Stover, born Apr. 1885.

VII. Jordan F. Stover, born Mar. 13, 1859. Mrd. Anna L. Bean, Dec. 28, 1882. Teacher, clerk and merchant. Children: **(VIII.)** Clarence Stover. **(VIII.)** Bessie May Stover.

VII. Jennie Stover, born ; died aged 6 days.

VII. Carrie Stover, born .

VII. Katie Stover, died aged 2 years.

Elizabeth mrd. second husband, Philip Protzman, May 27, 1883. Farmer at Finesville, N. J.

VI. Jemima Fretz, born in Bucks Co., Feb. 15, 1835; died Apr. 26, 1883. Mrd. George Gotlieb Ebert, Aug. 12, 1849. He was born in Germany June 27, 1821; died March 3, 1884. Mr. Ebert, Lutheran. Mrs. Ebert, Ger. Ref. Children: William, John, Ella, Mary, Charles, Warren.

VII. William Ebert, born May 3, 1850; died January 19, 1856.

VII. John Lewis Ebert, born Dec. 22, 1854. Mrd. Annie Hotel,—. She was born Jan. 10, 1847. Teacher and carpenter. Presbyterians. Children: **(VIII.)** Elmer Garfield Ebert, born Aug. 22, 1880; died May 28, 1884. **(VIII.)** Ella May Ebert, born Sept. 14, 1882.

(VIII.) Alice Magill Ebert, born Apr. 16, 1886. (VIII.) Jennie Valeria Ebert, born Jan. 13, 1888.

VII. Ella Ebert, born Sept. 5, 1857; died Mar. 4, 1883. Ger. Ref.

VII. Mary Catharine Ebert, born Dec. 22, 1864; died Feb. 25, 1865.

VII. Charles Ebert, born Oct. 31, 1859. He was well educated and at one time Principal of the Kutztown Normal School. He was mrd. and had one child, but afterwards separated from his wife.

VII. Warren Ebert born July 27, 1874. New Mennonite.

VI. Annie Fretz, born in Bucks Co., Jan. 29, 1837. Mrd. Joseph Funk, Nov. 23, 1857. He was born Apr. 1, 1831. Farmer. He, Lutheran. She, New Mennonite. Children: Adeline, Elmer.

VII. Adeline Funk, born Jan. 28, 1859. Mrd. Gideon Rosenberger, of Bedminster, Jan. 8, 1880. Farmer. Children: (VIII.) Joseph Rosenberger, born—. (VIII.) Minnie Catharine Rosenberger, born- .

VII. Elmer E. Funk, born August, 15, 1864. Mrd. Philena Zeigenfoss, June 12, 1884. Teacher. Children: (VIII.) Mamie Nora. (VIII.) Elmer Millard. (VIII.) Annie Ray, born June 22, 1889.

VI. John S. Fretz, born in Bucks Co., Pa., Nov. 6, 1839; died Jan. 1, 1887. Mrd. Ella Amanda Loux, Oct. 15, 1864. She was born Sept. 26, 1846; died May 14, 1873. Farmer and Miller. New Mennonites. Children: (VII.) Anna Laura Fretz, born July 23, 1865; died Apr. 2, 1873. (VII.) Katie Fretz, born Sept. 15, 1868; died Feb. 8, 1873.

John mrd. his second wife, Matilda Cope, Nov. 23, 1873. Children: (VII.) Howard C. Fretz, born Mar. 1, 1875; died Feb. 19, 1887. (VII.) Charles C. Fretz, born Nov. 30, 1876. (VII.) Sallie C. Fretz, born July 29, 1879; died Aug. 11, 1881. (VII.) Irwin C. Fretz, born June 19, 1885.

VI. Mary Fretz, born in Bucks Co., Feb. 2, 1842. Mrd. Jonas Loux, Jan. 26, 1861. He was born Jan. 16, 1839. Farmer. Ger. Ref. Children: Harvey, Lincoln, Eva.

VII. Harvey F. Loux, born Dec. 28, 1861. Mrd.
—, Sept. 1885. Teacher. Ger. Ref. One child: (VIII.)
Chester Arthur Loux, born Oct. 7, 1887.

VII. E. Lincoln Loux, born July 7, 1866. Teacher
and book-keeper. Ger. Ref.

VII. Eva Flora Loux, born Apr. 6, 1871. Ger. Ref.

VI. Catharine Fretz, born Oct. 4, 1844; died Nov. 3,
1846.

VI. Violetta Fretz, born Apr. 12, 1847. Mrd. Henry
Roth, Dec. 24, 1870. Ev. Assoc. No issue.

VI. Hannah Fretz, born in Bucks Co., Oct. 18, 1849.
Mrd. Monroe S. Weikel, in 1869. P. O., Leithsville,
Pa. Farmer and shoemaker. New Mennonites. Chil-
dren: Alice, John, Irene, Hattie, Meda.

VII. Alice F. Weikel, born Jan. 20, 1870; died Feb.
28, 1891. Mrd. Harvey R. Balliet, Dec. 14, 1889.
Mr. Balliet, mem. Springtown Union; Mrs. Balliet,
New Mennonite.

VII. John H. Weikel, born May 22, 1873.

VII. Irene F. Weikel, born May 8, 1876.

VII. Hattie F. Weikel, born Aug. 15, 1881.

VII. Meda F. Weikel, born July 15, 1883.

VI. Saloma Fretz, born in Bucks Co., Nov. 16, 1851.
Mrd. Andrew S. Hendricks, Oct. 29, 1870. Farmer.
Mem. Ev. Assoc. Children: Ella C., Charles F.,
Clara F., Franklin F., Laura F., Harvey F., Clay-
ton F., Stella F.

VII. Ella Catharine Hendricks, born July 2, 1871.
Mrd. Jacob M. Detweiler, Sept. 26, 1889.

VII. Charles F. Hendricks, born July 15, 1874; died
Apr. 6, 1876.

VII. Clara F. Hendricks, born July 22, 1877; died
Aug. 10, 1877.

VII. Franklin F. Hendricks, born July 6, 1878.

VII. Laura F. Hendricks, born Mar. 7, 1881; died
Mar. 19, 1890.

VII. Harvey F. Hendricks, born Dec. 16, 1883.

VII. Clayton F. Hendricks, born Aug. 30, 1886.

VII. Stella F. Hendricks, born Jan. 21, 1889.

VI. Caroline Fretz, born in Bucks Co., Nov. 12,
1854. Mrd. James D. Bergey, of Hilltown, Apr. 14,
1877. Blacksmith. Mems. Ev. Assoc. Children:

(**VII.**) Mary Catharine Bergey, born Mar. 22, 1879.
(**VII.**) Ella F. Bergey, born Aug. 18, 1885.

V. William Fretz, born in Bucks Co., Pa., Jan. 1, 1810; died Feb. 20, 1883. Mrd. Anna Myers, of Plumstead Twp., Mar. 12, 1838. He early engaged in farming and freighting goods by teams to Easton, Nazareth, and other points. Farming was his principal occupation. He was also the last of his name who owned and run his father's mill. As a business man he was financially successful. New Mennonites. Children: Mahlon, Albert, Elizabeth, Henry, Amos, Lavina, Sarah, Reed, Eli, Catharine, William.

VI. Mahlon Fretz, born in Bucks Co., Pa., Apr. 1, 1838. Mrd. Henrietta Althouse, Aug. 13, 1864. She was born Dec. 12, 1846. He has been variously occupied as farmer, teamster, agent, and merchant. Ger. Ref. No issue.

VI. Albert Fretz, born in Bucks Co., Pa., May 1, 1840. Mrd. Amanda H. Licey, of Hilltown Twp., Dec. 24, 1864. Blacksmith and farmer. New Mennonites. Children: Ella, Annie, Clayton, Aquilla, Abraham, Emma, Gertrude.

VII. Ella Jane Fretz, born June 20, 1865. Mrd. Harvey Bryan, in 1887. Farmer, of Bedminster, Pa. One child: (**VIII.**) Lillie Bryan, born Mar. 1888.

VII. Annie Elizabeth Fretz, born Aug. 20, 1869. Mrd. Moses Bryan, of Bedminster, Pa., Oct. 16, 1886. Farmer. Mrs. Bryan, New Mennonite. One child: (**VIII.**) Katie Bryan, born Apr. 1887.

VII. Clayton L. Fretz, born Sept. 8, 1874.

VII. Aquilla May Fretz, born Jan. 3, 1877.

VII. Abraham L. Fretz, born July 8, 1879.

VII. Emma Laura Fretz, born June 16, 1880.

VII. Gertrude Fretz, born Sept. 6, 1884.

VI. Elizabeth Fretz, born Dec. 16, 1841; died Mar. 19, 1860.

VI. Henry M. Fretz, born in Bucks Co., Pa., Oct. 15, 1843. Mrd. Sallie Haldeman, of New Britain, Pa., Sept. 1876. Miller by trade. He, Presbyterian; she, Mennonite.

VI. Amos Fretz, born in Bucks Co., Pa., June 12, 1845. Mrd. Catharine Fox, of Bedminster, Pa., Dec. 25, 1869. She was born Nov. 1, 1845. Engaged in the commission clothing business. Mrs. Fretz, Presbyterian. Children: **(VII.)** William Fretz, born July 1, 1870. **(VII.)** Jordan Fretz, born July 23, 1873. **(VII.)** Amos Fretz, born July 8, 1877. **(VII.)** Rosa Fretz, born Mar. 4, 1880. **(VII.)** Katie Alice Fretz, born Sept. 21, 1882.

VI. Lavina Fretz, born in Bucks Co., Pa., Feb. 10, 1847. Mrd. Simeon Landis, Jan. 21, 1871. He died in 1890. Harness maker at Blooming Glen, Pa. Mr. Landis, Old, and Mrs. Landis, New Mennonite. Children: **(VII.)** William F. Landis, born Nov. 4, 1872. **(VII.)** Allen F. Landis, born June 4, 1876; died Mar. 18, 1889. **(VII.)** Mary F. Landis, born Oct. 10, 1878; died Mar. 4, 1882. **(VII.)** Harriet F. Landis, born Feb. 22, 1883. **(VII.)** Reed F. Landis, born Dec. 13, 1889.

VI. Sarah Ann Fretz, born in Bucks Co., Pa., Sept. 7, 1848. Mrd. Christian Rosenberger, of Richland, Pa., in 1888. Farmer. Mrs. Rosenberger, New Mennonite.

VI. Reed Fretz, born in Bucks Co., Pa., Mar. 20, 1850. Mrd. Maggie R. Landis, of Lawndale, Pa., in 1876. She died in Jan. 1890. Farmer in Nemaha Co., Kan. He also does quite an extensive business in shipping horses and cattle from the West to Pennsylvania. Children: **(VII.)** J. Warren Fretz, born Oct. 14, 1877. **(VII.)** William L. Fretz, born Jan. 13, 1879. **(VII.)** Annie R. Fretz, born May 2, 1880. **(VII.)** Harry L. Fretz, born Jan. 15, 1881. **(VII.)** Arlington L. Fretz, born Aug. 28, 1883. **(VII.)** Leroy L. Fretz, born Sept. 30, 1885; died Oct. 10, 1885. **(VII.)** Floyd L. Fretz, born Nov. 21, 1887.

VI. Eli Fretz, born in Bucks Co., Pa., Dec. 1, 1851. Mrd. Emma Catharine Frantz, Feb. 24, 1881. Farmer. New Mennonite; Mrs. Fretz, Lutheran. Children: **(VII.)** Bertha Fretz, born May 6, 1884; died Sept. 14, 1884. **(VII.)** Charles F. Fretz, born Dec. 5, 1886. **(VII.)** John Fretz, born Sept. 22, 1888.

VI. Catharine Fretz, born Mar. 7, 1853. Mrd. Horace Swope, Nov. 25, 1885. Farmer in Tinicum Twp., Pa. Mrs. Swope, New Mennonite. No issue.

VI. William Fretz, born in Bucks Co., Pa., Sept. 6, 1856. Mrd. Laura M. Sames, of Springfield Twp., Dec. 25, 1880. She was born Mar. 8, 1860. Miller by trade. After his father's death he purchased the homestead farm, but finally sold out and went to Nemaha Co., Kan., where he is dealing in cattle. Lutherans. One child: (**VII.**) Sadie Fretz, born Feb. 5, 1884.

V. Mahlon Fretz, born in Bucks Co., Pa., June 12, 1813. Mrd. Mary Ann Grubb, of Montg. Co., Pa., May 30, 1841. She was born Oct. 20, 1821. His principal occupation has been farming, and he has otherwise been a skillful and useful man. He also had a military tendency, and was Captain of a Company of Militia for some time. He never belonged to any church, but was active in the building of the New Mennonite church at Deep Run, of which his wife was a member. In 1854 he and wife separated, and were divorced in 1872. Children: Jeremiah, Fenton, Susan, Sylvester, Mary, Hannah, Harvey.

VI. Jeremiah Fretz, born Oct. 21, 1842; died same day.

VI. Fenton G. Fretz, born in Bucks Co., Pa., Oct. 21, 1843. Mrd. Elizabeth Holloway, of Montg. Co., Pa., Mar. 12, 1867. She was born Feb. 6, 1842. He enlisted Aug. 29, 1861, in Company B, 6th Penna. Cavalry, known as "Rush's Lancers." He was thrown from his horse and wounded in a charge, in 1864, and was taken to the Hospital at Wilmington, Del., and was discharged from the service Aug. 17, 1865. He is at present Express Agent at Pottstown, Pa. Methodists. Children: (**VII.**) Jennie Fretz, born July 30, 1868. (**VII.**) Mary A. Fretz, born July 3, 1870. (**VII.**) Sarah M. Fretz, born Nov. 25, 1872. (**VII.**) Wilbur Fretz, born May 31, 1874; died July 15, 1874. (**VII.**) Ida Fretz, born Aug. 18, 1875; died Sept. 29, 1875. (**VII.**) Roy Fretz, born Oct. 19, 1876.

VI. Susan Fretz, born Nov. 28, 1844; died same day.

VI. Sylvester G. Fretz, born in Bucks Co., Pa., Oct. 30, 1845; died Feb. 2, 1888. Mrd. Catharine Swavely, in July 1864. She was born in 1847; died Oct. 24, 1875. Children: Anna, Rebecca, George, Sarah. Sylvester mrd. for his second wife Mary Lee, Sept. 29, 1878. She was born Oct. 12, 1844. One child: Thomas. Sylvester Fretz enlisted in Company I, 129th Regiment Penna. Vol., Aug. 4, 1862; and participated in the battles of Antietam and Chancellorsville. He was discharged Mar. 18, 1863, and re-enlisted July 11, 1864, in Company F., 197th Regiment Penna. Vol., and was discharged Nov. 11, 1864.

VII. Anna Fretz, born Dec. 17, 1865. Mrd. Reuben Eagle, of Montg. Feb. 2, 1884. He was born Oct. 15, 1859. Children: (VIII.) Laura Eagle, born Oct. 31, 1885. (VIII.) Harry Eagle, born June 2, 1887. (VIII.) Roy Eagle, born Aug. 1, 1888.

VII. Rebecca Fretz, born Aug. 13, 1867.

VII. George L. Fretz, born Feb. 11, 1869.

VII. Sarah M. Fretz, born Aug. 25, 1871. Mrd. Charles Engle, of Buckmansville, Pa., June 6, 1891.

VII. Thomas L. Fretz, born June 2, 1879.

VI. Mary Catharine Fretz, born in Bucks Co., Aug. 23, 1847. Mrd. George Spiese, Jan. 10, 1867. He was born Mar. 10, 1840. Attend Ger. Ref. Ch. Children: (VII.) Emma Spiese, born Nov. 18, 1867. (VII.) Lettie Spiese, born May 29, 1870. (VII.) Ida Florence Spiese, born June 15, 1874. (VII.) Harry Warren Spiese, born Jan. 15, 1877. (VII.) Fenton G. Spiese, born Mar. 7, 1879. (VII.) Mary A. Spiese, born Sept. 23, 1882. (VII.) William Earl Spiese, born Sept. 30, 1887. (VII.) Anna H. Spiese, born Apr. 1890.

VI. Hannah Eliza Fretz, born Sept. 5, 1849. Mrd. George Haus, Mar. 4, 1876. One child: (VII.) Anna Brown Haus, born Dec. 13, 1878.

VI. Harvey Fretz, born Sept. 16, 1852; died Apr. 1856.

V. Mary Fretz, born in Bucks Co., Apr. 12, 1815. Mrd. Henry Fretz, son of John and Susanna (Haldeman) Fretz, Oct. 4, 1836. Lived on a farm in Bedminster known as the "Low Lands," along the Tohickon Creek, until Apr. 1839, when they moved to

Plumstead Twp., on the farm known as the "Leatherman farm," where they lived until 1871, when they moved to a small farm adjoining the old homestead, where they still reside. New Mennonites. Children: John, Isaac, Amos, Enos, Ann, Lavina, George.

VI. John Fretz, born Aug. 6, 1837; died Sept. 8, 1839.

VI. Isaac Fretz, born in Bucks Co., Aug. 4, 1840. Mrd. Lottie Leech, daughter of George Leech, of Montgomeryville, Pa., Dec. 21, 1869. When three years old he became lame in his right knee, and has been afflicted ever since. He received a good education and taught school from 1858 to 1862. He then went into the commission business for two years; then went to Philadelphia and engaged in the retail grocery business, which he followed for a long time. He at present deals in butter and eggs. Baptists. Children: (**VII.**) Emma Fretz, born Dec. 17, 1872; died July 29, 1873. (**VII.**) Alice Fretz, born Sept. 2, 1874. (**VII.**) Hettie Fretz, born May 22, 1877. (**VII.**) Lottie Fretz, born Nov. 24, 1879.

VI. Amos Fretz, born Nov. 23, 1842; died Sept. 17, 1844.

VI. Enos Fretz, born in Bucks Co., Jan. 16, 1845. He remained at home and worked on the farm most of the time until the fall of 1869; then taught school for a few years. He was mrd. to Mary A. Rickert, of Hilltown, Dec. 3, 1873, and settled on the old homestead and engaged in farming, until Mar. 1882, when he removed to Milford Square, Pa., and entered into partnership with Nelson Leatherman in the mercantile business, in which he is still engaged.

VI. Ann Eliza Fretz, born in Bucks Co., Dec. 13, 1847. Mrd. Morris J. Davis, son of Wilson Davis, of Montgomeryville, Montg. Co., May 15, 1869. Dealer in produce in Philadelphia. Baptists. Children: (**VII.**) Ida May Davis, born May 25, 1870. (**VII.**) Henry Wilson Davis, born Aug. 23, 1872. (**VII.**) George F. Davis, born Aug. 31, 1874. (**VII.**) Mary E. Davis, born Jan. 24, 1876. (**VII.**) Addie L. Davis, born Aug. 5, 1878. (**VII.**) Clarence Oliver Davis, born May 26, 1881; died May 12, 1886. (**VII.**) Walter Cal-

(See Page 221.)

NEW
LIBRARY

ley Davis, born Nov. 11, 1883. (VII.) Raymond Davis, born Mar. 21, 1885; died May 21, 1886.

VI. Lavina Fretz, born in Bucks Co., July 6, 1850. Mrd. Isaac F. Rickert, of Hilltown Twp., . Farmer. They live on the old Rickert Homestead, in Hilltown. Children: (VII.) Clayton David Rickert. (VII.) William Henry Rickert.

VI. George L. Fretz, born Sept. 5, 1854. Mrd. Maggie, daughter of Valentine K. Clymer, of New Britain Twp., Jan. 29, 1876. Farmer. Ger. Ref. One child: (VII.) Ida Estella Fretz.

V. Samuel Fretz, born in Bucks Co., Feb. 12, 1819; died Dec. 25, 1884. He early identified himself with the printing trade, and rose step by step in his chosen craft, and at one time was editor and proprietor of the *Bucks County Intelligencer*, at Doylestown, Pa. He was also a mechanic of note, millwright, marble cutter, organ builder, dentist, and, added to these, during the latter part of his life he was engaged in teaching. In 1854 he went to Putnam Co., Ohio, and when taken sick he was teaching near Melrose, Paulding Co., Ohio, where he died, and is buried in the Mackling graveyard. He never married.

IV. Ann Kratz, born July 16, 1780, died Feb. 23, 1861, aged 80 yrs., 7 m. 7 d. Mrd. Henry Clemens, of Lower Salford, Montg. Co., Nov. 6, 1806. He was born in 1783, died Nov. 9, 1860, aged 77 yrs., 7 m. 28 d. Farmer. Mennonites. Chiadren: Mary, Garret, Catharine, Isaac, Elizabeth, Sarah, Jacob.

V. Mary Clemens, born in Montg. Co., Sept. 14, 1807, died May 15, 1852. Mrd. Jacob K. Godshall, May 9, 1826. He died- . Farmer. Mennonites. Children: Henry, Isaac, Anna, Barbara, Jacob, Abraham, John, Mary.

VI. Henry C. Godshall, born in Montg. Co., Sept. 1, 1828; died Aug. 18, 1884. Mrd. Anna Gehman, Dec. 17, 1853. She was born in Hatfield, Pa., Mar. 20, 1833. Farmer. Mennonites. Children: Lucy, Jacob.

VII. Lucy Ann Godshall, born Sept. 13, 1857; died Aug. 1, 1875. S.

17

VII. Jacob G. Godshall, born June 11, 1864. Mrd. Katie B. Kulp, Feb. 23, 1889. P. O., Telford, Pa. Telegraph operator. One child: (**VIII.**) Howard Godshall, born Apr. 1, 1891.

VI. Isaac C. Godshall, born in Montgomery Co., Pa., Dec. 29, 1829. Mrd. Anna Delp, Nov. 29, 1856. She died Sept. 27, 1889. Mennonites. Children: Catharine, Elizabeth, Samuel, Mahlon, Mary.

VII. Catharine D. Godshall, born Aug. 26, 1857; died Apr. 14, 1864.

VII. Elizabeth D. Godshall, born Sept. 5, 1859; died Sept. 24, 1859.

VII. Samuel D. Godshall, born May 18, 1863; died Aug. 13, 1863.

VII. Mahlon D. Godshall, born Aug. 20, 1865; died Sept. 12, 1865.

VII. Mary D. Godshall, born Jan. 6, 1871; died Nov. 20, 1889. Mrd. John S. Nice, Jan. 5, 1889. One child: (**VIII.**) Isaac Howard Nice, born Nov. 6, 1889; died Feb. 20, 1890.

VI. Anna C. Godshall, born Apr. 12, 1832. Mrd. Samuel Derstine—. P. O., Sellersville, Pa.

VI. Barbara C. Godshall, born Nov. 7, 1834. Mrd. Daniel B. Hackman, Nov. 11, 1855. He died Sept. 20, 1875. Merchant. Mennonites. Children: Jacob, William, Kate, Emma, Mary, Barbara.

VII. Jacob G. Hackman, born Nov. 11, 1857; died Jan. 31, 1860.

VII. William G. Hackman, born Mar. 5, 1859; died Oct. 20, 1889. Mrd. Lizzie K. Hunsberger. P. O., Souderton, Pa.

VII. Kate G. Hackman, born Oct. 15, 1862. Mrd. Josiah B. Dettra—. Res., Philadelphia, Pa.

VII. Emma G. Hackman, born Jan. 2, 1867. Mrd. Morris S. Landis. (See Index of References No. 37).

VII. Mary G. Hackman, born July 2, 1869. Mrd. William B. Freed, June 17, 1886. Marketman and laborer. One child: (**VIII.**) Lizzie H. Freed, born in 1886.

VII. Barbara G. Hackman, born Sept. 19, 1874.

VI. Jacob C. Godshall, born Jan. 26, 1837. Mrd. Barbara L. Godshall, daughter of Jacob Z. Godshall,

Oct. 29, 1859. Farmer and stockraising. P. O., Morwood, Pa. Mennonites. Children: Katie, Andrew, Ida, Horace, Rosalinda, Mary, Jacob, Reinhart.

VII. Katie G. Godshall, born Nov. 29, 1861; died Mar. 3, 1862.

VII. Andrew G. Godshall, born Mar. 29, 1863. Mrd. Ida S., daughter of Wm. H. Gehman, Dec. 11, 1886. P. O., Morwood, Pa. Children: **(VIII.)** Howard G. Godshall, born Nov. 27, 1887. **(VIII.)** Alverda G. Godshall, born Apr. 2, 1890.

VII. Ida G. Godshall, born June 15, 1865. Mrd. Sylvanus W., son of Henry Ziegler, Nov. 2, 1884. P. O., Morwood, Pa. Children: **(VIII.)** Jacob G. Ziegler, born June 4, 1887. **(VIII.)** Katie G. Ziegler, born Aug. 21, 1890.

VII. Horace G. Godshall, born July 21, 1867. Mrd. Lizzie B., daughter of Garret Clemens, Jan. 12, 1889. P. O., Morwood, Pa.

VII. Rosalinda G. Godshall, born Apr. 6, 1869. Mrd. Samuel B., son of Wm. G. Freed, Aug. 16, 1888. P. O., Morwood, Pa. One child: **(VIII.)** Lillian G. Freed, born Mar. 28, 1889.

VII. Mary G. Godshall, born Nov. 5, 1870; died Nov. 1, 1880.

VII. Jacob G. Godshall, born June 9, 1876.

VII. Reinhart G. Godshall, born Oct. 6, 1880.

VI. Abraham C. Godshall, born Apr. 10, 1839. Mrd. Anna O. Derstine, May 18, 1861. She died Mar. 21, 1866. Merchant at Lansdale, Pa. Reformed. Children: Marietta, William, Lincoln. Abraham mrd. for his second wife Lydia K. Hartzell, Nov. 30, 1867. Their children are: Martha, Harvey, Elizabeth, Naomi, Stella.

VII. Marietta B. Godshall, born Feb. 9, 1862; died Dec. 18, 1863.

VII. William Henry Godshall, born Sept. 14, 1863. Mrd. Marietta Gerhart. P. O., Lansdale, Pa.

VII. Lincoln D. Godshall, born Nov. 26, 1865. Mrd. Estella B. Hall. P. O., Denver, Colorado.

VII. Martha H. Godshall, born— 30, 1868.

VII. Harvey H. Godshall, born Sept. 14, 1872.

VII. Elizabeth H. Godshall, born July 5, 1878.

VII. Naomi H. Godshall, born Mar. 29, 1883; died April 9, 1883.

VII. Estella H. Godshall (twin to Naomi), born Mar. 29, 1883; died Aug. 15, 1883.

VI. John C. Godshall, born Oct. 2, 1841. Married B. Hockman, Nov. 2, 1867. She was born July 24, 1847; died Nov. 26, 1883. He married for his second wife Rebecca Troxel, Feb. 24, 1885. She was born May 10, 1856; died June 24, 1885. Married third wife Mrs. Susan Meyers, Aug. 18, 1887. She was born Mar. 23, 1860. Merchant, miller at Lansdale, Pa. Reformed church. Children all by the first wife are: (**VII.**) Wilson Godshall, born June 23, 1869. (**VII.**) Ella Godshall, born Aug. 4, 1871; died March 13, 1889. (**VII.**) Laura Godshall, born Nov. 1, 1873. (**VII.**) Mary Jane Godshall, born Mar. 13, 1876. (**VII.**) Perry Godshall, born Feb. 22, 1878. (**VII.**) Harry Godshall, born June 16, 1881.

VI. Mary C. Godshall, born Apr. 19, 1844. Mrd. Abraham M. Alderfer. (See Index of References No. 38).

V. Garhart Clemens, born Dec. 30, 1808; died—. Mrd. Elizabeth Nice. Farmer, and lived in Lower Salford Twp., Montgomery Co., Pa. Mennonites. Children: William, Anna, Henry, Mary, Jacob, John, Garret, Isaac.

VI. William N. Clemens, born Mar. 30, 1831; died Apr. 4, 1863. Mrd. Catharine Delp, daughter of Geo. and Susan Delp, Nov. 1, 1853. She was born Mar. 17, 1829. Farmer. One child: Lizzie Ann.

VII. Lizzie Ann Clemens, born May 5, 1856. Mrd. Lyman Rosenberger, son of David and Mary Ann Rosenberger, Dec. 4, 1875. P. O., Harleysville, Pa. Manufacturer. Children: (**VIII.**) Wellington Rosenberger, born Apr. 18, 1877. (**VIII.**) Harry Rosenberger, born July 3, 1879. (**VIII.**) Stella Rosenberger, born Nov. 17, 1880.

VI. Anna Clemens, born : died . Mrd. Henry K. Gottshall. (See Index of References No. 39).

VI. Henry N. Clemens, born May 12, 1838. Mrd. Fannie S. Schatz, Feb. 28, 1864. She was born June

4. 1843. P. O., Lederachville, Pa. Farmer. Mennonite. Children: Garret, Annie, Menno.

VII. Garret S. Clemens, born June 17, 1866. Mrd.
Sallie K. Nice, Oct. 25, 1890. P. O., Lederachville,
Pa. Carpenter. One child: (VIII.) Wellington K.
Clemens, born Mar. 16, 1891.

VII. Annie S. Clemens, born Oct. 28, 1868. Married
Frank M. Kuhn, Jan. 8, 1887. Children: (VIII.) Reinhart C. Kuhn, born June 17, 1888. (VIII.) Rosa C.
Kuhn, born Oct. 16, 1889.

VII. Menno S. Clemens, born June 25, 1872.

VI. Mary Clemens, born in 1840. Mrd. George D.
Alderfer, in 1862. He was born in 1836. Teacher and
farmer. P. O., Harleysville, Pa. Mrs. Alderfer.
Mennonite. Children:

VII. Alvin C. Alderfer, born Nov. 9, 1869. Mrd.
Mary L. Alderfer, daughter of Levi S. Alderfer, Oct.
25, 1890. P. O., Harleysville, Pa. School teacher,
land surveyor and leveler. One child: (VIII.) Bertha
May Alderfer, born May 8, 1891.

VII. Garret Alderfer, born in 1871; died in 1872.

VII. Lizzie Alderfer, born in 1873.

VII. Annie May Alderfer, born in 1875; died in 1882.

VII. George Alderfer, born in 1877.

VII. Harry Alderfer, born in 1881.

VI. Jacob N. Clemens, born in Montg. Co., Feb. 1,
1843. Mrd. Eliza K. Cassel, Apr. 17, 1869. She was
born Sept. 28, 1850. Farmer. Mennonites. Children:
Mary, Sylvanus, Jacob, Leahanna, John, Lizzie,
Norman.

VII. Mary Clemens, born May 28, 1870. Mrd. Frank
Bartholomew,—. P. O., Mainland, Pa. School
teacher. One child: (VIII.) Willis Bartholomew, born
Oct. 25, 1888.

VII. Sylvanus Clemens, born Aug. 22, 1872.

VII. Jacob Clemens, born Apr. 2, 1874.

VII. Leahanna Clemens, born May 6, 1876.

VII. John Clemens, born July 1, 1879.

VII. Lizzie Rachel Clemens, born Feb. 1, 1885.

VII. Norman Clemens, born Apr. 17, 1887.

VI. John N. Clemens, born in Montg. Co., Apr. 6,
1845. Mrd. Amanda S., daughter of John Alderfer,

Oct. 27, 1867. Farmer. Mennonites. Children: Sallie, Lizzie, Allen, John, Ida, Garhart.

VII. Sallie A. Clemens, born Oct. 22, 1868; died May 10, 1880.

VII. Lizzie A. Clemens, born July 27, 1870. Mrd. Edwin W. Krupp, Feb. 2, 1889. P. O., Franconia Square, Pa.

VII. Allen A. Clemens, born Mar. 24, 1872; died Jan. 24, 1874.

VII. John A. Clemens, born June 21, 1873.

VII. Ida A. Clemens, born Sept. 18, 1875; died Sept. 2, 1877.

VII. Garhart Clemens, born Nov. 18, 1881.

VI. Garret Clemens, born —; died— . Mrd. Kate Bergey,—. One child: (**VII.**) Lizzie Clemens, born—. Mrd. Horace G. Godshall. (See index of References No. 40.)

VI. Isaac N. Clemens, born Feb. 27, 1852. Mrd. Anna S. Alderfer, daughter of Jacob K. Alderfer, Nov. 1, 1873. Farmer. Mennonites. Children: (**VII.**) Lizzie A. Clemens, born Feb. 12, 1875. (**VII.**) Jacob A. Clemens, born Nov. 1, 1876; died Apr. 22, 1877. (**VII.**) Garret A. Clemens, born Jan. 17, 1878; died Sept. 21, 1878. (**VII.**) Harvey A. Clemens, born Aug. 23, 1879. (**VII.**) Isaac A. Clemens, born July 30, 1881; died Aug. 19, 1882. (**VII.**) Susan A. Clemens, born Aug. 1, 1883. (**VII.**) Clayton A. Clemens, born Jan. 22, 1886; died Sept. 21, 1886. (**VII.**) Allen A Clemens, born Oct. 9, 1887.

V. Catharine Clemens, born in Montg. Co., Pa., Dec. 21, 1810. Mrd. Joseph F. Tyson, Oct. 13, 1831. He was born Sept. 3, 1808; died Dec. 23, 1869. Farmer, blacksmith and Commission Merchant. Mennonite. Children: Henry, Enos, Anna and Daniel.

VI. Henry Tyson, born in Lower Salford, Montg. Co., Pa., Dec. 25, 1832. Mrd. Sallie Shepard, of Danboro, Pa., Nov. 13, 1862. She was born in 1833. Milk business, at 2409 Germantown Ave., Phila., Pa. Mrs. Tyson is a member of the Society of Friends. No issue.

VI. Enos Tyson, born in Bedminster, Bucks Co., Pa., Aug. 28, 1835; died July 1869. Mrd. Margaret.

daughter of Adam Myers, of Phila., Pa., in 1859. She died Aug. 1869. Children: Adam, Enos, Catharine, Harry, and three died in infancy.

VII. Adam Tyson, born Jan. 1, 1863. Time and Book keeper in Phila., Pa. Single.

VII. Enos Tyson, born in 1863; died Oct. 26, 1883.

VII. Catharine Tyson, born Oct. 1867. Resides at 2438 Germantown, Ave., Phila., Pa. Single.

VII. Harry Tyson, born Nov. 1868. Drives milk-wagon in Phila., Pa. Single.

VI. Anna C. Tyson, born in Doylestown, Bucks Co., Pa., Apr. 13, 1840. Mrd. John Bryan, Oct. 27, 1858. He was born Dec. 5, 1835. Grocer at 2364 Germantown, Ave., Phila., Pa. Methodists. Children: **(VII.)** Henry C. Bryan, born Sept. 27, 1859; died Nov. 8, 1859. **(VII.)** William Bryan, born in Phila., Pa., Nov. 12, 1860. Groceryman in Phila., Pa. **(VII.)** Charles T. Bryan, born in Phila., Pa., Oct. 5, 1862. Groceryman in Phila., Pa. **(VII.)** Rose Anna Bryan, born Feb. 4, 1865; died Feb. 1, 1870.

VI. Daniel Tyson, born at Danboro, Bucks Co., Pa., Apr. 20, 1847. Mrd. Hannah Sackler, Sept. 16, 1871. She was born Mar. 20, 1847. Foreman in Milk business in Phila., Pa. Res. 2436 N. 8th St. Phila., Pa. One child: **(VII.)** Sarah Tyson, born in Phila., Pa., Feb. 26, 1873. Member of the Methodist Episcopal Sunday School.

V. Rev. Isaac Clemens, born in Montg. Co., Mar. 1, 1813. Mrd. Mary Clemens, June 16, 1836. She was born in 1818. Farmer and minister. Mr. Clemens was ordained to the ministry of the Old Mennonite church, at Salford meeting house Jan. 27, 1853, and where he has since served as pastor. Children: Hannah, Henry.

VI. Hannah Clemens, born Apr. 28, 1837. Mrd. Henry G. Groff, M. D., —. A physician of prominence, who has for many years enjoyed a large and lucrative practice at Harleysville, Pa., where he now resides retired. Children: Isaac, Mary, Olivia, Ida, John, Hannah, Kate, Henry.

VII. Isaac Groff, died aged 10 months.

VII. Mary Groff, born Feb. 14, 1859. Mrd. Garret Landes, Aug. 1878. P. O., Souderton, Pa. Farmer. Mennonites. Children: **(VIII.)** Allen Landes. **(VIII.)** Harry Landes. **(VIII.)** Isaac Landes. **(VIII.)** Howard Landes. **(VIII.)** Mary Landes.

VII. Olivia Groff, born Aug. 22, 1861. Mrd. John D. Moyer, Sept. 29, 1882. Assistant Cashier of the Union National Bank at Souderton, Pa. Mennonites. Children: **(VIII.)** Willis G. Moyer, born Apr. 20, 1883. **(VIII.)** Alvan G. Moyer, born Sept. 6, 1886. **(VIII.)** Hannah May Moyer, born Dec. 1890.

VII. Ida C. Groff, born May 25, 1866. Mrd. Sheridan A. Metz, Oct. 8, 1889. P. O., Souderton, Pa. Clerk.

VII. John Wilson Groff, M. D., born Dec. 18, 1863. Succeeds his father in the practice of medicine at Harleysville, Pa., being associated with Dr. Keelor, both young men and rapidly growing into prominence as practitioners. S.

VII. Hannah Groff. S.

VII. Kate Groff. S.

VII. Henry Groff. S.

VI. Henry Clemens, born July 27, 1839; died Nov. 29, 1844.

V. Elizabeth Clemens, born Feb. 28, 1815. Mrd. John Landes, Apr. 6, 1834. He was born June 14, 1811; died June 2, 1852. Farmer. Mennonites. Children: Henry, Abraham, Jacob, Garret.

VI. Henry C. Landes, born Jan. 6, 1836. Mrd. Elizabeth Souder, Oct. 26, 1861. Farmer, and resides on the old homestead in Hatfield Twp., Montg. Co., Pa. Mennonites. Children: Emma, Morris, Edwin, Hannah, Henry, Lizzie, Jerome.

VII. Emma Landes, born in Montg. Co., Sept. 3, 1862. Mrd. Jacob K. Clemmer, Oct. 6, 1881. Farmer. Mems. of Mennonite Ch. Children: **(VIII.)** Mary Ellen Clemmer, born Apr. 13, 1882. **(VIII.)** Lizzie Irene Clemmer, born June 11, 1884. **(VIII.)** Emma Bertha Clemmer, born June 11, 1886. **(VIII.)** Henry Austin Clemmer, born Mar. 7, 1888. **(VIII.)** Hannah Alberta Clemmer, born Dec. 30, 1890.

VII. Morris S. Landes, born Feb. 28, 1864. Mrd. Emma G. Hackman, Feb. 27, 1886. Merchant. P. O., Souderton, Pa. One child: (**VIII.**) Stella H. Landis, born Nov. 17, 1886.

VII. Edwin Landes, born Feb. 17, 1866.

VII. Hannah Landes, born Nov. 8, 1868; died Sept. 11, 1869.

VII. Henry Landes, born Mar. 25, 1871.

VII. Lizzie Landes, born Aug. 29, 1875.

VII. Jerome Landes, born Jan. 9, 1879.

VI. Abraham Landes, born in Montg. Co., Pa., Apr. 24, 1838. Mrd. Annie Gerhart, Sept. 28, 1862. She was born April 6, 1843. Carpenter. Mennonite. P. O., Lansdale, Pa. Children: Simon, Carrie, Allen, Ella, Fannie, Catharine.

VII. Simon G. Landes, born Oct. 28, 1865. Mrd. Annie, daughter of John O. Clemens.

VII. Carrie Landes, born May 12, 1869; died Mar. 18, 1871.

VII. Allen Landis, born Mar. 13, 1871.

VII. Ella Landes, born Feb. 12, 1876.

VII. Fannie Landes, born Aug. 30, 1877; died Oct. 8, 1888.

VII. Catharine Landes, born May 8, 1882.

VI. Jacob Landes, born in Montg. Co., Pa., Aug. 10, 1840. Mrd. Ellaweira Hunsberger, Nov. 16, 1867. She was born Mar. 19, 1848. Cashier of the Union National Bank of Souderton, Pa. Mrs. L. Ger. Reformed. Children: (**VII.**) Rufus Landes, born Aug. 16, 1869; died Aug. 15, 1890, aged 21 yrs. less one day. Baptized in the Reformed Ch. (**VII.**) Arthur Landes, born Nov. 6, 1873. (**VII.**) Margaret Landes, born June 30, 1875; died July 29, 1875. (**VII.**) Lizzie Landes, born Aug. 26, 1876.

VI. Garret C. Landis, born in Montg. Co., Pa., Mar. 19, 1844. Mrd. Ella J. Moyer, of Dublin, Pa., June 13, 1872. Wholesale grocer of the firm of H. K. Kindig & Co., Phila., Pa. Baptists. Children:
(**VII.**) Howard Malcom Landes, born Apr. 9, 1875.
(**VII.**) Charles Yeager Landes, born Jan. 10, 1877.
(**VII.**) Naomi Grace Landes, born Feb. 14, 1879. (**VII.**) Lyman Landes, born June 21, 1884; died Apr. 5.

1885. (VII.) Leroy Clemens Landes, born Mar. 22.
1888; died Sept. 20, 1888. (VII.) Ralph Stanley Landes, born Nov. 6, 1890.

V. Jacob K. Clemens, born Nov. 9, 1820; died July
18, 1888. Mrd. Catharine Clemens, Mar. 24, 1844.
She was born 1820; died 1873. Farmer. Mennonites.
Children: Henry, Mary, Manasseh.

VI. Henry C. Clemens, born Mar. 31, 1845; died
Mar. 26, 1864.

VI. Mary Ann Clemens, born Aug. 13, 1846; died
Oct. 18, 1853.

VI. Manasseh C. Clemens, born May 11, 1856. Mrd.
Mary K. Bean, Sept. 21, 1882. P. O., Harleysville,
Pa. Farmer and feed merchant. Attend Mennonite
church. Mr. Clemens is a large landholder, and does
an extensive feed trade. He has erected a large
building with steam power, in which is located and
printed the "Weekly News" of Harleysville, edited
by the Dambey Bros., on the third floor. On the second floor a city merchant tailoring business is carried
on, and in the basement a hosiery business, where
from 15 to 20 young boys and girls are employed in
making stockings. Mr. Clemens is an enterprising
young man, and has done much towards building up
the village at Harleysville in which he resides. Children: (VII.) Minnie Clemens, born Dec. 19, 1883.
(VII.) Wilmer Clemens, born January 1, 1886. (VII.)
Harry Clemens, born Feb. 8, 1888. (VII.) Florence
Clemens, born Nov. 12, 1890.

V. Sarah K. Clemmer, born Aug. 25, 1817; died
Apr. 9, 1889. Mrd. Garret G. Delp, Dec. 3, 1839.
He was born Sept. 12, 1815; died Apr. 7, 1890. They
lived together nearly fifty years. Farmer. Mennonites. Children: Annie, Henry.

VI. Annie Delp, born Apr. 21, 1842. Mrd. Charles
M. Hildebrand, Apr. 10, 1880. He was born Nov. 9,
1857. Farmer. P. O., Harleysville, Pa. Mennonites.
Children: (VII.) Harry D. Hildebrand, born May 10,
1881. (VII.) Sallie D. Hildebrand, born Apr. 30, 1885.

VI. Henry C. Delp, born Feb. 1, 1846. Mrd. Kate
K. Frick, Oct. 12, 1867. She was born Mar. 9, 1847.

Farmer. P. O., Harleysville, Pa. Mennonites. Children: Jennie, Ellie, Katie.

VII. Jennie F. Delp, born July 3, 1869. Married Garret S. Nice, of Franconia, Pa., Nov. 17, 1888. He was born Sept. 10, 1864. Merchant. No children.

VII. Ellie F. Delp, born July 10, 1873.

VII. Katie F. Delp, born Jan. 21, 1876.

IV. John Kratz, born in Montg. Co., Pa., June 27, 1782; died Dec. 23, 1872, aged 90 yrs., 5 m. 26 d. Mrd. Catharine Johnson, of Skippack, Apr. 16, 1807. She was born Apr. 2, 1788; died May 23, 1842. After marriage they at first lived on that part of his father's farm owned by Jacob K. Freed deceased, in Upper Salford. They afterwards moved down to the Skippack, near Markley's mill, where he died. He was a farmer, and during his long and eventful life, he was successful in accumulating considerable property, and was said to have been worth upwards of $40,000. They were members of the Old Mennonite church, of which he was ordained deacon in 1843. He met his brethren for the last time in conference at Franconia in 1866. Children: Mary, Elizabeth.

V. Mary Kratz, born Oct. 4, 1808. Mrd. Abraham Detweiler, Jan. 24, 1826. He was born Dec. 11, 1799; died Jan. 17, 1888. Lived on the homestead of her father in Skippack. Farmer. Mennonites. Children: John, Lydia, Jacob.

VI. John K. Detweiler, born Jan. 28, 1827; died Oct. 11, 1888. Mrd. Lavina Cassel, Jan. 24, 1852. She was born May 15, 1826. Farmer. Mennonites. Children: Abraham, Eliza, Mary, Sarah, Mahlon, John.

VII. Abraham C. Detweiler, born Dec. 23, 1852. Mrd. Lydia S. Kulp, Jan. 1, 1884. She was born Sept. 22, 1856. Mennonites. Children: (**VIII.**) Percival Detweiler, born Oct. 14, 1885. (**VIII.**) Sallie Detweiler, born Sept. 7, 1887.

VII. Eliza J. Detweiler, born Sept. 9, 1854; died Jan. 27, 1878. Mrd. Aaron Gouldy, January 1877. Farmer. Mrs. G. Mennonite. One child: (**VIII.**) Mary Jane Gouldy, born Jan. 10, 1878.

VII. Mary Ann Detweiler, born May 16, 1856. Mrd. John K. Kulp, Dec. 19, 1885. Mennonite. Children: **(VIII.)** Alvin Kulp, born Apr. 24, 1887; died Mar. 1, 1888. **(VIII.)** Norman Kulp, born Nov. 18, 1888.

VII. Sarah Detweiler, born Dec. 10, 1859; died Apr. 17, 1861.

VII. Mahlon Detweiler, born Jan. 22, 1862. Mrd. Sallie Detweiler, Feb. 9, 1889. Mennonites.

VII. John C. Detweiler, born Feb. 21, 1867. Clerk. Mennonite. S.

VI. Lydia Kratz Detweiler, born Jan. 2, 1829; died Mar. 1, 1883, in Jacksonville, Fla.. Mrd. Anthony H. Seipt, Mar. 6, 1852. Formerly merchant at Skippackville, where he now resides, and is at present engaged in farming and running a mill. He is a descendant of the sect know as the Schwenkfelders. Children: Mary, Emma, Manilius.

VII. Mary Ann Seipt, born Oct. 29, 1853; died June 17, 1854.

VII. Emma Jane Seipt, born Feb. 10, 1855. Mrd. Samuel Wolfe, M. D., Dec. 27, 1877. Professor in Medical College in Phila., Pa. Children: **(VIII.)** Mott Leroy Wolfe, born Oct. 8, 1878; died Aug. 17, 1879. **(VIII.)** Claude Anthony Wolfe, born July 7, 1880. **(VIII.)** Russel Seipt Wolfe, born Aug. 4, 1882. **(VIII.)** James Harold Wolfe, born Apr. 26, 1884.

VII. Manilius Detweiler Seipt, born May 31, 1860.

VI. Jacob K. Detweiler, born May 6, 1833. Mrd. Mary Y. Cassel, Mar. 12, 1859. She died Sept. 9, 1867, aged 26 yrs., 11 m. 16 d. One child: **(VII.)** Mary Detweiler, died Sept. 21, 1867, aged 27 days. Jacob mrd. for his second wife, Elizabeth Landis, Oct. 31, 1868. She died Feb. 2, 1887, aged 41 yrs., 9 m. 18 d. Children: **(VII.)** Abraham L. Detwiler, born Nov. 28, 1869. **(VII.)** Jacob L. Detwiler, born Sept. 18, 1871; died Oct. 11, 1871. **(VII.)** Daniel L. Detwiler, born Sept. 8, 1872. **(VII.)** John L. Detwiler, born Feb. 16, 1875. Jacob mrd. for his third wife Sarah S., widow of David H. Allebach, Mar. 1890. P. O., Mainland, Pa. Farmer. Mennonites.

V. Elizabeth Kratz, born in Montg. Co., Aug. 31, 1813; died in Sussex Co., N. J., Mar. 21, 1855. Mrd. Martin Fretz. (See Index of References No. 41.)

IV. Mary Kratz, born Sept. 13, 1784; died Jan. 5, 1824. She became deranged at the age of 14 years.

IV. Abraham Kratz, born in Montgomery Co., Pa., Nov. 22, 1786; died June 3, 1868, aged 81 yrs., 6 m. 11 d. Mrd. Elizabeth Fretz (daughter of Martin Fretz, of Hilltown, Pa.), Nov. 2, 1813. Farmer and weaver. Lived in Upper Salford, Montg. Co., Pa., on the farm now occupied by John K. Clemmer. Mennonites. Children: Mary, Martin, Abraham, Elizabeth.

V. Mary Kratz, born Aug. 3, 1814; died Feb. 16, 1888. Unmrd.

V. Martin F. Kratz, born Dec. 9, 1817; died Nov. 15, 1846. Unmrd.

V. Abraham F. Kratz, born June 28, 1825. Mrd. Rachel, daughter of Christian Moyer, of Upper Salford, Jan. 4, 1852. She was born Oct. 26, 1833; died Sept. 1, 1867. Chairmaker and upholsterer. Mennonites. Children: Leah, Henry, Mary. Abraham mrd. for his second wife, Catharine, daughter of Jacob Boorse, of Centre Point, Montg. Co., Mar. 4, 1871. She died Dec. 30, 1885, and closed a life of more than ordinary endurance and suffering. Nine years previous to her death she was operated upon for a heavy tumor. Her friends and the local physicians and other members of the profession who witnessed the operation gave her up in utter despair, but the operator, Dr. Atlee, of Philadelphia, assured them that there was still hope for her. This hope had been partly realized when, after many days of pain and patience, she was again able to attend to her household duties and to enjoy ordinary health. The dread disease, however, though subdued for a time, was not conquered, and nearly nine years later caused her death. She was about 50 years old. Her remains were interred in the Lower Salford Mennonite burying ground.

> "Rest in peace, thy toil is o'er,
> Pain and sorrow never more
> Shalt thou ever know.
> But thy corpse beneath the sod—
> Thou, within the light of God,
> Shalt forever glow
> Like a planet when the sun is low."

Children: Sarah, Jacob, Evelyn.

VI. Leah M. Kratz, born Aug. 24, 1853. Mrd. William K. Cassel, of Upper Salford, Dec. 4, 1875. He was born Nov. 26, 1848. Farmer. Mennonites. One child: (**VII.**) Mary Catharine Cassel, born Apr. 9, 1878.

VI. Henry M. Kratz, born Apr. 18, 1857. Mrd. Mary, daughter of Philip Markley, Dec. 15, 1877. Mennonites. Children: (**VII.**) Irene M. Kratz, born Oct. 26, 1878. (**VII.**) Jennie M. Kratz, born Dec. 11, 1888.

VI. Mary Ann M. Kratz, born June 19, 1860.

VI. Sarah Alice B. Kratz, born Apr. 30, 1872.

VI. Jacob B Kratz, born July 12, 1873.

VI. Evelyn B. Kratz, born Feb. 14, 1875.

V. Elizabeth F. Kratz, born Sept. 30, 1831; died Feb. 6, 1877. Mrd. Jacob K. Freed, of Harleysville, Pa., Oct. 22, 1854. Carpenter. They lived on her father's farm until her death. Mennonites. Children: Abraham, Catharine, Mary, Isaac, John, Elizabeth, Joseph, Sarah, Anna, Henry, Infant, Jacob.

VI. Abraham K. Freed, born Aug. 24, 1855. Mrd. Deborah L. Zeigler, Sept. 2, 1876. Farmer near Lederachville, Pa. Children: (**VII.**) Elizabeth Z. Freed, born Mar. 14, 1877. (**VII.**) Mary Z. Freed, born June 16, 1879; died July 7, 1879. (**VII.**) Reinhart Z. Freed, born July 9, 1880. (**VII.**) Henry Z. Freed, born Feb. 24, 1883. (**VII.**) Dayton Z. Freed, born Jan. 25, 1885; died Mar. 23, 1885. (**VII.**) Bertha Z. Freed, born Dec. 28, 1886.

VI. Catharine K. Freed (twin to Abraham), born Aug. 24, 1855; died Oct. 11, 1856.

VI. Mary K. Freed, born Jan. 31, 1858. Resides with her father in Lederachville. Ger. Ref. Single.

VI. Isaac K. Freed, born Sept. 17, 1859. Mrd. Elizabeth Allebach, Feb. 2, 1882. School-teacher. Mennonite. One child: (VII.) Bertha A. Freed, born Apr. 18, 1885.

VI. John K. Freed, born Aug. 6, 1861. Schoolteacher. Resides at Hamlin, Kan. Member of the Christian Ch. S.

VI. Elizabeth K. Freed, born July 24, 1863. Mrd. John K. Clemmer, Apr. 15, 1882. Farmer, and occupies his father in-law's farm, the "Old Kratz farm" near Salfordville, Pa. Mennonites. Children: (VII.) Elmer F. Clemmer, born Apr. 2, 1883. (VII.) Jacob Howard Clemmer, born Mar. 16, 1887; died Aug. 20, 1887.

VI. Joseph K. Freed, born Aug. 4, 1865. He has taught school for some years, but is now a student at Ursinus College, Collegeville, Pa., preparing for the ministry of the Reformed church. S.

VI. Sarah K. Freed, born Nov. 5, 1867; died Jan. 25, 1868.

VI. Anna K. Freed, born Sept. 23, 1869. Married George Hartranft, in Feb. 1889.

VI. Henry K. Freed, born Feb. 21, 1872. Carpenter.

VI. A son born and died unnamed, Mar. 20, 1874.

VI. Jacob K. Freed, born Jan. 29, 1877.

IV. Philip Kratz, born in Montg. Co., Nov. 19, 1789; died Sept. 5, 1875, aged 85 yrs., 9 m. 16 d. Married Mary, daughter of Valentine Hunsicker, of Upper Salford. She was born Mar. 9, 1794; died Apr. 22, 1865. In 1833 he sold his farm on the Skippack road, and moved to Bedminster Twp., Bucks Co. New Mennonites. Children: Margaret, Isaac, John, Abraham, Mary, Elizabeth, Anna, Catharine.

VI. Margaret Kratz, born Nov. 11, 1813 (still living 1890). Mrd. John D. Hockman, Oct. 19, 1834. Farmer. Mennonites. Children: Jacob, Isaac, Henry, William, Mary, Sarah, Anna.

VI. Jacob Hockman, born July 9, 1835.

VI. Isaac Hockman, born Nov. 18, 1837; died July 18, 1840.

VI. Henry K. Hockman, born Aug. 15, 1840. Mrd. Maria Fretz,—. Carpenter. Children: (VII.) Lillie Hockman, born Mar. 1, 1867; died Jan. 7, 1872. (VII.) William Henry Hockman, born Dec. 17, 1869. (VII.)

Ella Hockman, born in 1874. **(VII.)** Clinton Hockman, born May 25, 1885.

VI. William K. Hockman, born Feb. 23, 1843. Mrd. Clementine D. Fretz, Mar. 5, 1870. Farmer. Children: **(VII.)** Maggie F. Hockman, born Dec. 14, 1871. **(VII.)** Clara F. Hockman, born June 17, 1874. **(VII.)** Infant daughter, died Dec. 23, 1878. **(VII.)** Infant, still-born, Feb. 13, 1884.

VI. Mary Hockman, born Oct. 18, 1846. Mrd. Jacob Kindy,—.

VI. Sarah Hockman, born June 18, 1850. Married Charles J. Roberts, Oct. 25, 1867. P. O., Dublin, Pa. Ger. Ref. Children. **(VII.)** Debbie Roberts, born Feb. 18, 1869. **(VII.)** Lillie Roberts, born Apr. 24, 1876. **(VII.)** Mamie Roberts, born Jan. 25, 1880. **(VII.)** Gertie Roberts, born Dec. 19, 1882. **(VII.)** John Roberts, born Jan. 7, 1886. **(VII.)** Lizzie Roberts, born July 12, 1890.

VI. Anna Hockman, born July 27, 1853. Mrd. Jacob A. Ruth, Oct. 19, 1872. P. O., Bethlehem, Pa. Shoemaker. Moravians. Children: **(VII.)** Elmer E. Ruth, born Sept. 4, 1873. **(VII.)** Flora R. Ruth, born Feb. 22, 1878. **(VII.)** Almeda Ruth, born June 8, 1890.

V. Isaac H. Kratz, born Dec. 31, 1817. Mrd. Sybilla B. Duke, Dec. 3, 1837. P. O., Doylestown, Pa. Tinsmith. Presbyterians. Children: Susanna, Mary.

VI. Susanna D. Kratz, born Sept. 21, 1840. Mrd. John Roberts, Nov. 22, 1857; died June 15, 1868. Children: Sybilla, Chrissie, Mary, William.

VII. Sybilla D. Roberts, born Sept. 21, 1858. Mrd. Edwin Barnes, Feb. 14, 1889. P. O., Hartsville, Pa. Farmer. Presbyterians. One child: **(VIII.)** Mary Emma Barnes, born Nov. 4, 1890.

VII. Chrissie Roberts, born—; died—.

VII. Mary Emma Roberts, born May 12, 1861. Mrd. Howard P. White, May 12, 1889. Second Steward of the Philadelphia Art Club. One child: **(VIII.)** Edward Earle White, born Feb. 1890.

VII. William S. Roberts, born July 6, 1864. Mrd. Alice Fell, May 26, 1886. Farmer. No issue.

VI. Mary E. Kratz, born Aug. 20, 1843. Mrd. William Hoffman, Sept. 22, 1864. Dealer in stoves and tinware, at Doylestown, Pa. Presbyterians. Children: Sybilla, Rosalia, Elizabeth, Mary, Isaac.

VII. Sybilla K. Hoffman, born May 6, 1866.

VII. Rosalia Hoffman, born Feb. 9, 1869. Married Frank S. Wilgus, June 19, 1890.

VII. Elizabeth B. Hoffman, born May 15, 1871.

VII. Mary Emma Hoffman, born May 23, 1874.

VII. Isaac Herbert Hoffman, born Dec. 26, 1877; died Oct. 16, 1878.

V. John Kratz, born—: died—. Mrd.—. Children: Isaac, Mary.

VI. Isaac Kratz, born   . P. O., Bedminster, Pa. S.

VI. Mary Kratz, born—. Mrd. John Crouthamel.

V. Abraham Kratz, born—: died—. Mrd. Diana—. Children: Hannah, Jerome.

VI. Hannah Kratz, born—. Mrd. Edwin Strouse,—.

VI. Jerome Kratz, born—.

V. Mary Kratz, born—. Mrd. Enos Fillman, dec'd. Children: (VII.) Isaac. (VII.) John.

V. Elizabeth Kratz, born Aug. 24, 1826; died Dec. 25, 1882. Mrd. Rev. Isaac Meyer, Oct. 6, 1833. He was born Sept. 1, 1812. In early life he was a blacksmith, after marriage he engaged in farming, now retired. He was ordained to the ministry of the Old Mennonite church June 12, 1843, from the active service of which he retired in 1890. For a period of about 46 years he faithfully preached the Gospel at Deep Run and elsewhere. Children: Enos, Abraham, Mahlon, Mary, Anna, Elizabeth, Sarah, Rachel, Isaac, Dilman, Christian, Hannah.

VI. Enos Meyer, born—; died in infancy.

VI. Abraham K. Meyer, born Feb. 19, 1836. Mrd. Sophia, daughter of Christian S. Myers, Jan. 23, 1863. He followed the carpenter's trade for 16 years, after which he purchased his father's farm and has engaged in farming ever since. Mennonites. Children: (VII.) Tillman Meyer, born Dec. 10, 1865. (VII.) Lydia Meyer, born Oct. 14, 1869. (VII.) Edwin M. Meyer, born Nov. 20, 1873. (VII.) Abraham Meyer, born Mar. 5, 1880.

18

VI. Mahlon K. Meyer, born July 29, 1838; died—. Mrd. Sarah K. Myers, Sept. 10, 1859. Children: Barbara, Eliza, Edward, Irwin.

VII. Barbara M. Meyer, born Jan. 23, 1863. Mrd. Henry L. Myers, Dec. 8, 1883. Children: **(VIII.)** Samuel M. **(VIII.)** Howard M.

VII. Eliza M. Meyer, born Nov. 22, 1866.

VII. Edward M. Meyer, born—; died in infancy.

VII. Irwin M. Meyer, born May 10, 1875.

VI. Mary Meyer, born Oct. 23, 1839; died May 22, 1872. Mrd. Jacob High, Apr. 9, 1859. He died Aug. 29, 1863. Laborer. Mennonites. Children: Mahlon, Lizzie. Mary mrd. for her second husband, Henry Wisler, Jan. 14, 1866. Farmer. Mennonites. Children: Mary, Emma, Rachel.

VII. Mahlon M. High, born May 13, 1863; died Dec. 1888. Mrd. Mary Krout, in 1882. Shoemaker and carriage trimmer. Ger. Ref. Children: **(VIII.)** Oscar K. **(VIII.)** Henry. **(VIII.)** Susan.

VII. Lizzie High, born May 26, 1860. Mrd. Isaac Bishop, Dec. 16, 1882. Farmer near Dublin, Bucks Co. Mennonites. No issue.

VII. Mary Ann Wisler, born Nov. 7, 1866.

VII. Emma Wisler, born Feb. 17, 1869. Mrd. Milton Meyers.

VII. Rachel Wisler, born July 23, 1871; died Feb. 9, 1872.

VI. Anna Meyer, born Dec. 14, 1841. Mrd. William Rush, Sept. 29, 1860. Farmer near Dublin, Pa. Old Mennonites. Children: Jacob, Lizzie, Catharine, Annie, Isaac, Allen, William, Amanda, Mahlon.

VII. Jacob M. Rush, born Apr. 4, 1862. Mrd. Mary G. Moyer, Aug. 4, 1883. Farmer. Mennonites. One child: **(VIII.)** Nora Lizzie Rush, born Feb. 20, 1885.

VII. Lizzie M. Rush, born Dec. 10, 1863. Mrd. Joseph A. Schuler, July 15, 1882. Carpenter. Children: **(VIII.)** Irwin R. Schuler, born Feb. 11, 1883. **(VIII.)** Howard R. Schuler, born Oct. 24, 1885; died Jan. 21, 1887.

VII. Catharine M. Rush, born Jan. 18, 1866. Mrd. Philip Musselman, Oct. 18, 1884. Shoemaker. German Reformed.

275 —

VII. Annie M. Rush, born May 27, 1867. Mrd. I. Newton Snyder, —. Carpenter.

VII. Isaac M. Rush, born June 15, 1871.

VII. Allen M. Rush, born Sept. 26, 1873.

VII. William M. Rush, born Nov. 3, 1878.

VII. Amanda M. Rush, born May 9, 1883; died Apr. 29, 1887.

VII. Mahlon M. Rush, born May 3, 1885.

VI. Elizabeth Meyer, born Dec. 19, 1843. Married Lewis Myers, Nov. 21, 1874. Farmer. Old Mennonites. Children: (**VII.**) Annie Myers, born Oct. 19, 1875. (**VII.**) Hannah Myers, born May 27, 1879. (**VII.**) John Myers, born June 1, 1881. (**VII.**) Isaac Myers, born June 11, 1885.

VI. Sarah Meyer, born Oct. 18, 1845; died aged 18 years.

VI. Rachel Meyer, born Aug. 28, 1847. Mrd. Jonas Mill, . Farmer. Old Mennonites. Children: Isaac, Lydia, Harvey.

VII. Isaac M. Mill, born . Mrd. Lydia Meyers, —. They have two children.

VII. Lydia M. Mill, born —. Mrd. John Derstine, —. They have two children.

VII. Harvey M. Mill, born —. S.

VI. Isaac K. Meyer, born Nov. 14, 1849. Mrd. Mary Amanda Bryan, —. Carpenter. Members of the Old Mennonite church. Children: (**VII.**) Allen Meyer, born —: died aged 5 years. (**VII.**) Oscar Meyer. (**VII.**) Addison Meyer.

VI. Dillman K. Meyer, born Apr. 20, 1853; died young.

VI. Christian K. Meyer, born Oct. 18, 1854. Mrd. Amanda Garger, —. Carpenter and undertaker, at Plumsteadville, Pa. Members of the Old Mennonite church. One child: (**VII.**) Edwin G. Meyer, born —; 8 years old (1889).

VI. Hannah K. Meyer, born Apr. 28, 1858; died aged 6 years.

VI. Anna Kratz, born Mar. 15, 1834; died Sept. 24, 1887. Mrd. Joseph S. Meyers, Mar. 19, 1854. He died July 11, 1876. Shoemaker, farmer. Mennonites.

Children: Sarah, Mary, Harvey, Willie, Peter, Pierson.

VI. Sarah K. Meyers, born Mar. 3, 1855. Married Noah K. Stear, Dec. 19, 1874. Farmer and Justice of the Peace. Lutherans. Children: **(VII.)** Ella Stear, born May 12, 1875. **(VII.)** Emma Stear, born Nov. 27, 1878. **(VII.)** Annie Stear, born June 4, 1881; died 1886.

VI. Mary K. Meyers, born Dec. 3, 1856. Mrd. Willoughby Bergey, Jan. 9, 1875. P. O., Dublin, Pa. Carpenter. Lutherans. Children: **(VII.)** Theodore M. Bergey, born July 7, 1875. **(VII.)** Harvey M. Bergey, born Feb. 7, 1881.

VI. Harvey Meyers, born Oct. 10, 1869. Married Chrissie Roberts, Jan. 8, 1887. P. O., Plumsteadville, Pa. Carriage painter. Children: **(VII.)** Jonas Arthur Meyers, born Dec. 25, 1887. **(VII.)** Abraham Lincoln Meyers, born Dec. 19, 1890; died Jan. 7, 1891.

VI. William K. Meyers, born Nov. 3, 1858; died Dec. 13, 1861.

VI. Peter K. Meyers, born Feb. 3, 1872. Married Mary Emma Gilbert, May 24, 1890. P. O., Church Hill, Pa. One child: **(VII.)** William G. Meyers.

VI. Pierson K. Meyers, born Aug. 13, 1874. P. O., Red Wing, Minn. S.

V. Catharine Kratz, born—. Mrd. Jacob L. Leatherman, Dec. 12, 1852. He was born Jan. 10, 1826; died Apr. 8, 1886. Farmer. Mennonites. Children: John, William, Lena, Emma, Mary, Isaac, Laura, Wilson, Elmer.

VI. John K. Leatherman, born Feb. 17, 1853. Married—.

VI. William K. Leatherman, born in Plumstead Twp., Dec. 24, 1856. Mrd. Kate Leonard, of Dover, N. J., May 31, 1887. Paper hanger and decorator at Doylestown, Pa. Methodist Episcopal Ch. No issue.

VI. Magdalena Leatherman, born Mar. 2, 1859. Mrd. Peter Strouse, Dec. 25, 1884. Carriage painter. Mr. Strouse, Lutheran; Mrs. Strouse, New Mennonite. No issue.

VI. Emma K. Leatherman, born Oct. 5, 1861. Mrd. Bramley Holden, —. Children: **(VII.)** William A.

Holden, born Apr. 12, 1878; died Apr. 15, 1878.
(VII.) Stella L. Holden, born Jan. 4, 1881. (VII.) Herbert L. Holden, born Mar. 18, 1883. (VII.) Howard F. Holden, born Oct. 2, 1885.

VI. Mary Ann Leatherman, born Nov. 10, 1863. Mrd. Sylvester R. Fluck, Dec. 10, 1881. Harnessmaker. Ger. Ref. One child, died Feb. 17, 1883.

VI. Isaac Leatherman, born Aug. 11, 1867.

VI. Laura Leatherman, born Oct. 23, 1869.

VI. Wilson Leatherman, born Apr. 8, 1873.

VI. Elmer Leatherman, born Sept. 8, 1879.

IV. Isaac Kratz, born Nov. 19, 1791; died Jan. 23, 1873, aged 81 yrs., 2 m. 4 d. Mrd. Anna Alderfer, daughter of Benjamin Alderfer, May 9, 1816. She died Sept. 12, 1884, aged 89 yrs. less 9 days. Lived and died on the old homestead in Lower Salford, where Milton H. Alderfer now owns. Farmer. New Mennonites. Children: Benjamin, John, Mary, Michael, Isaac, Elizabeth, Annie.

V. Benjamin A. Kratz, born Jan. 12, 1817; died Sept. 16, 1860. S.

V. John Kratz, born in Lower Salford, Pa., Nov. 9, 1819. Mrd. Margaret Oberholtzer, of Hatfield, Pa., Dec. 3, 1848. Farmer. Mennonites. Republican. P. O., Elroy, Pa. Children: Levi, Isaac, Lizzie, Mary.

VI. Levi O. Kratz, born Oct. 9, 1850. Mrd. Rachel Dresher, of Worcester, Pa., Nov. 29, 1873. Farmer. Republican. Children: (VII.) Irwin Kratz, born Nov. 8, 1880. (VII.) Warren Kratz, born July 12, 1883; died Mar. 22, 1885. (VII.) Katie Kratz, born May 21, 1888.

VI. Isaac O. Kratz, born Apr. 28, 1855. Mrd. Mary Ann Alderfer, of Lower Salford, Nov. 10, 1877. Farmer. Republican. Children: (VII.) Lyman Kratz, born Dec. 16, 1878. (VII.) Alice Kratz, born Aug. 2, 1880. (VII.) John Kratz, born July 16, 1882; died May 27, 1883. (VII.) Annie Kratz, born Mar. 25, 1884. (VII.) Melvin Kratz, born Feb. 7, 1886. (VII.) Maggie Kratz, born June 1, 1888.

VI. Lizzie Ann Kratz, born June 27, 1857. Mrd. Samuel Swartley, of Franconia, Pa., Nov. 10, 1879.

Republican. P. O., Line Lexington, Pa. Children: (**VII.**) Minerva Swartley. (**VII.**) Stella Swartley. (**VII.**) Nora Swartley.

VI. Mary Kratz, born Jan. 1, 1862. Mrd. Joseph G. Ruth, of New Britain Twp., Bucks Co., Pa., Jan. 1, 1884. P. O., Colmar, Pa. Children: (**VII.**) Maggie Ruth. (**VII.**) Ella Ruth. (**VII.**) Emma Ruth (twins).

V. Mary K. Kratz, born Dec. 14, 1821. Married Henry D. Kratz. (See Index of References No. 43.)

V. Michael A. Kratz, born Dec. 23, 1824. Mrd. Julian Klein, Dec. 9, 1847. Children: Annie, Lizzie, B. Morris, Katie.

VI. Annie Kratz, born in Upper Salford, Montg. Co., Pa. Mrd. Irwin W. Stetler, Feb. 25, 1873. P. O., Frederick, Pa. Merchant. Mrs. Stetler is a member of the Mennonite Ch. at Schwenksville, Pa. No issue.

VI. Lizzie Kratz, born —.

VI. B. Morris Kratz, born —.

VI. Katie Kratz, born —. Mrd. I. H. Smoyer, Aug. 11, 1883. P. O., Green Lane, Pa.

V. Isaac Kratz, born in Lower Salford Twp., Montgomery Co., Pa., Sept. 9, 1829; died Nov. 28, 1871. Mrd. Catharine W. Klein, Jan. 12, 1851. Miller. Mrs. Kratz, member of the Lower Salford Mennonite Ch. Children: Senorah, Sallie.

VI. Senorah Kratz, born Mar. 27, 1860. Mrd. Irvin Christman,—. P. O., Zieglersville, Pa. Merchant. (**VII.**) One child, died in infancy.

VI. Sallie Kratz, born in Montg. Co., Pa., June 4, 1866. Mrd. Allen K. Hunsberger, Sept. 25, 1885. P. O., 609 N. 43½ St., Phila., Pa. Telegraph operator. Mem. Evangelical Ch. One child: (**VII.**) Senorah Hunsberger, born Apr. 29, 1890.

V. Elizabeth Kratz, born June 27, 1835. Married John K. Shutt, Jan. 1, 1859. P. O., Harleysville, Pa. Miller. Mennonites. Children: Andora, Alonzo, Jacob.

VI. Andora Shutt, born May 6, 1862. Mrd. Isaac G. Koons, Mar. 15, 1881. P. O., Harleysville, Pa. Miller. One child: (**VII.**) Gertie Koons, died at birth.

VI. Alonzo Shutt, born July 20, 1868. He began teaching school in 1886, in which vocation he is still engaged.

VI. Jacob K. Shutt, born Nov. 4, 1870. P. O., Harleysville, Pa. Painter.

V. Annie Kratz, born in Montg. Co., Dec. 21, 1838. Mrd. Henry Quillman, Dec. 14, 1859. He was born Dec. 14, 1836; died Sept. 30, 1875. Hotel keeper. Ger. Ref. Children: Amelia, Warren, Anna. Annie mrd. second husband, Jacob Kenton, Dec. 21, 1886. He died Sept. 28, 1887. Hotel keeper. No issue.

VI. Amelia Quillman, born in Norristown, Pa., Aug. 13, 1861. Mrd. Ellwood Rogers, Mar. 9, 1878. Children: (**VII.**) Eva Alice Rogers, born May 20, 1880. (**VII.**) Helen Rogers, born Apr. 3, 1882. (**VII.**) Warren Roy Rogers, born June 7, 1885. (**VII.**) Samuel Larshaw Rogers, born Jan. 31, 1888. (**VII.**) John Carl Rogers, born Mar. 1, 1889. (**VII.**) Ruth Rogers, born Dec. 8, 1890.

VI. I. Warren Quillman, born in Norristown, Pa., Sept. 18, 1863. Mrd. Ida V. Spotts, Nov. 28, 1889. Clerk in National Bank of the Northern Liberties, Phila., Pa. Mrs Quillman, Baptist. No issue.

VI. Anna Frances Quillman, born July 1869. S.

IV. Elizabeth Kratz, born Mar. 9, 1800; died Jan. 11, 1888. Mrd. Henry Ziegler, Mar. 5, 1822. He was born Oct. 3, 1798; died Dec. 1878. Farmer. Mennonites. Children: Isaac, Michael, Abraham.

V. Isaac Ziegler, born May 21, 1823; died—. Mrd. Elizabeth Mattis,—. Children: Henry, Anna, Emma.

VI. Henry Ziegler, born—.

VI. Anna Ziegler, born—. Mrd. Harry Kulp.—.

VI. Emma Ziegler, born—. Mrd. Jacob Reiff,—.

V. Michael Ziegler, born Sept. 13, 1829. Mrd. Hannah Thomson, Nov. 9, 1856. Tailor. Independent Ch. Children: Henry, Edwin, Elizabeth, Malinda, Caroline, Hannah, Ella.

VI. Henry Ziegler, born Apr. 22, 1857; died Mar. 14, 1887. Mrd. Kate Moyer,—. Lutheran. Children: (**VII.**) Norman Ziegler, born Apr. 7.—. (**VII.**) Bertha Ziegler, born Aug. 10,—. (**VII.**) Wilmer Ziegler, born— . **(VII.)** Hannah Ziegler, born— . **(VII.)** Jesse Ziegler, born—.

VI. Edwin Ziegler, born Oct. 16, 1858; died—.

VI. Elizabeth Ziegler, born Feb. 29, 1860. Married Henry S. Wambold, Jan. 6, 1876. Children: **(VII.)** Harry Wambold, born Sept. 10, 1876. **(VII.)** Clinton Wambold, born Oct. 5, 1879. **(VII.)** Howard Wambold, born Apr. 22, 1885.

VI. Malinda Ziegler, born June 1, 1862. Married Henry Moyer,—. One child: **(VII.)** Ellsworth Moyer.

VI. Caroline Ziegler, born Sept. 3, 1865. Married Henry Bomer. Children: **(VII.)** Rosy Bomer. **(VII.)** Emma Bomer. **(VII.)** Hannah Bomer, born—; died—.

VI. Hannah Ziegler, born June 26, 1867. Married Levan Kramer, Dec. 13, 1890.

VI. Ella Ziegler, born June 21, 1871. S.

V. Abraham Ziegler, born Dec. 16, 1835; died Jan. 8, 1890. Mrd. Caroline Geisinger, Jan. 7, 1860. Mem. Ref. Ch. No issue.

TABULATED STATEMENTS

OF THE DESCENDANTS OF JOHN VALENTINE KRATZ,

FROM 1732 TO 1892, AS FAR AS RECEIVED.

Generation.	Children born bearing the name of Kratz.	Died.	Living.	Total of descendants born	Died	Living.
II.	1	1	0	1	1	0
III.	9	9	0	9	9	0
IV.	45	44	1	55	54	1
V.	128	82	46	248	171	77
VI.	298	90	208	1008	335	673
VII.	254	40	214	2187	516	1671
VIII.	6	2	4	858	131	827
IX.	7	1	6	24	3	21
	748	269	479	4490	1220	3270

The total number of descendants reported is 4,490. Complete returns of all born bearing the name of Kratz, would probably bring the number up to about 800, and the total number of descendants to about 4,800.

Descendants of John Kratz, son of John Valentine Kratz.

Generation.	Children born bearing the name of Kratz.	Died.	Living.	Total of descendants born	Died.	Living.
III.	1	1	0	1	1	0
IV.	6	6	0	6	6	0
V.	17	16	1	26	24	2
VI.	35	11	24	147	62	85
VII.	33	5	28	384	76	308
VIII.	1	0	1	223	23	200
IX.	7	1	6	7	1	6
	100	40	60	794	193	601

Descendants of Philip Kratz, son of John Valentine Kratz.

Generation.	Born bearing the name of Kratz.	Died.	Living.	Total of descendants born	Died.	Living.
III.	1	1	0	1	1	0
IV.	11	10	1	11	10	1
V.	21	17	4	44	35	9
VI.	39	12	27	129	55	74
VII.	33	4	29	257	59	198
VIII.	0	0	0	157	15	142
	105	44	61	599	175	424

Descendants of Abraham Kratz son of John Valentine Kratz

Generation	Born bearing the name of Kratz	Died	Living	Total of descendants born	Died	Living.
III.	1	1	0	1	1	0
IV.	10	10	0	10	10	0
V.	18	11	7	71	50	21
VI.	50	16	34	305	102	203
VII.	53	9	44	834	218	616
VIII.	0	0	0	454	72	382
IX.	0	0	0	17	2	15
	[illegible]	4	[illegible]	1692	455	1237

Descendants of Two Sons ... descendants of John Val. Kratz.

Generation	Born bearing the name of Kratz	Died	Living	Total of descendants born	Died	Living
III	1	1	0	1	1	0
IV	0	0	0	10	10	0
V	0	0	0	17	13	4
VI	0	0	0	62	23	39
VII	0	0	0	94	23	71
VIII	0	0	0	4	3	31
	1	0	0	218	73	145

Complete returns would bring up totals of grand descendants.

Descendants of ... Kratz:

Generation	Born bearing the name of Kratz	Died	Living	Total of descendants born	Died	Living.
III	1	1	0	1	1	0
IV	0	0	0	0	0	0
V	11	[illegible]	20	43	23	20
VI	[illegible]	[illegible]	88	100	[illegible]	112
VII	[illegible]	[illegible]	76	185	87	98
VIII	4	0	4	22	1	21
	28	[illegible]	185	370	125	251

Descendants of John Kratz ... son of John ... Kratz:

Generation	Born bearing the name of Kratz	Died	Living	Total of descendants born	Died	Living
III.	1	1	0	1	1	0
IV.	1	0	0	0	0	0
V.	24	13	11	47	26	21
VI.	30	4	[illegible]	190	30	160
VII.	43	0	87	483	103	380
VIII.	4	2	2	68	17	51
	125	37	88	617	146	612

4.

Ie pity show'd for sinners bl n l,
He came and p d the awful debt
Ie rolled the b r en from our minds,
Which none w l e'er regret.

5.

) who can such great love reject
Those dying groans refuse to hear,
Come, sinners come, once more reflect,
And to your Lord draw near.

6.

And when our life on earth is o'er—
Our sorrows ever at an end;
We'll gather on the heavenly shore,
Eternity to spend.

7.

There' there, at Jesus bleeding side,
From sin and death we shall be free
There evermore we will abide,
And praise for aye and aye.

Con anima.   mf
Music composed by REV. A. J. FRETZ.
Arranged by D. H ANDERS.
1. When the mists have rolled in splen-dor, From the beau-ty of the hills,
2 If we   err   in hu-man blind-ness, And for-get that we are dust,
3 When the mists shall rise a-bove us, As   our   Fa-ther knows his own,
And   the   sun-shine warm and ten-der, Falls in   beau-ty   on the   rills.
If   we   miss the   law of kind-ness, When we strug-gle   to   be   just;
Face to   face with those that love   us We shall know as   we are known,
We may   read love's shin-ing let-ter, In   the   rain-bow of the spray;
Snow-y   wings of peace shall cov-er   All the   pain that clouds our day,
Just be-yond the dark-en shadows Floats the gold-en fringe of day;

CHORUS.
When the mists have clear'd a-way, When the mists have clear'd a-way,
In the dawn-ing of the morn-ing When the mists have clear'd a-way,
We shall know as we are known Nev-er more to walk a-lone,
In the dawn-ing of the morn-ing, When the mists have clear'd a-way,

VALEDICTION.

FRIENDS AND BROTHERS OF A COMMON ANCESTRY.

Ere we lay aside this volume and consign it to some obscure corner of the library, let us commune together.

We have read of him, our worthy ancestor, of his immediate descendants, of our fathers, of our cotemporaries, of ourselves. They and we are now the substance of written history. Our names will be, to some extent, preserved from oblivion; and whether we approve or otherwise, it matters not.

To make history is man's evident mission; and if we make good history, we shall have no cause to wish it unknown. It should therefore be our aim to make clean history; not only on our own account, but on account of our posterity as well.

With what commendable pride may the honest, upright man look upon himself as the son of a noble sire; and how the paternal heart yearns toward a worthy son!

In view of this, it becomes our duty to endeavor to improve society, by each one contributing his moiety to that end. Are we accepting the task? Are we, the parents of the present generation, shouldering this burden of responsibility, and teaching our offspring in their turn to bear it too? Are we guarding our every word and deed, and inculcating on their minds just, moral and religious principles?

I fear that many of us have not an adequate conception of the onerous responsibilities involving us, as sons of the past and sires of the future. Possibly in that greed for gain which at the present time influences all nations and societies, many moral duties sink into comparative insignificance and are neglected. Be that as it may; when the accounts of human life are rendered up, our offenses will be found no less grave, nor the judgment less severe. He who will for a moment seriously pause and ponder, cannot fail to see, and, in all honesty, should admit, that as many of the young of this generation are being reared, thousands, aye, hundreds of thousands, of them are apt pupils of vice, and are, day by day, fitting themselves as apostles for the dissemination of immorality and crime.

Who is responsible? We, every one of us, in a greater or less degree; not alone as parents, but as elder brothers, as neighbors, or as strangers; consciously or unconsciously, we, and all with whom they come in contact, are daily and hourly teaching them by precept or example. Every untoward action of ours is seen and copied by some observing youth. Every unguarded expression is heard and repeated by some precocious juvenile. Is it any wonder, then, that morality does not keep pace with science?

We of the present day and generation are blessed with many conveniences that were not enjoyed by our fathers, and we should seek to transmit them to our posterity.

We are living in an age when the most valuable germs of ancient and modern wisdom, purified and concentrated, have advanced civilization far beyond even the elysian dreams of the "Eastern Magi."

Thus far in the history of the world, the present is the "Ne plus ultra" age of human enlightenment.

Search the archives of nations and find, if you can, a parallel to the progress of our own beloved America during the first century of its existence as a distinct power.

The haughty Nebuchadnezzar, when at the zenith of his grandeur, never dreamed that the "Great Babylon which I have built," could be surpassed; nor Solomon in all his glory with wisdom and knowledge; nor yet all the great and wise men of antiquity ever enjoyed or hoped to enjoy such comforts, such luxuries, such privileges, and such immunities as we of to-day.

Think for a moment of our illimitable resources; of our nation's vessels dotting every sea, its commerce carried on in every port, its products distributed throughout every land. Think of our vast continent traversed in all directions by iron bands of trade and travel, by innumerable threads of communication, by its hundred thousand highways and byways, and by its hundreds of rivers and lakes, natural channels of commerce. Think of its vast agricultural and animal products; of its exhaustless mineral deposits, developed and undeveloped, and of the countless thousands of useful mechanical appliances which, by man's genius, reduces human labor to a minimum and annihilates time and distance. Think of all this and assert if you can that the responsibilities resting on this people are not weighty. Who does not believe that the responsibilities of a people increase with their enlightenment?

The source of all our prosperity and power is evident. The daystar of Universal Christian Liberty has risen above the horizon of human events, shedding his refulgent glow o'er the awakening world, and humanity is emerging from the Plutonian darkness of ignorance and intolerance into the broad light of Christian love and fellowship.

Shall we go on and on increasing in knowledge, in wealth, in power, in grandeur? Not unless we continue in the way the Almighty has marked out for us. History furnishes many instances of ancient nations who knew not the God of Revelation, fallen to the dust from whence they sprang; and of others who, having known Him, departed from the way and likewise fell. Nineveh, Babylon, Egypt, Greece, Rome, all fell. From the very nature of affairs their doom was inevitable and they could not escape it. Their fabric, erected like the house on shifting sands, fell, and the fall thereof was great. Even God's "chosen people" sank from their high estate and calamities fell thick and heavy upon them. God's ways are mysterious and past finding out, but His laws are

Old Mennonite Church, Deep Run, Bucks Co., Pa.
(Second House.)

THE NEW YORK
PUBLIC LIBRARY

ASTOR, LENOX AND
TILDEN FOUNDATIONS.

plain and immutable. They must be obeyed or certain destruction will follow.

No people can have true prosperity, true peace, or be truly happy without true religion. Not that religion of fanaticism and fear that invests God with terrible powers, one to be worshiped and propitiated to avoid the visitation of His annihilating wrath; not that form of religion that compels men to conform to the law and will of God through fear of eternal condemnation. No; but that form of religion that acknowledges God as the God of Love and Tenderness, who made the covenant with mankind whereby they may be redeemed through the mediation of His Divine Son.

A happy, peaceful and prosperous people should be a vigilant people. Eternal vigilance is not alone the price of liberty, but of virtue and integrity as well. Man's arch-enemy is ever watchful, seeking whom he may destroy; and when our vigilance relaxes, in that moment we fall.

Let us each and all determine that, regardless of the course pursued by others, we, at least, will transmit to our children a name that carries with it no reproach; and if we would have them free from taints of vice, we must keep them from contaminating influences, from evil associates, from pernicious literature; withal we must teach them self-reliance, and cultivate in them the will power to stand alone and resist the inevitable temptations of life.

Let us give each and all of our children a sound, practical education. Among our two hundred thousand public schools, our three hundred and twenty colleges and universities, beside thousands of other educational institutions, every one may have it who will. In this country there can be no longer any plea for ignorance among our native born. This epoch is becoming more and more one of specialists in all branches of human industry. Human knowledge is becoming so extended, and the sciences and the arts are ramifying out in so many directions, that it is impossible far any one individual to learn but a tithe of it all. Yet the fundamental principles of all knowledge are the same; and they should be acquired by every one. Society demands it, and science demands it. Even now many desirable positions can be obtained only through competitive examinations for eligibility. In such cases, what hope of success can an unqualified person have? Absolutely none.

This is pre-eminently an age of advancement and our real duty is improvement in all that tends to elevate and benefit our race. If we, as a people, cultivate all arts and sciences, strive for supremacy in knowledge, practice the tenets of our fathers, preserve inviolate the institutions reared by them, grant justice and equal rights to all, heed the injunctions of Holy Writ, and follow righteousness, there is no limit to the height we, as a nation, may attain. But if we disregard these things and employ our faculties to propagate evil, calamities will overwhelm in the moment when we think not, and we too will sink to rise no more. May the day soon dawn when the emblems of Universal Peace and Universal Liberty shall crown the summit of every hill in every clime! when every knee shall bend, and every head shall bow, acknowledging that God is God, and that he rules supreme in love and equity.

A. B. FRETZ.

Jan. 15th, 1892.   Caldwell, New Jersey.

INDEX OF BRANCHES.

INDEX OF REFERENCES.

GENERAL INDEX.

ERRATA.

Page 133, read V. Silas Fretz, not VI.
" 134, " VII. Fannie Gehman, not VI.
" 142, " Lizzie C. Loux, born Jan. 1, 1882.
" 147, " V. John Fretz, not VI.
" 152, " Robert Nace died Mar. 24, 1887.
" 159, " Josephus Fretz, born Mar. 23, 1835. Not mrd.
" 164, " VI. Sarah Gross, not VII.
" 164, " Emma Lapp, born Oct. 15, *1863*, not 1763.
" 214, " VI. Amanda Kratz, not V.
" 214, " *Warren* Wismer, instead of Warrel.
" 220, " Annie C. *Kratz*, instead of Annie C. Moyer.
" 237, " Amanda *Nice*, instead of Amanda Fice.
" 239, " Valentine *Kindig*, not Kratz.
" 243, " Blanch M. Bibler, born Aug 6, 1878.
" 266, " Sarah K. *Clemens*, not Clemmer.
" 271, " V. Margaret Kratz, not VI.
" 275, " V. Anna Kratz, not VI.
" 273, (Children of Mary Fillman) read VI. Isaac, VI. John,
      not VII.

www.ingramcontent.com/pod-product-compliance
Lightning Source LLC
Chambersburg PA
CBHW021719110726
47902CB00005B/1255